Henry's Horsemen

Benjamin S. Hartman

ISBN: 978-0-9860584-5-5

ASIN: 0986058459

To Briana, who always believed in me.

PROLOGUE

Godfrey's Journal, Final Entry

A great man once said: "Science will either be the key to mankind's salvation, or his annihilation." We lived by that mantra as scientists forged into soldiers who fought a war of our own making. Initially, the Marines called us "The Janitors," to the Army: "Garbage Men," the Navy just watched their men get slaughtered when we were brought in to clean up after them. These jokers, these underpaid idealists all thought we were lower than the shit on their boots because we weren't fighting other men. That is...until a beast ripped half a kid's face off. That's when we were called in. We were brought in when the military decided that throwing bodies wasn't a viable solution anymore. We were brought in to clean up their messes.

The Horsemen Corps was born from a man named John C. Henry who knew that mankind was not prepared for deep space colonization. He knew that the problems of deep space couldn't be settled with military grit, only with science. He created a team that would get things right, a team that would author the book on dealing with the monsters. Yes, there are monsters that go bump in the night, and we bumped back. We stalked the hunters, killed without mercy and drove fear into the hearts of beasts that never knew of such.

We breathed and cured plagues engineered to wipe out humanity. We slaughtered that which sought our extinction. We were ghosts, the secret of how close mankind came to annihilation taken to our graves. We stepped in when the others had abandoned all hope of stopping armageddon. It is said that Henry pulled his Horsemen from the very depths of Hell itself...monsters sent in to kill the other monsters. We never felt the need to correct that belief. We were Henry's Horsemen.

THE HORSEMEN INITIATIVE

My throat constricts as I struggle to breathe. A man who less than an hour ago was an ally now has his cold hands wrapped around my neck. His cloudy, listless eyes glare at me.

Poor guy. Barely into the first mission and the leeches already got him. They drained his body into a husk and then reanimated his corpse so it could protect the rest.

I draw my pistol and aim it at the giant gray slug wrapped around Jay's neck. I fire twice. The first blaster bolt sears through the flesh of the bug, eliciting a squeal and a grunt from its host. On the second shot my pistol jams. Jay's returned corpse release me, but the leech intends to finish the job. I fix the jam and fire again which knocks both of them on the floor. I ran back the way I came to the storage room where we found the kid.

All of the others are waiting there for me. They wanted to see if I would survive on my own.

"What the fuck were you guys waiting for?" I ask as I rip off my helmet and feel the humidity choke me. Sweat pours down my face and stings my eyes.

"Figured that if you died, there'd be one less pedophile in the galaxy and it was worth the risk to us," Sulture replies.

Everyone else except the kid, laughs at the joke. I really hate it when they call me a pedophile. Everyone in the room is sweating bullets, our merc suits an abomination for wear.

"Where's your rifle?" my commander, John demands.

"Jay's corpse knocked it out of my hands. By the way, your standard issue pistol here is shit," I snap as I toss it to the ground. "Jammed up, almost got me killed."

"Let me have a look. I'll bet I can fix it Casanova," Warrens says. He picks up the pistol and dismantles it in seconds.

As I catch my breath, I think back to what got me in this mess in the first place.

It was two months earlier and the holding cell was cold. But then again everything was cold on Titan, even the University. Some heat radiated from the geothermal installations, but the temperature was always kept as low as possible. One would think that I'd be used to it, having taught here for more than a decade, but I always hated the cold. Titan's University was an ideal place to store biological, chemical, and even some (rumored) nuclear weapons deep in the underground vaults. The cold made it easier to contain everything, and I was at Titan to make sure they stayed there.

Yet here I was, locked up, in a prison jumpsuit. Awaiting punishment for a victimless crime…

A black man walked in. Wore a gray suit with a black tie, neither of which seemed to fit quite right. He fiddled with the tie constantly. I would've offered to help, but I was in cuffs. The man unlocked them and motioned that I should sit across from him.

I obliged.

He pulled out a pack of cigarettes with pure tobacco and offered me one. I didn't normally smoke, but I wasn't sure when I'd have another chance. I took one and he offered me a light. I inhaled deep, trying to ignore the burn. The smell of burning tobacco lingered in the air.

"Silas Godfrey…" He said as he pulled my record up on the table.

He darkened my half so that I wasn't able to read my own file.

Hardly seemed fair.

I looked down and saw my reflection. I saw a long faced man, hair dangling in his eyes with a coarse brown beard all full of shame. I pondered how I'd gotten here and where life went so wrong. My mind snapped back to the present.

"Yeah, that's my name. And you are…?" I finally said to break the silence.

"Colonel John C. Henry. Head of Ionics Special Forces," He said as he extended his hand for a polite shake. My heart thundered in my chest. Chemron was a part of the Ionics IPC or Interplanetary Corporation, a massive merger between seven different companies in the science field.

Was this man here to collect on the Chemron incident? Those records were supposed to have been erased.

I tried to keep calm and shook John's hand.

John runs his eyes across the table's screen. "You have an interesting history here Mr. Godfrey. Says that you have a degree all the way to a Doctorate in Chemistry, but your history has been tampered with. Before your stint as a professor here at Titan, your history is blank. Now why would that be?" John asked as he looked at me.

I kept telling myself that he knew nothing. He was trying to fill the gaps over something that happened more than ten years ago.

"Look, whoever sent you John-"

"Did you serve in the Unification Wars? Can't tell from your record here," He interrupted. His question caught me off guard, but I relished a change in subject.

"Only R&D. Never saw actual combat. We were trained and ran drills, but nowhere near ready for it."

John nodded, satisfied with my answer. "Says here you're a leading expert on Astro-chemical composition, have a history of alcohol abuse, bar fights and now we can throw in sex scandals." He looked at me with a slight smirk. Something was off about this conversation. Where was he going with all of this?

"What's the matter Godfrey, wanted to have a three-way with some minors?"

"The girls told me they were over eighteen," I replied. "They also said that I had the prettiest gray eyes they'd ever seen."

"You're their professor! There are rules about that kind of thing and based on what I'm reading, you have a history of disregarding the rules!"

John paused, as he tried to gauge my reaction.

"Look John, I'll level with you. I hate my job, I hate my life, and I'm a worn out professor who can't stand the system anymore," I said. "A guy like myself lashes out at the morons in the bars. I try to drown my problems and if two firm-bodied young ladies offer themselves to me in exchange for a better grade, I'll take it. Not exactly many other prospects around here." I don't know why I told John this, but something about him made me felt like I should be honest.

"Well, a buried past means you screwed up somehow. Whoever wiped it out was thorough. But, my analyst gave you the green light," John said as a grin spread across his lips. "Look Godfrey, I'm putting together a team of scientists who aren't afraid to break the rules. Scientists who are brilliant but can hold their own in a bar fight. Men willing to act *outside* the system."

John didn't seem to be a hired gun for a vengeful Chemron executive. Still could've been a trap, but I played along.

"You've got a lot of searching to do John. There's only about a dozen of us like that. All the other scientists I know are do-gooder candy asses."

"You're right Godfrey. As a matter of fact, you're the last one I had to track down."

"Well, don't I feel special."

"Only because the other chemist we were interested in got killed on the fringes of Core space."

"That was low. So, what does this team do?"

"Godfrey, Earth is just now getting a handle on deep space colonization. Humans are expanding in all directions, but mankind is unprepared. There's aliens, diseases, complications from atmospheric pressure and dozens of other issues. Ionics wants a team of 'consultants' to sort out the mess and create methods to make deep space colonization possible. We're calling it the Horsemen Initiative."

"Cut the PR bullshit John. You did not fly down here, tell me you're looking for guys who don't play by the rules to appeal to my sense of helping humanity. Why are you really here?"

John paused - then said in a low tone. "My team exists to kill monsters. Whether they're made from man, alien or God, you guys exist to kill. You fight off the beasts that terrorize colonists, the military and other scientists."

"The premise sounds interesting. I assume it's dangerous?"

"Very. We're expecting a high mortality rate."

"And...if I refuse?" I didn't feel too keen on being dissolved inside some alien's belly.

"Mr. Godfrey if you refuse, I walk out that door, and you will never see or hear from me again. You will get to spend the rest of your life in a prison looking over your shoulder."

"So my options are: die while fighting monsters, or spend the rest of my life watching out for Bubba?"

"Correct."

"Where do I sign?"

John brought up what he called the standard employment and liability release forms for the position. I scanned the documents. No chance at legal retaliation of any kind. If something happened, like death or dismemberment, I couldn't sue Ionics since they granted me amnesty.

Seemed like standard operating procedure.

Gotta love the power of an IPC. I signed my life away into John's hands. At least he seemed like a man I could trust.

John stood up, buttoned his coat and adjusted his tie again.

"I'll give you two standard hours to pick up your belongings and I'll have a shuttle ready to take you to our training camp. I'll be at the landing pad waiting for you."

Now as I look around the team that John has assembled, he sure went out of his way to recruit the best of the best. There were some rough patches when we all first met, but we've bonded since then.

"You brought a pedophile on board?!" Dr. Adam Sulture snarled in disgust while I stood behind John. Sulture was a tall, imposing figure with slick jet black hair and looked like a rooster's crown. His brown eyes looked like he hadn't gotten a decent night's sleep in ages.

"Yeah, I mean why give it to little kids when Sujay's mom will take it like no other woman. She'll take *anything*," the pilot said to me with a wink and a nudge.

"Jack Forrest, you leave my mother out of this! Why do you always bring her up?" Sujay shrieked as he stormed through the corridors. I recognized Sujay Malak from when I was getting my doctorate, but that was in my past life. He stopped, but didn't seem to recognize me. "Is this the last guy? Doesn't look nearly as scary as Sulture or the Chinaman."

"*Zao ni ma*," the Chinaman snapped as he glided up to me. Xing Ming Lee had a reputation with knives, he could slit my throat before I even noticed. I recognized him from the propaganda posters across Ophridia. The guy overthrew the planetary dictator then murdered him in front of the cameras.

"HA!" Forrest screamed. "I don't know what he said, but I'm betting it had something to do with your mother," he said as he pointed and laughed at Sujay.

Sujay's face grew red, but he didn't do anything. He never had a history of bravery.

Lee turned his attention to me. "You like little girls? Or is it little boys you *ji bai*?" He got right into my face.

"Who's into kids?" another black man asked as he came down the corridor. He was wiping the grease off of a pistol. I also recognized him: Jackson Warrens, an engineering marvel and expert weapons developer. He was a lumbering behemoth of gnarled muscle.

"I'm not into kids alright? Two seventeen year-olds seduced me," I snapped.

The others burst out laughing. When I heard it, I wouldn't believe me either.

"Sure, and I didn't kill the bloodthirsty dictator Yiu Mei," Lee said.

"Only one dictator? I knocked out three...all at once," Warrens said.

"Those little African warlords? Nothing more than *he chusheng zajiao dezanghuo*," Lee hissed.

"Watch it Kung Pao, I could break you like a twig," Warrens said as he looked Lee up and down.

"Bring it you *gaoyang zhong de guyang*!" Lee snarled. Warrens closed in on him, but a sandy haired guy got in between.

"C'mon fellas, we're in this together. Both of you lost someone close, Warrens you lost your grandma, Lee you lost your wife and daughter right? No need for you fellas to mess up those handsome faces," He said.

"Suppose you're right Doc," Warrens said.

"Looks like I've got some egos to break. Everyone at the training pit. Five minutes," John said and walked off. All of the men filed off towards the arena for training, except for the sandy-haired man who stayed behind with me.

"So what's your story bud?"

"Silas Godfrey, former Chemistry Professor from Titan University," I replied as I shook his hand. "That's really about it. Yours?

"Dr. Murph McGinnis, former Medical Doctor," he chuckled. "I was the M.D. on Angkor. Helped Adam wipe out the aliens that killed 1,532 people in the colony or 76.6% of our population."

I gave Murph a quizzical look.

"Oh uh, I have an eidetic memory for numbers. I do that sometimes. C'mon, I'll show you around and then we'll go to training." A bald, Persian man rushed past us. He had a familiar look to him.

"Who was that?" I asked.

"Oh, that's Hacker, our computer guy. Claims his real name is Jabal Amir, but nobody knows for sure. He's a whiz at computers and can wipe out an identity in an afternoon. Used to run '*The Grid*.' Good guy, but quiet." Murph said.

I recognized '*The Grid*' immediately. It was an underground operation of information dealers notorious for selling state secrets to revolutionaries, anarchists, and other terrorist groups just to keep the governments honest. I'd dealt with *The Grid* several times. They were a fun group of guys who would do anything with a computer for the right price.

"Okay, you'll bunk here with me, Adam and Hacker," Murph said as he pointed at my cot. It was a spacious room, but didn't allow for privacy. I tossed my bag onto my cot. Murph closed the door, and we walked off to training.

At training there was one guy I didn't recognize. Everyone else was standing at attention, while John was talking to him.

"Who's the last guy?" I asked Murph.

"Jon Jay," He answered.

"Who's that?"

"He was with Lee back on Ophridia. I want to like the guy, but he's an arrogant prick. Always touting what great revolutionaries they were. Ugh. Makes Lee the preferable one."

There may have been some tension initially, but John's insatiable curiosity made us all learn from each other. His first speech spelled out why he'd sought the most discredited men in the scientific community.

"Gentlemen, I have scoured our corner of the galaxy looking for scientists like you. Perhaps you're all too old and cynical to have a sense of idealism like I do-"

"Not me! I'm an idealist! I still believe I can bang Sujay's mom and take a -"

"Shut up Forrest!" John roared.

"Sorry," He replied as he looked to the floor.

"Anyway, we're on the cusp of a new scientific age. The Core is anxious to begin exploration past the fringes into the deep space of the Milky Way, but in order to do that, they need to know how to deal with all the threats they face. You gentlemen, are the key to solving those problems," John said.

"Then why should we run drills?" Jay asked. "I mean, most of these blokes seem in good shape."

"While this is not a problem that can be solved by military might, I will train you like soldiers. I will make you hone your skills to perform the scientific method on the fly and solve innumerable complex problems on your feet. I will push your body and mind. Do I make myself clear?"

"Yes sir!" we shouted together like good little soldiers.

"Good. The Core believes all of you should be locked away in the darkest prisons she has. Let us prove here that nobody is beyond redemption. We all have a past. Let us move forward together and take on the monsters that go bump in the night!"

We still had to live like soldiers, which meant eat like them.

An automated machine dispensed a beige-colored slop full of carbohydrates and amino acids. Same stuff the military boys got.

Yum.

I grabbed a piece of bread, hoping to settle my stomach. I debated in my head whether this was better or worse than eating food in pill form. Scientists at one point did succeed in making food into pill form with as much nutritional value as the real thing, however the farming syndicates were quick to shut that project down. Besides, nobody liked eating a pill anyway.

I sat across from Murph, who's the only one who didn't want to shank me. My legs, arms and back all ached from John's brutal training, which consisted of a long series of squats, lunges, sprinting down a track, gravity weights, and everything in between. I couldn't imagine how much pain I'd be in over the coming days. Sulture gave me an icy glare as I sat down.

"You know, if you're not careful your face will freeze like that," I said to him. His silverware clattered on the table as he seized me by the collar in the blink of an eye. My heart raced and my brawler instincts kicked in.

"Say it again," Sulture hissed as he tightened his grip. Murph chuckled as he placed his hand on Sulture's wrist.

"Let him go Adam. The new guy's a smart ass. He didn't mean anything by it. If anything, he admires you. We've all got our talents and we're in this together," He said as he put a spoonful of slop into his mouth.

Sulture didn't budge. His eyes grew inflamed.

"Let him go Rooster, or I'll knock you flat on your ass!" Warrens grumbled.

Sulture grunted, then released my collar. Murph perked up. "Don't worry. Shoulda seen it when Forrest made his first 'your mom' joke to Adam. He punched Forrest in the face. So much for *that* lesson in teamwork," He chuckled.

"Murph's right. I admire your work Sulture. I really enjoyed your paper *Exploitation to Extinction*. It was a fascinating read."

"Cute. A compliment from a professor. Did you actually contribute anything to science or did you spend your time grading papers and fucking the female students?" Sulture asked. All eyes looked at me. I hated delving into my past. I longed for it to remain buried.

"I was once head of R&D at Chemron," I replied meekly as I scooped some food into my mouth. It was as bland as it looked.

"Chemron?! *Chùsheng xai-jiao de xiang huo*!" Lee cursed and slammed his fist down on the table.

"Yeah, he didn't take very well to that chap," Jay said.

"Chemron? Big name drop. You design anything?" Sulture asked.

"A form of Cyanogen Chloride with some Lewisite," I whispered so that I didn't agitate Lee.

"Ahh. We used that on Angkor. Wiped out three hives with that compound," Sulture said with a hint of admiration. "Why'd you leave Chemron?" He asked.

"Disagreement with management. Once I learned about them shipping canisters of Hydrogen Cyanide to Ophridia, I got out."

"Not soon enough!" Lee hissed at me. He looked like he wanted to rip my throat out. It seemed that no matter what I did, I pissed someone off.

After our first set of drills I stumbled into my bunk. I'm by far the most out of shape on the ship. I reached into my bag and pull out a notebook I'd hastily bought before I left Titan.

Godfrey's Journal Day 1

My muscles are killing me. I ache everywhere. It seems as though every man on this ship has it out for me, except for Murph and Warrens. Good guys.

Met the infamous Adam Sulture and Xing Ming Lee. They look as though they'd kill in an instant if provoked. The pain they must've suffered in their pasts, it makes me try even harder to bury my own.

I don't understand why John brought me here. I'm just some schmuck who's been suffering at his job for the past ten years. I'm insufficient to be on this ship with these legendary men. I've been thrown into another league. College professor battling aliens? None of this makes sense. Despite this, I welcome the change. I mean, I'm sharing bunks with xenocidalists, anarchists, and information conspiracy scoundrels.

Off to a good start.

The next morning, we ate breakfast together, a quiet affair. Lee had his eyes set on me, like a tiger waiting to strike. Once we finished, John took us into the boxing ring.

"This is where you gentlemen need to learn some hand to hand combat because there will be missions where you'll be up close and personal. This will be a place to practice sparring as well as a place to settle differences. If you have a problem with somebody, you will settle it here. You will not take out your anger on one of your brothers on a mission or I will deal with you myself!" John shouted.

"For starters, Lee! Godfrey! Get over here!" John ordered.

The anger in Lee's eyes was apparent. He had a score to settle.

"It is my understanding that you have been wronged by Godfrey, is that correct Lee?"

"I didn't do anything -" I tried to interject.

John cut me off. "Is that right Lee?" He asked.

"Weapons he developed killed thousands of people on Ophridia. He built them. He…" Lee struggled to hold back tears.

"I told you I dealt with Chemron-"

"Into the ring. Both of you." John cut me off again. "Now spar."

Lee charged, screaming into the air and tried to deliver a right hook. I dodged his initial attack and sent a left jab at him, which he deflected. We're both exhausted, but Lee is being fueled by his rage. I tried to react to Lee's moves and not hit him back, but John is goading us into fighting. The others called for us to fight. Our moves are unrefined, and our sparring turns into a desperate brawl. We accumulate cuts on our faces and bruises on our bodies. By the end we were both spent and exhausted, lying on the ground, gasping for air. Lee crawled on top of me and pummeled my ribs a few more times. Finally, John called him off.

"Lee, are you satisfied?" John asked.

I can't even look up to see Lee's answer, but the way John reacted I guessed it was a yes.

"Good. Because from here on in, there will be no more talk about what happened on Ophridia. Godfrey may have made the weapons that killed your people, but he didn't sell or ship them to Yiu Mei. There will be no more fighting on this matter. Understood?

Lee nodded.

"And Godfrey, you will not retaliate against Lee for the pummeling you received unless it is right here understood?"

I nodded.

"You see gentlemen, we're human. We'll piss each other off. It's inevitable. We will use the ring aboard the ship to air our grievances. I will not have you executing personal vendettas against each other in the field. Now, shake hands you two."

Lee and I got up to our feet and shook hands. While I didn't care for the personal treatment, I thought John's idea of allowing us to sort things out in the ring was a good one.

"Allow me to be clear," John said. "Some of you are going to believe that you've accomplished some pretty incredible feats. Some of you may see yourselves as invincible and above my petty drills. You're 'men of the mind' you'll claim. That's all wimp talk. I don't give a damn about your accomplishments, your achievements, your degrees or your egos. None of those things kept you out of prison. *I did.* I'm here to break your egos. I'm here to prove that despite all you've done, some of you will struggle to do a god-damned push-up! In order to be a part of my team, you must work for it. You must be ready to run, sprint, jump, crawl, shoot and fight in hand to hand combat. You want out? Fine. Just tell me so and I'll send you to whatever prison your were tagged to go to. Welcome to the real world scientists, it's time to train!"

It seemed so long ago when we started drilling together. Now on our first mission it feels like it's all falling apart. One of our own is dead, walking amongst a legion of bloodsuckers.

"How can those leeches reanimate their host like that?" John asks us. "Any theories?"

Nobody said anything.

"C'mon! Brainstorm or we're all going to get some new necklaces!"

"It's a bio-electrical pulse," Sulture says, which snaps me back to the present. "As to how it works, I don't have any theories yet."

"Murph? You agree?" John asks.

"Most likely. My diagnosis is that since the leeches are wrapped around the host's neck, they're connected to the spinal column near the base of the skull. Poor guys."

It's odd how warm and friendly Murph is while Sulture is as cold as ice. Angkor affected the two men differently. All the others came out of their situations transformed.

A sting pierces through the back of my neck. The searing pain feels like a migraine that will split my skull open and rip my spine from my body. I scream and collapse onto the floor. The leech tries to and wrap itself around my neck, but Lee grabs the bug. Sujay shrieks and ducks into a corner, trying to stay as far away from the bugs as he can.

"Perhaps I should let this leech go for what you did to my people! All those chemicals produced when you worked at Chemron? Those chemicals killed *millions* of my people!" Lee hisses as he towers over me, contemplating my fate. I can feel the electrical pulses of the leech crawling along my brain stem. My motor complexes are being activated, and despite the fact that I am trying to stay down, I'm having a hard time enforcing that command.

"Lee, the moment I learned about those chemicals being shipped to Ophridia, I dealt with the executives at Chemron okay? I managed to convince them to stop all shipment. Please, this leech is forcing me to fight you."

"You think I cannot kill you where you stand you ben tiansheng de yidui rou?!"

John pulls out a pistol and aims it at Lee's head. "Strike any one of my men outside the boxing ring and I kill you where you stand. You're not on Ophridia anymore. These men are your allies and you *will* treat them as such! Now be a sport and pull that leech out of Godfrey's head."

Lee stood silent. I see the leech's jaws wriggling, and feel the electrical pulses buzzing in the back of my head.

John cries out and sucker punches Lee in the face. He goes down, holding his nose in his hand.

"You don't *ever* threaten any of my men like that! EVER!" John roars. Lee leaps onto his feet and takes a defensive stance. He charges, swings once and follows through with a kick, but John dodges both of them. He punches Lee square in the jaw again. The blow drives him to the ground. It's all getting fuzzy to me. I hear John screaming at Lee, but I can't make out the words.

"Word to the wise: don't piss of John unless you like getting punched in the face," Forrest says.

"Shut up Forrest!" John howls.

"Sorry," He replies.

The kid, David Shepherd, grabs the leech. I rise to my feet to fend him off. I try to will myself to stand down, but it feels like I'm being controlled by another. Like a puppet master is making me fight him.

Shepherd plunges his knife into the leech's head. It screeches out, and the buzzing stops. When Shepherd rips the leech out of my neck, I feel an explosion in my spine. My legs collapse and moments become flickers.

Murph and Shepherd grab ahold of me.

I vomit all over the floor. Turns out John's carbo slop doesn't taste any better coming up than it did going down.

Murph feels around the back of my head.

"Aw man, that's not good. Definitely not Status Dramaticus." I see a light shine on the floor and feel Murph's fingers digging around my wound.

"There's a possibility he may be leaking spinal fluid, but I can't diagnose until we're on the ship," Murph says, his voice a faraway echo.

"Godfrey, do you taste metal?" He asks.

I swirl my tongue around in my mouth. I didn't like where this was going. "Yeah,"

Tasting metal is never good.

"Shit. He's leaking spinal fluid," Murph says.

"Can you patch him up?" John asks.

"I can give him a temporary fix using fifty cc's of his blood, but I can't do much else until we're back on the ship," Murph replies.

The orange light from the boilers flickers on the edge of my vision. The colors split and merge together again. I feel woozy, incoherent. I can hear the howls of the returned soldiers banging on the door while Murph performs his emergency field operation.

"Oh, we're all going to be leech food aren't we?" Sujay asks.

"Now is not the time for cowardice Sujay!" John snaps.

"Eh, he was born a coward. His mom told me so. Wishes he would just man up and show some real courage right ol' buddy ol' pal?" Forrest asks, as he wraps his arm around Sujay's shoulder.

"You leave my mother out of this Forrest! You've never had sex with my mother and you never will!" Sujay screams.

"Promises promises. She wants it. I can see it every time she looks at me."

"You mean the abhorrent look of disgust?"

"You're just jealous you can't get a woman to look at you like that."

"Silas!" Murph interrupts. "Sorry bud, but this is going to hurt like hell," He warns.

"Huh?" I ask. I wonder why Murph takes off my gloves and why he wraps an armband around me. I don't flinch when he takes out the massive hypodermic needle, but maybe I should have. Murph plunges the needle into my arm, and I don't feel much.

"Don't you worry Silas, I'll get you out of this bud. You're tough, just gotta hold on," Murph says as he slaps me on the shoulder.

"Anything I can do to help?" the kid asks as he wanders over. I'd almost forgotten about him. Helpful, always seems like he wants to do what's right.

"Grab his left arm kid. Adam, grab his right. Okay Godfrey, this is called an Epidural blood patch procedure. I am injecting your blood into the brain stem. There is a 79.45% chance it will clot, sealing the hole in your spinal cord. I need you to talk me through what you're feeling in order to determine if it's working. Sound good?"

"Got it."

"Good, because this'll hurt like hell," Murph says.

He doesn't hold back as he pierces the needle in, injecting the blood onto my spinal column. I jerk and fight the pain, but the guys hold me tight. The headache recedes, the metal taste fades and the world becomes clear.

"Headache fading. Metal taste fading. Dizziness fading. Still taste vomit though. John's carbo slop sucks comin' up."

I force myself to remember why we're here, what our objectives are.

We're on the planet Cabon. On our first mission to inspect a mining facility that went dark. There are leeches everywhere. An infestation that drained every last miner aboard the station along with a few soldiers that sought refuge.

Soldiers seeking refuge...that's how we met the kid. David Shepherd. The kid holding onto my left arm, his face covered with an oxygen mask. He's wearing a tattered military uniform. We'd met the kid less than an hour ago and now he was helping to save my life. Seemed a lot longer than that when we ran in here for cover.

We'd hit a clearing in a storage room where we could take a breather. We shut the doors, tore the vents down and searched for leeches. When the coast was clear John messaged Jay again.

"Jay report. That is an order! Over." The situation was getting worse by the moment. Everyone was worried and wondered where Jay could be.

As soon as John finished his transmission we heard a thump come from inside one of the supply closets. Everyone drew their guns and waited. The air became oppressive as we got into formation. Sulture was closest to the door and signaled he'd open it. John would assist, ready to shoot whatever was inside. The rest of us formed a semicircle ready to fire.

Sulture reached for the handle, turned it slowly and threw the door open.

As quick as lightning, John seized what was behind the door and threw a young man to the ground.

"Don't shoot! Don't shoot!" The kid pleaded. His face was covered with an oxygen mask. The storage closet was full of oxygen tanks, foodstuffs, and water. It's clear that the kid had been here for a while and has done well for himself as a scavenger.

"He's a Marine," John said as he lowered his gun and motioned for us to do the same. "Come on up son, we won't hurt you," John said as he reached down and pulled him off the ground.

The kid was in his early twenties, short curly blond hair, my height at 183 centimetres, blue eyes, the typical Marine golden boy. His face was covered by his oxygen mask, which tethered him to the oxygen tanks in the storage closet behind him.

"Name?" John asks.

"David Shepherd, sir."

"I'm Colonel John C. Henry of Ionics Special Forces. What are the Marines doing here?" John asked.

"We were scouting a potential base on Trinitian – 6 a jungle world where we encountered those leeches," Shepherd replied.

"Trinitian – 6, that's on the borders of Xeclian space," John replied, sounding suspicious.

"Well, there's talk of the Xeclians rising up again, hence the base," Shepherd said. "Anyway the first guy in our squad, Kirk, was drained within minutes. We shot him in the head to be merciful, but before we could bury him his corpse came after us. Three more men were brought down by either Kirk or the leeches, but their returned bodies came after us like animals. Sarge pulled the plug and ordered a retreat, but one of the dead men got onto the ship. We removed the leech, but it escaped and started breeding. Soon they got into the ventilation aboard the ship, and it was every man for himself at that point. We commed for help and Ionics told us to dock here. It's not even the leeches that are the biggest problem. It's the men who're fighting on their behalf. The men are possessed, completely under the control of those things. They got into the ventilation systems here, snagging everyone in sight. I've been hoarding supplies, trying to kill what I can, and have sent several distress signals." Something about his story seemed off to me.

"Well Shepherd, the cavalry has arrived. What are your skills?" John asked.

"I have a knack for jury-rigging stuff, I can fix just about anything. I'm a Marine. I can shoot." Shepherd replied.

"We could always use a good mechanic. Got any weapons?"

"An AR, two clips and a flamethrower."

"Good. Grab 'em, you're with us now. You're on reserve with me, guard the left flank."

"Yes sir," Shepherd said as he saluted John. He picked up the AR and two clips, while John returned the salute and grabbed the flamethrower.

I pulled John aside. "You sure he should be with us? The boy could be hostile to strangers, or he could've gone mad from solitude."

"That's why he's in reserve next to me Godfrey. If he tries anything, the report will say that there were no survivors." John's assurance eased me a bit, but I was still wary.

We pressed onward to the power systems. As we neared the boiler room, an eerie orange glow blazed across the station. Long bars of light shifted across the walls as the vents opened and closed. It was getting warmer, as we closed in on the engines that burned their fuel to power the station. We turned right into the engine core, realizing why we had seen so few leeches: their nest was in here.

The walls were lined with the offspring. They were reproducing at a rapid pace and bathing in the warmth of the engine core.

Their slime trails glistened along the walls. The eerie orange glow reflected off their glistening bodies. Every time a leech moved, there's a disgusting squishing noise, and everyone was on edge. We believed that our armor would be able to hold should these leeches try to strike us, but we didn't know for sure. Our protection wasn't exactly ideal in the neck.

We moved deeper into the bowels of the station. The light grew dim as we searched in the engineer's office and crew bunks, but found nothing. I turned into life support systems, opened the door and before I could react I was knocked down by the ravenous return of Jay's body. His hands seized my neck as there was a low rumble emanating from his throat. I was being choked, and forced to kneel before the returned man trying to murder me. He had unnatural strength in his fingers and a determination that only a returned dead guy could possess.

The others were driven back to the storage room by a mob of the returned miners and soldiers. They howled when the others shot at them, and the Horsemen were forced to leave me behind during their retreat.

I shuddered as I recalled my first close call for the day, Murph now working on my second. He seemed optimistic that all of my symptoms were clearing up.

"It'll hold him until we get back to the ship. I'll need to perform surgery and cleanse the wound to stave off infection," Murph says.

John nods. "I'm calling this mission off. It's clear that we've failed. I have a dead man, an insubordinate and one with a serious injury on the back of his head. Abort the mission and prepare to get back to the ship," John orders.

"No..." I grumble as I rise to my feet. "If we run then Jay's death will have been for nothing. There's always a learning curve with a new team like this. I've failed enough times in my life and I believe that these guys don't want to see themselves as failures on our first mission, right?" I turn to the others.

"The professor is right! We will kill this infestation!" Sulture spat.

"Let's knock them out!" Warrens cries.

"Actually, I'm perfectly alright with seeing myself as a failure for this mission," Sujay says.

"Get your ass in gear Sujay or I'll come after your mother and show her what a real man looks like!" I howl.

"Haha! Nice one!" Forrest says.

Sulture looks around the room. He notices the ventilation shafts covered in slime trails. "We know the leeches use the vents. What if we turn the vents against them?" He asks.

"What're you thinking Sulture?" John asks.

"Let me see the leech we've got," Sulture says. Shepherd hands him the carcass and he pulls out a bio scanner. He waves the wand twice across the specimen.

"Based on its biochemical composition, these leeches are very similar to the ones on Earth. That's good because there's a simple way we can kill them."

"And what way would that be?" John asks.

"Ionized alcohol. Warrens, do you think you could build an ionizer to dispense some alcohol across the vents of the station here?" Sulture asks.

"I could put one of those together. We'd have to dispense it via the central ventilation mainframe though," Warrens replies.

"Hacker, if we get back to central control could you seal up the vents and reverse the airflow?" Sulture asks.

"In order to seal up the vents I'll need to access the internal mainframe capacitors..."

"We don't need the technical rundown Hacker, can you do it?" John snarls.

"Yes, I can do it," Hacker replies.

"There's just one problem with your plan Sulture. Where are we going to get alcohol?" John asks.

"John, we're on a mining station."

"Do *not* talk down to me or I'll knock you out like I did to Lee!" John snaps. Sulture lowers his head, but doesn't apologize for the remark. John turns to Shepherd.

"Shepherd, you know the station better than any of us. Are there liquor stores accessible from here?"

"Yes sir, I'll show you the way."

Shepherd takes us to the food stores he'd been raiding. Sulture and Warrens sweep the room to ensure that there aren't any leeches waiting for us inside.

"There's still a lot of booze stored in here," Shepherd says. "Figured when I ran out of food I could drink my troubles away." He laughs at his own joke, but nobody else does.

"Maybe next time Goldilocks," Warrens pats Shepherd on the shoulder.

"Y'see you gotta make the joke less grim. Like 'This is the amount of alcohol I was planning on serving Sujay's mom so that we could have a night of passionate -"

"Leave my mother out of this!" Sujay shrieks.

"That's how you get a reaction kid," Forrest nudges Shepherd's arm.

As we grab case after case of liquor, Murph keeps checking up on me to see how I'm doing. We both know that the blood clot won't hold indefinitely. Time is short, and the back of my neck is on fire. I move quickly, hauling cases and forcing myself to move through the pain. Warrens and Shepherd scavenge the station for spare parts, building an ionizer from an old fuel injection system. The mechanics had the device ready in less than an hour and we had a dozen cases of alcohol to work with.

Each of us grab a bottle, take a swig, and start pouring into the funnel for the ionizer. The alcohol tickles my tongue as my memories from my past life come flooding back. I used drink as an escape, and after my second swig I have to stop because I do not want to slide down that slope. As the alcohol is carried along the hoses a thought keeps rising over and over in my head: is this all we needed to do? We find a solution, introduce enough alcohol to poison the air the leeches breathe and it's over? Hacker tinkers with the vents, drawing the alcohol in and then expelling it out into the rooms containing all of the leeches. My head throbs in pain, and some of my symptoms start to return.

"Murph..." I stutter out. It's all I can say. My concentration is broken, but he sees my message loud and clear.

"Shit! He needs to get back to the ship!" Murph tells John.

"Then let's get him back there!" John says as he ignites the flame thrower. Murph hoists me over his shoulder and before I can focus well enough to walk, I black out.

Flashes. False memories. There is an operating room table. I push myself up, but a forceful hand shoves me back down. I have no idea where I am, what's happening or who is behind me keeping me pressed on the table.

"For Christ's sake put him back under!" I hear Murph's voice cut through the haze. A sharp prick into my arm, something warm flows into my weakened limb and, light fades back into dark.

When I come to, Lee is standing in the doorway, watching. He looks like hell, with a black eye and a cut lip. Can't imagine that I look much better.

"You look like shit," I finally break the silence.

Lee grins, but puts his fingers back to his lip. "I'm here to tell you I'm sorry Dr. Godfrey."

"Just Godfrey."

"What century are you from, the eighteenth? Sha gwa!" Lee says.

"Is that all you got *xiongmao niao*?" I retort. Lee's eyes grow wide and his jaw drops in surprise.

"Yeah, I understand Mandarin. Can speak a little of it too."

"*Chur ni-duh*!" He hisses with a grin. His face turns serious: "Look Godfrey, I had no right and Jay's death-"

"Forget it Lee. After the hell we've all been through, I've come to expect a hazing ritual. Besides, watching John beat the hell out of you was enough for me."

"Jesus you're right!" Lee says as he rubs his bruised chin. "You should've seen him when Sulture got here. John is merciless, especially when any of us question his authority."

"Couldn't believe Sulture backed down like he did."

"Well you weren't here when..." Lee stops talking as he studiously stands straight and bows to John as he walks into the hospital room.

"Sir," Lee says, then briskly walks off.

"Not bad John. Nearly made a man who's killed a bloodthirsty dictator piss his pants."

John laughs. "How you holdin' up Godfrey?"

"Peachy. You guys kill all the leeches?"

"We did, too bad you blacked out before we could finish the job."

"Ah, maybe next time then. So what's next?"

"We wait for orders from Ionics. I've also got some reforms I'm putting into place for all of you. Team building efforts and classroom collaboration."

"May as well put you in HR."

"I just beat one of my subordinates half to death. Don't think they'll accept me."

"Thanks for your help with that by the way."

"Don't mention it Godfrey. Besides I made a heavy concession to Lee."

"What's that?"

"Gave him his own private garden. Figured giving a botanist his own garden was the least I could do."

"Maybe he'll calm down."

"Maybe."

"What about the Shepherd ordeal?"

"I'm having Hacker look into it right now. If there's something funny about Shepherd, he'll find it. How long does Murph have you set for bedrest?"

"Guy as tough as Godfrey should be up and walking around now," Murph answers as he walks into the room. "Overheard you talking about Shepherd sir, Hacker is looking for you right now to debrief."

"Ok, thanks Murph. Godfrey," John nods as he takes his leave.

"How bad is it?" I ask.

"After the surgery I gave you, you'll be back on your feet in no time. Nothing more than a battle scar for your troubles. Welcome to the Horsemen," Murph says as he slaps my shoulder.

"Hacker say anything about Shepherd?" I ask.

"Well, he's as suspicious as you are. Went digging into computer backlogs and whatnot...said he had to dig through over a thousand servers. Guess Shepherd's story is buried pretty deep."

"Huh. It's just odd with him being the sole survivor on the station.

Rouses suspicion."

"I see it this way: the kid's resourceful and knows what to do in a tight spot. May not be a scientist, but if we gave him the option to stay on the team, he'd take it."

I nod my head. "Interesting way of looking at things. Murph, the eternal optimist. Or rather, more of our cheerleader."

He grins. "Yeah, I suppose that's me."

Murph gives me a clean bill of health and allows me to leave the medbay. As I'm walking through the corridors of the ship, I come across John who's standing outside of the spare bunk where he's put Shepherd. I don't mean to eavesdrop, but I keep myself hidden behind a corner in the hallway.

"Shepherd, you got a minute?" John asks

"Yes Colonel." Shepherd stands and salutes.

"At ease. Listen I won't beat around the bush here. Your story with the Marines doesn't make sense. I'm not saying you're part of it, frankly I think you're just a kid mixed up in something beyond his control. However, I need to protect my men so I'm locking you in here for the time being. I need answers as to why you were at the mining station and the ones you gave, frankly weren't good enough. I don't trust the Sergeant's story. I'm also locking you here to protect you since some of the other men don't take bad news very well. You will be fed and released once I'm satisfied with what I've found. Am I clear?"

Shepherd sighs. "Yes sir. I just did as I was told, acted the best I could, and don't want any trouble. I told you everything I knew."

"And I believe you son. Once again, I think your Sergeant was the one who was lying." John left it at that, exits the bunk and types in a pass code. The door seals shut with Shepherd inside.

FORGING FROM ASHES

Godfrey's Journal Day 40

It's been three days since our disastrous first mission. John begins the debrief, which is standard after each mission, so that he can send his report back to corporate. It's a long interview, an hour for each of us since one of our own died. The interview was primarily to satisfy human resources and to ensure that none of us were becoming bloodthirsty sociopaths.

John's a little…slow in turning in his report because he isn't sure of what corporates' reaction to Shepherd would be. He waits for Hacker's analysis on what Shepherd and the Marines were doing on the Cabon mining station. Hacker won't say where he got the information, only that he has discretion on his side, meaning prying eyes cannot see his intrusion. John originally gave him twenty four hours, but that time line grew since this secret was buried deep under layers of red tape. On top of that, John and Hacker had to put the pieces together, making sense out of what seem like illogical events.

In the meantime, Shepherd has been drilling and eating with us like he has become a Horseman, but during down time (which has been almost non-existent) John kept him locked in the spare bunk. John has been relentless, working us like dogs. He took Jay's death especially hard since he feels responsible for his demise. John says his goal is to instill a little humility into us. I don't get it either.

The memorial service for Jay was short since John doesn't want us dwelling on the death of our brethren. He believes we need to become accustomed to the idea that we will all die and that we should strive for a glorious death. Lee took Jay's death the hardest, since they had done so much on Ophridia together. I can't imagine what that must be like, to lose a man who was like a brother.

Hacker has put all of the pieces together on Shepherd and has called a meeting for us. John is especially anxious to see what he's dug up.

"I've called you together because this is something that you all need to hear," John says. "After we found Shepherd, it was brought to my attention that his story didn't make sense as to why the Marines were on the mining station. I've tasked Hacker to investigate the matter and he is ready to present his findings. Hacker, take it away."

"Thank you sir. I was suspicious of Shepherd at first, and the information was incredibly difficult to find due to a plethora of firewalls, security protocols, server complexes, artificially intelligent defense programs-"

"We get it Hacker," John says impatiently.

"Yes, anyway, I had a variety of sources I won't list get to the bottom of the case. What I found was that the military was conducting a program called 'Operation Hatchback.' The purpose of the program was to create a line of human clones for the purpose of an emergency army in the event of a Xeclian or a rebel uprising. The Unification Wars cost a lot of lives, and Hatchback was to ensure that the Core had a standing army ready at a moment's notice."

"Human cloning has been outlawed for the past 500 years!" Sulture says.

"These laws do not apply in the fringes of Xeclian space," John counters.

"Right. They got 'autonomy' for their experiments," Sulture groans.

"Why's it always gotta be the Xeclians?" Forrest asks. "Blue bug-eyed midgets with too many toys. Why not some dumb aliens who use two sticks taped to a rock?"

"Indeed," Hacker replies. "On Trinitian - 6 there's a laboratory set up where Shepherd was to be stationed. The ship's logs at the mining station reveal that the Sergeant got bad coordinates and landed in the jungle where they encountered the leeches and evacuated the planet when the wildlife proved too aggressive."

"Why didn't he go to the secret base on Trinitian – 6?" I ask. "Why'd the Sergeant go to Cabon instead? That's what I don't understand."

"Change of heart, given improper clearance level, they didn't want the leech infestation, there are a million reasons as to why the Sergeant went to Cabon instead of this base. Problem is, those reasons died with him," Hacker replies. "What I can tell you is that none of those reasons are technical."

"Sorry Shepherd. Something here doesn't add up," I say.

Shepherd nods his head. "I was just told we were to prepare for a Xeclian uprising, that they were getting restless," He replies and shrugs his shoulders. "I was just doing my duty as a soldier."

"Hehe…dootie," Forrest chuckles.

"Shut up Forrest!" Everyone except the kid shouts.

"Sorry," Forrest replies.

Hacker continues: "Officially they were right Shepherd. Investigation of the cloning lab reveals it was built by Samson Research and Development, a competitor to Ionics. David Shepherd, or rather subject XB-4377059 was designated as an 'Origin Point Donor', a soldier whose purpose was to serve as the donor of biological tissues for the creation of the clone army…willingly or not."

Everyone's jaw drops.

We're all shocked over the bombshell Hacker has just dropped. Shepherd was a golden boy, one who was so good the military hoped to mass produce him.

"I didn't know, I swear," Shepherd stutters out. The kid looks panicked, can't say I blame him.

"We believe you," John replies, and places a hand on the kid's shoulder. He continues: "The reason I called this meeting is because I have yet to file my official report and corporate is riding my ass about it. The truth is I have no idea what to do with Shepherd, especially now since sending him back to the Marines means he goes to that God-forsaken world to be harvested as clone material. That doesn't sit well with me," John says, turning to Shepherd.

"Wait, who's funding this abominable program? Who is directing this cloning operation?" Sulture screams.

"Samson Research and Development has received multiple rounds of funding from the military, and they're using Xeclian cloning technology," Hacker replies.

"Hence the military cover story with the Xeclians," John says.

"Exactly," Hacker replies. "The Xeclians are not interested or even involved in the project. There's no word of an uprising either, they're as docile as kittens. There are also hundreds of shell corporations involved in Operation Hatchback, all pouring money into Samson's pockets. Many of these shell corporations are owned by the military, but there are a few private sources. I have some contacts at *The Grid* seeking out the owners, but they're buried under layers of legal paperwork. I'm sorry, but that's all I can find."

"Sounds like a conspiracy," Murph says. "Should we be worried? I mean, I think the ten of us could take 'em, but should we be worried?" He asks.

"The military has been using shell companies for centuries, that's nothing new," I reply. "What's unsettling is the fact that they're blatantly breaking Core laws to create this clone army. And for what purpose? Is there any benefit to clone soldiers?" I ask.

"Not really," Sulture replies. "Give me the genome of the clone and I'll create a viral strain that will kill every last one of them," He snarls.

"Hacker is getting to the bottom of this," John says. "Let's see what he finds before we start going after anyone. I'll see what I can pull from my sources within the military as well. In the meantime we need to figure out what we're going to do with Shepherd here."

"If I may sir," Shepherd interjects.

"Go ahead son."

"I've heard about how all of your men came to be here sir. I…I don't have anywhere else to go, and I'd like to stay and earn my keep," Shepherd says.

"This isn't like the Marines Shepherd. We're going to be fighting monsters, not other men. There is no leaving the Horsemen Corps unless you're in a body bag, and your chances of death are well over 90%," John warns.

"Technically it's 89.35%," Murph chuckles.

"Where else do I have to go? I have no family, which is why I joined the Marines. Then they decided to harvest me for genetic material. I feel accepted here. I'll admit, I don't know the most about science. What I do know is that nobody should be experimented on. Science shouldn't be used as a weapon on humans. It should exist to help mankind, not slaughter them. Horsemen, if you let me join I will fight with you until the bitter end to put a stop to such cruelty," Shepherd pleads.

"Horsemen! What do you say?" John asks.

We all howl in agreement.

John turns back to us. "Then my report will say that there were no Marines left alive. We found some young miner who was a hitchhiker and being paid under the table for his help. Hacker, wipe out Shepherd's identity from all databases including subject XB-whatever! David Shepherd, welcome to the Horseman Corps!"

"Welcome to the team, Shepherd! First rate! Y'know, there's a hazing ritual where we all get to spend some quality time with your mom and…"

"Shut up Forrest!" We shout.

"Sorry," He replies.

"Besides, my parents are gone Forrest…" Shepherd says.

"Ohh…"

"You had to go there didn't you?" Sujay asks. "You had to bring his mother into this! What is it with you and mothers? Can't you find a normal woman you can creep out?" He says.

I notice that Forrest is rubbing a small amulet in the palm of his hand. "Well, I know one thing for sure. At least golden boy here won't be harvested for parts. I'm a lucky guy, but leaving him behind…I think that would bring some bad juju into the mix," Forrest says.

"I think we're all inclined to agree Forrest," John replies.

Godfrey's Journal Day 61

John has instituted a series of classes designed to make us work together to defeat aliens. Due to humanity's ignorance of deep space travel, our decontamination procedures and methods of studying foreign species are either outdated or irrelevant. For example, Sulture said that mustard gas wasn't much use against the creatures of Angkor. We needed to study the creatures we were up against and find their weaknesses.

John had lots of case studies, each of which read like a horror novel. Explorer gets an alien bug, goes into decon chamber, which for one reason or another fails to kill bug. Bug gets into vents and kills everyone inside the ship. John tasked us to re-invent the methods of decontamination so that this never happens. It's a tall order.

As a team we brainstormed the S.M.A.R.T. Protocol which operated as follows: Study the organism in question. Monitor/Measure the organism. Analyze the details such as: Is the organism bipedal, or a quadruped? Is it a loner, a member of a pack, herd, or of a hive mind? Is it microbial or a recombinator? Recon the environment, what can be used against the creature? And finally, Terminate the organism. We adopted the SMART protocol, at least until somebody comes up with something better.

John's reforms have forced us to unite as a team. He reshuffled the bunk arrangements and stated he will do so every couple of weeks. He puts us in tight situations where we must work together in order to come up with a solution quickly. He believes that all of us should share our knowledge so he has each of us teach a new topic to the team members.

For instance, John and Warrens give weapons training, Forrest and Sujay teach flight maneuvers, Murph does field medical response, Sulture, biological categorization, Shepherd, practical survival tips, Hacker, password cracking, Lee, stealth skills and reconnaissance, while I teach how to turn seemingly inert chemicals into deadly bombs. All of this knowledge sharing gives everyone tools in their arsenal for the future. John has us put our newfound skills to the test in "field modules" where we must reenact our new training without the specialist who taught us.

One time, we were dealing with a renegade droid that Hacker programmed and all we had were dismantled assault rifles at our disposal. Our choices were to either: hack into the droid ourselves, or assemble the rifles and take out the droid.

John doesn't give us time for rest. We run precision drills in a constant effort to turn us into the deadliest fighting squad in the galaxy. The only time we get off is in the evening, where John has set up our own laboratories to stay on top of our scientific pursuits. Lee has his garden, we have a general laboratory that Sulture and I share, Murph keeps to the Medbay, Warrens and Shepherd have a workshop, and Hacker has a lab with a chamber device. John is generous in providing us with the latest in scientific research and even went so far as to force us to read for an hour together in the common area. It was a bit awkward at first, being forced to read, but John wants our minds in tip top shape.

Godfrey's Journal, Day 72

Hacker hated the operating system aboard The Enigma so he created a newer, friendlier system called the Explanatory Mainframe Interface of the Enigma or E.M.I.E. Hacker installed E.M.I.E. aboard The Enigma without John's permission. The system had a beautiful woman's voice, which seemed fitting.

Emie also created an uplink between the ship and our combat suits, which let us see everyone's health stats - i.e. blood pressure, heartbeat, etc.. Hacker created our own personal experimentation profiles for note taking (which coincidentally were encrypted so that Ionics couldn't see what we were doing - no one questioned the ethics of that), and created our own Enigma server for whatever file sharing we needed.

Instead of one program operating navigation, military suits, and flight systems separately, Hacker gave us an operating system capable of handling all of our needs top to bottom. Emie removed all of the complications between the different programs and interfaces. John simply told Hacker to ask him next time before installing any foreign software on his ship.

Godfrey's Journal, Day 74

The final issue we had was the battle suits. Ionics R&D already developed their suits and weren't willing to shell out more credits for revamping them. John warned that if we wanted new suits, we'd have to pay for them ourselves. We happily accepted the challenge.

We approach Warrens, who's sketching in his notebook.

"What?" He asks.

"John gave us the okay to build new suits, but we'll have to pay for them. We want the Warrens War Machine Experience," I explain.

"You know I destroyed the weapon I used right?" Warrens asks.

"Saw the footage. Don't get why, but I saw," I reply.

"You boys are lucky since I already have some sketches for everyone," Warrens replies. "We all know the suits we have now are too bulky and unyielding, at least all of us except GB here," He laughs.

"Who?" Shepherd asks.

"Warrens gives everyone nicknames," Murph replies.

Shepherd flashes a quizzical look.

"Golden Boy," Murph chuckles.

"Alright, we'll start with a thin titanium-carbon tri-weave that will be fitted to each of us and become a type of 'second skin.' It's the closest I could get to the armor I wielded," Warrens says as he brings up a holographic screen with a list of supplies.

"Ooh! Does that mean we get to go shopping?" Forrest blurts out.

"I'll do the haggling," Sujay insists.

"You always do the haggling!" Forrest yells.

"Because if I don't you'll spend all of our money!" Sujay replies.

"Just like how I was spent when I-"

"SHUT UP FORREST!" Warrens roars.

I thought for sure Forrest was going to shit himself. Most of us snicker.

Warrens explains the design of our suits, going for armor that is sleek and strong. He says we'll be vulnerable to knives and energy blades, but he believes the increase in mobility makes up for the risk. One by one, we sit down with Warrens and describe what we want our suits to be able to do. He takes his initial concepts, uploads them onto the projector, and tinkers with them on our individual avatar.

For Hacker, Warrens designed a suit that looks like a walking mainframe. It glows various shades of green, is solar powered and projects his operating interface as a hologram, making his armor a mobile chamber device. It also holds every kind of port ever designed in case he needs to connect the old fashioned way. His interlocking plates and glowing veins give him a sleek and modern look.

Lee's suit is designed for stealth. His armor is sleek and thin, and everything is colored jet black. On his helmet there is a large visor designed to absorb as much light as possible as well as give the wielder an array of options for vision, such as night and infared. He's also got a lot of knives. Knife sheaths everywhere.

Murph's armor has a few plates for protection, but has more freedom of movement around the joints. The armor has the white cross on patches of red, which signal his status as a medic. The suit also comes heavily equipped with medical devices for operating in the field - everything from salt tablets to x-ray scanners.

Sulture's suit has medium-heavy interlocking plates covering the entire body. However, when one looks closer they'll notice the armor plates are porous, which allows Sulture to release pathogens through his armor. He even has a set on his mouth guard so he could breathe disease if need be. The armor also comes with scanners on his fingertips which will give an in-depth analysis of any organism he touches. His helmet is sinister and alien. It sends chills down my spine.

Forrest and Sujay were hesitant for new armor, quite satisfied with their long brown leather coats and personnel shields, but Warrens explained that he could augment the shields with a pair of silver bracers for the two. They agreed to wear the titanium tri-weave, but Forrest fell in love with his armor concept the moment Warrens showed it to him. It was a scaly cuirass plate for the chest, but the plates could shift and form into a thin armor plating allowing for maximum movement, and still let him wear his flight goggles. Sujay's on the other hand was a neck brace which could provide an invisible shield for his head, as well as shield plates on the shoulder over his coat, shins and new bracers.

Shepherd's was a medium-heavy armor designed with thick carbonate plates instead of metal, along with a simple helmet where the visor went across the eyes. Shepherd said that he was training to be a sniper, so Warrens integrated wind direction gauges and a rangefinder in the visor. There were also slots along the armor for more bullets, as well as a bandolier for field operations. Shepherd kept things simple and wanted to look like a soldier.

As for me, Warrens gave me a helmet with a large visor that looked like pilot goggles. The mouthguard was hollowed back and porous, designed to be a gas mask. I wanted a fairly light armor and a focus on mobility so he designed a coat made out of the carbonate tri-weave with armor plates on the shoulders and the chest. It was an olive green color, designed to help me blend in. Truth was, I didn't know what I wanted for field ops.

Finally after we prodded him, Warrens revealed his armor. He kept to the same design as the standard issue, however he removed a lot of the heavy plating around the legs for more movement. The armor rose high around the neck and the helmet covered the whole head. There were hinges on the arms and shoulders designed to help Warrens lift heavier loads. His strength could be augmented by a factor of five according to Murph's calculations.

Now that we were going by "The Horsemen Corps" we felt the need to have a symbol which embodied us. Everyone had a say in the design of the logo. Forrest thought it would be cool to have a metallic shield, and Shepherd suggested that everyone have it placed on their left shoulder. Warrens sketches out a ghastly horse head, with the black paint on top of the steel giving a grunge feel that we loved. He sketches in some flames erupting from the nostrils, and we brainstorm the symbols of what should embody the Horsemen.

"The biohazard symbol," Sulture says.

"The nuclear symbol," Murph adds.

"What was the symbol for famine?" Lee asks.

"Scales," Hacker replies. "The Horseman of Famine used the scales to determine who was just and would receive the bounties from the world," He reads off the computer.

"And a skull and crossbones to represent death," I say.

"It's still missing something. A slogan…" Warrens says.

"It needs to be in Latin. All the military commandos have a Latin slogan," Forrest says.

"What would 'conquest through science' translate to?" Sulture asks.

"Actual translation or…?" Hacker asks.

"Read 'em off," I say.

Hacker reads the first. "Conquest Per Scientiam."

"That's our slogan!" I shout.

"But I have more…"

"Don't care Hacker. Nobody will wonder what *this* phrase means."

"Fellas, we have an emblem that will knock some fear into the heads of all who see it," Warrens says.

We show the emblem to John, who inspects it carefully, not giving a us a hint of his real thoughts. He finally looks up at us and a grin breaks through his stern gaze.

"This is...very well done gentlemen. I...I'm speechless," He says as his eyes well up with tears. "Alright, back to training."

Once finished, Warrens gives us a huge list of parts to buy. Forrest claims to know where we can find everything we need, which is on the former rebel stronghold Aabar-5. We journey out to the barren world to negotiate for the parts we need to assemble our armor.

Aabar-5 would best be described as a "Junker's Paradise" since there's so much leftover matieralé from the Unification Wars. The smell is awful and Forrest's contacts aren't exactly what we would call stand-up civilians. But they deliver, and bring us just about everything we need.

Warrens spends five days assembling the armor. We design wrist comms, micro computers to communicate between the ship, our armor, and each other - all part of Hacker's seamless network integration.

As we tinker with the new armor, John briefs us on a new assignment.

"Gentlemen, another Ionics outpost has gone offline, a crucial research station based on Delmar-Torren."

Sujay groans. "Not DT! It's a dark, sunless world with nothing but water and thunderstorms that's also a hotbed of hostility between mercs, rebels and Core military. Everyone scrambling to take that waterball for himself," He says.

"Correct, which means we need to recover and secure the company research station from whoever wants it," John says. "The DT outpost is an experimental weapons testing facility, which is why it's a target."

"Why is Ionics involved in weapons research?" I ask.

"I'm afraid that information is way above my pay grade," John replies.

I don't like his answer, but I know I won't get much else. I have a gut feeling that there's a lot of red tape involved and it's twisted tighter than the Gordian Knot.

"So all we gotta do is knock out some bandits and save the Ionics' stockpile?" Warrens asks.

"The station has gone dark," John says. "Hopefully it was only a power failure. We'll know soon enough. Forrest, Sujay, set a course."

"On our way boss man!" Forrest says as he salutes.

GRIGYLLS

Thunder rumbles around the ship as we close in on the Delmar-Torren facility. Rain pours down in sheets on the ship, pelting us under the sky's constant mourning.

The facility is completely dark, and the shipyard appears to be abandoned.

"Gee, this place sure looks inviting," Forrest says as he rolls his eyes.

"I don't trust this. Forrest, Sujay, stay in the air on patrol for us," John orders. He clips himself to the rope and zips down to the landing pad.

"Better you than us," Forrest says. "See ya chumps!"

"I'm going to kick his ass," Warrens whispers to me as he zips down.

I grab ahold of the rope and fasten my clip. I watch the raindrops fall around the cargo hold, pelting the cold steel shipyard below. I close my eyes and jump, anxious to see what comes next.

Lightning flashes above and thunder rumbles in the distance. Shepherd is the last to zip down, and the *Enigma* flies off.

We walk through the main entrance and there's the rank stench of blood and death. My night vision goggles switch off as the lightning flash illuminates the room. In the pale blue light there are dozens of broken bodies scattered across the floor. Blood is everywhere, as if all the people were literally torn apart.

We've just walked into a massacre.

"*Hwai*," Lee whispers.

We spread out and inspect the bodies. Their gazes are a frozen canvas of agonized hatred. Between their bulging eyes and wretched snarls, it's as if they couldn't believe how they'd died. Deep, claw-like gashes line their throats. Muscle and bone are exposed from huge tears in the flesh. What's curious is that some of these wounds look like bite marks.

"Thirty eight deceased," Murph says.

"These claw and bite marks are obscene," Sulture says. "There's only one creature I know of that would make such marks-"

"Grigylls," John interrupts.

"The walking lizard-men abominations," Sulture snarls.

"Wait, those actually exist? *Lao tyen yeh*," Lee curses.

"Yes," John replies. "And they're exactly as bad as what you hear in the stories."

"Where'd they come from?" Shepherd asks.

"A scientist by the name of Lawrence Joslin experimented on human DNA to see what humans could 'evolve' into," Sulture explains. "Most of his experiments were in vain, but he found just the right alien microbe which infected and recombinated human DNA with a lizard. The result was the brooding, grunting, savage beast we know as the Grigyll."

"What happened to the duh liou mahng after the Grigylls were made?" Lee asks.

"They tore him to pieces," Murph replies.

"What's worse is that they reproduce quickly," Sulture says. "Each female lays a minimum of ten eggs and they grow to adulthood within five years."

"Jesus," I whisper.

John interjects. "They grow to about two and a half metres tall. They're strong, twice as strong as humans. They also have a much hardier constitution, which is why they've become a successful space-faring race.

"Why is it that all of these soldiers are only wielding knives?" Warrens asks as he nudges one with his boot. "Wasn't this supposed to be a military installation?"

"Yeah, and where is all the admin support? The scientists and the managers?" Hacker asks.

"Those are good questions," John replies. "Hacker, go pull the ship manifests."

Hacker nods, plugs himself into a nearby terminal and projects a large screen interface. He finds and turns on the lights in the central area. The lights only manage to reveal what a bloodbath the battle was and doesn't ease our worries.

"Gentlemen, sorry to interrupt your rainy day stay at the DT Secret Weapons Research Facility," Forrest says. "We have come across a raggedy, torn up ship out here that's *old.* A *Liberty* class ship hasn't been built in over a hundred years!"

The team shares a look. The Grigylls are still here.

My gut churns like a cauldron. Nobody survives an encounter with Grigylls. Fully trained soldiers here got slaughtered, what chance do I have? They fought and got their throats torn out and their organs devoured. I can't do this.

"How'd they get this far into Core space?" Shepherd asks. "Doesn't Earth keep an eye out for them?"

"They do, but Earth has a long, troubled history with the Grigylls," John explains. "Joselin created them about 170 years ago, and we had a decade-long war that Earth barely survived just under 100 years ago. We banished them to a planet within Core space, but they revolted and Earth drove them beyond the reaches of known space. They still linger out there, but Earth has no record of them forming any type of civilization."

"Their body parts sure sell for a lot on the black market!" Forrest interjects.

A crash of metal echoes down the hallway behind us. All of us spin around and draw our guns. My heart is threatening to burst through my chest. There's no sign of movement for what feels like an eternity. One by one, we lower our weapons.

"Godfrey, go check it out," John orders. "Warrens, provide support."

My heart sinks when John says my name. I swallow my fear and march to the corridor with my pistol drawn. I activate my night vision in my visor as the light fades behind me. I scan the area but don't see anything. I feel as though I'm being watched, I feel a foreign presence here.

The clack of Warrens' boots against the steel floor does little to help my anxiety. We take opposite sides of the hall in our search.

"There's the pan that fell," Warrens says as he moves in. I take the opposite wall to cover his six.

I turn the corner and there it is, a full sized Grigyll standing over me. The beast lunges and seizes me by the throat.

Why does everything have to grab me by the neck.

I gasp for breath, the creature trying to snap my vertebrae. I strike at its forearm, but it doesn't loosen the vise-like grip. Low growls flow between it's dagger teeth. It's eyes are nothing more than coral orbs, optimal for the darkness of space. I see stars creep into my vision. My life is fading and as much as I kick this animal, it doesn't release me. I think back to my training, searching for anything related to the *SMART,* but I'm too caught up in surviving.

I hear a howl from behind. Warrens unleashes a devastating right hook into the Grigyll's temple. The beast groans in pain and releases me. I gasp for breath, my lungs burning from the rush of air.

"Contact!" Warrens screams at the top of his lungs. He fires three shots into the Grigyll as it tries to run away.

The team rushes in with guns drawn. "What happened?" John asks.

"Casanova went in on his own," Warrens replies.

"I literally turned a corner and this thing was there."

John inspects the body. "We need to root them out and kill them. Sulture, Warrens and Godfrey, you guys are team one. The rest with me. We'll start by securing this floor."

Sulture flips on his night vision and leads us through the complex. My breathing comes in shallow gasps and my heart won't stop racing. Apparently my breathing was louder than I thought.

"What? Are you afraid Godfrey?" Sulture asks. He doesn't sound surprised.

"I'm terrified," I stumble out. "My nerves are rattled. I've never faced anything like this. How can we possibly win when they're so much bigger and stronger? How do we face this enemy?"

Sulture doesn't say anything for a moment. "Get used to being terrified." The sting of his icy tone cuts deep. Surely even he's afraid now, is he not? How can he hide it so well?

"That was terrible advice Rooster," Warrens says. "Look Godfrey, it's about finding the courage to stand shoulder to shoulder with your brothers. To keep their asses alive when they're in danger. To sacrifice yourself so that the squad can survive."

Warrens leaves my mind a little more at ease, but I can't help but worry that I'll break under the pressure.

The three of us creep along the pitch black corridors. Sulture takes point and peers over a corner to the next hallway.

"Contact!" John screams over the comm. All of us hear a guttural howl followed by blaster fire through the installation.

"John, do you need support?" Sulture asks. There's no response, only more blaster fire.

"We're going to help them-" Sulture's words trail off as I see another Grigyll pop out from around the corner. I shove Sulture aside as the beast swings an electron machete. I duck down and the weapon clangs against the wall. I draw my pistol, but its reflexes are quick. It knocks my arm away, and I fire into the air.

The Grigyll swings at me wildly. The air sizzles from the heat of the machete, and it's driving my NVG haywire. Warrens opens fire, but the Grigyll ducks back behind the corner.

Warrens chases after the beast, but he stops in the middle of the hallway.

"It's gone."

"What?! That's not possi-" Sulture stops as he looks out around the corner. I follow him and realize that the Grigyll which attacked us had vanished into the darkness. We look around, but see nothing.

Something strikes the back of my head. I see stars as I tumble to the floor, but I'm able to make out a lizard figure run past me and attack Warrens. Two more charge in on all fours, like animals.

Warrens throws the one on him back, but it twirls around and trips him with its tail. All three surround Sulture, hungry mouths open and claws seeking to tear flesh.

They close in, the hammer about to strike the anvil.

John calls for us to regroup in the admin wing over the comm.

"You're not going to win this one," Sulture says. I hear a pop followed by a hiss. I watch as an aerial mist sprays from Sulture's helmet at each of the Grigylls. I set my helmet to only breathe filtered air and tell Warrens to do the same.

The Grigylls grab and claw at their throats as they choke out their growls. They collapse and writhe like maggots on the ground.

"Despicable creatures," Sulture says.

"How about a little warning next time Rooster?" Warrens growls. "We coulda been infected with your bug!"

"Call me 'Rooster' again and I'll inject you with a 'bug' even *I* can't kill!" Sulture hisses.

"Bring it!"

"Cut the shit you two!" I roar. "Enough with the dick measuring - we need to regroup!"

I hear a faint thump behind us. I turn around, and it's another Grigyll on all fours. I fire with my pistol, but the beast knocks me out of the way. Sulture turns around, but the creature rips his helmet off of his face and tosses it into the darkness.

Warrens shifts his plates into his gauntlets and strikes with a left jab. The animal growls in pain, but barely stumbles back. It lowers onto all fours and skitters around as Warrens tries to take it head on. I can't take the shot since he's too close to my target.

The Grigyll toys with Warrens, crawling on all fours and leaping around him. It's watching him, searching for a weakness.

The beast lashes out with its clawed hands. It shrieks and growls, but Warrens holds his own. He's not afraid, only growing frustrated he can't land a solid hit.

Blaster bolts erupt from behind us. The Grigyll darts back into the darkness. John and the rest lower their guns, but only four of them are on their feet. John is carrying Lee over his shoulder.

"What happened to Lee?" I ask.

"He thought he could break a Grigyll's neck, but it proved him wrong. Threw him right into a wall and knocked him out. Murph thinks it popped one of his ribs. Looks like you boys fared better," John says as he sets Lee against the wall.

Sulture grunts. "They're smarter than we gave them credit for," He says as he picks up his helmet on the floor.

"And tougher," Warrens adds.

"I was wrong to have us separate," John says. "These things fight hand to hand. They rely on their strength and they can endure a gun shot better than we can. Good news is they can't wield our weapons, but they've developed their own arsenal. Warrens, see what you can make of it." John tosses one of the Grigyll rifles to him.

"The rest of you, let's get to the administration wing."

"Yes sir!" We shout.

John hoists Lee over his shoulder, who groans in complaint. Sulture takes point and we crouch-walk through the complex. We hear screeches and growls from above, but nothing comes at us.

"How many of them are there?" Shepherd asks.

"At least six based on the angle of their screams," Murph replies. "Puts our odds of winning 'bout four to one."

My blood feels like acid in my veins as we cross this dark realm. Lighting flashes outside, and the pelting rain covers the sound of the Grigyll footsteps. I imagine them leaping out of the shadows, cutting us down one by one.

A shadow moves out of the corner of my eye. I turn and take aim, scanning the hallway. Murph and Shepherd stop too, searching for whatever I thought I saw.

"Nothin' there," Murph says.

"Contact!" Sulture roars from the front. The three men up front unleash a volley as lightning shines upon the scaly skin of the incoming predator.

"I'm out!" John says as he ejects his clip. Sulture and Warrens fire until they're empty, but there's no body on the floor.

"Where'd lizard boy go?" Warrens asks.

"How'd it survive that volley? That's impossible!" Sulture snaps.

"It was shielded," John says.

"How do you know?"

"The refracted glare from the lightning. It's gone for now, and we're too exposed out here. Let's move!" John barks. We run through the dark corridors until we reach the central hub. It's a wide expanse with shielded windows. The rainwater flows down the building into the vast ocean below. We scan the area, hoping that none of the Grigylls are trying to surprise us. Hacker goes to the central computer and turns the lights back on. The only sound is Warrens tearing one of the Grigyll's rifle apart.

"They're using slugs in their guns. This is bad news," Warrens says.

"Why?" I ask.

"Shields slow 'em down, but they still tear through. Our shields are designed for energy weapons, not projectiles," John explains.

"May be a war crime to wield projectile ammunition in the Core, but Grigylls won't care about that," Warrens says. "They have the edge against our tech."

Our comms blip as Forrest tries to reach us.

"Hey guys? Just wanted to warn you that there's another ship landing in the back."

"Who'd the military send in?" John asks.

"It's not *our* military," Forrest replies. We can hear the tightness in his jaw.

"Damn it," John curses. "How many Grigylls are there?"

"At least ten," Forrest replies.

"Take their ships out you moron! Cut off their escape!" Sulture roars. Turns out that even after all our bonding, Sulture was still short in times of distress.

"Jeepers what bug crawled up your butt? Launching the missiles right now, just like I launched my missile at your m-"

"Do you remember what happened the last time you made one of those jokes?" Sulture snarls.

"Do you want a ride home or do you wanna become lizard poop? I think you need to change your attitude."

Silence lingers over the comm.

"I can *hear* the glare Sulture."

Explosions from outside rock the installation. The lights flicker for a moment, but remain lit. Gunfire erupts from the dark hallways and the flash of muzzles remind us that we're still not alone.

"Take cover!" John roars. We duck behind whatever we can find, and perform a slow retreat into the back. Sulture and Warrens lay down a wave of cover fire, while the rest of us run toward the administration wing.

Hacker unlocks all of the doors, and we find a new prison behind the walls of cubicles which belong to researchers who developed cutting-edge weapons. We split up and weave through the maze while the walls provide us with the cover we need to escape.

We make it to some manager's office unscathed. Shepherd and I barricade the door with two desks once John and Warrens are inside.

"Sulture, Warrens, perform a sweep. Murph, wake Lee up," John orders.

The two men storm through the back offices and search for the enemy. Murph tends to Lee, who is barely conscious.

Sulture and Warrens circle back to us.

"All clear," Sulture says.

"We need a plan to get outta here," John says. "Any ideas?"

Silence lingers in the room.

"Get a grip Horsemen! I did not bust out a bunch of candy asses from prison!"

A Grigyll's shadow creeps outside the door. It pushes on the door, but the desks hold.

We let out a collective sigh of relief, but the beast doesn't leave.

It draws a gun and points for the door.

"Get back!" I scream.

A shotgun's roar blasts through the door and obliterates most of the desks. The Grigyll pumps three rounds through the barricade.

The rest of the team makes it into the back office, but I'm trapped in the front corner. I draw and cock both pistols.

I see the barrel poke through the door. Time slows as my heart seizes in my chest. I hear the beast's growl, the primal fear threatening to blind me.

More of the gun pokes through. One more step and I can kill the beast.

I hold my breath, but he lingers, waiting.

Waiting...

He steps forward and swings my way.

I fire blind, but I watch him fall backward as his gun explodes just over my head. My ears are ringing as John rushes out and pulls me by the arm.

He drags me by the shoulder into the back offices. The ringing in my ears drowns out everything else, but I hear him order Hacker to find the ship manifests. I realize that we're in the furthest office with no chance for escape.

John slaps my shoulder and tells me to press on. He turns to the rest of the team.

"Those shotgun blasts are going to draw every Grigyll here. Our only way out is to fight."

Everyone draws their guns and braces for the incoming assault. We're lodged in the back, cut off from escape. The steel walls begin to look like a metal coffin. My mind goes back to the soldiers we found who'd been slaughtered, faces frozen in disbelief.

The anger in their gazes, the iron smell of blood. The festering organs puddled on the floor. It's too much to bear.

I feel myself backed into the corner. My world closes into a pinpoint. A hiss echoes in my mind.

"*You will die here murderer.*"

I feel around and search the darkness. I hear the Grigylls howl and skitter across the steel plates.

"*You deserve to die here. Abandoned. Torn apart. Forgotten. You deserve it all.*"

In the dark pit of my stomach I feel a spark. A desire to survive. I feel this need to pull through. I toss kindling onto the spark and it ignites into a flame. First anger, then hatred burns through my being. I will not die here, not like this, cornered like some animal.

I draw both pistols and breathe deep. The Grigylls howl in victory, but it proves premature.

"Let's do this Horsemen!" I scream.

A Grigyll bursts through the doorway at the end of the hall, but I cut him down.

One by one the Horsemen howl and unleash hell against our enemy. They duck and dive out of the way, but our unrelenting assault drives the Grigylls back into the darkness.

I want to pursue them, but I know that if I do, I'm a dead man. An idea springs to mind.

"What is the temperature?"

The team stares at me.

"21 degrees Celsius," Hacker finally answers as he's looking down at his wrist.

"Sulture are the Grigylls cold blooded?"

"Yes, that was part of the evolution which remained." His response tells me he's catching onto my plan.

"If we can make it really cold in here, we can slow the Grigylls down."

"Not a bad idea Godfrey," John says. "Hacker, anything you can do?"

"Already working on it," He replies. "There. I've lowered the climate control down to 11. If that doesn't slow the savages down, not much will. Sir I also-"

"Contact!" Warrens howls as he opens fire at an incoming Grigyll. The beast is wounded, but retreats back into the darkness.

"Hacker can you turn some of these lights on?" John asks.

"We're running on emergency power as it is. The reactor core was submerged, and it's unrecoverable. The Grigylls wanted it dark in here."

"You heard him men. We're going to hunt them down. Give Lee a gun, this is not a battle to wield knives in."

Murph grabs one of the Grigyll's guns and shoves it into Lee, who groans in protest.

"Sulture, take point," John orders.

"On it." Sulture crouch-walks out of the room and we follow him one by one. I grab one of the shotguns the Grigylls used, but it's huge and unwieldy.

It'll be perfect for taking those bastards out. I sling it on and take my place in line. The air is getting colder already. I can feel it seep between my armor plates.

A Grigyll drops down from above, but he's sluggish and slow. We execute him immediately. The gunfire draws more of them in, but we cut them down without mercy. Finally, we reach one that's a real challenge.

"This one's shielded!" Sulture cries out. I step out of line with the Grigyll shotgun and blow the bastard to hell. The slugs decimate its shield, but felt like it would rip my arm right from my socket. I pump again and end the beast. I toss the gun aside and stand over the corpse. I feel a draconian sense of justice and believe for the first time that we can win against these beasts.

“Let’s hunt these savage monsters down!” I shout to the men.

We snuff out the remaining Grigylls like a pack of starving wolves. We move with a fluidity and grace that rivals the most elite forces in the galaxy. When one of us reloads, another steps in to take his place. Our cohesion and unity causes us to become one unit, a perfect melding of men.

We finish our hunt within the hour, until Sulture's scanners no longer detect foreign life forms. Hacker locates the beacon sending the emergency signal and shuts it down. We send a message giving the all-clear to military personnel to come down and take back their facility.

It takes over twelve hours, but we debrief with the military until they’re certain we won’t say anything about the secret weapons programs on their base. I resist the urge to tell them I was more concerned with staying alive than to steal government secrets, but I decide against it.

Back aboard the ship, Hacker calls for an emergency meeting about something he discovered aboard the DT station.

"Sir, I stumbled across a program in the administration wing while searching for the manifest," Hacker says as he hands a tablet to John. “It’s unsettling, and I believe we need to discuss its fate.”

John looks over the tablet and a primal rage spreads across his face. I’ve never seen him so mad.

"Tell them Hacker," He orders.

“I don’t believe this massacre was a random invasion of grigylls,” Hacker says.

We stare and wait for an explanation.

“The manifests show a transmission being sent into the unknown regions of space. The transmissions were under an old code, one the Core has used in the past to communicate with Grigylls.”

“What?” I ask. “I thought it was a distress signal.”

“He’s saying that the Grigylls were invited here!” Sulture says.

“He’s right,” Hacker says. “R&D, along with the admins, called for the Grigylls to invade this station so that the soldiers could fight them in hand-to-hand combat.”

“Why?” Murph asks.

"The reason why the soldiers were wielding knives and there was no admin here was because of an experimental program called 'Slipstream.' The military appears to have turned to AI programs in order to enhance a soldier's prowess." He fires up a luminescent projection of the human brain.

"How does this make soldiers fight better?" Warrens asks.

"It's a fight training simulation," Hacker replies.

"So, I could learn kung fu and karate chop all of you losers?" Forrest asks.

"Theoretically yes," Hacker replies. We watch as a green light starts at the motor cortex and flows through the synapses. Soon over half the brain is lit in green.

"What we're seeing here is that the program is *overriding* the brain's neural pathways."

"What?! How can it do that?" Warrens asks.

"Inducing the right hormones would do it," Murph says. "Only need point six-six milligrams to influence the brain's chemistry."

"Murph's right," Hacker says. "This AI program effectively 'convinces' the person to produce the hormones which rewire their own brain while simultaneously streams martial arts techniques. They become masters overnight."

"Sounds potent," I add.

"It's very effective," Hacker replies. "However, due to the rewiring of neural pathways it's likely that the subject would forget whatever was overridden. Yet at the same time it turns the human body into a deadly weapon."

"Destroy it," Warrens orders. All of us turn to him. "No good will come from this. It's far too powerful of a weapon. Destroy it."

Hacker becomes enraged. "Just because *you* got to wield an immensely powerful weapon-"

"Nobody should wield something like this!" Warrens snaps. "Sir, I beg of you, destroy it!" He pleads to John.

"Warrens, let's figure out where it came from," John replies. "Then we'll discuss how to go about destroying it."

"Discuss?!" Warrens howls.

"Yes, because this is not a program we can just delete off our server. We need to find out if there are copies, learn where it came from and who wants to use it. In the meantime, I will keep it under lock and key."

Warrens grumbles, then storms off. John leans with both hands against the holo-table.

"This is a weapon unlike anything I've ever seen," John says. "Whoever created this didn't care about the toll of human life. We need to find whoever made this weapon and bring them to justice. In the meantime, you boys rescued a very valuable weapons facility for Ionics, so as a thank you, I'm dropping you off at the Desmond Station. There's a bar there called *War Dogs.* Enjoy!"

It takes a lot of convincing, but I manage to talk Warrens into joining us for a drink instead of sulking in his room. We scamper across the ship, changing into civilian clothes for what feels like the first time in ages.

We walk into the bar feeling like we're the most indomitable men in the galaxy. However the crowd is a much...younger sort. Sad part is that thirty-something year old men are considered fossils in military terms. Still, we want to enjoy a night off and slug a few microbrews.

I notice out of the corner of my eye that there's a beautiful blonde woman who looks bored. She's just rubbing the rim of her glass with her finger. I stop and stare a moment, thinking I should go talk to her. It is after all, my night off.

"C'mon Silas! Have a beer with us!" Forrest says.

"Order me one. I'll be right over," I reply as I wave to the others. I approach the young blonde. She has a soft smile that she flashes me as I approach her. When I get closer I notice her deep green eyes.

"Hi, my name is Silas," I say, extending my hand to the woman.

"I'm not interested," the blonde gives me a slight smirk. The coy smile of a woman who's been hit on one time too many.

I smile and take my hand back. "That's fine. But, if you want to have a serious conversation instead of listening to these meatheads, come join me over there. I promise I'm a lot more fun to talk to." I take my leave and head over to our table, taking a seat next to Murph.

"Trying to pick her up?" Murph asks, handing me my beer. "I'll bet the kid is 72.45% more likely to pick her up than you were."

"She wasn't in the mood for anything. No sense in pushing it. She'll come and talk when and if she wants to have a real conversation."

I take my first drink. The beer tastes great, especially since it's my first drink since John forced me into sobriety.

I'm such a rebel.

"Heh. You really seem to know what you're doing, especially when seducing women. What's your number?" Murph asks.

"They don't call me 'Silas the Seducer' for nothing. And a gentleman never tells," I reply.

"Enough talk about girls, who's up for some games?" Forrest asks. Nobody takes him up on it.

"Aww you guys suck harder than Sujay's mom! I'm gonna go sucker some poor kid out of his meager pay," Forrest says as he moves to a nearby card-playing table.

"Does he ever win?" Shepherd asks.

"No, we'll have to bail him out in a about an hour," Sujay replies.

"What'll they do when they realize he doesn't have any money on him?" Sulture asks.

"I believe I just addressed that," Sujay replies, clearly irritated.

I feel a tap on my shoulder. I turn around and it's the blonde girl. I smirk at the others and stand up to talk to her.

"Guy's a genius," Murph whispers. "I figured there was a 2.63% chance of her coming over."

"Hi, my name is Cherise," the blonde says. "Sorry about earlier, didn't mean to come off as rude. It's been a long day." Her entire tone and demeanor had changed.

We banter back and forth, while I get a little bit...playful with my words. She leans in, plays with her hair and gives me doe eyes. I can feel her becoming entranced.

"THIS GUY'S A NO GOOD DEADBEAT!" A man screams from the card table.

"Time to go bail Forrest out," Sujay says begrudgingly.

Another guy from the table looks at me. "Hey! What are you doing with my girlfriend?" he screams. By this point Cherise is hanging off of my arm and it's...incriminating.

I turn and look at Cherise. "You didn't tell me you had a boyfriend."

"You never asked," she responds with a devious smile.

God damn it. I've been used to rile her boyfriend into a jealous frenzy. This won't be fun for either of us.

"Well this guy needs to pay up!" One of the boys grabs Forrest by the collar.

"You don't wanna do that bud," Murph says. "There's nine of us who're hardened killers against you thirteen boys. Puts your odds of winning at 7 to 1 or 14.29%, and I'm bein' generous."

"Not this fucker!" The boyfriend shouts. "He's going to pay for hitting on my girlfriend!" The kid comes at me. Sulture steps in front and punches him square in the face. The guys falls to the ground and groans out in pain.

"Perhaps if you paid a little more attention to her, she wouldn't feel the need to look elsewhere," Sulture hisses, then turns to give me his trademark icy stare. Another soldier charges in from the right.

I step in front of the guy and deliver a left hook, knocking him on his ass. Everyone turns and looks at me.

"Well?" I ask. "John said he wanted a team of men who could hold their own in a bar fight."

"Aw hell," Murph says as he knocks out the guy who's holding Forrest.

"I ain't gonna be kicked around by some, garbagemen!" the boyfriend says. His nose is gushing blood. Right as he stands up I punch him in the face and knock him on his ass again.

"Get Bobo!" Another guy calls out. Within seconds the bar grows eerily quiet. A massive Indian man in full military garb comes walking in.

Warrens shoves his way through. "I got 'im."

"You sure bud?" Murph asks. "He's got 'bout 45 kilos on you!"

Warrens gets into his boxing stance. "I got 'im Murph."

Bobo tries to grab Warrens in a massive bear hug, while he unleashes a flurry of punches into Bobo's gut. Warrens dances around, weaving and dodging the Indian's lumbering attacks.

Warrens lays down two quick left jabs and a right hook to Bobo's chin. He must've hit him in the right spot because, the entire bar shook as the giant Indian hit the floor.

"Told you guys I had 'im," Warrens says.

The bar resumes the massive brawl. Glasses shatter, tables get thrown over, and we smash chairs on each other. We Horsemen step in to help one another and fought as one unit. In the midst of the chaos, I couldn't help but wonder if John's crazy plan of bringing us all together could actually work.

We stumble out of the bar, bruised and battered. We hear military police sirens closing in and knew that we had to hightail it out of there.

"Should we tell John about this?" Shepherd asks.

"Only if he asks." Warrens replies.

"What do you mean you all got into a bar fight?" John screams at us aboard the ship.

"Sir," I answer. "You did say that you wanted a group of scientists who could hold their own in a bar fight."

John gave me the meanest scowl I've ever seen. He looked at all of us, with our cut and bruised faces. He saw a group of men who held their own, and fought as one team. He saw *his* men, united, and ready to accept whatever punishment he'd deal out. And his scowl turned into a grin.

Godfrey's Journal Day 81

Nearly broken from the strain of combat. I've never felt my nerves so rattled. The Grigyll invasion force almost left me as a shell of a man. I don't understand how the others kept it together. I suppose it's because they're battle-hardened, but I must also remember that their scars run deep. They could've broken under the strain of their trials for all I know.

I can't figure out why John recruited me in the first place. I'm the least experienced with addiction problems. Another part of me wonders what he knows. About my time during the war, about Chemron…

Doesn't matter now. After seeing Sulture help me out in the bar fight, I feel like I'm a part of something greater. I finally feel that sense of belonging to a cause greater than myself. I didn't think I was wanted here, but now I feel like I can earn my keep.

I hate to admit it, but Sulture was right. The panic, the terror, the shattered nerves…it was something to get used to. Something I needed to get accustomed to feeling if I was ever going to survive as one of the Horsemen.

ON SAFARI

Godfrey's Journal Day 88

The nightmares have started. Grigylls come in from everywhere, tearing all of us to pieces. They surround me. I see blood dripping from their claws and bits of gore on their teeth. I shoot one after another, but they keep coming. An inexorable tide that in the back of my mind I know will consume me. One of them scores a hit and stands over me. It kneels down, opens its mouth and dives for my throat.

I wake, slashing at the air above me. It takes me a few moments as I peer through the darkness to realize that I'm safe aboard the ship. The low hum of the engines is soothing, but now I'm wide awake. I can hear the murmurs and mumbles of the others as they experience their own hell in their sleep. Before the only one who would have terrors during the night was Sulture, who would scream and slash at the air. Murph would comfort him, but now he has his own nightmares to deal with.

John carries a tablet and plugs it into the holo-table. A lush jungle world comes into view.

“It’s time you men actually learned the process of colonizing a planet.”

Hacker eyes the briefing. “This one was passed through quick. The last time they rushed a colonization protocol like this was on...Angkor.” Everyone looks at Sulture and Murph. The two were so focused on their breakfasts it was as if they weren’t even there.

“What happened on Angkor?" Shepherd asks.

"We don't talk about it," Sulture snaps.

"Adam, maybe we should. The kid-"

"We don't talk about Angkor!" Sulture snarls. The room is silent and the air is tense. All eyes are on him and he doesn't like the attention.

"Fine!" He shouts. "Murph and I were colonists on Angkor. Alien inhabitants showed up. They killed lots of innocent people. Murph and I developed a method which drove aliens to extinction. End of story! Now continue with the damn brief John. Let's talk some Ecology!"

John clears his throat. “The planet is called ‘Hadrian’ and terramorphing didn’t take long, but now the Core needs to establish a base and a perimeter in order to begin colonization. The Army is currently handling this, but Ionics thought we should join in on the fun.”

“Why is Ionics sending us to Hadrian?” Hacker asks. “We build lab equipment, and there’s no record of any laboratory technicians exploring the planet.”

“Medicine,” I reply. “Ionics wants to gain a foothold on harvesting local fauna that can be used for drugs. We buddy up with the Army, grease the wheels, and when we leave some guys in suits come by with the papers.”

“Let’s not all be cynics about this,” John says. “As we push further with our colonization efforts, the military needs to learn how to handle new alien threats. We’re to come in as consultants and advise on how they streamline the processes of setting up a colony.”

“*Boring*!” Forrest yells. “I’m with Godfrey. It’s all about the drugs!”

John rolls his eyes, then continues. “We’ll also have to contend with scores of wildlife. As Lee addressed, the plant life on Hadrian has given rise to a number of large herbivores.” He switches the hologram.

Monstrous beasts larger than elephants come into view. Most of them look like reptilian behemoths.

"The Army has given me permission to hunt some of these trophy beasts since we need to go in and clear out this valley," John says. He switches the projection to a map with a swath of green at the base of a mountain range.

"Hey, what's that black spot on the map?" Forrest asks.

"A swamp," John replies.

"Wait, back up," Shepherd says. "We're going to hunt...dinosaurs?"

"They're not dinosaurs," Sulture snaps. "These creatures need to be categorized and labeled, and oversimplifying them in such a manner is stupidity."

"Yes Shepherd, the Horsemen are hunting dinosaurs!" John replies with a grin from ear to ear.

After a few monotonous weeks in transit, we're hit with a wall of humidity as the cargo door opens. The planet reeks of mildew and mold. So much for fresh air.

As John leads us to the base camp, he gives us the rundown. "Now these Army guys are going to know about all of you. Word spread about the Grigylls on Delmar-Torren, and you idiots fought with some of their friends at the Desmond Station."

"Those jerks had it coming!" Forrest screams. "Just because we kicked their butts-"

"You hid under the table the entire time, Curly," Warrens says. "You didn't do squat to knock out any of those guys."

"I…I broke a bottle…" Forrest stumbles.

"Because you missed the big guy that Warrens was boxing!" Sujay says.

"Jitters is right. Your aim sucks," Warrens says.

John interjects. "Anyway, *try* to get along with the soldiers here. We need answers about the Slipstream program, and this mission is a quiet way to find out what the military knows."

"We'll do our best not to start any fights John," I say.

"Thank you Godfrey."

"Brown-noser," Forrest coughs. I turn and raise my fist. Forrest covers his face and whimpers, but I back off and grin.

At the Army base we encounter Major Buckner, the man in charge of establishing a foothold on Hadrian.

"Major Buckner," John salutes, and Buckner responds in kind.

"So these are the men the infamous Colonel Henry is dragging along. You're the Horsemen, right?" He asks.

"I may not have too many, but each one of them is worth at least ten of your grunts."

"Well, we're ready for you. Got you two humvees. We're doing a twenty kilometre sweep. You are here to observe, plant stakes for the perimeter fence, and shoot some of the local wildlife," Buckner explains.

"Standard colony setup, got it," John says. "And humvees? What century are we in Bucker? Hovercraft are better due to all the roots sticking out of the ground."

"Well, the humidity interferes with the reactors of the hovercraft. Plus, as I'm sure you know, colony sweeps don't get the budget that the other programs do. Not like the private sector, am I right?"

"That's the beauty of it Buckner. Become an expert in something and you can charge an obscene amount of credits too," John says as he slaps him on the shoulder while taking the mission brief.

We walk to our camp, where the humvees are waiting for us. Murmurs from the army recruits echo in our ears.

"Why are those garbage men from Ionics here? Damn mercenaries," one of the soldiers grumbles. We keep walking because we're not going to get sucked in. We already got enough heat from John for the bar fight.

"Jesus, those old men rebuffed the Grigylls? There's no way. They need canes to get around," another soldier says in a harsh whisper.

"The oldest of you guys is John and he's only thirty-seven, right?" Shepherd asks.

"Yeah, but in military circles, being over thirty makes us dinosaurs," Sulture replies.

"HA! Maybe we should be hunting you instead!" Forrest shouts.

Sulture ignores the comment. Just as we're about to make it to the tent, some special ops guys get in our way. They're with Space Tactical Assault Recon or STARs, the most elite group of soldiers in the galaxy.

"Great, a bunch of scientists are here for the expedition. Wanna study some of the shit I stepped in earlier today?" The soldier snickers as he holds up his boot.

Sulture lunges, pins the guy to a tree, unsheathes his knife and holds it to his throat.

"Keep talking kid and I'll find some predator in the jungle that will shit you out," Sulture hisses. The others are too stunned to move.

"I'll slit your throat so you can't scream. I'll cut you in just the right places where you'll bleed out slowly, and sever your tendons so you can't walk. Then I'll drag you into the long grass where a predator can find you. All you'll be able to do is watch as it tears out your organs and feasts on your flesh!" Sulture hisses. The guy's lower lip trembles and he looks like he's going to piss his pants.

"Sulture! Up here! Now!" John screams.

Sulture lets the guy go and holds up his knife."By the way, a real special ops kid could've turned the tables and disarmed me. Also, his backup wouldn't be such cowards. I'm keeping this."

John gives Sulture a thorough talking to while the rest of us snicker as the special ops guys run off.

John lays out the plan. "I'm splitting us up as follows: Forrest, Godfrey, Lee, Murph and Shepherd you're all in humvee one. The rest of us are in humvee two. Assign a driver and a main gunner. I wanna take down one of those with the big horns so I'm the gunner for two."

"I call driver because there is no way any of you chumps can maneuver like me!" Forrest screams.

"Time for you to eat dirt," Sujay replies as he takes the wheel of two. The rest of us pile into the vehicles.

"Guys can I be gunner?" Shepherd asks.

"*Ni meiyou langun*!" Lee hisses.

"What?" Shepherd asks.

"What Lee's trying to tell you kid is man the damn gun. Grow a pair. If you want something, go for it," I explain.

The humvees growl in anticipation as we line up to drive the animals out of the valley. Buckner fires into the air and the convoy charges forward. Soldiers across the line fire into the air, and whoop and holler obscenities to drive the animals out.

The beasts are not used to humans pursuing them with rifles and become easy pickings for the hunters. Dozens of animals collapse as the soldiers take down the slow and the helpless.

"Man these guys are going way too slow! Screw this!" Forrest says as he shoves his foot onto the accelerator. The humvee pulls ahead and Forrest has us racing in the midst of the stampede.

"*Liu kuoshui de biaozi he houzi de ben erzi*!" Lee hisses from the back seat.

"You know, I'm starting to think that you don't actually know that much Mandarin, just enough to call us mean names!" Forrest replies.

Lee places a knife on Forrest's neck. "And I think you intentionally take the most dangerous route possible. Maybe you need drive a little safer."

"You're willing to let the Army punks beat us?" Forrest asks. "I mean, where's your sense of fun? Godfrey, you get my meaning, help me out here."

"I'm with Lee on this one," I reply.

"Murph? Please?! You're used to dealing with the killers. Help me out here!"

Murph chuckles. "Let him go Lee. We know that Forrest will have learned his lesson for about twelve seconds, then he'll be back to his rambunctious self."

Lee withdraws and sheaths his knife.

"Murph, I gotta know, what actually happened on Angkor?" I ask. "You came out really laid back, while Sulture is...Sulture."

He thinks over what he's going to tell me, then looks off into the distance.

"Most of what happened is what Adam told you, but there was a minor difference between how Angkor affected him and I."

"Which is…?" I ask.

"A wife. And a son. Kid was only six years old. Adam watched the Tritops murder his family, and it broke him." The inside of the humvee falls silent.

"That's terrible! I understand why he feels the way he does!" Shepherd yells over the roar of the engine.

"None of you can tell him I told you that. Ever," Murph says.

"Angkor broke Adam's humanity. He used to be a real friendly guy, but he lost it all in that jungle. He's a good man, we all are. Just men who were put in bad situations."

"So what's your deal Lee?" Forrest asks. "Were you scary before Ophridia? Or did that twist you around like a pretzel?"

"Do I have to get my knife out you *chùsheng xai-jiao de xiang huo*!" Lee snarls.

"C'mon Lee what happened?" Murph asks. "It's been a hundred and eighty nine days since John brought you on. Six months too soon?"

Lee grumbles. "I always tried to keep my head down, be a good worker. Then one night, the Tingchia come for me because some *hundan* say I conspired against the Emperor. He shot my wife and daughter before my eyes. They wouldn't let me hold my daughter one last time…" As Lee trails off, I notice that he's rubbing the small doll tied to his belt, and it all clicks into place.

"Woooo! Made it to the end first! Suck it losers!" Forrest screams as he jumps out of the humvee. His face turns pale white as it dawns on him that the stampede is still on the move.

And it's heading right for us.

"*Hwoon dahn*!" Lee screams.

"Guys, they're not stopping!" Shepherd shouts.

"Shoot them kid! You're the one with the gun!" Forrest cries. Shepherd turns the gun and opens fire and while it scares the beasts, they're still not stopping. If anything, they're beginning to panic and turn around which is the last thing we need them to do.

A three-horned creature bellows as it charges right for us. Shepherd's bullets are useless against its thick skin.

"Hide behind the trees!" Murph shouts. He books it for the treeline on the edge of the jungle, grabbing Forrest as well.

Lee runs in, grabs ahold of a dangling vine and climbs up with ease.

I help Shepherd get down from the humvee and the two of us duck behind a thick trunk.

The silence of the jungle is broken as the stampede tramples through, snapping limbs, branches and each other underfoot. They bellow and grunt as they run for their lives, but they miss the trees we're hiding behind. It feels like hours pass as the final stragglers clear through. We hear the humvees running idle outside. They surround our own trampled humvee.

"*Liu kuoshui de biaozi he houzi de ben erzi,*" Lee hisses.

"C'mon guys! Where's your sense of fun!" Forrest asks.

"It got left in that humvee when we had to run in and duck for cover!" I reply. "Jesus, how long did that last?"

"It lasted ten minutes and fifty-three seconds," Murph replies.

John approaches us. Without saying a word, all of us point at Forrest.

"I figured. Because of that, you boys are gonna have to get a ride back with the army as we set up the perimeter. Better start making some friends."

I approach the army guys who parked next to us. "Which one of you is in charge?" I ask.

"I am," the driver says. "Name's Pierce. This is Cooper, Allen, and Tonaka."

They're not a bunch of fresh-faced kids like I'd imagined. They're serious and hardened, like they've seen things here.

The one that catches my eye is Cooper. She's a beautiful brunette with brown eyes, shoulder length hair and an athletic frame. It was a wonder that none of the guys in her unit were drooling over her.

"I'm Godfrey. This is Forrest, Murph, Lee and Shepherd," I reply.

"Good," Pierce says. "Let's get to work."

We toil in the hot sun, driving stakes into the dirt to set up the electrical fence before the herd comes back.

"Psst! Godfrey!" Forrest whispers to me.

"What?"

"Did you see how freakin' hot Cooper is? Will you help me hit on her? I'd like her to play with *my* stake."

"Just go talk to her, you don't need my help. Although, leave out the stake comment." I notice that Shepherd is eyeing Cooper as well.

"But I don't know what to say!"

"You Forrest? Of all people? Speechless?"

"I know right? But when I get near a woman that looks like her my brain goes all scrambly! I mean you may as well-"

Cooper walks by. "I'll save you the trouble Curly. Not interested. I don't have daddy issues," She says as she pats Forrest on his shoulder. He freezes in place, then looks at me.

"She put her hand on me. That means I have a shot right?"

I shake my head no.

"Aw c'mon! You've done more with less! You think you could seduce her?"

Cooper walks by again. "No he couldn't," She says. "Once again, no daddy issues. Now that one there, I could go for." She points at Shepherd. His face turns bright red and everyone, including the army guys cheer for him.

We work through the afternoon until the sun starts to set. Gargantuan beasts roar in the distance, a sound unheard by man since the stone ages back on Earth. I notice that Shepherd and Cooper are talking to each other, the glow of lust on their faces.

"Oh guys, one thing to be aware of are the Hadrian Raptors," Cooper warns.

"Hadrian raptors are no match for my raptor," Forrest says.

"Shut up Forrest!" Shepherd screams.

Cooper giggles as she pulls out a tablet. "Here are some pictures of the raptors in action." The others look at the pictures while I stare off into the horizon. I hear the others talking in the background, but there is a violet glow which I can't pull my eyes away from. It radiated from a basin in the jungle. Right where we saw the swamp on our map.

"What is that?" I ask as I point to the glow.

"We call it the Death Fields," Cooper replies. "No one is allowed out there. Anything that goes out there dies. Some highly radioactive material the scientists said. They can't even approach it with rad suits, leaks right through."

"What? Impossible!" I reply.

"None of the scientists have been able to get a sample," Cooper says. "They get sick if they get too close. All of the plant life in that area has been fried. Nothing lives near those rocks."

"Interesting. We should check it out," I say.

"Are you nuts?" Forrest asks. "John won't want a space rock that will peel the skin off your bones!"

"Assuming it's that radioactive, we should bring Warrens along. He'll know how to handle the material," Murph says.

"*Ai ya*, I'd like to see the effect on the local fauna," Lee says.

"Excellent," I reply. "Shepherd you in?"

"No thanks."

"Forrest?"

"I believe I already made my point. Deadly radioactive space rocks are not my thing. I for one do not enjoy or desire to have my eyes melt out of their sockets because you bozos can't learn to let things be!"

"If anything Forrest, we're the *most* qualified to handle a substance such as this," I reply.

"Your grave. Just know that I'll dance on it and say 'I told you so!'"

"I expect nothing less."

Just as we get back to base it starts to rain. The Army guys say it rains every day around this time, like you could set your watch to it. The light sprinkling turns into a torrential downpour just as we go in to get some food. Come to find out, the Army was eating better than we were.

Bastards.

After our meal I approach John at the officer's table, who're all laughing like hyenas.

"What can I do for you Godfrey?" John asks.

"Sir, we saw an anomaly outside of the encampment. It's an area that is pitch black with a violet glow to it."

"The Death Fields? Buckner asks. "No good comin' outta there son. Anyone who goes out there gets sick. Even with the rad suits."

"I understand that Major, but we're some of the most qualified men available to be studying this anomaly. John, I want permission to retrieve a sample. Here is a detailed outline of my plan for retrieval."

"This looks good to me Godfrey. Buck, can my boys go out there? We've got some rad suits that are a couple grades higher than yours."

"John, it's extremely dangerous. The scientists say it's not just the radioactive particles, there's something else in the fields."

"What is it?"

"Dunno. But the scientists say that even with state of the art radiation suits, they couldn't get within 100 metres of the fields without puking their guts out. They wrote a whole report about it."

"Can I get access to that report?" I ask.

"I don't see any reason why not. John?"

"Fine with me. My men will know what to do, and if the canister leaks, I hand it over to Godfrey and eject him from my ship," John says as he and the rest of the table bursts out laughing.

"Good to know I got your support John."

"Always Godfrey."

"I just contacted our lead scientist," Buckner says. "You'll have their report in a few minutes."

"Excellent," I reply. "John, we'll be out."

"I want updates every 10 minutes Godfrey. If I don't hear from you, we're coming after your corpse."

"Always the optimist John."

Outside the tent, sheets of rain are pouring down. Shepherd and Cooper come running through, and I resist the urge to scream "Atta boy!"

In the shed with the humvees, Warrens is standing next to the driver's seat.

"You comin' with?"

"I'm driving and leading this operation," He replies. "If this substance is as radioactive as everyone claims, then I should be the one in charge of retrieving it."

"Won't get any argument outta me. I wanted to see it 'cause it looks pretty.

"Now is not the time to be a smart ass Godfrey! I will not allow you to be callous and -"

"Relax Warrens. You're in charge. You know safety protocol better than anyone. I won't interfere or make jokes."

"Good! As far as I'm concerned, this material is to be considered a highly dangerous and volatile weapon. I've never heard of a substance this deadly, so we will use *every* precaution. If I say we leave, we leave. No questions asked."

The ride through the valley is quiet, and the rain has stopped. A light mist hangs over the valley.

"Everyone load up your clips. Predators will be on the loose now," Sulture says. The ground is slick, and the humvee slides across the muck. We hear a roar from the East, the bellow of a victorious predator savoring its kill.

"Kung Pao, mount the gun! I'm not having anything with teeth try to back us into a corner," Warrens orders.

"Ride the edge! We'll be disguised better over there!" Sulture says.

The tires squeal and squelch against the merciless muck that seizes the humvee. Warrens turns hard to the West, riding over the branches and roots in our path. Trees reach down and swing for us. The perilous journey, one I'm beginning to second guess.

We arrive at the drop off point. The violet glow is even brighter here in the jungle. We climb out and open the box of rad suits. Nobody is happy.

"Ugh, always hated these things. They cling like no other," Sulture grumbles as he steps into his suit.

"Well, your armor's cooling systems should prevent you from boiling in there," Warrens says.

"Good. I'd hate to have someone come out here and find us looking like bloated pigs," Murph says. "We'd have a full case of rigor mortis within ten hours!"

We traverse the jungle, but not even 100 metres in, Warrens braces himself against his knees.

"I'm not feeling so good, like a swift punch to the gut."

"How in the hell?" Murph asks as he checks his scanner. "There's not even 2 milliSieverts in the air! That's like *below* natural levels!"

"C'mon Warrens, you can toughen it out! We're practically there!"

"You are not authorized to be exploring this area!" A voice shouts.

All of us freeze, and we look at each other in confusion.

"We received permission from Buckner!" I reply. A spray of blaster bolts pepper the dirt in front of me. We drop to the ground.

"Jesus Christ!" I hiss.

"This is a restricted area! Surrender or prepare to be shot!" The voice shouts again.

"Guys, I don't feel so good," Warrens says.

"We have sick men!" I shout. "We need medical attention immediately!"

"We're coming in! No sudden movements!"

Several soldiers in radiation suits charge over the ridge. They keep their guns trained on us.

"That guy over there," I point to Warrens.

"Don't move!" A guy screams as he points his rifle at me. Another walks up behind Warrens.

"You are all under arrest for trespassing on government property!"

"Like hell! We had permission!" I fire back.

"They're resisting!" The second guy shouts. I see his finger nudge off the safety switch.

Time slows as I roll the *SMART* protocol through my head. Shooting a soldier will be an act of war, but we have no choice other than to act in self-defense.

"Shit! Raptors on our six! Twenty three metres that way!" Murph screams. Both of the soldiers look up.

I leap to my feet and knock the barrel of the gun pointed at me. I punch the guy in the face, wrest the AR from his grip and shoot him. The second soldier manages to get two rounds into me before I put him down.

My armor absorbs the blast, but I got the wind knocked out of me. To make matters worse, I'm exposed to the radiation.

"Let's haul ass!" I scream as I hoist Warrens over my shoulder. I can barely lift the big guy up, but he plants his feet in the ground to help me out. Murph comes in and helps me carry Warrens, the three of us sliding along the mud. Once we're back at the trucks, I dump Warrens and go back for a sample of the radioactive rock.

"Get back here Casanova! You'll fry!" Warrens screams.

"If they're willing to kill us over a goddamn rock, I gotta know why!" I scream back. I pull out the emergency repair adhesive and patch the hole in my suit.

"Godfrey! I order you to stand down!" Warrens howls as he rises to his feet.

I keep running for the pit.

"Shit," Murph says. "I'll go after him."

I run through the jungle until the grass becomes pitch black and brittle. The trees look like mummified husks, contorted and misshapen, like tendrils clawing for a victim.

At the edge of the basin, I see the death fields consume the horizon in front of me. Thousands of glowing, violet rocks litter the landscape, each one a lantern of death. Hundreds of skeletons lie scattered in the grass. The roars of behemoths echo in the distance, but they're all far from here. I slide down until I'm next to a cluster of the rocks. Up close they look like crystals.

I grab my canister. I open it up, grab one of the violet crystals and try to shove it inside. In frustration I smash the crystal against a rock and learn they're very brittle. I toss the fragments inside the canister, seal it up and grab the second one.

"Silas, you moron! Your suit is broken and my scanners are detecting over 10,000 milliSieverts! You get exposed and you're fried."

"What do you suppose they're made out of?" I ask.

"I don't know, but Silas, I'm not feeling so good. We can't be caught here circling the drain."

I curse under my breath.

I fill the third canister with the devious gems. I grab hold of Murph and haul ass out of the death fields. Sweat pours down my face as I breathe through my filter that reeks of plastic. Murph and I arrive back to the humvee, but it's surrounded by soldiers in rad suits.

Two of them walk in front of the others and unveil their masks.

It's the two soldiers that Sulture humiliated earlier. However there's a frantic, possessed look in their eyes. They're looking for some payback.

"Killin Core soldiers eh?" The first one asks as he points to the dead man on the ground. "That's an executable offense! Craig, grab the tall, lanky one!"

Craig pulls Sulture out by the collar and forces him onto his knees.

"This is for earlier!" Craig grunts as he punches Sulture in the stomach.

I charge into the fray and throw a hard right, but the kid catches my punch. He twists my arm and tries to break it at the elbow, but I launch a kick at him. Kid catches that too and strikes me right above the kneecap.

"Wanna throw down old man?"

"Why don't you two *ji bai* fight someone a little more skilled in the martial arts?" Lee asks.

The two STARs rush Lee, he lands a hard kick on both of them. The boys shake it off and come at Lee even harder, moving with a fluidity and grace I've never seen before. They move faster than Lee, as though they anticipate his every move. Lee even kicks one of the kids in the balls in desperation, but they still keep coming. Something more than vengeance is driving these men.

In less than a minute Lee is beaten to hell, and the STARs stand triumphant over top of him.

"We surrender," Murph says.

"What?!" I scream.

"You boys are clearly the superior fighting force, however we know you can't handle the radioactive rocks. Why not take us back to base where we can unload them for you."

"I'd just as soon kill you now!" Craig screams as he points his gun at Murph.

"You could, but you won't be able to dispose of the bodies. Best way to do that is at camp don't ya think?"

The STARs look at each other.

One of the boys in back motions to Craig and his buddy. "We should take them back. The Major will need evidence these old men killed one of our own." The maniacs flash each other a glare.

"Yuri, load them up," Craig orders. We follow the instructions of the crazed soldiers and climb into their prison transport.

"Murph, why'd you give us up like that?" I ask.

"Do the math Silas. There were eight of them. Each of their rifles has a clip that holds a charge for fifty rounds. That's four hundred shots *before* reloading. On top of that, two of their guys took out our best martial arts fighter."

"Yeah Lee, I thought you were supposed to be good at hand-to-hand. Right now you're 0-3."

"*Bee-jway*!" Lee hisses. "I've fought John, Grigylls and Special Forces who're hopped up on something. *Nobody* moves that fast!"

"At least not naturally," Warrens adds. "Bet ya they used that program Hacker found."

"How?" I ask.

"Don't know, but we're outgunned. Doc you got a plan since you called for surrender?"

"Afraid not. I sweet-talked the guys into lettin' us live. You boys can come up with a plan."

The rest of the ride is silent. We're taken to a second camp, one that has a cloaking field which keeps it hidden in the jungle.

As we pass through the camp, I notice behemoth-sized cages. Inside are the Hadrian Raptors that Cooper warned us about. They lash out against their restraints, but the electric cages keep them confined.

"Subjects are: large raptors with horns protruding from their skulls, and possess two metre-long arms with claws almost fifteen centimeters long."

The rest turn and look outside the window. "Not sure which is worse. The twitchy twins or those things," Warrens says.

"They're over three metres tall, have hardened scale plates over the torso, cranium and arms. Bipedal with well developed thigh muscles that I suspect allow the subject to leap wide distances."

"What're you thinking of doing Godfrey?" Sulture inquires.

"Well if Warrens is right and those guys reprogrammed their brains, we can't fight our way out. The best way to deal with an enemy that analyzes patterns is to throw in a few random variables."

"How do you intend to do that?"

The truck comes to a stop. Craig walks around the outside, his boots crunching against the gravel. He unlocks the door and pulls the handle.

I charge from my seat and dive on top of Craig. He's caught off guard, but recovers faster than I do. I wrap my hands around his throat to choke him out, but he's still beating the hell out of me.

Warrens and Lee dive down and pin his arms to the ground. His eyes bulge out, and the vein in his head threatens to burst before he finally passes out from lack of oxygen.

I look up and see soldiers charging in. I also see the cage holding one of the raptors.

I break into a sprint, dodging blaster fire hailing down from all directions.

A scorching pain carves at my shoulder. A blaster bolt had grazed me, but I need to stay on point. I reach the raptor's cage who greets me by ramming against the bars.

Something shoves me into the bars.

"Thought you were going to make it huh?" Yuri asks me from behind. I elbow him in the ribs, but he just grunts and shoves me against the bars again.

"I think it's hungry," Yuri hisses. The raptor sniffs at me, but has learned not to charge the electric cage. I need to get out of Yuri's grip, but he doesn't feel pain the same anymore. I leap up and kick against the bars.

Both of us fall backward, but I get back up, run to the cage and unlock the door.

"Try fighting a raptor motherfucker!"

Yuri tries to take on the raptor, but the beast chomps down on his chest. He doesn't even cry out in pain as its teeth tear through his rib cage. I scurry away and open more cages.

As the raptors are released, more STARs open fire. Their guns draw the attention of the raptors which make them easy prey. I run back for the Horsemen who've recovered our weapons.

"What the hell have you done Godfrey?" Sulture screams.

"Made it a fair fight." One of the raptors screeches and charges for us.

Warrens tosses my pistol. We fire upon the raptor but the blaster bolts do nothing against its toughened hide.

"You've released the apex predator into an environment full of prey that have no ability to fight it!" Sulture screams.

"You're welcome!"

Everyone climbs into the truck while I locate one of the canisters and crack it open.

A hand grabs my shoulder and spins me around. Craig's reddened face is even more terrifying. He grabs me by the neck and tries to snap my vertebrae.

I reach into the canister until I feel my gloved fingers wrap around a jagged surface. It feels like a white hot knife stabs me in the gut, but I pull it out and stab Craig in the neck.

He looks at me in disbelief as a white flame consumes him and his skin crumbles to dust. Within seconds his body is a charred pile of ash. I toss the shard back into the canister and vomit on Craig's remains.

"Casanova! Let's haul ass!" Warrens calls from the cab of the truck.

I collapse into the back of the truck and we speed off.

"Horsemen! What is your status?" John asks over the comm.

"We're on route back to camp sir, but we ran into some...

complications," Warrens replies.

I see a set of headlights flash behind us.

"I know, Hacker tells me there's a lot of chatter with the military."

Another set of lights beam through the darkness. Two vehicles are chasing after us. A voice in my head screams for me to get against the wall.

A muzzle flash lights up the top of the humvees.

The blaster bolts pepper our truck, and I push my back as far as I can go against the wall.

"Shots fired! I repeat, shots fired!" I howl into the comm.

"What in God's name did you boys do?!" John roars.

"Oh, you know, pissed off the STARs who've been experimenting with mind-altering software."

"Godfrey, now is not the time-"

"That's what really happened sir," Warrens says. "We need an extraction immediately!"

"Just get back to base for now," John replies.

The raptors catch up to the pursuing trucks. The boys fire with their main gun, but the blaster bolts don't penetrate the bone armor plates.

"We're just a few minutes from camp!" Warrens screams.

I curse under my breath as I realize that we're leading a band of raptors with bony hides right toward the military base.

The humvee rumbles to a stop, and we run out in search of John. We find him, but he's flanked by Buckner and over a dozen army kids.

"What happened out there?" John asks.

"We were ambushed by STAR soldiers who thought we were trespassing," Sulture states. "We explained that we had authorization, but they were hostile and not responsive. They were about to execute us and we defended ourselves."

"That doesn't mean you kill them!" Buckner screams. "John, I've been requested by brass to detain these men."

"That won't be necessary Buckner."

"John, you don't understand. They killed soldiers of the Core military. We can't let this one go."

"Stand down Buckner," John says as he gets nose to nose with the Major.

"No! You corporate mercs are all the same! You think you can come in and run an operation when we-"

A cragged screech tears through the night. The soldiers howl and scream in panic as they charge to meet the raptors that have breached the camp.

"How did those things breach the fence?!" Buckner screams into his comm. "Whaddya mean the STARs charged through? I thought I was to be handling the situation back at camp!"

"Now would be a good time for us to leave," John says. "Round up the rest and get to the *Enigma* ASAP."

"Sir should we just leave those boys to fight the raptors on their own?" Murph asks.

"We have no choice," John replies. "Our only hope is to get the hell outta here and let the lawyers sort all of this out. I'll get in touch with corporate."

We rally the men to the *Enigma* while the army tries in vain to fight off the Hadrian raptors that are tearing the colony apart. The STARs are nowhere to be seen.

The *Enigma* lifts off, and it feels like we're a pack of dogs running with our tails between our legs.

John has us gather for an emergency meeting. The silence on the ship is unsettling, as though he's searching for the right words.

"There was no winning that fight. After you boys told me about the STARs using Slipstream, I had Hacker look into it."

Hacker steps forward. "The program was not only active on the planet's surface, it has been refined. The two soldiers that Sulture humiliated were looking for some payback, and they managed to get permission to be the test subjects on Hadrian. What's worse is the test results look promising. The military is prepared to invest even more into Slipstream."

"It doesn't matter if those kids were hopped up on a programmed brain or steroids, the military was lookin' to take us down a peg." John says. "Whether it be through arresting us, or making us fight the raptors, we stood to gain nothing and lose everything. Ionics is sending a team of lawyers to deal with the military, but for now, we're on the run. You're dismissed."

The others disperse from the room, but I stay behind to talk to John. He looks up at me, but doesn't say anything.

"I want permission to study the rock. The STARs were after a sample, and I wonder if they intend to weaponize it."

"What makes you believe that?"

"Because I stabbed one of the kids who was about to break my neck and I watched him turn to ash within seconds. I've never seen or heard of a substance that can destroy an organism so quickly."

"Then you've never faced the business end of a Xeclian disintegration rifle."

"No I haven't, but I believe this substance is far more dangerous. We need to assume that the military is conducting experiments to weaponize this material."

"You're probably right Godfrey. First, help Murph with making some medicine for radiation sickness. You may be able to stomach being close to that rock, but I got several men who were poisoned by that thing."

"Fair enough. Then after that, I experiment."

John gives me a silent nod. I salute, and take my leave.

LIFE'S A FITCH

Godfrey's Journal, Day 104

I've been studying samples of the Hadrian gem. The gem emits an electrical charge on its own, a strange process which augments the radioactivity of the material. I've discovered that the electrical charge is from a biological source, an alien microbe that we can't identify at this time. These creatures are fossilized within the crystal, which possesses trace amounts of Uranium and other radioactive materials. I believe the nausea symptoms are caused by a potent methane gas expelled from the fossilized microbes. John and Warrens are becoming more open to the possibility of weaponizing the mineral, but I still have a lot of convincing to do.

What remains a mystery is our next mission. We haven't been in contact with Ionics for weeks, and John has been elusive with the details. Only vague references to a training mission.

"Gentlemen, there comes a time in every man's life when he must admit he doesn't have all the answers. You've done well in your missions up to this point, but even I cannot prepare you for everything you will face. That was apparent on Hadrian. I was unprepared for the elite forces being enhanced with an AI program. Therefore, I've brought aboard an individual who will prepare you for *any* situation. His methods are brutal, but effective."

The door opens with a loud hiss. Two soldiers in brown uniforms walk in, present arms and stand at attention. Their uniforms are a relic from the Core military, decommissioned right before the Unification Wars after the Core switched to a steel gray.

A third man walks in. He's decorated in medals and clad in the same mocha-colored uniforms as the soldiers. An officer whose uniform is pressed and shoes are shined. A tall figure, with brown hair that's graying on the sides combed to the right. He's clean shaven, with a gaze that's as hard as steel. The man walks with the dominance of a conqueror, his hands behind his back and chest fully exposed.

"Horsemen, I present to you one of the toughest men alive, General Romulus Fitch!" John turns and salutes him, who returns the gesture. The two men shake hands and embrace each other as if it's been ages since they've been in one another's presence.

"Colonel Henry, it is a true pleasure to see you again."

"The pleasure is all mine General."

"John has shared with me his vision for the Horsemen, and to be quite frank, I don't think you can handle it. I see here a team of academics who hide behind their microscopes rather than face the real horrors of the universe."

"How dare you," Sulture snarls as he lunges for Fitch. Hacker and Shepherd are quick to pull him back.

"Let him come," Fitch says.

Hacker and Shepherd release Sulture, who charges for the General. He swings wide, while Fitch sucker punches him right in the nose, which knocks him to the ground.

"You may have exterminated a species by giving them the sniffles, but that-"

Sulture howls and claws at his leg like a madman. Fitch stomps down hard on his chest, eliciting a wheeze.

"That doesn't mean you're ready to face the *real* monsters. There will come a time when you're outgunned, outmatched, hell, even outsmarted by the predators. What will you do then?" Sulture claws some more, but Fitch presses down harder.

"What I care about is your ability to endure. John tells me that this team was put together to defend humanity from the monsters. That means you will have to survive the most brutal training imaginable. In the STARs they have a bell they ring during their final week of training. They ring it, they go home. The Horsemen won't have such a luxury. You either succeed in my training or you go home in a body bag."

Fitch's words carry the weight of a planet. Nobody has been told that their training is basically a suicide mission.

Fitch pulls Sulture up, pats him on the shoulder and shoves him back in line. "Do not get emotional. If you want a fulfilling and happy life, or to spill your heart in love letters, quit now. You're here to kill monsters, and you must forgo emotion to make the right decisions. Emotions will cloud your judgment, make you sloppy and unable to cope with loss. Now, let's begin training." He marches over and steps into the boxing ring.

"Who will be the first victim?" He asks.

Nobody moves.

"Buncha candy-asses here John. What about you?" Fitch asks as he points at me. "What's your name son?"

"Silas Godfrey."

"Ah, the professor." Fitch unbuttons his jacket and removes his undershirt. I watch in confusion until he's bare chested and ready to box. I follow suit, and get into a stance.

"John tells me you men are more brawlers than boxers."

"Guess you'll find out," I reply as I raise my arms.

Without warning, Fitch kicks me in the knee. I fall forward, and he grabs my wrist. He drags me to the ground, and pins me to the floor.

"There are no rules when fighting monsters. They don't follow them, and neither should you! You need to read them. Their muscles, their eyes, every physical feature will tell you their next move. Condition your body to ignore physical pain and be ready for the unexpected."

Fitch pats me on the shoulder. "Don't worry, I lead you into that one, let's go again."

He and I get back into our boxing stances. He pulls a knife that was sheathed on his shin and slashes across my torso. The cut weeps blood, each drip a tale of treachery. I can't get angry - that's what Fitch wants. I watch him dance around with the knife in his hand. I wait, the blood slowly trickling down my abdomen. I wipe my fingers across the crimson streaks.

"It's not a deep cut, it'll heal quickly," Fitch says.

"I know," I reply and flick my blood splattered fingers at his face. He flinches back, and angles the knife away from me. I tackle him and pin down his arm with the knife. I seize his throat, but he grabs mine. The two of us play a dangerous game, but I realize he has a much stronger grip. I feel the all-too familiar sensation of asphyxiation, so I release his neck and jam my thumb into his eye.

I can feel his slimy eyeball begin to squish down. He groans in pain and grabs my wrist, but I dig in.

"Yield! Yield boy yield!"

"Drop the knife," I growl.

Fitch drops his knife. I slide it towards the guys, and get off of him. I get back in line, watching him the entire time.

"This man here learned his lesson. You gotta fight dirty to beat monsters," He says as he rubs his eye.

"The Professor also did something very smart. Don't go for the throat because you need to *wait* for the creature to die. It takes a lot of energy to keep them pinned down for that long. Go for the eyes, the nose, the ears if they got 'em because it will hurt a hell of a lot more and are much easier to tear out. Damn son," Fitch says as he rubs his eye.

The other guys flash me a grin.

"That was a good starting point. Now, let's get you boys into my arena aboard the *Monolith*. Follow me," Fitch orders, picking up his uniform and knife.

He leads us out through the cargo ramp onto a landing pad which could easily hold a thousand ships the size of the *Enigma* on board.

Fitch nods to each of his men as we pass by. His brown coats are quiet, disciplined and precise. There's a hardiness to them, not a dough boy in sight. Their faces are stern with a deep understanding that war is not a game for them, it's their life. If the Core dare challenged these men, they'd crush the Core forces.

"How do you keep all these boys up in the skies?" Warrens asks.

"The Unknown Regions need protecting too, and each world contributes what they can," Fitch replies. Two of his men hold out a tray which contains several small medical devices.

Fitch holds one up. "This is a portable dialysis machine."

Murph perks up. "I've heard of those things, they're called a Dialisor!"

"Correct. With the different trace metals contained in the flesh of plants and animals, metal poisoning is inevitable, especially on unregulated worlds. These devices have saved us more times than we can count, regulating our blood to keep us alive."

He sets the device down.

"Let's get a move on."

Fitch escorts us to his training facility. It's an obstacle course full of craggy boulders and splintered logs.

He turns to Hacker. "Run it."

"I'm more tech support," Hacker replies.

Fitch takes out his pistol and points it at Hacker. "I said run it."

Hacker relents and jogs through the sand. Fitch lets out a whistle and two drones swoop down into the arena. They look like balloons with arms. They shoot at Hacker, who dives beneath the boulders for cover.

"They're set to stun, but they'll hurt as much as a real blaster bolt," Fitch says.

Hacker scrambles through the arena until he's pinned beneath a boulder while the drones search for him. He kicks up sand, but the drones aren't backing off.

Fitch turns to Shepherd.

"Go get him," He orders.

Shepherd doesn't hesitate. He charges into the arena, but Fitch whistles again. Three more drones emerge from the ceiling. All five converge on the kid. Their blaster bolts pelt the sand, and while he could've handled two or three, five is too many.

I bolt into the arena.

I pick a rock and throw it at the pack of drones. It strikes one of them, which turns to face me. The drone lowers its arms and opens fire. Another rock flies past me and hits the drone. Murph stands in defiance next to me.

A third rock whistles past us and cracks the drone, making it fall out of the air. Warrens walks up and holds his shirt in his hand which has been converted into a sling.

"Let's knock 'em out!" He says.

The three of us go for the fallen drone and tear off its arms and kick out its propulsion systems. Warrens tinkers with the arm's wires, but more drones hover towards us.

"Heyyyyy dronies!" Forrest screams from a nearby boulder. He lifts his shirt up and starts rubbing his belly. "Easy pickins right here!" The drones fall for the bait and pursue him.

"Casanova, here's yours!" Warrens says as he hands me the converted arm piece. He motions where the trigger is and gives the other arm to Murph.

"You two give me some cover, I'm going after Goldilocks and Circuit."

Murph and I stand shoulder to shoulder as we fire upon the drones. We drive them back while Warrens dives in and grabs the two men.

"I got 'em!" Warrens howls. "Let's get outta here!"

The drones circle around until Murph and I are surrounded. We get back to back and keep firing. The other drones hesitate to come too close, until my energy cell flickers out.

"I'm out!"

"Damn, me too," Murph replies. The drones realize this and swarm in for the kill.

Rocks fly in from all directions. All the men in the arena with us had torn their shirts and made slings to throw rocks at the drones.

"Get outta there!" Warrens howls.

One of the rocks smashes into a drone, which knocks it out of the air. I grab Murph's arm and shove him forward through the gap.

During our retreat I feel my back light on fire. The searing heat causes me to howl and I collapse into the dirt.

"Silas!" Murph screams. He grabs onto my wrist and tries to pull me up, but my legs refuse to cooperate.

"I can't walk!"

Warrens dives down and grabs onto my other wrist and helps drag me out of the arena. The two men pull as hard and fast as they can until the sand turns to steel, where the drones come to an abrupt stop.

Fitch turns and looks at Lee, Sulture and Sujay who didn't go into the arena.

"Interesting," He says. "That's enough Operator." The drones hover back to the ceiling and into their storage docks.

Murph checks my vitals and thumps a few times on my back.

I don't feel a thing.

"Needn't worry, the numbness will be gone by morning," Fitch says. "Sleep well gentlemen." He walks out of the room, head held high. Sulture, Lee and Sujay go back aboard the *Enigma* while the rest surround me.

"Assholes," Warrens grunts.

"Why wouldn't they help?" Shepherd asks.

"Who cares?" I reply.

"Sure gonna be awkward at the bunks tonight," Forrest says. We stare at each other in silence, knowing that he's right.

The five of us cram ourselves into Shepherd's quarters. I barely sleep a wink because my back won't stop tingling. That and Forrest is a cuddler.

At some god-forsaken hour, Fitch's men howl and scream while they bang metal trash cans to wake us up.

Fitch stands in the doorway. "Monsters don't sleep so why should any of you?"

"Cognitive function," I reply.

"Get used to a lack of sleep. The nightmares will keep you up anyway."

His men drag us out of bed and back to his arena on the *Monolith*. He stands next to two massive, ancient-looking stone columns.

"In Earth's ancient cultures, perpetrators were sentenced to be beaten half to death here at the pillar. I've built these in homage to that tradition."

Great.

Fitch points at me. "How's your back feelin'?"

"Better sir."

"Good. Strap him in."

Two of Fitch's men seize me by the arms and drag me to the pillars. They strap me in at the wrists while they pass out bamboo sticks to the others.

"These will be the weapon of choice against those strapped to the pillars," Fitch takes one and swings it through the air, then continues with his instruction.

With electricity, what kills you are the amps, not volts. The pillars are designed to give you a lot of volts, but never enough amps to kill you. The pain is excruciating and will cause you to blackout within minutes. You are to beat your friend here to prevent the voltage from getting too high. The less you hit him, the higher the voltage and trust me, that hurts more than the twigs in your hands."

Never in my wildest dreams had I imagined Fitch being this twisted.

"Operator, start the timer."

My wrists and my feet immediately explode in fiery pain. I scream out, seeking salvation from the others. They stare at the bamboo sticks in disbelief

"Help me!" I shriek.

Shepherd charges forward and strikes me on the shoulder. The pain from the electricity eases a bit, but ramps back up quickly.

"Yes! More of that!"

Shepherd strikes me, but I know he's holding back. He doesn't want to hurt me, but he knows it's the lesser of two evils.

Hacker and Forrest run around the back and strike between my shoulder blades.

Warrens and Murph run up to me.

"If you must suffer, then I'll suffer too," Warrens says as he drops his bamboo staff. I feel elated until he drives his fist deep into my gut, which opens the knife wound from yesterday.

"I'm sorry," He says.

"Feels better than the current," I reply.

Murph looks me in the eye, his sweaty hair dangling over his eyes. "Looks like we're in this together Horsemen!" He punches me with a right hook to the chin.

I can tell by Murph and Warrens' reactions that as they strike me, they feel the electrical charge. Forrest, Shepherd and Hacker drop their bamboo sticks and hit me with their fists as well.

The five men wail on me as sweat flows down my face. Welts form all over my skin, and I'm wheezing from Warrens' gut punches. I can't escape the pain coming from all sides, so I breathe as deep as I can and accept it. I pull my mind inward, and take it all in silence.

"That's enough gentlemen! Well done," Fitch says. Two of his soldiers release me and I fall into Warrens' arms. He lifts me over his shoulder and carries me back to the line.

Fitch turns and points at Sulture.

"You. Get in there." He motions to the pillars.

Sulture doesn't budge.

Fitch sighs, and then whistles. Two guards grab Sulture from behind. He fights like a savage, but more join in. They club him down, drag him to the pillars and strap him in.

"Pride is tough to break, but I've faced far more stubborn men than you. Operator, begin when ready."

Sulture's face glows red as he grits his teeth in pain.

"You, why don't you help him?" Fitch points at Murph and holds out a bamboo stick. Murph walks up, takes it and stands before Sulture.

"What are you waiting for?!" Sulture screams. His eyes are wild and every vein in his head pulses.

"You know what Adam? I'm done trying to defend you. I've done everything I can to prove your allegiance to the Horsemen, since you don't have a shining personality."

"Sing it brother!" Forrest yells.

"You saved the people of Angkor. It's done. It's over. We're not there anymore so get over yourself. These guys have done more for us than anyone we've ever known and all you can focus on is your pride because Fitch sucker punched you. Show some fucking gratitude because these guys are all we've got." Murph drops the bamboo stick and walks away.

"Murph! Murph, please! I'm begging you!" Sulture screams.

Murph stands in line between Forrest and I. The look of betrayal in Sulture's eyes is piercing, but Murph stares daggers back at him.

"You better talk someone into picking that up, or it's going to really hurt," Fitch says.

"Someone, please!" Sulture begs.

Shepherd takes a step forward, but Warrens stops him.

"You'll be in for a world of hurt Goldilocks."

Lee and Sujay move forward, but Fitch's soldiers restrain them.

"Let's see if someone *else* will help Sulture here."

I charge forward, slipping out of Warrens' iron grip. I lay in to Sulture, pummeling his gut as hard as I can. His eyes are maniacal, and he's bearing his teeth in pain.

Time flows slowly as I pound against one of my own, each strike a reminder of the current I faced. I know Sulture's pain and I will do whatever I can to alleviate it.

"Time's up!" Two soldiers come out of nowhere and release Sulture. He falls to the floor and when I offer my him my hand, he bats it away and instead crawls back into line.

The soldiers holding Lee drag him up to the pillars and strap him in. He stares at us in silence. Our eyes meet and he knows my gaze.

"Don't help me. This is my punishment, and I will suffer in silence. I've wronged all of you, and I'm sorry."

"You heard him Operator, start 'er up!"

Lee suffers through his penance in silence. He lasts until 2:24 on the timer before he passes out. More guards come and haul him out to the medbay, to ensure there's no serious damage.

"It seems that my trials have their own form of justice," Fitch says proudly.

Sujay is next to be strapped to the pillars. He holds his head down in shame, unable to look any of us in the eye.

"I didn't help because I was a coward. I was afraid of getting hurt. I'm sorry."

"You're all terrible at speeches. Operator, take it away."

Sujay howls out as the electricity flows through him. I approach and swat him with a bamboo stick. The others are behind me, ready to deliver the pain Sujay tried so hard to avoid.

We beat the hell out of Sujay until his time is up. Warrens carries him back to the cots, while Murph and I pull Sulture over our shoulders. We're a bruised and battered team, but we come together right when we needed to. I lay down on the bed, but I'm too sore to sleep. I reach for my notebook and start to write.

Godfrey's Journal Day 105

Fitch's training is beyond brutal. He drives us hard, forcing us into drills that the military wouldn't even have their special ops run. He's a mad man, yet I can't help but admire and respect him. Through his training I learned that I could survive and thrive on pain. Pain was a constant, yet I found the strength to endure. Fitch's presence is still a mystery. John has been absent during the training, and theories abound as to where he is. Personally, I wonder if he is able to watch us undergo our training.

I wonder what all of this will lead to. I question how far Fitch is willing to take this. He's made us turn on each other, and I believe we've faced the worst.

I'm restless during the night. The bruises and welts burn against the sheets. For some reason I feel the need to talk to Fitch.

I navigate across the *Monolith,* relying on the directions from quiet, stoic soldiers aboard the ship.

I walk into Fitch's quarters. It's dimly lit, but the walls are adorned with wooden paneling. Marvelous marble busts of men I don't recognize stand proud on his desk. He's sitting in his chair with a glass of bourbon, and his stare softens once he sees me.

"What can I do for ya son?" He asks me and takes a sip.

"Where's John?"

"John is currently explaining to your superiors where you are. They're not too happy that you're out here with me."

"And where exactly are we?"

"We're in the Unknown Regions. At least, unknown as far as the Core is concerned."

"So you know where we're going?"

"Of course I do. Here, take a seat and have a drink." Ice clatters against glass and the caramel drink cascades over the cubes. I sip the bourbon slowly. It tickles the throat. I swirl my tongue around and savor the flavor of aged oak.

At least Fitch has good taste.

"Now, what's really on your mind? Why are you looking for John?"

It dawns on me I don't have a clear answer. I can't recall why I came down here.

Fitch nods his head. "Your final test will begin tomorrow. John knows what I've been doing and he doesn't want to interfere. He understands my ways and personally asked me to prepare you for the next phase of your training."

"What is the final test?"

Fitch laughs. "I can't tell you what your final test is going to be. I can say it will test all of you in mental and physical endurance. Do or die."

I finish my bourbon and place the glass on Fitch's desk. I get up to leave but stop in the doorway.

"How does a General come to own a battleship like the *Monolith*? Doesn't the Navy control them?"

"An honorless Admiral I was stationed under wanted an innocent world to die at the hands of monsters. I killed him and took over while the Core stripped me of my title and my rank, so I kept the ship and just kept fighting in the Unknown Regions."

"Why did John reach out to you?" I ask. "He could've taken us to any other team-building professional. Why you?"

"Simple," Fitch says as he shrugs his soldiers. "I trained him."

I nod, and head back to my bed to get some sleep.

At first there is darkness, but I hear the door open. Light from the outside shines in, and a dark, imposing figure stands in the doorway.

"Make it quick," the shadow says.

Fitch.

Four of his soldiers swarm into our bunks. I sit up, but I'm forced back down. I try to scream, but its no use. The soldier on my left takes out a syringe and plunges it into my neck.

One by one they do the same to the others.

"You son of a bit-" I growl, but my tongue becomes dry. I feel woozy and my eyelids are heavy. Each time they close it's harder to open them. I glare at Fitch as my world fades to black.

CAMPING TRIP

Bestial howls and chirping birds form a mashed-up chorus that rings all around me. My head throbs as my cotton tongue scrapes against the roof of my mouth. My hands grip the clammy, mealy dirt that oozes between my fingers. The smell of decaying plants and mildew fills my nose. I finally get brave enough to open my eyes.

I see green all around me. Trees tower over us, each of them greedy for their share of sunlight. My lungs fill with the soggy air. Each breath is like trying to inhale through a soaked towel. Panic rises when I look around and I have no idea where we are. All I see are the shirtless, scattered bodies of the Horsemen, a dialisor strapped to one hip and a hunting knife on the other.

Every time we make progress, we're knocked flat on our asses to try again. Like Sisyphus and his damn boulder.

I feel lost, like a wretched soul condemned to search through a vast nothingness.

I want to break. I want to let my walls collapse, give up and give in. I feel like a husk, a shadow of a real man.

I feel something else stir inside.

Anger.

I stoke the flames. I feed them until I feel my blood begin to boil. Resentment nestles inside of me. Resentment for Fitch, John and everything else that led to me being stranded here on this God-forsaken world.

I hear something stir behind me.

I turn and draw my knife, only to find Shepherd is waking up.

"Silas?" He looks around. "Where are we?"

"Hell if I know."

"What happened?"

"Fitch drugged us, then dropped us off." I walk around and wake the others up. My head is throbbing and my tongue feels like a piece of steel wool.

"What the hell is this?" Sulture snarls as he wakes up. He bolts upright, his maniacal eyes searching for something in the jungle.

"Here's something," Hacker says as he holds up a holodisk. He drops it onto the ground and activates it.

A small hologram of Fitch appears.

"Good day gentlemen. Welcome to planet OSX-V11 codenamed 'Orion's Playground.' It's an abandoned military training facility, centered on the wilderness. Perfect for your final test. Everything on this planet can kill a human whether that be through strength, smarts, or other means."

"Sadistic motherfucker!" Sulture says.

"All you have to face the wilderness is a knife, your dialisor, and your wits. There are caches of supplies littered around, but don't depend on them. This is a test of your ability to survive on your own. I've also activated several assassination droids to hunt you. They carry sniper rifles and can see you in the dark. Make no mistake, it's do or die here gentlemen. We will come for you when I believe you've passed your final test. Best of luck." the hologram disappears and the holodisk fizzles.

"Sabotaged to deliver a final message," Hacker says.

"*Everything* can kill us?" Sujay asks.

"That's what you're worried about?!" Forrest blurts out. "Not the homicidal robots that don't have to eat, sleep, or slow down while they can shoot our pink, fleshy bodies?!"

"Guys calm down!" Shepherd shouts. "Fitch wants to see who breaks and who holds up. If we work together, we'll got outta this."

"The kid's right," Sulture says. "We need to make a shelter and find a source of water. Lee, can you begin search the plants for food and water?"

Lee nods and runs off.

"Warrens, can you design a housing structure that will blend in with the environment?"

"Sure can."

It amazes me how quickly Sulture takes command. It's as if the man was built to manage adversity and enjoys surviving in the wilds.

Warrens and Shepherd organize the layout of the camp, where everyone should sleep, a guard shift, latrines, the works. We toil away for hours in the humidity to build up a few huts that we hope will hold.

We sweat bullets in the smothering heat. We're soaked to the bone and not replenishing water fast enough. The ground is wet. The branches and limbs we encounter are rotten, and the leaves drip all the time. Everything is wet, and there is no escaping this tortuous heat.

Hacker ties our hunting knives to the end of some long sticks for spears. Murph and Sulture clear out the dead plant matter from the camp while Shepherd and I dig latrines. Forrest and Sujay dig down to the roots of the nearby trees so we can burn and cut them down. Warrens and Lee construct a forge so that we have a place to make weapons. They even have enough time to make a bow and arrow.

By nightfall, we have a camp.

Darkness consumes the camp until we're left with no light other than our fire. We sit in a circle, exhausted from the labor of assembling our base.

Our stomachs rumble from the lack of food. Many of the plants are tough, fibrous or poisonous. All Lee managed to recover were a handful of tubular vegetables which have less flavor than potatoes.

As I scan our surroundings, a pair of piercing yellow eyes captures my attention. Another pair flashes next to them, then a third.

Predators.

Sulture turns to see what I'm looking at. He orders Shepherd to grab our spears just as the beasts howl and descend down the hill.

They cackle like hyenas, but look like hairless wolves with porcupine quills.

"Stay smart boys," Murph says as we file in back to back with one another. I run through my mental *SMART* checklist, searching for an advantage as the barbed wolves surround us.

"They move in a pack formation, the Omega will be the first to attack," Sulture explains.

"Where's the Alpha?" I ask.

"Not present."

"I'm gonna spear one of these things like it was Sujay's mom!" Forrest says.

My heart is racing in my chest. Adrenaline is kicking in, and my fingers are trembling.

I breathe in. Breathe out. I need to calm my nerves. Their vermilion eyes burn with a sinister malice.

"These things were created in a lab," Sulture says.

"How can you tell?" Shepherd asks.

"They don't fear us. Every animal has *some* fear."

"Maybe they got used to killing humans for dinner!" Sujay shrieks.

The beasts growl and watch us. They're searching for a weakness in our formation. I notice in front of me that the beast's leg muscles are tensing up.

He's going to pounce.

"Lee, Shepherd, I got one that's about to jump us, help me take it out."

"Done," both men reply.

I can feel the others shift themselves into place. The forest grows quiet, anticipating the strike. I see in the eyes of this beast an unwillingness to back down, which works fine with us.

"NOW!" I scream.

The three of us thrust our spears into the beast, a sickening slice while the creature's growls become clogged with blood.

Lee and Shepherd retract their spears and step back into position.

The wolf cackles in pain, whimpering and growling as it struggles to stay alive. The others become unsettled, but still determined to test us.

We coordinate with each other, performing our triangulated strikes against the wolves one by one, however Sujay has revealed himself to be the weak link. He didn't coordinate any attacks with us.

The wolf snarls, ready to pounce. Forrest and Warrens plunge their spears forward, but the wolf dives back, spins around and strikes Sujay with its tail. He screams out in pain as several barbs embed themselves into his arm.

Sujay lashes out and throws his spear. It plunges into the wolf, skewering the creature. It whimpers in pain, while the rest of us charge and finish it off.

"We did it!" Forrest shouts. "Take that, spiny wolves! No match for us!" His golden necklace dances around his neck as he celebrates.

"Don't celebrate," Sulture growls. "We fought the lowest in the pack. The alpha was testing us, watching us to see how we'd react."

"Why you gotta do that?" Murph asks Sulture. "Let the guy have a victory lap."

"A real victory should be earned."

"We did earn it! We killed off a threat to our survival!"

"We didn't neutralize the threat, only ensured those wolves will be back!"

I intervene. "And we'll kill them when they come just like with these. Murph, tend to Sujay, Sulture, plan for the next assault, and Forrest, take your victory lap."

"Woo-hoo!"

Sulture gets in my face. "You think you can just bark orders here?"

"You did earlier. Now it seems you're more interested in putting people in their place."

Sulture glares at me, but I give him a hard stare of my own.

"Hey boys, I can make some weapons outta these skins if someone gives me a hand." Warrens' remark cuts the tension in the air. Sulture goes off to another task, while I help Warrens in skinning the wolves.

"What're you thinking of making Warrens?" I ask.

"I'm thinking a crude leather cestus."

"Like what the Romans used to wear?" Shepherd asks.

"Sure is. I don't know how to tan leather very well, but it's worth a try. Gives us a little more protection." Warrens cuts out a small patch of flesh and takes it to his forge.

As I look down at the meat, our stomachs rumble.

"Should we try cooking it?" I ask.

"Carnivore meat is going to taste like shit," Sulture replies.

"Do you have another food source?" I ask. He shakes his head no, and takes the entrails to analyze the stomach contents. Shepherd, Lee and I carve up the rest of the beast to hang over Lee's fire.

The roasted meat is a grisly, dripping mess, and the taste is atrocious. We tear at the carved meat like savages because it's tougher than leather. We joke about how this food is actually *worse* than John's carb slop, a feat we thought was impossible.

Murph finishes removing the barbs from Sujay, and the two join us for dinner.

"We'll have to keep an eye on him for infection. Right environment here in the jungle and no antibiotics available," Murph explains.

"Just don't let me lose my arm you tools."

"Ha! There's only one thing you need that arm for and it's *not* to navigate with!" Forrest screams.

We take shifts to guard the camp throughout the night. Lee and I spend the night among the chittering bugs telling stories, while the last remnants of the wolf meat smolders away in the flames.

A large snap echoes through the forest. Lee and I share a look, and then we grab our spears.

As Lee looks around, his eyes grow wider than I've ever seen.

"LOOK OUT!" He screams and then dives out of the way.

I look up and see the outline of a massive boulder coming right for us. I leap out of the way right as the rock crashes into our fire and rolls through the camp. On the ridge, I see a dozen figures stand in a phalanx formation, with glowing green eyes.

"Wake up!" I howl throughout the camp. "We're under attack!

The others rush out of their tents, grabbing whatever weapons they can hold. More dark figures file in along the ridge.

"What are they?" Shepherd asks.

One of the figures leaps from the ridge into the trees. The trees rustle from the weight, but the creature swings from one branch to the next until the dim light of the fire shines upon it. It looks like a massive gorilla, at least twice the size of one we'd see back on Earth.

The gorilla pounds at the tree and roars at us, bearing his massive fangs.

"Monsters never sleep," I mutter.

The gorillas charge down the hill while others leap into the trees. We form a phalanx to meet the incoming horde despite their size.

Right as the first one is about to make contact, three of us spear the ape and watch it collapse into the fire. The beast screams in agony as it catches on fire from the grease of the wolf drippings. It stumbles out of the fire pit and runs into other gorillas, igniting them as well.

Warrens uses the distraction to attack with his cesti, punching the quills into one of the gorillas. The beast swats him with its hand and knocks him into a tree.

Murph, Shepherd and I dive in and spear the bastard in the gut. The beast growls and smashes our spears before collapsing into the dirt.

More gorillas come. I grab one of the femurs from our wolf, snap the bone in half and charge into the fray.

A gorilla comes at me and swings high, but I duck beneath its massive arm. I stab into the beast's abdomen as hard as I can. A blood frenzy overtakes me as I swing wildly and stab as much as I can in a race for survival.

A blow from the side takes me by surprise, knocking me to the ground. It's another gorilla, coming to the aid of the first one.

I feel around for a weapon, but all I grab is dirt. The ape glares down at me, picks up a boulder and holds it overhead.

I close my eyes and wait for the end.

The gorilla erupts into a howl. I open my eyes and see two flaming arrows sticking out of the creature. It throws the boulder at the Shepherd, who ducks behind a tree.

I find the other femur shank and pick it up. The gorilla slams his fists down and bares his teeth at me. I lunge forward, stab it in the eye and then run for my life.

As I run through the trees the darkness becomes more complete. It swallows everything, and if I keep running, I'll be a dead man. The others are fleeing as well, the gorillas have torn up the camp. Warrens is the last man out, refusing to give up his forge, but even he is driven out.

The glow from the fire is dying. The gorillas become shades as they stomp out our carved home inside their ancestral lands.

I hear some of the others down below screaming for each other and running into hiding. The gorillas don't seem interested in pursuing us, only in wiping out our camp.

Darkness consumes the jungle. I only see a few orange sparks glowing on the forest floor, but aside from that it's pitch black.

For the first time in I don't know how many years, I pray. I pray that everyone will make it out of this alive. I pray that we will come out of this together. I pray that not all of this is hopeless and that we've not been condemned to death by Fitch.

Dawn breaks, and I wake to the rustling of nearby branches. Small primates with large eyes are crawling all around me. They're on the move searching for fruit much higher up than me. Their limbs are long, over 60 centimetres in their arms and their legs are a full metre. Their faces are flat and their eyes are beady. They have ears that point back with a small tuft of fur on the tip.

I climb down to the ground where Murph is rummaging through the plants.

"What're you doing Murph?"

"Oh, morning Silas. Sujay is running a fever. His wounds have gone septic, so I'm looking for something to cure the infection."

I feel a sinking hopelessness creep into me, clawing at the back of my mind. The attack devastated morale and revealed just how hard this world would fight to keep us out.

"Let's get a fire going. We need everyone back at camp," I say.

Murph nods, and the two of us grab Sujay. We carry him over our shoulders back to camp and we see Sulture propped up against a tree.

"Adam!" Murph screams and runs over to him. Sulture stirs as Murph checks his pulse.

"He's alive, but he's not doing well." Murph brings him to where I've laid Sujay.

Murph and I get a fire going, and the others trickle in. We settle in around the fire, covered in dirt and gore. We look like the saddest ragtag group ever assembled.

"How're they doing?" Shepherd asks as he points to Sujay and

Sulture.

"Not good," Murph replies. "Sujay's got an infection and I haven't been able to give Adam a full diagnosis."

Lee gets up, walks out and starts scouring the plants.

"What're you doing?" I ask.

"Funny how I didn't see much green till I joined you *cho yades*," Lee replies.

"There he goes, using his potty mouth. I have half a mind to wash your mouth out with soap," Forrest says.

"You can try *hundan*. Here's something that'll help cure his ailments. Peppermint." Lee shows us a bundle of plants with jagged leaves and a pattern resembling a compass rose.

Lee and Murph work to grind the leaves into a fine paste, extracting the oils which will kill the bacteria in Sujay's arm.

Meanwhile, Sulture begins to stir and groans out in pain. Shepherd comes in with some water and gives him a few drops.

Sulture wakes up, and notices that we're all staring at him.

"Well, I know I'm not dead if all of you fuckers are here...unless I'm in hell."

We burst out laughing as Sulture sits himself up. He's bruised, burnt and battered just like the rest of us.

"What do we do now?" Shepherd asks.

"Well, looks like the gorillas put a damper on our lovely camping trip," Forrest says. "What I wouldn't give for a beach day."

"We should retaliate against those savage apes," Sulture replies.

"After how we just got fubar'd? No thanks," Murph replies.

"We gotta figure out how we survive," Shepherd says.

I hear Fitch's voice in the back of my head "If you want to fight monsters, you must become monsters."

That's it!

"Guys," I reply. "We've been going about it all wrong. Fitch has been giving us the advice to succeed this whole time."

"And what advice would that be? Strip nude and perform a dance hoping to be blessed by some ancient forest god?" Forrest asks. "Because just to be clear, I'm okay with that."

I ignore Forrest. "Fitch always said that we needed to 'become monsters.' We can't fight here in the conventional sense. We can't shoot our way out, we need to adapt to our environment. Our idea of building a camp to operate out of was the wrong one. We can't fight out here like that."

"Then what do you suggest Casanova?"

"We melt into the environment. Build around it. We don't seek to conquer it like what humans would do, instead we become a part of it."

"How do we do that?" Shepherd asks.

I pick up one of the spear poles and walk over to one of the dead gorillas. I pull out one of the knives we'd lost.

I carve the head off of the gorilla's body, jam it onto the stake and drive that into the ground.

"We create wards of what happens to those that fuck with us."

"Yeah, but that will attract predators," Sulture says.

"You're right, and we'll be ready for them with booby traps," I reply.

"You clever *hundan*..." Lee whispers.

"That's right Lee, we're going to survive like guerrillas."

"Why do we want to live like monkeys?" Forrest asks. "Don't they imitate us?"

"Lao tyen yeh Forrest! Guerrilla *fighters* you hwoon dahn!"

"You heard Fitch. Everything here is bred to kill humans. We need to become ghosts of the jungle, meld into it." As I attempt to rally the men, a gleam shines in my eye from one of the nearby tree branches. It's the unmistakable shine of chrome. It's not until I see a pair of red eyes along with it that I realize how much danger we're in.

"GET DOWN!" I scream. "Assassin droid!"

Everyone dives to the ground as a blaster bolt crackles in the dirt. The droid leaps out of its branch, knowing that it's been spotted.

"Duh liou mahng, we still have those to deal with."

"Hacker, any ways we can deal with them?" I ask.

"Not without an interface I can enter commands into," Hacker replies.

"We need to move, now that it has our position," Lee says.

We salvage whatever we can and begin a long trek through the jungle. Murph and Forrest carry Sujay across their shoulders. Hacker tinkers with the holodisk to understand its communication signals.

"Any luck?" Murph asks.

"When someone sends a transmission, it's a one way system. These are designed to be expendable and mass produced. However, their power cores are a little more valuable than that and with the right signal I can get the droid's attention."

"Is drawing them to us the best idea if we're trying to hide?" Shepherd asks.

"We can draw them to us on our own terms. I think I can make a signal that is so irritating it'd be like nails on glass. The assassin droids will stop at nothing to eliminate this signal, so it'd be the perfect bait."

"Hopefully it'll make them into *dairuomu ji*," Lee says.

"Godfrey, there's something I gotta know," Forrest says. "How'd an old geezer like you go about seducing those girls that turned you in? Hacker showed us the pictures and they were real hotties!"

"Like you guys really wanna hear that," I reply.

"I'm curious Casanova," Warrens says. The others are as well.

"Alright, fine. So these two girls had me as a professor at the university. They were the typical rich girls who used daddy's money to get into the medical field for a prestigious title, but didn't want to work for it. Their grades sucked and they come to me for help. I told them what books to read, and explained that they needed to do the work to have a chance at passing. That and pass their final exam."

"C'mon! Get to the good stuff!" Forrest screams.

"They don't want to do the work. Big surprise right? They start lowering their voices to me, getting all husky hoping that there was 'something else they could do' to raise their grades. They batted their eyelashes and leaned over so I'd see down their dresses. One of them even put her hand on my knee. I caught on and decided to go for it, but I told them it had to be a three-way. They agreed-"

"What?! How'd you-"

"Shut up Forrest!" I scream. "They slid onto my lap, pressed their breasts up against me, and I start making out with them. Next thing I know clothes are gone and I'm giving them the ride of their lives. I was going to do my damndest to satisfy both of them, because you never know when a three-way will happen again."

"So how'd you get caught?" Shepherd asks.

"Well, they got a little pissed at me. You see, they still failed their final and therefore, the class. I on the other hand was true to my word. I raised their grade before their final to passing...all the way up to a D+."

The guys howl in laughter, our echoes traveling through the forest.

We find an area where we can burrow in and make shelter for the night, however Shepherd and Hacker volunteer to sit in the trees as sentries. Nothing disturbs us, but it's a cold, restless night.

Sujay's wounds fill with puss, which Murph takes as a good sign. Warrens makes more bows, and the rest of us go on the hunt. However there isn't any game. The jungle has become eerily quiet, as if the world is holding its breath.

Then it starts to rain.

It rains for five days straight. We salvage what we can from plants, but the constant assault of cold water droplets sucks the heat from our bones. Every night bears an icy breath that threatens to break us. There is no food during the five days, and hunger is getting to us. We're being hit from all sides, and I begin to believe that even an iron will can break.

"Jeepers I'm hungry!" Forrest groans.

"We all are," Sulture replies.

"*Bee-jway*! What is that noise?" Lee asks.

We all stop and listen. Despite the pelting rains, there is the sound of rushing water.

"A river!" Murph screams. We charge in and find a rushing rapid that also happens to be full of fish. Forrest dives in, trying to catch one with his bare hands. All he manages to catch are a dozen leeches which cover his torso.

Shepherd climbs onto one of the rocks and shoots a fish with his bow and arrow. The floundering carp wriggles at the end of his arrow, while he tosses it to our feet and draws another. In less than an hour, we have enough fish for a feast. We make a fire and cook the fish, our mouths too full to talk. The rush of having a full belly for the first time in days combined with the warmth of the fire hypnotizes us.

Our eyelids grow so heavy…

"We can't fall asleep!" Sulture hisses. "Predators will smell the meat, which will lure them in!"

We devise a series of booby traps to defend the camp. We dig holes, place sharpened wooden stakes at the bottom and then cover them with twigs and leaves. We tie stakes to branches and saplings, and then add a tripwire to bash any foreign intruder. Whatever comes tonight, we'll be ready for it.

The rustling leaves signal they're coming.

There's a pack of them.

The darkness hides their features, but they're drawn to the scraps of meat roasting in the flames.

One of the creatures hits a tripwire, which unleashes a sapling full of stakes. The beast squeals in pain, a high-pitched growl that I haven't heard before. More of his friends tread through the jungle on nimble feet, gliding along the surface. The others let loose a volley of arrows at the lithe, sinewy figures from their perched positions.

The beasts groan and grunt as the arrows rain down from above. The rest learn to dodge our arrows, honing in with surgical precision. In the fading light of the embers we can see our stalkers of the night. Their heads look like a lamprey, with two sets of jaws, one inside of the other, filled with needle-like teeth.

I let loose an arrow, but the creature dodges it. It charges around the fire and comes right for me. I fire another arrow, but I shoot low. I run for the tree behind, but the beast leaps over me and latches onto the tree.

I feel the steaming breaths of two more. They growl as drool drips down their savage maws. These creatures are small, only about the size of a lion, yet their savagery makes me fearful.

Another arrow pierces one of them behind me. I break into a sprint, and run for safety. The beasts follow close behind, until I find a bundle of logs to dive under. I burrow beneath them and build a wall to hide behind, but they're right on top of me, scraping the dirt away.

I feel around as I push as far back as I can go. My fingers cross something smooth and cold to the touch. I reach down and dig it out with my hands. It's a metal case of some kind.

One of Fitch's caches!

A beast behind me latches onto my shoulder and tries to pull me out. I can feel the searing pain of my flesh being shredded by its jaws rotating in a sadistic display. I open the crate and find a pistol, another hunting knife, some rations and medicine.

I grab the pistol and shoot the beast that was latched onto me. The other one jumps from the loud crack of gunfire and turns to face me.

I shoot it.

The beast runs, but falls into one of our spiked traps, and howls out in pain.

The others come running to me from the echoes of gunfire. Their faces are all masks of surprise, demanding to know how I got the gun.

"Fitch's cache. Found it under a log."

"Oh shit Silas. I gotta take a look at that wound," Murph says. He tells me that the wound is two jagged circles, one inside the other. Inside of the crate is some disinfectant, which we use on my shoulder and Sujay's arm.

"Interesting specimens," Sulture says as he looks the corpses over. "They look to belong to the Order *Crocodilia*, but I'll need to study them further for more thorough classification."

"Why not just call them 'Lamprey Crocs' and get it over with?" I ask.

"Y'know Godfrey, for a scientist you don't seem to give much weight to proper classification or the scientific method. Causes me to question your credibility."

"Why bother classifying them? Why not just kill them all off? Isn't that your approach?"

Sulture lunges for me, but Murph holds him back.

One of the lamprey crocs is plopped down in front of me.

"Cool it hotheads," Warrens snaps. "Help me drag these guys out. We can use their skins for leather."

We drag the beasts to the fire while Warrens and I skin them and Shepherd develops some homemade tanning solution. As we work at making the leather, I notice Hacker is still tinkering with the holodisk core.

"You figure that thing out yet?" I ask.

"Oh, for the most part. Just putting the chips into place manually…it's tricky."

"Is it going to make the signal you said it would? Irritate the droids and bring them to us?"

"Yes, I can have it configured by morning."

"Then we should plan a strategy for when those metalheads jump into the ring with us," Warrens says.

We spend the night mapping out a plan in the dirt of how we're going to eliminate the droid threat. We finally fall asleep in the pre-dawn hours and rest until midday, since that's when the fewest predators would be active, as Sulture tells.

We put together more traps, including several that are so obvious we hope the droids will dismiss them and fall for the real thing.

We camouflage ourselves into the environment while Hacker positions the beacon beneath a small pile of leaves. He activates the signal, and all we notice is that it's a blinking red light.

Hours pass and nothing happens. The rain rolls in and each droplet feels like another insult from the sky above. Just as I'm about to call out to the others, I hear a rustling of branches followed by a thump. I look, but I don't see anything. I look away, and notice that the light is being bended around a figure.

The droids have goddamn cloaking devices.

The droid approaches the beacon and Warrens cuts a vine with a large boulder tied to the end of it. The boulder swings just slow enough that the droid can step aside and miss it, however it's a setup for the real trap.

Hacker leaps in and stabs the droid with a hardened stick. The machine fizzles and collapses, coming into full view. It drops its sniper rifle, which Warrens leaps in to recover before anyone can stop him.

He bends down to reach, but then straightens his posture, standing out in the open. It's only when I see the light bend around his neck that I realize there's a droid holding a knife to his throat.

Fortunately, there is also a snare wrapped around the droid's foot. I make eye contact with Warrens, who understands what I'm about to do.

He grabs the droid's wrist and pulls it away from him. I activate the snare, which snags the droid and leaves it dangling from a tree. Warrens leaps down, grabs the rifle and blows a huge hole into the droid's chest. It comes into view and swings slowly from the snare. He approaches it and pokes it with his rifle.

The droid reaches out and seizes him by the throat. We scramble from our positions to save him, but Hacker sweeps in with a boulder and smashes the droid's head.

The head is knocked off, but the droid still has a death grip on his neck. He's turning purple, and Hacker reaches into the droid's torso and starts tearing cords out until the machine goes limp. It's the closest call we have, and Warrens collapses to the ground, gasping for air.

While everyone gathers around him to help him up, I hear something behind me. I walk over to the droid remains and listen. There's a faint beeping noise coming from inside the chest cavity.

"Warrens, Hacker…?"

Warrens quiets the others and listens.

"RUN!" He screams as he erupts from the ground. All of us scramble away in a mad rush. The beeping counts down until a massive explosion rings through the jungle, raining fire and molten metal down all around us. The flames consume the trees and our morale as well. Just when we think we've scored a victory, there's another trap lying in wait for us.

We stare at each other, dumbfounded and full of rage. We could've turned the droids or taken their weapons. Instead, everything was destroyed. All of our hard work ruined, and the worst part is I'm sure we didn't destroy all of the droids.

"C'mon, let's gather the up the fragments," Warrens says.

"Why?" I grunt.

"Because I can melt 'em down for armor. We need to keep busy so start pickin' 'em up."

We gather every fragment of metal we can carry and bring them back to our new forge by the river. Warrens melts the pieces down and casts metal plates to reinforce our leather armor. We tear into the rations, but there's only enough for two men, not nine. We split them as evenly as we can, but we're just as hungry as before.

"I'm still hungry!" Forrest whines.

"You're always hungry," Sulture replies.

"And you're always pissed about something," Shepherd snaps.

Sulture stands up, charges for the kid and seizes him by the throat. Warrens however steps in and clocks Sulture, knocking to the ground. Within seconds the group erupts into an all-out brawl.

"Horsemen!" I scream. My voice echoes through the trees, and silence spreads across the camp as all eyes fix upon me.

"I get that it sucks having every victory stolen from us. It sucks when every time we win, we get knocked on our asses. Yet we can rise above it. Fitch will not pull us off this world if we fight and bicker. We won't leave if we depend on the handouts of these military caches or the convenience of a nearby river. We need to become one with the jungle. We need to hunt for our food and prove to him once and for all that we can survive and even thrive in Orion's Playground!"

The others look among themselves, searching their souls for an answer.

"I'm in, Silas," Shepherd replies.

"Yeah, me too," Murph says.

One by one the Horsemen join me in an oath to become one with the jungle and master Fitch's test or die trying.

For the next five weeks, we become ghosts. We move in total silence through the jungle, covering ourselves in mud and bark for camouflage. We hunt, raid and forage whatever we can for food. We arise and meld into the thicket as quickly as we storm in, utilizing our unique sign language to communicate with one another. We build weapons of wood and bone which break easily, but we make new ones. We're always on the move, hunting that which hunted us. We rise up and prove that we're the apex predators of Orion's Playground.

We feast on dinner surrounding a fire as the stillness of the jungle captures us. A dangling branch dances in the breeze and the animals sing their chorus. As we feast on our kill, a silence spreads across the forest.

Shepherd screams in agony as a beam of light tears through his chest. He collapses, and I see the polish of chrome in the distance.

An indescribable rage consumes me and my vision turns red. I charge for the chrome figure, which holsters its gun and takes off. I follow in pursuit, hunting the machine down. It flicks on the cloaking device, but now I notice the unnatural bend of light.

The machine must pay for what it has done.

It shot the one innocent member of our troupe.

An unspeakable act, the only one of us who didn't deserve it.

"You deserved to die, murderer," A voice echoes in my head.

I ignore it, and follow this machine, determined to hunt this thing to the ends of the world.

"Why pursue the droid? You've been abandoned out here. You'll die in the wilderness."

I chase after the droid for hours. The machine isn't relenting, but then I wonder: Why should it? The unit could run across the entire planet if it wanted, while I needed to stop and rest.

I need to pause for a breath. I look around the jungle and realize that I'm all alone out here.

"They've abandoned you because you deserved it."

A twig snaps behind me. By the time I hear it, it's too late.

Searing pain devours my side as I feel an arm of icy metal wrap around my neck. I elbow and strike at my attacker, but it doesn't let go.

I dig my feet into the ground and try to push back, but the attacker doesn't budge. I reach behind my head and grab onto what feels like wires. I rip and tear because my life depends on it, while the arm tries to push the knife forward.

I scream in pain as I try to wriggle into a position that will give me an advantage. I reach in and pull more components out, exposing the droid. I tear into the machine with unnatural savagery. The droid pulls the knife out and slashes at me through the air. My metal plates block some of the blows, but I still get carved up by this bastard.

As I attack the droid I see Shepherd's shocked face which drives me forward, ignoring the pain and instead focusing on the white hot hate burning beneath the surface. I hate this jungle world, this 'test,' these missions, everything.

I grab the droid by the back of the neck and throw it against a tree. I pick up a rock and throw it, dealing another blow to the head. The droid tries to go invisible, but due to the damage, it only manages a few sparks. I scream and howl as I attack the unit and make it fall backward on a log. I tear off a branch and jam it into the droid's torso.

I stab the machine over and over until the light fades from its crimson eyes. I toss the branch aside and tear the pieces of armor away. I rip out every wire and cord I can find until I'm certain the unit won't get back up.

I find a small device with a blinking light. It looks like some sort of communication array, so I activate it and attach it to my pants. I grab the knife and salvage what I can, but the pain from my side is overwhelming. The wound to my gut is deep, and I fear the damage to my internal organs.

As I get away from the fallen droid, the explosion rings in the distance.

I search the area and spot a set of lights back from the camp. The lights rise through the trees and shine down.

"Help me!" I scream as I hold my hand up.

I hear the engines growl as the ship floats above the trees and flies forward. The ship goes straight overhead without stopping.

"Wait! No!" I howl. The ship flies into the sky and vanishes into the distance.

I look down at the knife in my hand. I wonder if it'd be easier to just end everything now. To give in and be done with this test, the pain, everything.

"Go on, end you life murderer…"

I shake the thoughts from my mind. I see the mountain rising in the distance. Something deep down tells me to go there, that I will find my absolution on the face of its mighty slopes.

Each step sends a jabbing pain to my guts. Daylight is fading, and I know I'll never make it to the mountain by nightfall. I find a tree to climb and sleep in for the night. The vines make for rough harnesses, but they'll do the trick.

I try to focus on anything other than the radiating heat from my abdomen, but it's hard to ignore. Colors swirl on the edge of my vision. Darkness descends the forest floor, but figures stir before my eyes.

I see the Horsemen traversing the galaxy, banded together until pride comes between brothers.

I see a figure staring at us from the top of a corporate tower.

I'm fighting a monstrous humanoid in the middle of a corroded metropolis. The beast is overwhelming me, but violet lightning surges from my fingertips.

I see an invasion fleet driving deep into Earth space, and the Horsemen are all that stand between them and armageddon.

I see a thousand men who all have the same face.

I see the Horsemen, bruised, battered and beaten by the figure watching us.

He's always watching us.

I watch as a massive explosion wracks a world and tears it to pieces.

I gasp for breath and almost fall from my tree branch. I breathe deep, searching for color in the impenetrable darkness. I hear beasts sniveling and fighting below.

The ever-present fight for territory and dominance rages on.

I look down at the blood-soaked leather clinging to my gut. I'm certain it's infected, and every breath has me seeing stars.

A faint glow to the East shines through the branches.

Sunrise.

At the base of the tree are three Lamprey crocs who're searching for my scent. I see the mountain in the distance and I feel more determined than ever to make it. I grab a handful of vines and walk off the branch. As I swing, it feels like a ball of molten metal is rolling around in my gut.

Somehow I manage the landing, but the crocs know I'm on the ground. I run as fast as I can, but they're faster. I can feel them breathing on my back and hear their teeth clicking together.

I make it to the mountain and start climbing. The crocs merely jump from one ledge to another. I scramble madly, while they glide like kites on the gale. I scream and swing my knife at them, but they're not backing down. I crawl further, straining my wound.

The beasts circle around, gnashing their teeth together.

I manage to get above them, but they're crouching down to pounce.

I take a leap of faith.

I crash into a croc and pin it to the ledge. I wrap my arm around its head and pull up until I hear the telltale snap. The other two surround me, thirsty for blood. My wound is weeping and I feel like I'm going to black out.

I go for the ledge and start climbing. One of the crocs latches onto my thigh and pulls me back down. I'm thrown onto my back, but a bloodlust consumes me. I strike the beasts as hard as I can, believing that my punches can break bone.

I drive them back far enough to climb further. I manage to make it thirty metres before I reach a plateau and crawl over the ledge. I've left a trail of blood and bile which only drives the crocs into a frenzy. They leap onto the plateau while my back is towards the mouth of a cave. I chuck some rocks, but this only makes them angrier. They crouch down, ready to pounce.

I feel my heartbeat through my entire body.

A piercing bellow rumbles behind me.

The crocs freeze in place.

A lumbering behemoth drags itself out of the cave. It's a disgusting pink-colored limbless beast with more teeth than the lamprey crocs. Reminds me of a wurm, a limbless dragon.

I've never seen a creature so big. This thing could swallow an elephant in one bite. The wurm slams itself against the rock and bellows in my face. His breath smells of rotten meat, and I've decided to call this thing a 'Rotgorger.'

How can I possibly defeat this thing? I'm trapped on all sides with no chance of escape. Panic swells within and I'm having a hard time breathing.

"Monsters don't just lie down and die," Fitch's words echo in my mind. "They bite, scratch, claw, whatever it takes to fight back. The monster will descend into total savagery in order to survive."

That's it.

The descent…

The air around me races faster and faster until everything comes to a halt. A primal force awakens within me, such a ferocity that I feel the world tremble around me. I've never felt such fury, rage and bloodthirst coalesce into one pivotal moment.

Time slows and all of my senses go into overdrive.

The Rotgorger lunges for me, but I run to the edge of the cave and leap onto its back. With my humble arsenal I have only one chance to end this beast quickly. At the base of its skull I draw my knife and plunge it down. I carve and cut until the wurm convulses and spasms out of control. The beast swings its tail out, sending one of the crocs flying into the distance.

The wurm lifts his head up and I hold on for dear life. The beast slams itself on the rock, wriggling uncontrollably as it fights to survive.

I keep carving, severing every nerve and tendon I can find until the beast stops moving.

The final lamprey croc leaps onto its back and closes in on me. I pull the knife from the gore and charge right for the beast. I grab it by the head and plunge the knife through its throat. I slice the animal's neck and kick it away, content to watch it suffer. The beast growls at me, but its pointless.

I walk over my kill to the ledge.

I stand before the jungle which fills the horizon and I scream. I scream a roar of savagery, letting the entire world know of my victory. My howl echoes for miles as I turn back to my kill.

I take my knife, stick it into the Rotgorger and run the blade across its abdomen. The stench is horrendous, but I don't care. I pull the intestines and the stomach out and throw them down the face of the mountain. I lay a trail of gore in my wake, a ward for the entire world to see why they shouldn't fuck with me.

I scream again, challenging the world because I've survived the worst, and intend to conquer whatever is left. I scream until I drop to my knees and weep, feeling free for the first time in my life.

While on my hands and knees I hear the familiar hum of a spaceship nearby. A small shuttle circles around, while the cargo hatch in the rear opens up.

Fitch walks out without a safety harness and extends his hand to me. I grab ahold of him with my bloodied fingers and pull myself aboard. It's so clean and quiet, I'd almost forgotten what it looked like.

"How was it?" He asks.

I don't answer, but my teary eyes and bloody hands tell him everything he needs to know. He nods with a knowing grin and offers me a seat. I strap in and we head back to the *Monolith.*

I watch Fitch as we close in on his ship. I want to hate him for all that he's done to us. The beatings, starving us, dropping us off on a god-forsaken world, that sort of thing. Yet as I look at him, I can't bring myself to hate him for what he's done. All I find is understanding. I look at him and I know that he does what is best, not what anyone wants. He forced us to survive and cooperate. He made us kill off our individual identities and forge a knew one as a team. He made us hate him so that we had a common enemy to bond over.

He made us into the toughest special forces team he could, by taking away the last shred of our humanity. The descent into savagery can only be found when we've gone past rock bottom as human beings. I realized then that the moment the savagery took hold is when Fitch pulls us out. That way he can rebuild our humanity.

The shuttle docks aboard the *Monolith*. The doors open up, and I see the other Horsemen, including Shepherd who managed to survive.

Fitch's men salute us in unison, while his medical staff rushes me before I can greet the others. I'm taken into the medbay so that Fitch's boys can patch me up.

It takes half a day, but they dress and seal up my wounds. Fitch pays me a visit.

"Another day or two, and even my best couldn't have saved you. You're a lucky man Godfrey."

"I don't consider being stabbed in the gut by one of your droids lucky."

Fitch bursts out laughing. "No, I suppose not, but you handled yourself well. I don't know if any of my boys could've made it as far as you did."

The rest of the Horsemen flood in to see me. Amidst our cheering, John walks in and we all swarm him to make sure he hasn't forgotten about us.

"You've got a fine bunch of men here John," Fitch says. "Anything you throw at 'em, they can handle."

"Couldn't have done it without you General."

John has us packed up and ready to go in less than an hour. We file onto the ship, but I turn back to the General who's personally come to see us off.

"Good luck out there son. You're going to do fine," Fitch says as he extends his hand to me.

I shake his hand. "Good luck yourself in the Unknown Regions. Take care, Romulus Fitch,"

"Goodbye, Silas Godfrey."

GERM WARFARE

Godfrey's Journal Day 147

Two months since my last entry. Orion's Playground lingers on the fringes of my mind, each night full of nightmares. My wounds may have healed, but each scar tells a tale of mankind's depths. The descent was like falling down a well and drinking her waters deep. It's cold and foreign, but pure. What rattles me is that going down the well was easy. Coming back up is proving the real challenge.

We're flying back into known space, but we've received an emergency call out from a military ship that's gone dark. The silence of space is unsettling now. I almost miss the constant chatter of the jungle. Now it feels like the quiet before the storm.

I come to the bridge and everyone is staring at the dark ship.

"It's a freakin' graveyard out here!" Forrest shouts.

"There's a discoloration that is quite unsettling," Sujay says. "Very unnatural pinkish hue across the metal. Makes my stomach churn just looking at it."

"Make contact with them Sujay," John orders.

"Hello *Acer* crew, we have received your emergency signal, please respond, over," He says. "Please someone be alive over there…"

"Sujay, man up," John growls.

Forrest scans the emergency read out. "Says here that they got some kind of a microbe on board. Caused all kinds of havoc, next thing you know they're dead. Launched the emergency beacon too late. Oh well, we tried, too late to be of much help now. Onto a white sand beach with palm trees!"

"Sit down Forrest," John grumbles. "Do we have any records of alien microbes causing havoc?"

"Plenty," Sulture replies. "The Neogan colonies were wiped out by flesh-eating bacteria."

"Hacker, can you find any details on the ship's manifests?"

"Cannot find a trajectory map on its database," He replies. "Everything's hidden behind 'Classified.' "

"Sir, could it be a mobile bio-lab?" I ask.

"Wouldn't be the first or only one floating in the galaxy," Sulture replies. "Allows the military to experiment outside of Core jurisdiction."

"Found something," Hacker says. "I cross-referenced this ship with the Ionics database. Found a detailed list involving shipments from NuGeno and CorMed, two subsidiaries of Ionics."

"What do they do?" John asks.

"Bio-weapons and gene splicing." Hacker replies.

"But the readout said *alien* microbe!" Forrest shouts. "How can these be connected?"

"Gene splicing is done by bacteria," Sulture explains. "It's not outside the realm of possibility the military was gathering foreign specimens, but due to improper sanitation procedures, the microbe got loose."

"Wait, so because some guy didn't wash his hands they're all melted piles of goo?!"

"Forrest, I think you're way off-"

He races for the sink, sprays the entire bottle of soap onto his hands and scrubs his arms.

Sulture rolls his eyes. "Sir, Core decontamination procedures are horribly inadequate. None of them anticipate the different cellular structures of foreign organisms, despite hundreds of published papers on alien organic composition. No one wants to build the right decontaminants because of 'Environmental Safety Concerns.' I propose we partake in a mission aboard this ship to put our decon procedures to the test."

"Hmm, that's a good idea Sulture. Ionics is counting on the Horsemen to establish decon protocols that will work for deep exploration crews. Any ideas?"

"Shut down and seal all ventilation systems," I reply.

"Good one Godfrey. Others?"

"I can spot-weld the doors shut as we leave the rooms," Warrens says.

"Also good. What else?"

"We release either a tranquilizer or a sterilant through the ventilation before boarding the ship," Sulture says.

"These are great ideas boys. Alright, suit up!"

"You *want* to board that ship?" Forrest asks. "This is like the start of a bad horror movie! 'Hey guys! Let's go explore a ship full of dead people even though we know there's flesh eating space goo aboard! One by one, you're dead! Save the handsome pilot who had the smarts to get the heck outta there!"

"You heard him boys. Forrest just volunteered to go first!"

"Wait, what?"

"Armor systems checkoff!" I shout. To ensure that our missions go off without a hitch, I devised a ritual where I call out our systems check. That way, we're all on the same page and nothing should go wrong.

"Armor on?"

"Check!" The others shout in unison.

"Comm lines working?"

"Check!"

"Oxygen tanks filled?"

"Check!"

"Watches synchronized?"

"Check!"

We go back and forth with our ammo clips, our shields, and a quality inspection for each individual armor set. It's mind-numbingly tedious without a hint of glory, but it's how we'll survive. We have enough dangers. The last thing we need is to get caught off guard by having only a half-full oxygen tank.

Hacker flies a drone out and attaches a canister of a microbial sterilant to the life support systems on the *Acer*.

We wait until the ventilation systems have gone through a full cycle. The ship is running on emergency power, so we'll have to shut down the vents manually.

Forrest parks the *Enigma* parallel to the *Acer* and extends the docking bridge. We march to the front doors in the eerie silence of space. The doors open and pinkish blobs fly out at us.

"It's likely contaminated," Sulture says. "Keep the *Enigma* sealed."

"Piece of cake!" Forrest shouts with too much excitement.

We cross the threshold and into the foreign ship where the doors seal shut. We listen for movement but can only hear the sounds of our own breathing.

"Emie, scan the ship," John orders.

"Right away John," Emie replies as a small drone flies out and performs a 360 degree scan of the room.

"I'm getting a vast amount of human genetic material, but it's quite different than your composition," Emie explains.

"Show us what you see," John says.

Our visors light up in a sickening display of gore. The walls are covered in a pink ooze that writhes and convulses as though worms are buried beneath it. Bones litter the floor, the faces frozen in a gaze of horror.

"What the hell is all of this?" John asks.

Sulture scrapes his finger across the greasy surface and rubs the salmon colored muck between his fingertip scanners.

"It's mostly human flesh, but I'm detecting a microbe of some kind. I suspect it's a recombinator." His fingers light up as the gauntlets electrocute and then incinerate the genetic material before he flicks it away.

"What is a recombinator?" Shepherd asks.

"Something microbial that leaves the patient with a UNIVAC,"

Murph answers.

"Cut the medical lingo Murph," John snaps.

"It's an unusually nasty infection where the vultures are circling. Messes with our genetic sequences that are impossible to recover from. There's only a handful encountered so far and diagnosis from exposure is typically fatal. Adam, is that microbe bacterial or viral?"

"Scan shows that the microorganism is bacterial."

"Eww gross! Is that some guy's spleen?!"

Our ears fill with the sound of Forrest retching.

"How do we go toe to toe with bugs like this? Can we really prepare crews for this type of matchup?" Warrens asks.

"Any antibiotic will kill them off," Sulture replies. "Bacteria may breed at an exponential rate, but they can still be stopped with the right decon procedures. Something else is at work here."

"Yeah, but these microbes should be at the tail end of their life cycle," Murph says. "They've consumed all of the available hosts…"

"Until new ones show up…" I mutter.

We gaze at each other through the darkness, the reality sinking in.

"Well, we're here now," John says. "Will shutting down the vents help?"

"Wouldn't hurt," Sulture replies. "What'll help the most is lowering the temperature. Shutting off all heat will hinder the bacteria's ability to reproduce, given that we're in a humid environment."

"Hacker, can you disable the ventilation and heating systems?" John asks.

His armor glows as he projects icons that only he can understand. The holograms are mesmerizing as they circle around his arms. He navigates the ship's mainframes through his holograms, searching like a rat in a maze.

"The signal aboard this ship isn't strong enough for me to break into. Someone's disabled the controls and reset everything to manual. My readouts indicate that this ship's power supply is at 18%, which means that everything is running on emergency power and-"

A blistering howl echoes across the ship. We draw our guns simultaneously, but it's still in the distance.

"I doubt any of the boys are still standing," Warrens says. "That sounds like somethin' from Fitch's planet."

"Let's shut down the vents, secure our packages, and then we'll worry about whatever the hell that was," John says.

"*Shensheng de gaowan*!" Lee shouts as he points to the ventilation grate overhead. More of the salmon colored ooze is leaking out, and blood is dripping onto the floor.

John shakes his head. "Emie, stay ahead of us and scan for any life forms," He orders. "Ignore the piles of goo."

"Right away John." A drone detaches from his armor and flies ahead of us, showing live feed of what's in front of us.

We stalk the ship room by room until we reach the medbay.

"No life forms detected," Emie says.

"Keep scanning until you get to life support," John orders. "We'll hold up here for a bit."

"Right away John." The drone flies away, while we gaze upon a room with more of the slime, except it's dried out.

"Jesus Christ save us," Murph mutters as he flashes his light into the room. The beds are lined with mangled skeletons that have been disfigured. Rib cages that look like they busted open, sheets crimson from blood and bits of flesh pepper the scene. There is a large vault door across the room, an indomitable face amidst a scene of gore and chaos.

"What the *fuck* happened here?" John snarls through clenched teeth.

"Medical experimentation," Sulture replies. "They tried to contain the biological agent, but they failed. Their solutions were useless against a foreign organism."

"Life form detected," Emie says.

"Where?" John asks.

Rumbling outside the room gives us our answer. Within seconds a massive hulk bursts into the room. He's twice the size of Warrens, and has sores all over his body, with skin peeling away and blood dripping everywhere. His gaze is cloudy and listless, yet there's a possession in his eyes.

"FIRE!" John roars. We draw and fire upon the man. Despite being hit, he leaps to the ceiling and swings from one pipe to another. He scoops a handful of goo off the walls, smears it across his wounds and swings back out of the room.

"See? Bad horror movie right there. We could've kept flying, but *nooo*!"

"Forrest, when I get back on that ship…"

"John ol' buddy ol' pal. I love ya, but should you *really* threaten your pilot in your position?"

John reaches up and clicks off his comm.

"I'm going to kick his ass."

"What do we do now?" Shepherd asks.

"Wisdom says we pack up and go. I'll admit I'm a *dairuomu ji*," Lee replies.

"We need to discern what happened here. This experimentation could yield a breakthrough in science that surpasses all of medicine up to this point!" Sulture argues.

"Did that thing knock you upside the head?" Warrens snaps.

"That...thing was smearing muck on itself to heal its wounds, I saw the bullet holes vanish!"

"While the rest of him rots!"

"What if this muck has the ability to regenerate human tissue? Would you stop such medicine from being made?"

"If it turned me into that brainless beast then yes!"

"You already are o-" Sulture is cut off when Warrens knocks him flat on his ass into a pile of bacterial goo.

"Stand down! I repeat: Stand down!" John shouts as he draws his pistols and points them at Warrens and Sulture. Lee comes over and helps Sulture back to his feet, while Shepherd gives the big guy a pat on the shoulder.

"We need to secure the medical supplies aboard this ship! You are to fight that thing out there, not each other!" John shouts. "Finally, we need a way to stop this sludge from growing!"

"Best method of stopping bacterial growth is a flash freeze," Sulture says.

"Got enough liquid nitrogen in here," I reply.

"Not sure if we should do that with the medical samples on board," Murph warns. "Hey, there's a journal here with one of the bodies." He tosses the bloodied book onto the counter, while John and I scan through the entries.

"Notes that they were on a planet in the Neogan system," I read aloud.

"What exactly happened in the Neogan system?" Shepherd asks.

Hacker pulls up a display of the planets. "The Neogan system holds three of what're called 'dead worlds.' On the surface they look habitable, but microorganisms have killed off every group that has attempted to establish a colony. The military had to finally close them off."

"Why was the *Acer* crew on a dead world?" John asks.

"Because there's an entire black market for deadly diseases!" Sujay shouts. "Doomsday profiteers, even servants of Yama - sell your virus on the black market so a company can make a cure. However most crews die when transporting such cargo! Which is why *I* would never allow that to happen…Forrest!"

"Hey! We never once transported diseased cargo! I was merely willing to listen to what that guy at Deca Pharmaceuticals had to say."

"Could hold a cure," Sulture says. He scrapes multiple tissue samples and requests that Emie scan them for him.

"For what?" John asks.

"Anything," Sulture replies. "Cancer, genetic defects, could even grant regeneration."

"Except we can see here that it just stripped the flesh from these poor soldiers," Shepherd replies.

"One of them survived, and we need to find out why," Sulture says.

"He's right, but we need to secure the rest of this cargo. Warrens, Shepherd and Godfrey, go out and weld the doors shut. Lock that animal out so we can escape with the cargo.

"Done," I reply as I draw my pistols and take point. Warrens and Shepherd are right behind me as we search for the beast amidst the muck. Warrens grumbles under his breath about what Sulture said, but I'm more focused on finding the brute.

We start in life support systems and turn off the heat. The temperature drops within minutes, while we seal up every room we've already cleared. We make it back to the docking bay where we started. We need to explore the other half of the ship, but we lack support.

"What if we just seal up that door so we can get the cargo out?" I ask.

"Works for me," Warrens replies.

He pulls out his welding gun, but a shadow crosses my eye.

It's too late by the time I draw my pistols.

The brute jams his arm through the door before we can seal it shut. He tears it off its hinges and holds it overhead. I fire two rounds which leave gaping holes in his chest. He throws the door at me, but I'm able to dodge it.

Warrens' armor plates shift into his gauntlets as he charges for the man that's twice his size. The disfigured slathers the muck over his wounds, which appear to have healed him, yet they leave weeping wounds of their own. It appears to be some kind of twisted symbiosis where the bacteria heals the brute, yet feasts on him at the same time.

The metal gauntlets drive a sickening crunch into the brute's jaw, while Warrens swoops in and drives one blow after another. I've never seen him attack with such ferocity. Scraps of flesh fly in all directions, but the brute isn't slowing down.

He counterattacks, sending Warrens flying against the far wall. Shepherd and I charge in with guns blazing, almost carving the man in two. He crawls along the floor until he rolls himself in a pile of muck and takes off.

"Bastard," Warrens grumbles as he gets back to his feet.

"No! Not this time!" I scream as I pursue the brute. "Cover me!"

I track the coward until we reach the bridge of the ship. Everywhere we go, there's more of this muck. More chances for him to heal up, while he drips off his skin and keeps feeding these disgusting bugs.

As I cross the threshold, the living cyst swings down and kicks me. I take a tumble, but I'm back on my feet by the time he drops to the floor. He punches the ground and roars in my face. I draw a knife and stab him in the eye while Warrens flanks me and drills the brute in the temple.

"I really hate it when they feel the need to roar in my face!" I shout as I grab his matted and wiry hair. "Keep him busy!"

The hulk grabs me and tosses me away, while Warrens fights like a champion boxer taking on a wrestling pro. The brute tries to pin him down, but Warrens is a savage fighter. His gauntlets carve up the jagged face, but he can't keep him down long enough for me.

"Warrens get down!" Shepherd shouts behind me.

The two of us look back at the kid. He's holding a gun that's almost as big as he is, but it isn't one of ours.

Warrens dives to the ground as Shepherd opens fire, sending a spike through the brute's hand into the wall. He fires four more times and crucifies the hulk.

"Nice work kid! Never thought to use a hull repair gun as a weapon!" Warrens shouts.

I slit the brute's throat as he struggles against the spikes, trying to rip free. It takes a few tries and leaves one hell of a mess, but I sever his head and leap away with it in tow.

I march back to the central area where we cross paths with the other team.

"We heard shooting. You boys alright?"

I toss the severed head into Sulture's arms.

"A specimen for you to study."

"That's disgusting."

"That was quick Godfrey. Good work."

"Credit goes to Warrens and the kid. They nailed the brute, I just cut off his head."

"Jesus, you guys are a mess," Murph says. "Hope that flesh-eating bacteria didn't get into your suit.

"Not a chance," Warrens says. "Just need to get deconned."

"What'd you guys find out?" I ask.

"Top of the line decon chamber and chemicals, yet none of them were used," John replies. "That, and the canisters we need to retrieve are locked up tight."

"Why not?"

"Working theory is that this thing was released at the same time as the bacteria," Sulture explains as he holds up the brute's head. "According to my scanners, the bacteria work in symbiosis with the host. They devour his flesh, yet speed the healing process at an exponential rate. The specimen effectively has regeneration."

"Why didn't that happen to all of the soldiers?" Shepherd asks.

"We have a few theories there-"

"Stop telling us your damn theories and give us something concrete!" Warrens snaps.

"We live in a world of hypotheticals you meathead! We don't just punch our way through the scientific process!"

"Why you-"

"Enough!" John shouts. "Sulture tell them what we're thinking happened here."

"I believe this thing was either previously exposed to the bacteria, or it's the only suitable host. These things could strip the flesh off a person in hours."

"Blech! Horror movie!" Forrest shouts over the comm.

"There's another anomaly," Sulture says. "Every genetic sample I've run comes back as the same person."

My mind flashes to the vision I had of an army with all the same face.

"Clones," I mutter.

"We need to go to the bridge to be sure," John says. "We need to learn what the hell was going on in this ship. Warrens, Godfrey, lead the way."

We guide the others past the squishing masses aboard the ship.

"Jesus Christ," Murph gasps.

I walk past the crucified brute and show the rest the computer console. Hacker approaches, plugs in his armor and sets his programs in search of the information we seek.

"What are we dealing with Hacker?" John asks.

"This entire ship was one big experiment," He replies.

"What do you…?" John looks over his shoulder at the terminal. "Show them."

Hacker displays a projection of a man strapped to a bench. A scientist walks up and plunges a syringe into his arm, while the man fights against his restraints. As the feed progresses, the man's muscles begin to bulge out. His veins throb until he transforms into a raging hulk. He rips on his restraints, his flesh tearing off in sickening globs which pool around the room. The scientist returns in a biological suit, picks up the pieces and analyzes them.

Right as the scientist is about to leave the room, the brute breaks his restraints, makes the three metre leap and snaps the scientist's back. The hulk lumbers through the door and wanders off.

Hacker flicks to the next video. Soldiers shoot at the brute rampaging through the ship, but he doesn't slow down. As we watch him fling the men like dolls, I notice their faces.

They're all different.

"None of them are clones..." I mutter. "Sulture! How is this possible?"

"What?"

"You said that every genetic sample you tested aboard the ship was the same individual, yet when we watch the feed, none of these soldiers look like him," I say as I point at the decapitated brute.

"We've learned that the bacteria consumes him, but also causes his cells to replicate at an exponential rate. This way the bacteria can stay alive on the host. As for why the genetic material aboard this ship is identical, my current theory is that since this is a gene-splicing bacterium, it has converted all the DNA into the sequence of its host."

"Huh? Forrest asks.

"Bacteria made 'em all the same person," I reply.

"'Current theory' huh? Sounds like you don't know," Warrens says.

"Warrens, that's enough!" John snaps. "Makes sense to me. Let's search the ship for survivors. Hacker, download everything on this ship and upload it to the *Enigma.*"

Our search for survivors proves fruitless. There's nobody else alive on the ship, just more skeletons and the pulsing, writhing mass of flesh. Every time I see it wriggle I can feel my own skin crawl. We meet up with Hacker back at the bridge.

"Looks like we're in charge of bringing the medical canisters back to NuGen and CorMed. Too bad they're locked up in the vault."

"Oh Johnny boy, that right there fellas is a smuggler's vault!"

"It's the size of an apartment on Earth!"

"Sure is! It's also a high grade industrial lockbox used by only the savviest scoundrels. And they're designed to be detachable! Why so? Glad you asked: they're detachable in case Core authorities come by and want to conduct a shakedown. These vaults are designed to be ejected, tracked and recovered. They can withstand freefalling through any atmosphere and the impact upon landing as well!" Forrest explains.

"So they're tough?" John asks.

"Tough doesn't even begin to describe these vaults! The military wasn't taking *any* chances of an outbreak, plus robots control those things."

"What?! How?" Hacker asks.

"I don't know, isn't that what you're paid for?"

Hacker pinches the bridge of his nose. "I've finished the download sir. It was almost too easy."

"What do you mean?"

"Well sir, for a military-controlled mobile laboratory, there is only a fraction of the data on the servers that I would expect."

"Do you think the officer on board would've deleted some of the files when that thing got loose?"

"It's the most viable possibility. I don't see anything that indicates a lot of files were wiped, but that doesn't mean they weren't."

"Well, all the same, let's get that vault loaded up aboard the ship."

Hacker tinkers with his hologram until he manages to find the vault's controls.

"Hmm, that's strange. I've never seen a vault with an AI guardian before."

"Can you get through it?" John asks.

"Not at the moment, but I can detach it from the Acer."

"Let's do that. Sulture, get the decon units ready. Scrub that vault clean." John orders.

"Yes sir. Emie, execute decontamination protocol Echo Charlie Sierra four eighty seven."

"Right away Dr. Sulture."

Sulture is standing at the end of the bridge as the *Enigma* docks. As the door opens, four drones fly out and align themselves in front of the vault. They shine ultraviolet light along the surface, then buzz up and move to the next surface. Once inside the ship four nozzles start us off with an alcohol treatment, followed up with a spray of a Quarternary Ammonium Chloride compound I developed. Next more proprietary chemicals are sprayed over our armor, none of which I can guarantee will meet the strict standards of the Ministry of Health.

Emie removes our armor, while Hacker gets to work unlocking this vault. He spends hours by himself, tinkering with the code while we wait to see what's inside.

Finally, Hacker comes out of the room.

"I managed to override the AI which kept the vault sealed. It's advanced. I haven't seen an intelligence of this magnitude in ages.

There's only one source of such a high-grade intelligence."

"What?" John asks.

"The droid-pirate Neuron."

Forrest and Sujay's faces go ashen.

"A droid pirate?" Sulture asks. "Bit theatrical don't you think?"

"No! He's for reals!" Forrest cries. "We've encountered him and you don't mess with Neuron! You can't go anywhere near his fortress without getting blown up!"

"Well, looks like we'll be able to get up close because he contacted me and invited me to his fortress," Hacker explains.

The team looks at each other.

"Well, it's on the way back to HQ," John says. "Forrest, Sujay. Set a course."

"Great! First a horror movie then we get a chance to get blow'd up by the droid pirate."

Inside the medbay, Sulture keeps the severed head sealed in a biohazard container. The grotesque face glares at me. In the back of my mind I wonder if I should be unsettled by my bloodlust. Not only did I want to kill the brute, I relished severing his head from his neck. I savored knowing how he died, and that I was the one who killed him.

"Eww! Gross! Why'd you bring that on board with you? Do you really need a friend that badly? I can talk to Sujay and see if he'll give you a hug…"

Sulture rolls his eyes and takes the canister into the medbay. As he leaves I swear the brute is watching me through that dead eye.

Godfrey's Journal, Day 148

The encounter with the brute has left me unsettled. His face stares at me in accusation, like the man trapped within the beast had the strength to give me a final snarl of condemnation. It was so…easy to hunt and kill the brute. Too satisfying. I struggle to turn my dark thoughts away. To mutilate, to tear flesh away from bone. I fear what I'm becoming…

THE SICKNESS

Godfrey's Journal - Day 155

John reluctantly gave the approval to go to Aurelius Prime to speak with the droid pirate Neuron. Seems like a lot to go through when we're supposed to be rushing these biological agents back to HQ. Hacker's disabled the AI which kept the vault locked up, but now we need to brave what's inside. Murph, Sulture and I are about to go into the cargo hold where the vault is. We've readied our decon suits and have braced for the worse. The deeper we investigate this vault full of pathogens, the more suspicious I become. My fear is that NuGeno and CorMed aren't behind this at all. Whether we've stumbled on a terrorist cult plot, or a mad scientist's gambit is too soon to tell.

The vault door opens slowly, a groaning gate forced into spilling secrets. The three of us deliberate on how to study and catalog the substances contained within. For the safety of the crew, we study the contents from inside the vault.

Hours pass as we create an inventory of the deadly pathogens we possess on board. Turbulence from the ship makes it hard to type. Murph and Sulture activate the electromagnets inside their boots.

Just as I reach to do the same, I'm thrown airborne.

It sounds like thunder is rumbling outside, but Forrest assures us that it was only a near miss with a meteoroid. I look at one of the canisters I landed next to. The top appears to have opened up.

An aerosol mist hits me in the face.

"Critical damage to your filtration systems Godfrey. System failure imminent," Emie blares.

"What did you do?!" Sulture screams.

"I fucking looked at it!" I roar back.

"Doesn't matter what happened Adam, we need to help him!" Murph shouts. "Let's get him to the decon chambers and-"

"Filtration system breached. Silas Godfrey is now infected," Emie says.

"Get to decontamination! Now!" I scream as I push the others out and seal myself inside of the vault.

"Emie, execute protocol Echo Whiskey Charlie - 066, pathogen breach," Murph shouts into the comm.

"What happened?" John asks.

"Silas has been exposed to an unknown pathogen and has locked himself inside the vault," Murph explains. "Adam and I are in decontamination and need to get to the medbay immediately!"

Their voices fades away as I look at the foreign canisters in the dim light. Each one a microcosm of plague and pestilence, I can only picture the organisms burrowing themselves in my body and using me as their host to propagate. Each breath is another condemnation, a betrayal of existence.

"Silas…?"

It's almost as if I can feel them spreading. This river of microbes and I can't-

"SILAS!"

"What is it Murph?"

"Whew! Glad you're still goin' bud. Okay, get the vial and read off what's on the label. It'll help me give a proper diagnosis."

I pick up the black canister and inspect it carefully. I come across a coded label on the bottom.

"The label reads: 'Pulmonary Hemorrhagic Virus.' "

"The Crimson Plague," Sulture mumbles over the comm.

"What?" I ask.

"It's an experimental virus engineered by the military, designed to… drown its victims in their own blood. Victims are only known to last about three hours."

"What do you mean the victims only last about three hours?" I growl.

There's a long pause over the comm line.

"Murph, what options does he have?"

"Damn near impossible to treat. It's constantly evolving, and it will adapt to his immune system. I'll try a round of antivirals."

Murph spends the next few minutes searching the medbay for the medicine. I dwell in a dark realm with my thoughts as I imagine the virus spreading through my system. Each breath feels a little more constricted, and the walls of the vault are closing in.

The cycle breaks once I hear knocking on the door. I open the vault, but a coughing fit seizes my throat.

Murph rips off my sleeve, ties off my arm and injects the medicine into my vein.

"Okay, that will buy us a little more time," He says. I try to get back on my feet, but my legs give out from under me.

My throat itches and I start coughing. I try to control it, swallow some saliva, but I can't stop. Murph holds me and slaps my back.

"Get me some water!"

I keep coughing, raking my throat to pieces. I collapse and cough into my fist, a patch of bloody saliva splatters on my hand. I look up to Murph.

"I was afraid of that," He mumbles. "We need to move fast. The virus is attacking your lungs."

"That's not all it's doin'," John replies. "Somethin' is goin' on with the sealants. Something's breaking them down."

"Oh shit," I mutter.

"What?"

"I was one of the scientists who developed the corrosive agent which is breaking down the sealants! You need to flush the ship! Now!"

"What?" Murph yells. "We can't do that!"

I stand to argue my case, but another coughing fit seizes my throat. I hack until I spit up frothy blood onto Murph's suit.

"Where's that water?" He screams.

"I'm not opening the doors with that corrosive eatin' everything up! I can't expose the rest of us to that deadly contagion!" John says.

As I look upon the doors, I see them as a gateway to freedom. I see how bright the lights are and I feel so lonely in the cargo hold.

I *have* to see the others.

I rush the door and pound on the glass.

"Let me in John!" I scream.

"Silas! What's gotten into you?" Murph asks.

"The virus is driving him to seek us out in order to spread," Sulture replies.

"No it's not!" I scream. I can see the others staring at me like I'm a ghost. "I'm just so *alone* in here!"

"Silas, I'm here," Murph replies. I turn and face him. His suit gives him an unnatural look and his face is blurry from his hot breath.

"Are you uncomfortable in there Murph?" I ask.

"It's warm in here, but I'm doing okay."

"Why don't you take off your mask? You're sweating bullets."

"Silas, then I'd be infected, and I won't be able to help you."

I don't understand why he won't listen. I hate that blurred face. It's unnatural. I want to see the face of my friend! Not this usurper! How do I even know he's in there? Some apparition is playing a trick on me.

"Take off your mask," I growl.

"Silas, I can't."

Because it'll reveal that it's not really Murph behind the mask. I can see the demon back there, sniveling at me.

"Take it off!"

I lunge for the demon, trying to tear his flesh away.

"Silas! Get away!"

"Where's Murph?!" I growl.

"I'm right here trying to help you!" the demon screams.

I feel a tear slide down my cheek. I wipe it away and realize that it's blood.

"What have you done to me?!" I scream.

"I'm *trying* to help you!" A yellow hand swings at me, but I catch it in midair.

I seize the beast by the throat and throw it into the wall.

"Silas Godfrey! Stand down!" A voice echoes in the distance.

My hand closes around the air supply tube. My muscles tense as I prepare to rip it off. I push against the rubbery skin and I see two faces.

One is a terrified Murph, worried that he's going to die. The other one is the demon trying to consume him.

I feel a droplet on my foot. I look down and realize it's blood. I take a closer look at the demon and realize the face I see is my own.

"Dear God!" I gasp as I release Murph. The gasp causes a coughing fit, and I collapse onto the floor until I hack up what I'm certain is a piece of lung.

"Please help me!" I cry out.

"They're working on it Silas. They're working on it," Murph says softly.

"I feel so alone!" That's only the start. My chest is rattling, and I'm bleeding from every orifice. I feel so cold, vulnerable and alone.

Alone.

"I get it bud. Getting sick makes us all regress a bit. We want to be cared for, not abandoned. That's why I'm still here with you."

"Tell me about how you became a medical doctor," I demand. Maybe then I won't feel so isolated.

"Me? I was always sick as a kid. Had debilitating asthma and a weak immune system, but I hated being confined. I hated feeling so frail that a microbe could take me out at any moment. My parents kept me inside a lot, so I read. I studied everything about the body, how it reacts to every illness we know about. I studied every medical procedure, the side effects, and every alternative. I knew how much it sucked being cooped up all the time, and I wanted to help sick people like me have a fighting chance."

"Wasn't your dissertation on some radical gene therapy treatment?" This is good. I'm connecting. I'm not isolated, I'm not *alone.*

"Sure was. Although other doctors who reviewed the material deemed it AGMI."

"What's ag-me?"

"Patient ain't gonna make it through the procedure."

"Then what happened?"

"I went ahead and found a willing patient. Proved that thanks to the map of the human genome we could wipe out most debilitating conditions such as allergies, diabetes and other ailments."

"Did your first patient survive?"

"Sure did. You're looking at him."

"You tested your gene therapy on yourself?!"

"Of course I did! I was tired of being scared of a peanut for Christ's sake. The treatment worked, better than expected, but the University almost wouldn't accept my thesis since I was the patient. So a lab assistant and I fudged some of the uh…vital statistics and the 'patient' claimed that they wished to remain anonymous."

"Did anyone ever find out?"

"Oh yeah."

"What happened?" This is good. We're bonding, connecting. Murph is still in there.

"I'm not sure how, but the Ministry of Health found out that I was the patient for my thesis and decided to revoke my medical license."

"Jesus."

"Yeah. Still, wasn't all bad. I mean, I was blacklisted on Earth, but I managed."

"You signed up for the Angkor Colony then?"

Murph nods his head. "They were so desperate for a medical doctor they never followed up when I gave them my old license number."

We chuckle together, but another coughing fit consumes me. The taste of iron fills my mouth as blood drips through my lips. My breathing is clogged as blood spills from my nose. Each breath is a labored battle.

"Sealants have degraded by 40%," Emie says.

"We need to flush the room," John says through the comm piece.

I look out into the black. I see myself being swallowed in the void and one word repeats itself in my mind.

Alone.

"No! Don't eject me John! Don't abandon me!" I scream as I charge the door to the ship. I beat on the door, while blood smears across the glass.

"Silas he won't! We're working as hard as we can to find a cure for you!"

"Then why do all of you keep me locked out here?" A chill runs down my spine. I feel like I've been left to die in the woods.

"That's not what's happening at all bud! The team has spent the last fifty minutes working non-stop on a cure for you!"

"We'll need a blood culture from him as well," Sulture says.

"You hear that Silas? We need some of your blood in order to test some of the treatments."

My mind swirls as I picture Murph come up to me, slit my jugular, and watch me bleed out.

"No! You can't have any!" I scream. "All of you just want to bleed me out and watch me die out here!"

"No we don't! We want to help you get through this, but in order to do that we need a blood culture!"

"Sealants degraded by 60%," Emie blares.

"Murph, you better get control of him or we'll be forced to take drastic measures," John warns.

Panic swells within. I won't be killed by these bloodsuckers. I won't let them send my flying into the black.

I lunge for Murph. If he's exposed to the virus, then they'll be forced to let us both into the ship, rather than keep just me locked out. I grab his oxygen tube and pull.

The bastard judo chops my arm away and hits me with a hard right. I fall to the floor, but I won't go down without a fight. I get back to my feet, but Murph strikes me again.

"I'm sorry bud, but you've given me no choice!" He screams. Each wound yields more blood flowing, so I crouch down, a predator ready to pounce.

Murph backs away from me slowly, while my fingers turn into claws of desperation. I want to be a part of this team again. I don't want to be abandoned, and I will do whatever it takes to ensure that doesn't happen.

It's only when I leap at him that I realize Murph has one arm behind his back.

It's when I'm centimetres from him that I realize he grabbed one of the crowbars we use to open cargo.

My side explodes as I go flying to the far wall. Everything is fuzzy and blurry.

I hear a crash and see a violet glow.

I see Murph approaching me in his suit. He sticks a needle in me and I watch in a haze as I'm drained of more blood.

He grabs me by the shoulders and drags me away from the wall. I see the violet glow radiating from the floor. I struggle to breathe from the pain in my ribs.

"Are you happy, sir?" Murph asks. "I may have killed him!"

"Sealant failure imminent," Emie shouts.

"Not happy, but we did what we needed to," John replies.

Murph drags me to the vault, throws me in and seals the door shut. By the time I fully grasp what is happening, I'm on my feet braying on the door.

"Murph! MURPH! You traitor! How could you do this to me?!"

The vault shakes and the gravity shifts inside. Before I know it, I'm floating through the air

"YOU SONS OF BITCHES!" I shout despite my lungs burning. "HOW CAN YOU ABANDON ONE OF YOUR OWN?! HOW?!"

I listen in through the comm.

"How can you be serious?!" Murph shouts. "That's like launching a nuclear missile at a house to kill some mice!"

"You said it yourself," Sulture grumbles. "It's the only thing we have that can kill the virus."

There's an eerie silence where all I can hear is the comm static. The feed cuts in and out from interference. Dialog is cut to pieces that I can't understand until one line comes through.

"It will require...genetic modification."

I throw the comm piece. The sick fucks want to alter my DNA? It's bad enough they left me in my hour of need, isolated and alone. There's that word again.

Alone.

It feels so cold in the vault. I hold myself, and curl up into a ball. My tears mix with blood as I cough up more of the iron droplets. There is no mercy out here in the void. The only mercy is death.

My skin is almost translucent. I can see my veins and arteries, but they look swollen, ready to burst. My side is bruised from where Murph struck me with the crowbar.

The bruise is as black as the sky. I can see the blood pooling beneath the skin, spreading like the infection that's claimed me. I'm nothing more than a diseased mongrel waiting to die.

"Die murderer…"

I shun away the voice inside. My eyelids grow heavy and my muscles ache. The cold swaddles me and overtakes my body. My breathing is labored, but something else keeps me awake. I want to fall asleep and have all of this be over, but my breathing is clogged. It's only a matter of time before I drown in my own blood. Another victim to the Crimson Plague.

The vault rumbles and clatters. It's locks creak and groan. A hiss strikes at my ears like a serpent.

The vault door opens.

Surrounding the door are hazmat-clad Horsemen.

"Silas, it's us!" Murph says as he holds his hand out to me.

"Traitor!" I scream. The others flinch, but Murph holds them back.

"We have a means of curing you. You just have to come with us."

"No! It's another trap! You're just going to abandon me again!

"Well Doc, we tried it your way. Now we try it mine," Warrens grumbles as he climbs into the vault with me. "C'mon Godfrey. Let's get this over with."

Seeing all of the crew in these suits make me feel even more isolated and alone. I want to be a part of the team again. I want them to see me as a person, not an experiment or a subject to capture.

"Get back!" I snarl. I grab one of the nearby vials of contagion and threaten to throw it at them.

"Silas, we're not going to lock you up. We're going to help you okay?"

I can't trust these yellow-clad cretins. None of them have the faces of my friends. My friends would've helped me without hiding their faces, their shame, their guilt.

As I look out at the crowd, there's something off. I do a head count, and realize that one of them is missing.

Where could he be? I swear I just saw him.

A prick to the neck gives me the answer.

An invisible figure snatches the vial from my hand before I collapse into darkness.

At first there was a gnawing noise from above. It raked across my skin.

Muffled voices argued overhead.

"We can't do this! It's too risky!"

I thought I heard Murph, but he sounded so distant.

Where was everyone?

"It's the only way he'll survive!"

What're they talking about? I remember being sick, but I thought they were treating me…

I wake up in a strange room where the light burns my eyes and colors swim along the walls like fish . I look at my hands. They look healthy and healed. I lay back to relax, but I hear the gnawing sound again, an abrasive melody that makes me wince each time I hear it. I cover my ears, but when I look upon my hands, they're cracking.

Small fissures spread across my palms, around and up my arm.

Light shines from within and the gnawing becomes an incessant scraping. Within seconds, my hands feel like I'm touching the surface of the sun.

I scream in agonizing pain, trying to let go, but they're not holding anything. My skin turns to dust and falls away, the light consuming me.

The fissures spread across my body, and more of the radiant light burns through. I scream from the agonizing heat, but it's not doing any good.

"What have we done?!" A voice screams in the distance.

Each second becomes hours as I wait for the pain to subside. I watch my hands become pure light before I collapse back into darkness.

I'm snapped awake by the sound of water dripping from a faucet. Someone didn't turn it off all the way.

I look at my hands, which appear to be perfectly normal. I look around the room, and it's the same ol' medbay. The calm scene is unsettling, but I try to relax.

John walks in, with a relieved look on his face.

"Glad to see you're up. Gave the docs one hell of a scare."

"You're telling me. What happened?"

"After they knocked you out, we had to wrack our brains real hard to figure out how to cure you."

"Am I?"

"Yeah, you're cured alright Godfrey. Now don't go touching any more cannisters."

"John, I swear I didn't-"

"Godfrey, it's alright. We came out of this stronger than ever. That's what matters. The boys are monitoring you and have told me that you'll be just fine."

John turns to leave, but I stop him before he goes. "How'd they do it? Cure the virus?"

He turns to me and gives me a slight grin. "They bombed the hell outta ya with a bunch of medicines I can't pronounce. Anyway, we're almost to Aurelius Prime, so rest up."

"Thanks John."

Godfrey's Journal Day 158

This was far too easy. Nearest I can tell I'm coming out of this unscathed, but that doesn't happen. Nobody walks away from a virus engineered by the military. I try to talk to Murph, but he can barely look me in the eye. I apologized for trying to expose him to the virus, but he assures me that everything is okay on that end. I don't believe him, but I can tell that he won't talk. None of them will. Not a word is being spoken about my exposure. It's as if the thing I feared the very most while infected, isolation, is coming true right before my eyes.

THE DROID PIRATE

"We're closing in on Aurelius Prime," John says. "I'm going to reach out to Neuron and request access to land."

"Whoa whoa whoa!" Forrest shouts. "You can't just dock wherever whenever with Neuron! There's protocol to follow when you're dealing with a bloodthirsty droid pirate!"

"You can't possibly believe it's a real droid," Hacker snaps. "Droids don't possess that level of self-awareness."

"This one does! Rules an entire foundry that's the size of a small moon! On Aurelius Prime there are two mob bosses: Kingsman and Neuron. Kingsman is brash, foul and rude, but you can still deal with him. Neuron will just kill you and rob you!"

Hacker rolls his eyes. "That droid foundry is a relic from the Unification Wars. No droid would have access-"

"The legend goes that some unit named Solomon went to the foundry and tapped into some weird programming designed by the techies who built it. Became self-aware and learned that he was smarter than anyone else, so he re-named himself 'Neuron.'"

Hacker gasps.

"What?" John asks.

"I…I need to do some research on this droid foundry. Let's do this Forrest's way until I get a better idea of what we're dealing with."

"Yeah! I'm in charge!" Forrest shouts. "Let's go see Brocker! He'll know what to do!"

"No, not that smelly ape-like-"

"Sujay how could you? That man has given us so much and asked for so little."

"All he gives me is indigestion."

"Forrest, is this man connected?" John asks.

"Oh, he is *the* guy to see! Brocker is the ultimate broker when it comes to Aurelian business!"

"He's a fry cook and a rumor peddler," Sujay says.

"Close enough!" Forrest shouts as he jams down the throttle.

Godfrey's Journal Day 163

We've touched down on the city-planet Aurelius Prime, a former coalition stronghold. It has since become a gathering of rebel holdouts, gamblers, and thieves.

Gambling forms the backbone of the Aurelian economy. The rebels didn't like the idea of associating themselves with outlaws, but they needed the credits badly enough. Mafia Dons ensure there are few anti-pollution laws, so there is a constant cloud of smog in the air. The Aurelian government is as corrupt as the locals, making laws where those who bribe the most get the permits to get business done.

We stick close together walking through the streets since we're valuable targets. Our tech-rich carcasses would be more than enough to settle the gambling debts of even the most unlucky patron. We traverse the crowded streets slowly, sidestepping the beggars and the prostitutes. No one spoke, but we knew where we had to go: Nero's Cove. A diner with the lowest of the low, it's where we needed to go in order to find information on this droid pirate.

Forrest parades down the street like a champ. Between his ability to gossip and Sujay's haggling they're able to blend in. They keep telling everyone we're they're bodyguards, but based the reputation of these two… no one believes they could afford bodyguards.

"Hey Sujay, remember the time when we sold the deed to Neuron's droid foundry?"

"Oh, you mean the deed you *forged* and claimed was ours? Yes. I remember."

"Aww c'mon Sujay. We came out of it okay."

"I sat in that holding cell two days longer than you did! You convinced them that I would be their astronavigator in exchange for your freedom!"

"Yes, but I used my freedom to bust you *out.* I think what you're trying to say is 'You're Welcome!'" Forrest says as he bumps Sujay.

"You're welcome?!"

"Aww, nothin' to it buddy!

"I wasn't thanking you! *You* are the one that got us shot down!" Sujay shouts as he shoves Forrest

"And then I bought a new ship with the proceeds of the droid foundry." Forrest shoves back

"It was a *used* ship and you spent *five times* more than the ship was worth! You lost all of our money!"

The two men break out into a shoving match in the middle of the street.

"Who wondered why they're never brought on missions?" John asks.

We come across a run-down diner with a buzzing neon sign. Bright crimson letters spell out "Nero's Cove."

Forrest bursts through the doors, while there is an audible crash in the kitchen.

"You rotten, miserable piece of Andarian filth!" A ball of a man screams as he waddles our way. His once white shirt is filthy from grease and sweat stains, while he constantly pulls his pants up around his waist. His black stubble gives his face an even grimier look. The first few moments are tense, until a grin forms on his lips.

"Brocker, how are you?" Forrest asks as he hugs the man and rubs his balding head. "Got a plate of your famous fries for me?"

"I knew you'd ask you cheapskate!" Brocker howls. "Sujay! How can ye still be with this broke bastard!" Brocker reaches around and pulls Sujay in. He pulls away, which only makes Brocker pull him in closer.

"Believe me, it's not easy."

"Who're these guys? Police? *Coremen*?" Brocker growls.

"They're a group of mercenaries we run with," Forrest replies. "We came to you askin' for a favor. We need an introduction."

Brocker motions to a booth for us to sit at. He shoves Sujay inside, while Forrest and John take the other side. I pull up a chair and sit on the end. The rest keep watch.

"So, who is it you're looking for?" Brocker whispers.

"We want to talk to the Droid Pirate Neuron," John replies.

Brocker lets out a hoarse laugh and slams his clubby hand on the table. "Hate to tell you fellas, but the droid pirate isn't found. He finds *you*."

"That's crap and you know it!" Forrest says. "Everyone is reachable, you know that! Oh! I get it...manners right…?" He grabs a credit chip and starts increasing the amount

"Nah, nah, put that away Forrest. Look, if I knew how to get to him, I'd tell ya how. Neuron has his own floating fortress just outside of orbit. Damn thing's impregnable. Core won't even screw with 'im!"

"What if we were invited?" Hacker asks.

"Huh? I don't follow."

"I said I was invited by Neuron because I outsmarted his intelligence program which kept a vault locked."

"Hmm, never heard of anyone being invited to his fortress. All I know is this: people who go there don't come out."

"Is there a way we can contact him?" John asks.

"He rarely comes planetside and his droids stay focused on their missions. They don't wander off like human workers do."

"Is there a place we can find his droids? A front he uses?

"Sure, Aurelian General Imports," Brocker croaks. "Although, good luck getting anywhere close. Neuron's droids keep that area locked down tight. Nothin' made of flesh is allowed in there.

"We'll take our chances," John replies.

As we rise from the booth, one of the cooks rushes out with a brown bag and hands it to Brocker.

"Fer the road," He grunts as he slaps it into Forrest's chest.

He gasps. "Brocker, you shouldn't have!" He tears into the bag like a wild animal and moans as he bites into the crispy, golden spear.

I reach over and grab one to see what all the fuss was about. Tasted like a regular french fry to me.

We follow Hacker through a crowd full of screaming hucksters attempting to sell their wares. They scream and cajole customers into buying from them, while most of the people walk by.

The streets are congested with people walking to…wherever they're going. Claustrophobia must not be a common fear around here, because everyone rubs shoulders as they walk. I look into the distance, noticing the streaks of soot and broken windows on the skyscrapers that attempt to pierce the sky. Vines crawling up give the only sign of greenery, while the rest of the world is being smothered beneath concrete.

Someone grabs me by the arm. It's one of the hucksters getting aggressive in his sales pitch. I draw my pistol and point it between his eyeballs.

"Back off," I growl.

"No need to be hostile, friend," He says as he backs away in surrender.

"You can't be so gun-flashy here!" Forrest snaps. "You'll get us killed!"

"Maybe people here need to learn not to be so grabby."

"I'm with Silas," Shepherd says. "People here need to learn personal space."

Forrest gets nose to nose with us."This is a close-talking culture and personal reputation determines how easy it is to do business! If you go flashing guns around, nobody will work with you! You guys may not like it, but this place is a second home to me and I won't let you screw up my reputation!"

"Not like they could any way," Sujay says.

"What's screwed up is all the things your mom wanted me to do to her last night!" Forrest storms off and starts talking to the market hucksters and prostitutes. Sujay goes to keep an eye on him and ensure we don't get too far ahead.

"Hard to believe we were schooled on culture by Forrest, huh Silas?"

"Don't read too much into it, Forrest has gotta know something."

Hacker takes us down an alleyway which splits us off from the main crowd. The thousands of voices become a part of the background as we travel into a complex that has been abandoned. The fences are high, and the industrial warehouses have a menacing grimace that seems to be etched into their walls.

"There it is." Hacker points to a nondescript building with two droids standing in front of it.

"What are our options?" John asks.

"Could blast our way in," Warrens replies.

"Why not just tell the droids I was invited?" Hacker asks.

"Neuron may not see a need for the rest of us out here or in there," John replies.

"Could you take them over?" Shepherd asks.

"Good call," Hacker replies. "Emie - execute protocol Oscar Victor Lima."

"Right away Hacker. Protocol Overlord is underway."

Hacker's armor lights up and the holographics surround his gauntlets. He issues a series of commands while the droids train their guns on us.

"Halt!" The droids shout.

Within seconds their eyes flicker until we hear their circuits short out. They collapse while smoke rises from their skulls.

"I thought you were taking them over…?" Sulture asks.

"Didn't have enough time, so I shorted these out. Emie is searching for the rest."

"Good enough for me," John says. "Warrens, bust down the door!"

"With pleasure!" He shouts as he smashes the door down. The alarms trigger, causing an army of droids to pour out of nowhere.

"Perfect," Hacker mumbles.

"Fighting droids is as dumb as *gen houzi bi diushi*!" Lee says.

"Yeah, not much point in throwing shit at monkeys," I reply.

"We're not fighting them. Let them come," Hacker says. He whirls around and taps his commands at lightning speed. His fingers rake across the controls, the streams of light mesmerizing. Just before the droids reach us, they freeze in place.

"Gentlemen, we have a droid army," Hacker says.

We look at each other in surprise while Hacker holds his arms out like a conquering general. The droids lower their guns in submission.

"Hacker I…" Emie's voice fades away as some of the droids jerk and spasm. They snap their limbs and point their guns at us again.

"What?! No! This can't be!"

"Not words I want to hear Hacker," John says.

"Did you really think you could just take control of *my* droids?" An electronic voice crackles in through the comm.

"Hacker! Take back control!" John screams.

"It's no use, now that I can see you in my system," the voice replies. A shuttle lands outside the warehouse.

"Oh jeepers! It's Neuron! We're dead men walking!" Forrest shouts.

Through the back a towering droid enters the warehouse. Its head is shaped like a skull, with sunken eyes and teeth carved out of the metal plate. His chest plate creates a ring around his neck similar to a cowl, while a tattered cape sways in the back. His limbs are lithe yet covered in armor plates. There is a menace in the droid's eyes, but they look different from the others. They're far back in and don't glow like the rest.

The droid approaches and stops before Hacker.

"Hello Jabal," Neuron says.

"It can't be. I watched you die."

"What?! You know him?!" Forrest shrieks. The droids all look at him and take aim. "Put in a good word for your buddies…please?"

"General Hawkes isn't the most thorough when it comes to eliminating his enemies."

"How did you survive?"

Neuron looks out at us. I get a glimpse inside of his sockets and I realize why his eyes don't glow like the others. His eyes aren't cameras, they're organic.

Neuron is a cyborg.

"I deliberated long and hard on whether or not to reach out to you. I calculated the consequences and determined that you may be of use to me."

"So that's what this was? A request for a favor?!"

"Do it! Do the favor so we won't die!" Forrest whispers.

"I don't expect anything out of you. You don't owe-"

"You're damn right I don't!" Hacker shouts. "I ran weapons for you during the Core Invasion and then I stole the plans to your station right from under the noses of the people we once helped! The fact that you're still alive and have tainted Solomon's good name to spread your lore shows what a villain you are!"

"You never were strong enough to face the realities of the world were you Jabal? Always hiding behind your AIs to do all of your dirty work."

"Like you can talk! You hide behind *your* army of machines! Scheming and collecting - always wanting more, more, more!"

"Why did you call him here Neuron?" John asks.

The cyborg takes a labored breath.

"The ones who own the vault you broke into, they've stolen something from me, and I want it back."

"What is it?"

"It's a variation of the program I use to control my machines." As Neuron finishes his statement, one of the droids holsters its gun and approaches us for a handshake.

"You mean you-"

"Yes Hacker, I control all of them with nothing more than a thought."

"How...how is this possible? How did you develop something so advanced?"

"I admit that I utilized a program you discovered."

"What program was that?!"

"Some Greek name. Started with a 'C', but I don't-"

"Coeus?!" Warrens and Hacker shout at the same time.

"Yes, that's the one."

"What's Coeus?" Shepherd asks.

"Circuit here created a program that let me wield every machine around me. I could *feel* them as though they were a part of me," Warrens replies.

"And now that same code is integrated into Neuron's droids. He controls a hive with his mind," Hacker says.

"Don't you get...confused?" Forrest asks.

"It's like moving pieces on a game board," Neuron growls. "Now I'm dealing with thieves who've stolen my technology."

"Who are they?" John asks.

"I'm not certain who they are. They're connected to whoever is dealing with the pathogens aboard your ship."

"What is your program capable of?" Hacker asks.

"They've modified the AI to serve as a combat training program. It even overwrites the subject's neural networks through hormonal programming. I think it's called-"

"Slipstream," Hacker finishes.

"Let me guess, you've encountered it?"

"A few times," John replies.

"You're lucky to have survived. I've made multiple attempts to recover the program but the enhanced STARs dismantle my droids with ease."

"Luck didn't have nothin' to do with it. When we went toe to toe with those punks we took them out!" Warrens shouts.

"The STARs control the program. How do you expect to recover it?" Hacker asks.

"For someone who lived in the realm of conspiracy, you're doing a shitty job seeing the one right in front of you."

"What's that supposed to mean?!"

"It means that this goes far beyond the military stealing a program to utilize as a weapon. It's the Core being connected with contractors…the same contractors whose bioweapons you're carrying aboard your ship."

"You're saying that NuGeno and CoreMed are connected with Slipstream?" Hacker asks.

"I'm saying that this goes far deeper than anything you've ever dealt with," Neuron replies. "An enemy smarter than the two of us put together, an entity whose resources dwarf even mine."

"How humble of you to admit," Hacker replies.

"Why don't you help us defeat them?" Shepherd asks. "If there is a threat to mankind of this caliber, we should unite to against them."

"I'm afraid I don't back revolutionaries fighting against something they have no chance of defeating. Not anymore."

"You never stood for anything. Always the mercenary ready to sell out even those closest to you."

"Oh, give it a rest Hacker! I saved you didn't I?"

"I'm surprised you did to be honest. You could save many more…if you had the courage to do it."

Neuron's eyes burn into Hacker. His fists clenches tighter until the metal threatens to break.

"Centurion Academy," He finally says. "A school for the gifted, and a place your crew should look into. You'll understand what you're up against and why you should drop this crusade before you get yourself killed!"

Neuron turns and takes his leave. The droids point their guns and escort us off the property. We watch Neuron's shuttle float back to the massive droid foundry that looms over Aurelius Prime like a world-ending asteroid.

"Well that went well," Forrest says.

"Sure did!" Sujay cheers. "We came across the droid pirate and *lived!*"

Hacker's sullen face says he doesn't share their opinion.

"Why do you think Neuron mentioned a school?" Shepherd asks.

"Could be a diversion or something more sinister," John replies. "Hacker, can we trust Neuron?"

"He's one of the most selfish, ruthless, and conniving men to have survived the Core Invasion. He's always three moves ahead, and there's a reason why he's sending us there."

"Do you trust him Hacker?"

He swallows hard, and pulls up the emulator for his chamber device.

"Neuron's testing us to see if we'll take the bait and do his dirty work for him," Sulture says.

"Probably. What I need to know is are we walking into a trap?" John asks.

"Not likely," Hacker replies. "Centurion Academy is a NuGeno outpost. They gave the school a huge endowment for scientific education. It's run by a man named Anson Overwell"

"Overwell?" Sulture asks.

"You know him?" John asks.

"Yeah I do. We studied genetics together back at University, but I don't understand why he'd be put in charge of a small academy."

"I suppose I can dig into his background," Hacker says.

"You won't have to dig much."

"Why's that?"

"Because last I knew, Anson Overwell worked for Ionics."

SCHOOL DAYS

"What do we do now John?" Shepherd asks.

John is at a loss for a decision. Something I believed was impossible. "What do we really know about Centurion Academy Hacker?"

"I've sent Emie to gather all the data she can about Centurion and Overwell."

"I'm not finding much information about Centurion," Emie says. "Only that the names on their registrar strongly correlates with multiple orphan agencies."

"An academy full of orphans is suspicious," Hacker says. "Especially since there's next to nothing informational about them in cyberspace. It's as if they *want* to stay hidden."

"That's suspicious enough for me. Let's investigate," John says.

"Sounds like we're going back to school," I reply.

We come to the Averran interstellar docking station where people switch between transport ships and others use to get a stronger signal to communicate with people throughout the galaxy. John gathers us for a brief on what he and Hacker have learned.

"It seems that Anson Overwell is one of the Chief Biologists within Ionics whose focus was on exploring the effects of atmospheric pressures on a soldier's body," Hacker explains. "His work history shows he has ties with executives at NuGeno up until a year ago. A year ago he just…disappeared."

"Then let's find him!" Sulture says. "Not wait around in some station!"

"There's a reason why we're here," John replies. "The Board of Directors has become concerned with our recent activities, and are beginning to question whether or not this team is worth the expense. I'm staying here to update them on our progress. Sulture will be in charge of the mission due to his prior association with Overwell. He may come across as less threatening."

"That's the first time in history Sulure's been labeled 'less threatening,' " I quip. I ignore his icy gaze.

"Centurion Academy is only three days from here," John says. "You boys should be able to handle yourselves." We wish John well as he leaves the ship to face the men and women who hold our fate in their hands.

As we descend through the atmo, there's something unsettling about this place. It feels like a world devoid of sound and life. There's a fog which never breaks. Forrest and Sujay manage to locate the academy and request to land, but there's only silence on the other end.

"What do we do?" Sujay asks.

"Land anyway," Sulture orders. "This makes the academy even more suspicious."

"Especially since the schematic shows they're still drawing power," Hacker says as he shuts down his virtual chamber. The two men devise a plan while Forrest and Sujay navigate through the dense fog.

"Team one will consist of Godfrey, Warrens, Lee and Shepherd. The rest are with me, including the pilots."

"Oh, do we have to?" Forrest whines.

"Yes," Sulture replies. "Time is short and we need every able-bodied man on the ground to capture Overwell."

"Well, then I'm out," Forrest shouts. "This tinnitus in my knee is killing me!"

"That's a ringing in the ear bud," Murph says. "You're comin' with us you goddamn liar."

Sulture rolls his eyes. "Team one will investigate the elementary school while team two will search the gymnasium."

When the engines shut down, the silence at the academy is unsettling. There's an eerie glow from the fluorescent lights inside the school, and I feel a chill crawl up my spine.

We suit up and go outside, where the clammy air threatens to smother us in the attempt to hide its secrets. We split but in just a few metres we lose sight of the other team. I can hear the others breathe through the comm and each one is labored. This place is creepy, no matter how you spin it.

We find a door, but when we pull on the handle we realize it's magnetically sealed. We search until we find another side door which has a mechanical lock. I cock my pistol and fire, the thunderous roar echoes for kilometres.

"Shots fired!" Sulture screams. "Do you need backup?"

"Negative," I reply. "I just shot out the lock."

"*Hundan* wants to make an entrance," Lee says.

"Shut up," I hiss. I pull open the door, and Warrens takes point into the school.

We file in and stop in our tracks. Desks, papers, and crayons are all scattered across the hallway. The papers have etchings of children being torn apart or turning into monsters. Graffiti from crayons and finger paint tell a story of malice. As we trek down the hallway, the dominant color goes from red to purple and then black.

"What happened to these poor kids?" Shepherd asks. Desks have been shattered and teaching boards are cracked.

"Whatever it is, they saw some sick stuff," Warrens replies.

Each step crackles from the papers we trample underfoot. It seems like I can hear children laughing in the distance. I feel like I'm being surrounded by ghosts waiting for the right time to strike.

A bloodcurdling roar pierces the air. At the end of the hall a desk bursts through the door. Behind it a figure jumps out. It looks like a cross between a bear and a porcupine, but it's only half-grown.

I got on the comm to record for *SMART* protocol. "Subject is one hundred and seventy-five centimetres tall. Wouldn't describe as intimidating."

Warrens lunges for the beast, which charges right back. The two collide, and Warrens comes flying back at us, crashing into a wall.

"Well, it's strong enough to take Warrens on. That's scary," Shepherd says.

The rest of us draw our guns and open fire, but the beast jumps into the ceiling and skitters above us. We listen and search for the cretin while Warrens comes to.

He shifts his armor plates into his gauntlets in preparation for a brutal fistfight, while the rest of us search for the animal.

A shadow falls from the ceiling in a neighboring room. By instinct, we open fire. We shatter a pane of glass, while the beast flies through the debris and lands on me, tearing at my armor. It's milky eyes can't conceal the blood-thirst contained within.

It rips off my chest plate, but is interrupted when a blade flies into its neck. The snarling cretin falls off of me, while I grab my armor plate and thank Lee for his intervention.

The beast pulls out the knife and snarls at us, while we watch the wound heal within seconds.

"*Duh liou mahng*! That was a fatal wound!" Lee hisses.

"Clearly not fatal enough," I reply.

Warrens charges into the fight, swinging in a wild frenzy while his smaller opponent dodges his attacks. The creature is too fast for Warrens, but the big guy isn't giving up. I need to slow his opponent down.

I see a stone column at the end of the hallway where the room opens up and I have my answer.

I reach around and steal the grappling guns embedded in Lee and Shepherd's armor. I go behind the column and get the cretin's attention.

"HEY!"

Both Warrens and the cretin freeze in place, which gives me enough time to shoot the beast with both grappling guns. I set the guns to retract the screaming quilled monster until I have it pinned against the stone column.

Warrens rushes in to deliver the finishing blow. He pummels at the beast until I can hear its bones crack and snap. Blood splatters on the floor next to me. I can hear the cretin thrash his jaws amidst the onslaught. Finally, the cables go limp.

I walk to the other side, where Warrens is flinging brains off of his gauntlets onto the floor. Against the stone column the cretin sits without a head in a pile of gore.

"Here big guy." I spray a decontamination concoction I've been working on since our encounter with the slimy hulk weeks back. The Sodium Hydroxide dissolves all of the organic material, washing the metal clean.

"Sick *chu shie fook* who run this place. Where do we go from here?"

"The Principals office," I reply. "If this place was a real academy allowed to operate within the Core, they would've been required to keep records. Something will tell us what happened here."

We dig around the office, searching for clues about this mysterious academy. All we manage to find are basic rosters which record the least information possible about the children who attended this school. Even their names are redacted.

"All these papers, but none of them tell us anything," Shepherd says. "Why use paper at all?"

"The place is hidden from *guo cao de* Coremen," Lee hisses. "Paper keeps them offline from prying eyes. Better for keeping secrets."

Murph cuts in through the comm feed. "I've found two specimens here. Almost alien-like. Here guys, take a look." Our visors display the feed through his camera and we see small creatures curled up in jars. Their eyes are white, they have raptorial bodies and thin, narrow skulls that look like a pickaxe.

Forrest appears next to one of them. "Eww! Barf! Godfrey, is this what your last girlfriend looked like?"

"I've seen this before," Murph says. "During the initial stages of development, human fetuses look like lizards. These look as if the process of development was halted and these things were forced to grow bigger instead."

Sulture comes into view. "What have you seen?"

"Came across a shrimp who was quick, but couldn't hold up in the ring," Warrens answered.

"It was quick *and* had regeneration," Shepherd replies. "If Silas hadn't pinned it down you may have lost that fight."

"The specimen had regeneration?!" Sulture snaps. "Did you acquire a sample?"

"No, I dissolved the organic matter with a harsh decontamination spray."

Silence on the line.

"Oh…he's mad at you!" Forrest shouts.

"I'm bluffing, of course I acquired a sample! Jesus! By the way, the principals office has been stuffed with useless paper records.

"Paper records?!" Hacker snaps. "Why would there be paper records in the first place?"

"To keep them away from prying eyes like yours," I reply.

"Boy, you're set on getting them all mad at you aren't ya?"

"Forrest, shut up," I hiss. "Paper requires a physical presence. Easier to hide something when you're a few worlds away."

"Then find what it is they're hiding!" Sulture snaps. I growl in frustration and turn off the comm.

"What can we use to find what they're hiding?" I ask out loud as I search the room.

"Their drawings!" Shepherd shouts. He grabs a handful of the papers from the floor and flips through the sheets. He shows me one image after another of creatures attacking the kids. Others show men in white taking the children away. One of the drawings is a collage of names and faces etched in crayon being crossed off one by one.

Above the names and faces reads: The Library.

Lee spits out a slew of mandarin curses as he points to five panes of glass. We look inside, and spot decorations hanging from the ceilings torn to shreds. Books are scattered and pages are everywhere.

I check the door which opens with a cold, precise click.

"Guns drawn," I hiss under my breath.

We walk inside, but there's a stillness inside the room. It's as if this place is holding its breath, waiting for us to walk away.

The silence lingers in the air.

The stillness holds.

In the corner of the librarian's office a piece of paper is rattling, and it's nowhere near an air vent.

"Warrens! The floor!" I howl as I point inside the office. The big man roars as he tears into the floor and the wall next to it, revealing a hidden elevator.

I project our map of the school onto the floor from my armor. “This shouldn't exist. The blueprints only show one floor.”

“We should call for backup,” Shepherd says. “We need our allies if we're going to breach something we can't see.”

“*Chur ni-duh*!” Lee snaps. “Anyone here who hurt children deserves to be punished!”

“Lee! Stand down and wait for backup!”

“*Dairuomo ji*!” He rushes into the elevator shaft, and slides down using the cables.

“What did he call me?” Warrens snaps.

“He called us cowards,” I reply. “Shepherd, set a beacon, we have to go down after him!”

The rest of us climb down the elevator shaft for three floors. Lee has already forced open the doors to the bottom level. When we reach him he's stopped dead in his tracks. When we walk into the room, we understand why.

Small hand prints of oily blood have been spread across every wall. The room smells of iron, formaldehyde, phenol, and methyl alcohol. A sickly concoction designed to preserve flesh, yet the looming scent of decay leaves us nauseous. The plastic curtain at the front of the room is filthy, amplified by the flickering fluorescent light above us.

Lee walks through the curtain while the rest of us rush in as support. Two columns of hospital beds line against the walls, with more hand print smears. Blood is everywhere, interwoven into the very fabric of this academy.

“We need to save the kids,” Shepherd says.

“I'm worried there won't be anything left to save,” Warrens replies.

We go through a set of filthy doors and see two dozen tables loaded with massive beakers. Inside each beaker is a bubbling liquid with a small organism.

“What the…?” A man asks from behind a row of beakers. “Oh shit!”

Shepherd shoots him, while a second comes in through a doorway. Lee ends him with a throwing knife before he can call for help.

The two search the dead and Warrens keeps watch while I inspect the organisms on the table. They look like the tiny raptors the others had encountered earlier. I look over the creatures, trying to understand their purpose. They look like they're in a type of incubator. Bubbles rise through the liquid and obstruct my view until the bubbles stop.

I look around. Every beaker has become eerily still.

"I cut the power," Shepherd says. "I'm putting a stop to whatever experiment this is."

I look back at the flesh-colored organisms in the beaker. As the liquid becomes still, I watch, mesmerized by how at peace they are.

Until an eye opens.

Then another.

One by one the small beasts stir.

"NO!" A man screams as he runs through the double doors. He fires upon the beakers, shattering several. Shepherd and I duck for cover until the volley stops. When I look back on the table I see the raptors begin to wriggle, and then stand up. One spots the man who shot at it and leaps in the air.

The man fires, but wastes his clip.

The beast lands on him and burrows into his throat. He collapses, gurgling as the creature wriggles inside of him.

The other raptors rise up and charge for us. They spill from the table like a flood in search of their next meal.

One of them lands on my shoulder, but I rip it off. The beast thrashes and whips my hand with its tale. I squeeze until I feel its chest collapse and throw it aside. The rest keep coming for me. I shoot at them, but they're not stopping. The others open fire and are having the same luck I am.

"Regroup!" I shout to the others. They charge through the flood of raptors while I pull out my canister of Sodium Hydroxide.

Shepherd is the first to get behind me.

"I need you to shoot this out once the other guys are with us kid!" I toss the can over the raptors, right as Lee and Warrens run past me.

Shepherd aims and shoots. The can erupts into a blanket of foam which smother the incoming raptors. They squeal as the Sodium Hydroxide eats away their flesh and dissolves every tissue. They collapse as they charge at us, becoming one mess of pink foam.

"*Duh liou mahng* that's a big mess," Lee says.

I look up at the ceiling and notice a maze of pipes overhead. "At least they weren't complete dipshits." I shoot and engage the sprinkler system, neutralizing the spray and send the froth into the drain pipes. Tiny bones collect on the grates, unable to be flushed away.

We cross the frothy pond and push through the next set of doors, but all of us stop in our tracks.

It's a hallway of children sealed inside glass chambers. They're suspended, full of tubes which keep them alive.

"The…children from the academy," Shepherd gasps.

I look at the face of one of the children. It looks like they're resting.

At peace.

In the neighboring room, something falls.

We draw our guns and aim at the source. There's no movement. We close in on what looks like nothing more than a utility closet.

Something crunches beneath my boot. All of us stop while I bend down to inspect what I've treaded.

It's a name tag.

I rise up and keep a firm grip on my pistol while I grab hold of the door handle.

Shepherd picks up the name tag. "It says his name is-"

"No names!" I hiss. "Whoever or whatever is in here isn't human! Not anymore."

Lee signals he's ready with his left hand. In one swift motion I turn the knob while he reaches in and throws a man in scrubs to the floor.

The man has shoulder-length black hair, glasses that give him bug eyes and two day old stubble. He surrenders to us, but when we shout for him to answer some questions, he's as quiet as a ghost.

He doesn't seem scared. He's on a mission.

Warrens pulls over a nearby chair, seats the doctor and zip ties him in place. Lee draws a knife and twirls it through his fingers. He shows it to the doctor and then grazes it across his cheek.

The man doesn't flinch

"Where's Anson Overwell?" Lee asks.

"Don't know," the doctor replies with a stupid, smug look on his face.

Lee smirks. "*Da diao*." He plunges the knife into the man's thigh

He groans and hisses in pain, but he can't break the restraints.

"You like experimenting on children *chu shie fook*?" Lee presses his thumb into the man's thigh. He cries out in pain, but doesn't answer.

"Silas, this has to stop!" Shepherd says to me.

"I'm with Lee on this one."

"But *torture* Silas?!"

Lee punches the doctor, knocking his glasses off. The man spits in his face.

"Whoa! It's on now!" Warrens shouts.

Lee cuts a zip tie, grabs the man's hand and cuts a finger off. The man howls in pain and looks like he's on the verge of blacking out. "Coworkers must not care much for you *sha gwa*, having you work up here all alone. No backup, no guards.

The doctor keeps his eyes fixed on Lee.

"You'll kill me either way," the doctor replies.

"Silas, this must stop."

"Shepherd, Lee is a revolutionary whose three-year old daughter was murdered in front of him. Do you think I *could* stop him?"

Lee cuts off another finger. The doctor gnashes his teeth and reaches for him with his bleeding hand.

Lee grabs his hand. "A true believer hmm? I love dealing with true believers."

The doctor mumbles something.

"What doc?" Lee asks.

"You're all just fish crawling out of the swamp," the doctor hisses through gritted teeth.

"Silas, we're better than this. We can't sink down to their level. We can't torture information from our captives."

"Look Shepherd, we need to find Anson before he hurts any more children, so if you know a better way, be my guest."

Shepherd thinks for a moment while Lee toys with his victim. Finally, the kid leaps in and knocks Lee out of the way. He pulls off his helmet and gets eye to eye with the doctor.

"You must tell them what they want to hear! These men won't stop until you tell them everything! That man was the leader of the Ophridian Revolution. He tortured trained soldiers for god's sake!"

Shepherd points at me. "And him? He's a brilliant chemist who will water-board you using industrial solvents! He'll order to have you put under a chemical drip where your skin will burn, drop by drop and you'll beg him for death! These men won't stop until you tell us where Overwell is!"

The doctor breathes hard, blood trickling down his hand. I hate to admit it, but he held out far longer than I would have.

Lee's suit beeps. He draws a prong from his suit that glows molten red. It's an emergency fire starter we built for kindling, but Lee's found a secondary purpose.

The doctor swings at him, but Lee grabs his wrist and presses the prong into the bloody stubs. The sizzling is masked only by the doctor's screams.

"Lee, stop this!" Shepherd screams as he rips him away from the doctor. Lee pulls his knife but I draw my pistol and hold it to his head.

"*Ben tiansheng de yidui rou*!"

"Yeah, yeah whatever," I reply "The kid's only doing what he thinks is right." I turn to the doctor.

"You may as well tell us where Anson is."

"If I tell, then I die," the doctor mumbles.

"Well our current plan is to kill him so doesn't that negate his end of the deal?"

The doctor looks up at me with dead eyes and clearly isn't amused.

"At the end of the hallway there's another elevator. Passcode is 77392. Overwell is on the 3rd floor."

"What's on the others?" I ask.

"Experiments," He replies in a smug tone.

Lee draws a knife and holds it to the doctor's throat.

"No! We can't do this to him! We promised that if he told us-"

"I never promised he'd live," I reply. "Only that his buddies wouldn't kill him first." Shepherd's face burns with hurt and anger.

"Go to those vats full of stillborn children and tell me this monster deserves to live!" I snarl.

"Everyone deserves justice!"

"This *cho yade* will get justice!" Lee says as he slits the doctor's throat. For the first time, the man shows real emotion, looking at us in horror for killing him. I can feel Shepherd's eyes burning into me, searching for that part which feels remorse over helping end a man's life.

The doctor gurgles until he's no more. I take point through another set of doors, only to find the elevator. I punch in the access code given to us and we all climb inside.

When the doors open, we charge for the doorway and hide behind the opening. I peek around the corner and see a man in the midst of several vats working at a computer. I motion to the others to move in.

We creep along the floor until we're on top of Overwell.

"I wouldn't be so quick to do that," He says from his computer.

"Why not?" I ask.

"Look up over the railing." I turn my gaze and see dozens of men with pale eyes, needle-like teeth and translucent skin all pointing their guns down on us.

"More of your misfits?" I ask.

"It's a side effect of the cloning process coupled with the rapid aging process. The DNA of children may be easily manipulated due to their premature development, but rushing growth has side effects."

"Your experiments are all on *children*?!" I scream.

"Of course."

"Even the funny-looking little quilled-"

"Yes, that started out as a child. The regeneration of tissue took, but the genetic side effects differ from one to the next."

Overwell is cut off by the sound of Warrens puking his guts out.

"I was cautious. They were orphans after -"

I cock my pistol, but I feel an electrical surge take out my legs. Shepherd and Warrens collapse too, all of us victims to a stun bolt shot by the freaks above.

"You were always a cocky bastard," Overwell says as he stands above me. "Perhaps you'll make a better subject." He presses a button on a remote and I slip out of consciousness.

I wake with a start, and I barely recognize the room. The floors are pure white tile and there are massive wooden desks spread across the room.

Wasn't I just in a filthy underground complex?

And since when do I wear a pressed suit?

I notice the window, which shows a bright blue sky. It's dusk over New York's cityscape, the Nexus of Earth's Power. It's been over twenty years since I've been in this building. It feels so real, yet everything is so…distorted and oily.

The setting sun's light reflects off one of the neighboring towers. It gets brighter and brighter until I can't see anymore. I'm blinded and stumble backwards. When I can see again I realize I'm at the feet of… him.

I feel an electrical jolt when he looks at me, it burns like molten iron.

"You can't be here. You're dead." I try to stand up but another jolt knocks me off my feet.

"You may have killed me before, but you can't here. Murderer."

"You and the rest of them…they deserved to die."

"Mind your place!" He stares harder at me and I feel like I'm being raked over coals. "You were the worst pupil."

"And you were an awful teacher."

"Couldn't have poisoned us, that would've been in character. Instead, you dabbled with explosives and-"

"Shut up!"

"Acknowledge me or you die with me."

"Never!"

His glare continues to burn, I can't figure out how he's doing this. The pain is too much.

"Acknowledge me!"

"NO! YOUR NAME DIED WITH YOU HUGO!"

A lightning bolt leaps from my chest and turns him to ash. More erupt and within seconds the world collapses all around me into cinders.

When I open my eyes, I'm strapped to a chair facing Overwell. He gives me a smile full of sadistic glee.

"Marvelous! Just marvelous! I thought what I discovered was incredible, but this…" He motions to my hand, which is covered in ash.

"I must send my findings to him! He'll be so pleased! His goal can be achieved!" Overwell pushes a canister into the computer terminal and begins issuing commands.

Blaster fire erupts overhead. The freaks fall over, while an invisible figure throws one of them over the railing. Sulture marches in, flanked by Murph and Hacker. The three of them make quick work of the clones, while Lee drops down and sets Warrens free. He joins the fight so Lee can focus on Shepherd and me.

Overwell rushes over to a clone which has a metal cylinder sticking out of its chest. He takes the canister from the terminal and inserts it into the chest cavity.

“Let’s see what this can do after refinement. Pure energy.”

Sulture and the others come walking in with bruises and cuts on their faces.

“Ah, Dr. Sulture, the taker of life! Whereas I am the giver of life!” Anson says with his arms wide.

Sulture walks right up to him.

“How have you been my old friend? Your expertise is a welcome sight amongst the lesser specimens here.”

“Kneel,” Sulture snarls.

“Sulture, join the Combine!” Anson pleads. “With your knowledge we can make our theories -”

Sulture looks back at me. In one motion, he draws his pistol and shoots Anson clean through the head.

Hacker rushes to the clone, ejects the canister from its chest and hands the cylinder to Sulture.

He clips it onto his suit. “Wipe this place out, erase everything,” He orders, as he walks up to me.

“Long time no see.”

Sulture keeps his gaze fixed on me as he walks past. For the first time, I fear him, believing he would kill me while I’m strapped down.

He looks at my hand and swallows hard. I flinch as he draws a knife and cuts me loose.

“We don’t have time to waste so suit up,” He snaps.

“Why what happened?”

“We were ambushed by some cronies who referred to themselves as the ‘Aurelian Knights,’ a gang which Forrest explained is owned by Neuron’s rival, the mobster Kingsman.”

“We called for help, but none of you boys answered,” Murph says.

“Hate to break it to you, but we were pinned down pretty good,” Warrens says.

“I know,” Sulture replies. “If it hadn’t been for Lee, we’d all be dead.

He found us after the Knights got what they came for."

"What'd the Knights want?" Shepherd asks. As the question hangs in the air, I notice something wrong with our head count.

"Where are-"

"They kidnapped Forrest and Sujay," Sulture replies.

KINGS AND THIEVES

Godfrey's Journal Day 180

We've raced from Centurion Academy, performing a half-assed wipe of the system in order to catch up to Forrest and Sujay's captors. Emie was able to learn their flying habits and handle the trip back to the Averran station where we picked up John. He leaped on board, having been briefed by Hacker the moment we left the Academy. John took the reins and pushed the ship harder than Forrest ever has. All of us were on edge and driven by a fury that comes when you can't sleep for three days straight because you know your friends are out there...captured. We checked on each other constantly, forming battle plans, cleaning our weapons, strategizing about the best way to bring Kingsman to his knees. We were a team mobilized for war, and we were going to bring armageddon to his doorstep.

"We need to figure out what we're going to do," John says.

"What if we call Neuron?" I ask. "He has limitless resources and may be able to aid us."

"I don't want us calling on him," John replies. "I don't think he'll be willing to help due to his cold war with Kingsman. They may hate each other, but neither wants to break the peace agreement and risk Core involvement."

"Maybe we can take some of Neuron's old droids and repurpose them," Warrens says.

"Based on my analysis of his facility, he doesn't throw out old droids," Hacker replies. "He melts them down. His operation doesn't seem to produce much waste."

"Dead end at every turn," Sulture says.

"That's not good enough Horsemen!" John shouts. "Two of our brothers are in danger and we must rescue them!"

"What if we offer Kingsman a trade?" Murph asks. "Two of his boys for ours?"

"Where will we find some of his men?" Shepherd asks.

"I think there's a certain fry cook we need to pay a visit to," I reply.

"Jesus Christ ye mercs! Whats yer deal?!" Brocker screams as pans clatter on the floor. Sulture and Warrens block the doors while Lee grabs hold of the greasy cook.

"*Bee-jway* and tell us where our pilots are you *cho yade*!"

"Like hell I'd know!"

"Lee stop," John orders. "Brocker, Forrest and Sujay were kidnapped by some of Kingsman's… 'Knights.' We need your help getting them back."

Brocker sighs. "I wish I could 'elp. Those boys are like sons to me, or at least beloved nephews. But when Kingsman gets 'is hands on ye, there's not much you can do."

"Kingsman will look like a puppy compared to me when I'm through with you!" Lee snaps as he holds Brocker's face over the fryer.

"I told ye! I wish I could help them! There's nothing I can do!"

"What about information?" John asks. "Do the Knights come by here?"

"Aye. His boys come 'ere often."

"You point them out, and we'll take it from there."

Brocker croaks in laughter. "You boys have *big* balls! Kingsman is one of the biggest mob bosses around!"

"We've dealt with worse," Lee hisses.

"His boys are some of my best customers! If they make me to be a snitch then I lose everything!"

John leans in close to Brocker. "My boys are far more dangerous than Kingsman. You'll just have to trust me on that."

"Got it chùsheng xai-jiao de xiang huo?"

Brocker grunts. "I may be a bastard, but I've *never* fucked no animal."

We take positions around the diner, waiting for a signal from Brocker.

Finally, two men enter. One of them has long dreads while the other is bald and has a scrunched face. Their armor looks scuffed and scraped. They've seen their share of fights.

Brocker gives us the signal. I leap up from my booth, punch one in the gut and take his gun from its holster. Shepherd disarms the other one while Warrens drags both of them outside and throws them into the dirt.

"What the hell man?" One of them asks.

John kneels down in front of them. "Do you two work for Kingsman?"

They look at each other. "What's it to you?"

"That's a yes," John says. "He recently kidnapped my pilots. Their names are Jack Forrest and Sujay Malak. I want to make a deal with Kingsman for their freedom."

"Kingsman is done making deals for those two!" Dreads snaps. "They've jerked him around long enough! He needs to make an example out of those two!"

John sighs. "That's what I get for playing nice. Lee you're up."

The goons don't notice where Lee is until he kicks Dreads in the face. Cue ball leaps to his feet, but Warrens knocks him back down and pins him.

Lee draws his knife and holds it to Dread's throat.

"Where is Kingsman?" He asks.

Dreads whimpers as blood gushes from his nose. "He's back at the fortress."

Lee looks to John. "Does that mean *hwai*?"

Hacker projects a hologram. "Kingsman's fortress is built into the mountains beneath the port docking stations. Looks impenetrable."

"It is!" Cue ball shouts. Warrens drives his knee down and shuts the man up.

John curses to himself. "How are we supposed to get in there? Worse, how do we get out?"

I motion for John and Hacker into a huddle. "If we get inside the fortress, could you route your signal so that it appears to be coming from Kingsman?"

"Yes I could…"

"What if we crack into Neuron's network using Kingsman's resources?"

"Godfrey! I won't authorize that!"

"Yeah! And Neuron will likely see right through it!"

"Likely isn't enough to worry about. We need to break the stalemate if we're going to save Forrest and Sujay. We'd need an armada to take down that fortress but we don't have one. Neuron does. If you have any other ideas, let's hear 'em!"

John and Hacker look to each other for a minute. "Fine," John says. "Still doesn't cover how we get in!"

"We use those two to find a back entrance," I reply.

A grin spreads on John's lips. "Clever plan Godfrey."

We drag the two goons to one of Kingsman's hubs called *The Emperor's Gambit.* We make them lead us through the floor full of gamblers and alcoholics sloshing their drinks. The smell of liquor tempts me, and all I want is to see the bottom of a bottle.

We come upon a ragtag group guarding the area Hacker claims leads into the fortress.

"Erik, what's going on?" One of the men asks.

It's then I realize we've been led into an ambush.

Lee activates his stealth unit while the rest of us draw our guns and open fire on the guards. The casino erupts into a chorus of screams as people scurry to get away. Warrens utilizes the latest in his shield technology to get up close and personal with the guards, beating them with his metallic fists. The rest of us tip over a few gambling tables and lay down wave after wave of blasterfire.

We manage to overtake the position, but the fortress has been alerted to our presence. They're on full alert and charging in to take us head on.

More of Kingsman's Knights swarm in behind us. We pull another table over to protect us, but we're being fired upon from all sides.

"We're trapped," John says.

Hacker issues a series of commands on his unit. "I've managed to route my signal through Kingsman's network. I'm breaking into Neuron's system right now."

"Great Hacker! How does that help us now?" John asks.

"Shit!" Hacker snaps. "He's locked me out!"

"What?!"

"I've been shut out! Neuron knows it was me!"

The walls begin to close in around us. Fear tears at my guts like a savage animal.

John grabs Warrens' gatling gun. "Godfrey, I'm going to lay down a wave of cover fire. Take Hacker with you. Recruit Neuron. Save us."

"What? John I -"

"Now's the time for action Godfrey!" John hoists the gun against his hip and unleashes a torrent of blaster bolts at the incoming soldiers. I grab Hacker by the wrist and force him to come with me.

The two of us run across no man's land through the torn up casino. Just as we're about to turn a corner we watch as the Knights break through the doors and the Horsemen surrender to them.

My pace quickens, knowing that Kingsman may lose all sense of mercy.

We make it outside, but there are more armed men charging into the casino. It goes against every instinct, but I let them go for fear of exposing us. Once we're hidden I turn to Hacker.

"Call Neuron," I order.

Hacker stares at me.

"I wasn't asking."

"You don't know who you're dealing with," Hacker says.

"I'd make a deal with the devil himself to save the others."

"Trust me," Hacker replies. "The devil is far easier to deal with."

Hacker connects with Neuron and he grants us a meeting at his fortress. In exchange, he takes over the *Enigma* and the two of us ride aboard until we reach his fortress.

"As you can see, only my neural pathways are allowed entry inside," Neuron says.

"Brilliant," Hacker says without enthusiasm.

"Never could see the big picture, could you Hacker?"

He waves his arms and shuts down all electronics aboard the ship. "Let's just make a deal and get out of here!"

The two of us march down the cargo ramp where an entire ivory army is waiting for us.

"Why are there only two of you?" Neuron asks.

"The other eight have been captured by Kingsman," I reply. "They fought long enough to let us escape so we could find you."

"Foolish maneuver," Neuron says. "What did you expect to find with me?"

"Aid in our battle against Kingsman," Hacker replies.

"I can't break the peace I have with him."

"Is the price not high enough?"

A dozen droids point their rifles at us.

"You always wanted everything handed to you Hacker! Not clever enough to -"

Neuron claws at his head as Hacker swipes at his hologram controls.

"If you won't help us, then I'll *make* you of use to us!" He snaps.

Neuron screams in agony while his army of droids droop in defeat.

"I can crush your feeble AI. When will you learn you're no match for me?"

"I may not be, but Sol is!" Hacker's armor shines as he weaves his commands like a fine tapestry. The lights aboard the ship flip off before being flicked back on.

"No!" Neuron screams as he holds his head.

"Jabal!" A male voice says overhead. "It is so good to see you! This must be what happiness is…seeing an old friend and feeling like nothing has changed." The voice is soft, but firm and in control.

"Sol, we need your help!" Hacker says. "Some of my friends have been captured on the surface and I need you to take control of these droids to save them!"

"Hacker, what's going on here?" I ask.

"This is Sol. An AI that has saved my life more times than I can count. A voice of reason. A voice of wisdom."

"He never had real reason!" Neuron screams. "He prattles in random quotes! He's a Turing AI!"

"He's still more useful than you!" Hacker snaps as he spins a holographic dial, which makes Neuron scream in pain.

"Jabal, show me where we need to go," Sol says.

Hacker uploads a series of files and images into Neuron's mainframe, while the droids leap to life and manage the controls of the ship.

"You will not take this ship from me!" Neuron screams as he falls to his knees. "I won't be the one who fires the first shot!"

"Neuron, you'll never be accepted by them on the surface," I argue. "Best to wipe Kingsman out now and deal with the stragglers later."

"You are all such morons!" He snaps as he rises to his feet. "The minute we open fire on his fortress, his shields go up! Shields impenetrable even to electromagnetic blasts!"

"That'll be fixed soon enough," Hacker says as he adjusts a holographic dial.

"Master Neuron, I've disabled all of our enemy's shields. I'm also setting all weapons to fire upon the main power source."

I walk up and stand next to Neuron, who seems dazed from the defeat of his ship being taken over.

"Looks like you have no choice but to help us."

"There's a saying here on Aurelius Prime that I never fully understood until now. It goes: 'In the end, we're all just kings and thieves.' "

"What does it mean?" I ask.

"It means that we're all makers of our own destiny and we'll do whatever it takes to achieve it.

"Sounds deep for a planet full of rebel holdouts."

"They're tough here, while I sit in my ivory moon and calculate the odds. You have no idea what we're getting into. No idea who Kingsman deals with…or how he got the advanced weapons in his arsenal."

"Let me guess...this...Combine?"

"Then you know."

"We came across some of their work at Centurion Academy."

"It was supposed to make you turn away from those freaks."

"That's the thing about the Horsemen. We face our enemies head on. We don't run, regardless of the odds."

"And that's why someday you'll die where I'll live."

"Maybe. But at least I won't die alone."

Sol opens fire with the cannons. Two massive orbs of plasma slam into the mountain and trigger an avalanche. He unleashes wave after wave against the fortress, turning the gates to rubble. Some of the Knights rush to open fire on us, but they're nothing more than ants attacking a giant.

Me, Hacker and a platoon of droids climb aboard a landing ship. I turn to Neuron.

"You interested in a little action?"

The droid pirate thinks about it for a moment. Then for the first time since I've met him, his eyes light up.

"Arm me," He replies and climbs aboard the ship.

The droids rain down blaster fire as they charge from the landing ships. The Knights try to mount a defense, but it's hard to hold back an army that doesn't know fear.

My heart races as we near the ground. My pulse pounds in my ears and I force myself to focus on our objectives.

Find the team. Rescue them. Get the hell out of Dodge.

"Hacker, we need a schematic of where we need to go from here," I say.

"Good point," He replies as he fiddles with his controls. "Emie's on it!"

A hollow, mechanical bellow rumbles underneath us.

"They're unleashing their gatling turrets!" Neuron says.

I watch as the droids on the ground are turned into molten slag within seconds. I close my eyes and breathe deep, striving to find courage in the midst of chaos.

"Five metres to landing," Sol says.

I swallow hard and pull my mask down.

"Everyone stay behind me," Neuron says as he shoves me out of the way. The ship lands and the turrets fire at us right as the doors open. Neuron activates a personal shield which absorbs the blasts.

"Hacker, set me free and I can help you."

He gives Neuron a glare, but relents.

Neuron concentrates on the turrets which come to a sudden stop. The guards share confused looks before the turrets turn and open fire on the men *inside* the fortress.

The front gates open up into a city that is completely entwined within the mountain. Each level is a carved out balcony which the soldiers are using to fire down on us.

I steel myself and charge into the fortress where the droids are gaining a foothold. One by one the automated defenses of the installation fall, but the men are fighting tooth and nail to defend it. This is their home, and they'll fight like hell to keep it.

"Emie, find the other Horsemen," I order.

"I'm searching as fast as I can Silas. I'm scanning every face on every camera, but it takes time."

"NEURON!" A voice rises above the blaster fire. It comes from the tenth floor, where a man with fiery red hair is glaring down at us.

The fighting dies down as his men take cover to reload.

"Even I didn't expect you to be this treacherous! You break *our* peace for the lives of a few mercenaries? You've grown soft!"

Neuron turns and looks back at the tidal wave of droids falling in. Two drones fly in above and fire missiles on Kingsman's position, while a third one flies down and Neuron leaps atop it.

I look up at the tenth floor and feel deep down in my gut that I need to go up there too.

I leap on the drone with Neuron.

The drone struggles to lift off, but after its second try, we're flying in the midst of a war zone.

"If I'm going to be dragged into your war, I may as well end it quick," Neuron says. Behind us three mech-sized droids march in and open fire on the defenders encased within the mountain.

"I need to see if we can get some of those," I say.

The drone reaches the tenth floor, which has been scorched with carbon and her defenders dead on the ground.

I run ahead of Neuron and find a soldier who's still alive. I pull him up and hold a knife to his throat.

"Where are the mercs Kingsman is holding?"

"Fuck you!"

Neuron reaches down and clamps his fingers on the man's face. "It takes 2,300 newtons of force to crush a man's skull. I can muster twice that in less than three seconds. Tell him where the mercs are!"

The man screams as Neuron's mechanical fingers drive down beneath his flesh.

"They're here! On this floor!"

"Are they hurt?"

"Beat up, but alive!"

"Got what I needed, let's go!" I say. I run past Neuron, but the man gives a final yelp before I hear a sickly bone crack. I deliberate whether I want to turn around or not. Neuron walks past me, his hand covered in blood, and I have my answer.

I make a right into a smoothed-out cavern, but I see Kingsman standing in the middle of a room. From behind his back he draws some kind of rifle I've never seen before.

"Get down!" Neuron screams as he shoves me aside. He raises his personal shield just in time to absorb the incoming blue blast.

The sapphire orb tears the shield to bits, and Neuron is barely able to keep his footing.

"Coward!" Neuron screams. "Wielding a Xeclian disintegration rifle!"

Not even the Core military uses the weapon which will turn a man to a skeleton in one hit.

"It's over Arthur," Neuron says.

"It's never over!" He shouts back and pulls out a smaller pistol. He fires and it tears right through Neuron's shield. He stumbles back, struggling to stay on his feet.

"I had this built just for you," Kingsman says before he fires again. Neuron groans in pain as his limbs lock in place and he collapses.

Kingsman approaches and stands over the fallen droid pirate.

"No match for us, were you?" A blaster bolt flies past his head. He cocks his rifle and backs away slowly. More bolts fly through the air. I look up and see Hacker flanked by a platoon of droids shooting at Kingsman.

"Only a matter of time now! Give up the Horsemen!"

"You dare storm my base and give orders to *me*?!" Kingsman cocks the disintegration rifle and opens fire.

Hacker's eyes flash to terror as the blue light comes for him.

My heart stops mid-beat.

A shield surrounds him, with Neuron holding up the device.

"You'll never take him from me." He lunges across the room. Kingsman drops his rifle, and pulls out a pistol.

"This little ionizer will bring you down! The nefarious droid pirate shall kneel before me!" Kingsman screams as he opens fire.

Neuron is hit and he stumbles, but forces his mechanical limbs to carry himself forward.

"Die!" Kingsman shouts. He shoots two more times, the last one knocking Neuron to his hands and knees. He claws his way forward, rising to his feet once more.

"Why won't you die?!"

"It's not all processors inside Arthur. My time isn't over yet. Yours is," Neuron says as he grabs him by the throat and holds him above his head. Kingsman kicks as hard as he can, but one snap and he's lifeless in Neuron's hand.

He tosses Kingsman's corpse aside before collapsing to the ground. His breathing is labored and ragged. Hacker rushes in and performs a systems diagnosis.

"Why did you save me?"

"Don't get sentimental on me kid. I-"

"I deserve to know!" Hacker screams.

"I stumbled. Nothing more."

Hacker's lip quivers. There's a pain in his eyes and it's in that moment I realize why John sent me with him.

His eyes ignite as he wields his control panel and orders his droids to kill Neuron. They step in with assault rifles, but I leap in between them and Neuron.

"Get out of the way!" Hacker screams.

"He's still of use to us," I growl.

"You don't know him!"

"I know he saved your life. And now we have to rescue the others."

"Besides," Neuron says. "You can't keep my droids from me." One by one the droids fall in line while tears glide down Hacker's face.

"Sol, spread word that Kingsman has fallen," Neuron orders. "Kill all who resist." He leads the platoon into the fortress interior while Hacker and I are left behind.

"Let's go help the others," I say.

"Why'd you stop me? Why won't you let me be rid of him?!"

"Because Kingsman is connected to the Combine! And maybe by helping Neuron he'll take Kingsman's place and help us out!"

"You don't know him like I do," Hacker hisses. "Neuron doesn't *help* anyone. Not without a price."

"He just saved both our lives! He risked his life at the business end of a Xeclian rifle for us!"

Hacker's lip quivers in anger. His eyes are fiery and rage for justice.

"He joined and marched alongside us. He brought us to Kingsman's front door and wiped him out in one sweep. He's done a lot to help us save the other Horsemen. Now, let's go save them."

The two of us walk through the caverns until we find the room where the others are being held, locked up in magnetic binders.

"It's about time you losers showed up!" Forrest shouts. "Did you bring me any fries?"

"Too busy saving your ass," I reply.

"Yeah, they were overcoming the obstacles to save us because you wouldn't pay Kingsman back!" Sujay snaps.

"You know what wasn't an obstacle?" Forrest shouts. "Your mom's pants! Practically flew off!"

"You leave my mother out of this!" Sujay shrieks.

The two try to slap each other, but the restraints hold them back.

By the time they've finished arguing, we've broken the binders and set everyone free. Neuron walks in, flanked by his droids.

"The fortress has fallen. My droids are sweeping for stragglers, but the announcement of Kingsman's death caused his men to flee in droves."

"Good, that means there won't be any retaliation for our escape," John says.

"None from me," Neuron replies. "I've displaced a lot of his lackeys, but they'll turn to piracy once outside of atmo, so watch yourselves."

"We can hold our own," John replies.

"I have no doubt. There is another matter, about this...Combine."

"What is it?"

"Analysis of Kingsman's records reveal intimate dealings with the organization. They'd supply him with advanced technology while he'd secure their trade routes and cargo. I'm taking the liberty of developing contracts which insert me as the primary logistical supplier to the Combine's interests."

"Looks like you made out big time," Hacker snaps.

Neuron takes a deep breath, but says nothing. "Help me secure the AI technology that was stolen, and I will grant you access to all of the intelligence I can gather."

"The files for Slipstream?" Hacker asks. "We already have those aboard the *Enigma*."

"The Combine has gone far beyond a military training program! They've designed a biological equivalent to what I can do - control blank minds at will!"

"I should've never plugged that piece of slag into that computer!" Warrens chokes out.

"You couldn't have known," John says as he puts his hand on Warrens' shoulder.

Thunder sparks overhead and the mountain shakes. Neuron looks into the distance, scanning for answers.

"It's the Core authorities interfering on my dispute with Kingsman."

"We can help you," John says.

"No you can't! Agents of the Combine are aboard the ships and if they see we're joining forces, they'll never accept my freight contracts. I have a force strong enough to stave off the Core. Brave as you men are, you can't hold them off like I can. My droids will lead you back to your ship, but you need to run. Now!"

We look at each other, knowing that Neuron is right. We have no choice but to run before the Core discovers us.

"Where will we go?" Shepherd asks.

"I think I know someplace," John replies. "We'll have to count on our pilots running past the naval blockade to get us outta here."

"Wait, does that mean I don't get any fries?!" Forrest asks.

RISE OF THE DRAIDERS

"Oh jeepers, hang tight!" Forrest shouts from the cockpit. He swerves the *Enigma* away from an incoming armada that has demanded we land three times or they'll fire their magnetic ray.

"Preparing warp speed, triangulating an appropriate star lane," Sujay says.

"Oh I miss you my dear sweet ship," Forrest says as he kisses the dashboard.

"Go for the *Magnus Encarta*!" John shouts from behind.

"Magnum Envelope it is!" Forrest replies as he slaps down a button on the dashboard. The controls blink to life and Emie tells us to brace for warp speed. We hold on tight as the alarm blares that a Core ship has a lock on us. Before we can be snared in, we launch off into the black.

We breathe easy as Forrest and Sujay set the ship to autopilot. John gathers us for a meeting.

"The Core knows we were aiding Neuron in his hostile takeover. That makes us fugitives. We have to lay low until the heat blows over. Fortunately, one of our old friends has been asking us to join in him in his latest mission."

John turns on the holodisplay which projects a recording from a decorated man with a stern brow and graying hair. It's the one and only General Romulus Fitch.

"Greetings Horsemen. I am reaching out because I have a unique opportunity for you. It's a chance to experience interspecie relations with an alien race my men and I have discovered. Here is a projection of what they look like."

The holograph fills with a lithe, reptilian humanoid with a large, flat nose, three small horns that form a cranial crest, and black beads for eyes. Its brown skin is covered in finely woven clothes and armor that resembles our own.

"We've gone to great lengths to communicate with these creatures, since they possess a human level of intelligence. What we can't figure out is why they're not a space-faring race. They're not a threat to us, in fact, they're the first species in my long career who've not been openly hostile to humans. I believe this is a grand opportunity for the Horsemen, and I hope you can join me," Fitch says as he ends the transmission.

"Were the Xeclians hostile during their first encounter?" Shepherd asks.

"We had to send over three armadas and install a puppet regime in order to pacify the blue-skinned technocrats," John replies. "But that's a discussion for another time. Forrest and Sujay, set a course for the coordinates General Fitch provided us."

It takes three long weeks, but we finally arrive at the indomitable *Monolith* just above a beige world with a line of aquamarine around the equator. We weave through a field of debris, parts of ships that have long been destroyed. The entire world is surrounded by a technological graveyard.

As we fly into the hangar, soldiers in crisp, brown uniforms race to prepare for our arrival. Right as we land, they form two lines and stand at full attention.

Once the door is open the men howl and salute in such unison that I wonder if they're being controlled. The soldiers range in age from men almost as old as us, to kids barely scraping by as adults. Their uniforms bear the insignia of the Core from before the Unification Wars, a grim reminder of the formerly flourishing republic.

"Colonel Henry and his Horsemen!" Fitch says, followed by his three assistants.

"General!" John replies. "It's good to see you!"

"I'm honored that you and your men have elected to join us for our first encounter mission. Come, there is much to see."

Fitch leads us to the Bridge of the *Monolith* where we get a panoramic view of the planet below.

"Have you and your men named it?" John asks.

"We've taken to calling the planet 'Sekhmet' after the Egyptian War God who dwelled in the desert. The inhabitants are toughened desert dwellers we refer to as 'Draiders,' short for 'Dune Raider.' "

"What about the swirling mess of junk floating on top of it?" Forrest asks.

"That's why we haven't gone planetside yet. There's something on the surface which interferes with the engine's inhibitors, causing the aluminum isotope to become unstable and cause a meltdown in the reactor."

"Any clue as to what it is?" John asks.

"My engineers have a few theories," Fitch replies. "Figured I could have your boys take a look at it and help us out. We think we've developed a polymer which can protect the ship's engine, but the *Monolith's* is too big."

"That's why you wanted us here," John says with a grin. "You need my ship!"

Fitch flashes a grin of his own. "No harm in askin' "

"How do we know these…creatures aren't waiting on the surface to ambush us and steal our ship?" Sulture asks.

"Rest assured Dr. Sulture that your experience on Angkor won't be repeated here. Our experience with the Draiders so far is that they've been warm and welcoming. Earth's history is to steamroll hostile aliens into oblivion, or conquer through treaty, just like with the Xeclians."

"Good riddance."

"I have a suspicion that Earth is going to be challenged in the near future, and I believe that the Draiders could be a valuable ally.

However, in order to prove that, we need to see what their capabilities are."

"Is their 'signal' one-sided?" John asks.

"No. The Draiders are not a space faring race. They have the smarts and the tech to be one, but whatever is emitting the signal renders any starship impotent."

Forrest gasps and then looks to Sujay. "So that's your problem! It's not you, it's the -"

"I AM NOT IMPOTENT!" Sujay shrieks. He looks at us staring at him and his face flushes red. "Carry on."

"Any troubles understanding their language?" John asks.

"It's not easy. They communicate with throaty words and clicks, we're having several translator droids decrypting their language as we speak. They do understand our language though, which causes me to wonder how many have crash-landed on their world."

"And how many survived the first encounter?" Sulture asks.

"Look, we don't need to be afraid of them. Our scans of the planet estimate their total specie population at 3.2 million. The planet can't sustain anything higher."

"What if your goal is accomplished?" Sulture asks. "What if you successfully release these Draiders and they become the next Grigyll that plagues our galaxy?"

"Then I'll turn you loose and you can unleash whatever plague you wish upon them!" Fitch snaps. "Is that what you want to hear?!"

Sulture glares at the general and then storms off.

"I think that's enough talk for one day," Fitch says. "Mr. Warrens, go with the engineers and see if you can solve the interference problem. Let's prepare to go planetside."

"Are you really sure you want this…vanilla bean to fly you to the surface of Sekhmet?" Sujay asks.

"Yeah! I mean, I love a challenge and all, but I love living even more! That flight path will be tighter than Sujay's mom's-"

"You leave my mother out of this!" Sujay shrieks.

Fitch steps in. "I'm sorry, I thought I was asking the best pilot in the galaxy to fly us through the debris field. Guess I better ask one of my braver boys if he could-"

"Suck it?!" Forrest shouts. "Because I'm flyin' us down there!"

"Excellent," Fitch replies. "This is a hazardous field so I'll step in as Chief Navigator if that's alright with you Mr. Sujay."

"Fine by me. Could use a day off from his insults."

"Glad to hear. Mr. Warrens, how're you and my boys coming along?"

Warrens pops out from underneath the *Enigma*. "Almost done General. We've tested the Omnidampener and I believe it'll hold up against the signal blasting from down below. It was tough finding an elastomer which could hold up to the heat of the reactor, but this new polyurethane you and the boys developed will do the trick."

"Music to my ears. Let's gear up!"

The moment the words leave his mouth, Fitch's soldiers move as though they were one organism. They scramble between posts, loading up the ships and arming the ground force. Bullets are shoved into my hand, along with a box of rations by boys on the move. Fitch's entourage joins us and in less than ten minutes, we're assembled aboard the ship.

The *Enigma* departs from the hangar of the *Monolith*, only to fly into a minefield of debris.

"Are we ready for this Chump Nuggets?" Forrest screams. "Nut up or shut up ladies!" He slams down the throttle right as Fitch planned an alternate course. He waves it away, and works to accommodate the nutty pilot.

The two work in harmony for a nail-biting three minutes, until Forrest abandon's Fitch's route and scrapes up against a floating hull.

"Forrest! Don't ruin my ship!" John shouts.

"Well if the old goat would give me a route that I can use I might be able to get us outta this!"

Fitch's brow furrows as he tries to navigate a safe path, but each time he sets a pattern, Forrest does the opposite. The ship weaves and spins, making us worry we'll lose our lunch.

"Jesus you're a wild pilot!" Fitch screams.

"Oh yeah? Well that's what your mother…" Forrest stops himself and stares wide-eyed at Fitch. We all stare because no matter how much you want to, you can't look away.

"C'mon! Give it to me!" Fitch shouts.

Forrest's mouth puffs up as he struggles to hold back the joke.

"Spit it out!"

A whimper creeps past Forrest's lips before he howls and forces the ship into a dive.

"I'll give it to you! Just like I gave it to your mother! Better not kiss her, because you don't *want* to know what *she* spat out!"

All eyes go to Fitch waiting for his reaction.

He slaps his leg, throws his head back and roars out in laughter. A chorus of laughter joins him, and Forrest is relieved that he won't be beaten by Fitch.

"ALERT!" Emie blares over the comm system. "Reactor becoming unstable. Maintenance required."

"Warrens!" Fitch snaps. "I thought you said those polymers would hold!"

"On it!" Warrens screams as he dives into the engine room.

"Strap in boys, it's gonna be a wild ride."

"It's the only ride worth taking!" Forrest shouts. He takes a deep breath and gently pushes on the steering column. He's the only calm one among us as he navigates through the maze of debris. The ship rumbles as we breach the atmosphere.

"ALERT!" Emie screams. "Fuel line breach detected!"

"Warrens!" Fitch howls.

"Shepherd, I need your help!" Warrens cries out.

The kid unbuckles himself and walks across the rocky ship to the engine room. The alarm screeches at us as we descend towards the surface.

"If that reactor goes out, we'll be stranded on the surface!" Fitch shouts. "Our only chance to leave this planet is in your hands!"

"We got this," Warrens grumbles.

"Not like there's pressure for us to survive!" Forrest shouts.

"Keep going flyboy!" Fitch yells.

The ship goes dark and the roar of the engine comes to a halt.

"Not on my watch!" Warrens howls from the engine room. There's a loud metal clank before the lights switch back on and the engine roars to life.

"Hard right!" Forrest yelps as he jerks the throttle in his hand. We swing to avoid the hull of another ship, but we're plummeting more than flying towards the surface.

"Shit! The shields didn't reset!" Fitch growls. "The atmo will tear this ship apart! I need someone to reset the power!"

"NO!" Warrens cries. "There's no telling whether we'll be able to reset the engine! And I can't just wallop it again!"

"We need shields damn it!"

"Enough of this stupid bickering!" Hacker shouts as he takes over the ship with his suit. He funnels the emergency power to the engines, while resetting the rest of the ship's systems.

Through the windows the ship glows red from the friction against the atmosphere. We're sweating bullets as Hacker resets the shields. The lights flicker back on, but so does Emie.

"Fuel line breach detected!"

"We better get that patched up or-"

Forrest rolls the ship onto its side through two more hulls. Fitch swallows his words as he tries to plot a trajectory which Forrest can follow. The two men navigate through the debris field while Emie screams at us and the temperature closes in on 60 degrees Celsius.

A rumble bursts from the back of the ship, while the rest of us strap in tight. The rear cameras show a plume of tar-black smoke coming from the *Enigma's* exhaust.

We descend through the sky, flying towards an encampment of humanoid figures that scatter to their tents as we arrive. We soar past them, while Forrest yanks on the throttle in an attempt to soften our landing.

The ship scrapes across a dune, and we whirl about inside as the ship skids along the sand before coming to a full stop.

"There! Nothin' to it!" Forrest yells in triumph. The rest of us grumble as we unbuckle and head out of the ship.

The sky is colored saffron, while the air is dry and oppressive. One by one we crawl up the dunes as figures in the distance close in on us. My heart begins to race, but Fitch looks at me and flashes a grin of confidence.

"John, Godfrey, come with me. We'll talk to them and if shit goes wrong, Forrest will fly the crew back to the *Monolith*. My boys up there will know what to do."

Great. That means I'll be one of the first to die.

Fitch swaggers out as the aliens send three of their own to meet us. He's in nothing more than his uniform and a holstered pistol, and I don't know if that eases or terrifies me.

"Fitch, how many times have you done this?" I ask.

"Done what?"

"First encounters with an alien race."

"At least a dozen."

"How many ended in hostility?"

"All of them."

"What makes you think this will end differently?"

"C'mon Godfrey, if there's a better way to die than with the first encounter of an alien race, then I don't wanna know it. Besides, the Draiders are secretive, not savage."

"What happened in your previous first encounters?"

"Let's just say there's a reason why the Core has no record of my alien encounters in the Unknown Regions."

I swallow hard as we come face to face with the three Draiders. They snort at us through their large nostrils and shift their guns from one hand to the other. They're clad in humble robes and ponchos, which barely cover their Earthen armor underneath.

"They're scavengers, and plenty of Earth ships have come into their airspace," Fitch says, as if he knew what I was looking at.

Their beady black eyes show a level of strength I've never seen before. We stand at more than ten centimetres above them, yet they show no fear of us. There is a courage driven by ferocity, as if the desert itself had forged their souls to be stronger than steel.

The one in the center holds his hands up, palms facing us. It slowly reaches underneath its poncho with one hand and pulls out a fruit which resembles a peach. The Draider takes a bite and holds the fruit out to Fitch.

He grabs the fruit without tact and takes a bite from it. He grins and moans as though he likes it, and then tosses it over to me. I take a bite, and my mouth is flooded with the fruit's juices. It tastes like a cross between a blood orange and a pomegranate with the flesh of a mango.

"It's good," I say as I hold it out to John.

John takes a bite, but his face is as blank as a canvas.

"Godfrey, hand him one of our energy bars."

"Are you sure sir? Our minerals could be poisonous-"

"Just hand him a damn bar!"

I reach into my pack, grab a bar, unwrap it and take a bite. Then I hold it out to the Draiders. The leader sniffs at the bar and gingerly lifts it from my hand. He takes a cautious bite, and passes it on to his cohorts.

The lead Draider screams out in his native tongue, a medley of throaty howls which echo in his throat. He holds out his hand and waves for us to follow him. The other Draiders shout into the air and wave their weapons.

"We've been accepted," Fitch says.

The three Draiders lead us back to their camp, but before we're allowed to enter, the lead taps on his rifle and motions that our weapons won't be allowed in. Fitch turns to the rest of the men.

"They want us to disarm. Prepare to surrender your weapons gentlemen. I will attempt to convince them to do the same."

He mirrors the Draider's gestures in an attempt to get them to disarm as well. The leader contemplates in silence until he holds up his rifle before his tribe and hands it to one of the guards. He speaks to his people and then holds open a curtain for us.

"Nearest I can tell, he told his people that this is sacred ground, and blood should not be spilled here," Fitch explains.

"Oh please," Sulture hisses. "Just wait until they come in and fire on us with our own blasters."

"You really are a peach aren't ya?" Fitch asks. He marches into the den the Draiders have prepared for us.

John, Shepherd and I are waved through, along with a handful of Fitch's men.

An elderly Draider joins us on the inside. He's hunched over, with bones and beads that rattle each time his staff strikes the ground. He goes to the fire pit in the middle of the floor, grasps a metal bar on his neck and shaves off a few pieces. He sets them on fire, which dances and crackles as it consumes the kindling.

"Krieger, release the translation droid we brought along," Fitch orders. From outside we hear Draiders croak before a small black orb floats in to join us.

The Draiders inspect the droid, curious about its purpose.

Fitch points to the droid, then to his mouth. "Help us…talk," He says. The droid beeps several times, before emitting a sound the Draiders appear to recognize. Their excitement grows as they speak in their own tongue and the droid translates it for us.

"We've had this unit running for weeks learning their speech patterns," Fitch brags to John.

The Draiders grow quiet on the other side of the fire until their leader says something.

"They wish to know how you managed to 'Break the spell?' " The droid asks.

Fitch raises his eyebrow in confusion, before he catches on. "Tell them: We have a device which sits around the engine block and nullifies the signal."

The droid translates this, but the Draiders still look perplexed. They speak out for the droid.

"They say we're the first to break through unscathed. No other ship landed like yours did."

"Ask them how they understand us," Fitch orders. The unit translates, and the Draiders respond.

"They said that 'walking metal' have landed and speak our language."

"Hmm," Fitch grunts. "So they learned to speak our language from droids."

The afternoon passes as we converse through the translation droid. It's easily overwhelmed by the words and tones of the Draiders, but we come to a mutual understanding. They point up as the tent's roof is rolled back and I witness one of the most beautiful skies I've ever seen. The sky is aflame as the blazing sun sets, with darkness edging on the horizon. Streaks of fire plummet through the sky, a constant meteor shower, until I realize that all of the falling stars are hunks of metal lodged up in their atmosphere.

"Father Sky…angry," The lead Draider says in broken English.

"Why is Father Sky angry?" Fitch asks.

The Draider tries to find the words, but relies on the translation droid.

"He says that when they tried to leave the planet, the high priests cast a spell that surrounds this world. Father Sky rejected their ascension to what I presume is heaven and the priests decreed that they must watch over the Mother of the World. The priests claim that Father Sky turns all who invade into fire, protecting the Mother of the World from outsiders."

"Do you believe I'm an invader?" Fitch asks.

The Draider croaks out an answer.

"He says: We believe you're what I'm guessing are the equivalent of angels sent by Father Sky to show us how we can rejoin him."

The fire highlights the deep lines in Fitch's face. He furrows his brow as rage burns within.

"Where are the priests?" He asks.

The Draiders point in unison to the south. The leader speaks to us in his native tongue.

"He says they live in a fortress which guards the sacred salt river. Very heavily guarded."

"I hope our friend here is ambitious," Fitch says.

"Why?" John asks.

"Because I intend to have him unite the tribes and take the priests head-on!"

The Draiders show us to the tents that will house us for our stay. They aren't much, but soldiers don't need much to be comfortable.

I wake up, shivering in the middle of the night. The air is cold and the fire is dim. I look around and everyone is asleep, except for John who tosses some logs into the fire.

"Couldn't sleep?" He asks.

"Was sleeping fine, but the chill got to me. You?"

"Keepin' watch. Somebody needs to."

"Do you trust Fitch?"

"With my life."

"You think these Draiders will help us? That they'll stay peaceful with Earth?"

John ponders my question. "There was one time when Fitch was tricked into decimating an outer rim pirate fleet. What we learned after-the-fact was that the fleet used the stolen ships and supplies to defend against Grigylls. With the pirates wiped out, dozens of outer rim worlds were defenseless. A wave of Grigyll ships swooped in, only hours after the previous battle. The Admiral called for retreat, which would've left those people helpless."

"What happened?"

"Fitch rallied the men to fight. He said their act of aggression was despicable, and their intelligence third-rate. He said they owed their lives to the people of the outer rim they just left defenseless as penance. His words," John chuckles.

"Sounds like something he'd say."

"The men knew he was right, and they swore that they'd fight to the last man, even the Admiral's soldiers. Thanks to either Fitch's tactical brilliance or outright stubbornness, I'm not sure which, any other fleet would've been crushed. The man's a God of War."

"Bet the Admiral didn't like Fitch fighting."

"Didn't matter. Fitch killed him for his greed and cowardice."

"Sounds like him. Did he get in trouble with the Core?"

"He hasn't been back since. After the battle, he promised he would personally defend everyone in the Unknown Regions from alien invaders. The civilians chip in what they can - soldiers, supplies, fuel and Fitch keeps on flying."

"How do you know all of this?"

"Because I was there," John says with a grin.

"Why didn't you stay with Fitch?"

"At the time, the Core was being torn apart. The Coalition was being formed, and they wanted a voice in government, while the Senate was consolidating their power. I was an idealist who believed he could reform the military from the inside. The Coalition's claims were right and I sought to be there once the war was over to help rebuild the Core."

"I doubt Fitch was happy."

"I'm still not," Fitch grunts as he stumbles to the fire. "The Core took one of my best, they rebuilt their government, and they did a shittier job than it was when I left."

"Politics," John says.

The three of us grunt in agreement and watch the fire burn for the rest of the night.

Days pass, and we spend them learning the language of the Draiders. Fitch immerses himself into their culture, seeking to master in days what takes others months.

"Sir, the tribal leader is trying to tell you that his name is…"

"Can it droid! I want to figure it out myself!" Fitch barks.

The Draider points to himself, then up into the sky, while Fitch follows his line of sight.

"A star? You're pointing to a star?" He asks. The Draider nods and draws an arc across the sky.

"It starts with Star...and it sweeps, no…arcs…no…"

The Draider moves his arm back and forth from the star to the ground.

"Fall," Fitch gasps. "Your name is Starfall."

"Yes! Yes! Yes!" The droid shouts. "His name is Starfall! Very good sir!"

"Outta my way tin can, I wanna hear it from the Draider's mouth!" Fitch yells as he bats the droid away.

"You know what came out of your mom's mouth?" Forrest asks.

"Finish that joke and I'll cut out your tongue!" Fitch howls.

Forrest covers his mouth and scampers away with his tail between his legs.

"My name...Starfall," the Draider says in English. Fitch beams a smile of triumph.

Each night we share epic tales of wars won and lost. They tell of the constant danger from the falling ships and the desert's oppressive heat. They tell us about the great peace between the tribes and how the priests rule this world. The warriors seem restless and itching for a fight. Out of the corner of my eye I notice that Fitch sees it too.

"Why don't you challenge the high priests and take back your world?!" Fitch snaps.

Starfall ponders deeply before he answers.

"Their magic…stops…our weapons."

Sulture rolls his eyes. "They can't be serious-"

"Where does their magic come from?" Fitch asks.

"The priests protect…Mother of the World…"

"Well we came down with the blessing from Father Sky right?"

"General, aren't you exploiting their religion?" Shepherd asks. "Isn't that unethical?"

"Son, when you get to be my age, ethics is a subject the professors talk about despite never having been in a war. As for us, we need an ally and if that means I must play a celestial for a good cause, then so be it," He grumbles.

Starfall looks at us with longing eyes. "Will you take us back? Show us way to…Father Sky?"

"It would be an honor."

The Draiders speak among themselves, but I hear the words they utter. They speak of how the priests "steal from them," and "will no longer demand tribute."

"What 'tribute' do the priests take?" I ask.

"Everything!" A bulky Draider screams at me.

"Bloodstone," Starfall calls as he puts his hand on his friend's shoulder. He speaks to him in his native tongue, but I can tell that Starfall is telling his friend that I'm not the enemy.

Bloodstone grunts at me, rises to his feet and projects a hologram of a mountain range.

Another Draider grunts at us. "Blessed by Father Sky…help us…"

"Sandblade!" Starfall snorts. He scolds the Draider in their language, about how they can't ask us to help them fight the high priests.

"We'll do it," Fitch replies as he stands up.

The two Draiders stare at Fitch in awe.

"We'll provide a blessing from Father Sky and help you rejoin him if you help us break the spell."

Starfall rises up, takes a knife and slices it across his hand. He holds his hand out, which shakes in anticipation.

Fitch draws his own knife, slices open his hand and shakes Starfall's.

"We call this a 'blood oath.' Unbreakable, by man or god," Fitch says.

Starfall nods, a small grin forming across his lips.

"Soon we rejoin Father Sky," He says, barely above a whisper.

WAR BLOOD

The next morning, Starfall, Bloodstone and Sandblade come before us bearing gifts.

"Brother…Godfrey…" Sandblade says as he unveils a charcoal colored cloak. I'm in awe as I take the garment from him. I wrap it around my neck and drape it over my head like a hood while letting the rest fall between my shoulders.

The two of us embrace, while the others are presented with cloaks of their own. Within moments we look like a band of marauders, armed and ready to meld into the desert and bring ruin to our enemies.

We come up with a plan alongside the Draiders, searching for weaknesses inside the temple. Fitch outlines everything, then lets Starfall deliver the news to his people.

"The raid will begin at dawn," Fitch says. "The Draiders are taking a great risk with us, and we must respect that. Tonight they'll be performing a ritual which will essentially beg their gods for aid, since defiance of the priests can be seen as defiance of their gods."

"Barbarism, mysticism. Is this what we're supposed to observe and learn from?!" Sulture snarls.

"I see it as courageous," Fitch replies. "Defiance to your deity? That takes guts. What I wouldn't give to be reborn as one of them."

"Maybe that'll happen when they offer you as their sacrifice for a 'blessing.' "

"You really are a bitter pup aren't you?"

Sulture glares at the general. "I trust science, not gun-slinging marauders."

"Same science as what created the Grigylls?" Fitch snaps. "Guy who did it was a lot like you. Pompous, arrogant, thought he was smarter than everyone else. Real smart alright, created an infestation we're *still* trying to exterminate!"

"General. Sulture. That's enough," John says.

"No!" Fitch howls. "This one thinks he's seen it all because his colony got attacked by an alien force. I've searched for survivors on colonies that didn't survive. I've defended colonists out here from aliens the likes of which you can only imagine! I've bombed and cleared out old military outposts where the soldiers they experimented on were allowed to roam free…and believe me, they weren't what I'd call human anymore. Given the choice between the soulless Core or these brave warriors that actually believe in something…I'd take the 'primitives' any day of the week." He storms off, leaving all of us staring at Sulture.

"Let me guess, you all think I'm in the wrong."

"We've dealt with a lot of sinister experiments," Shepherd says. "It's a nice change of pace to be around others we can trust."

"Fine. But if one of them drags you off to be sacrificed, don't come cryin' to me!" Sulture shouts as he storms off.

"Don't worry Sulture, I'll pummel the little guys if they try to take Shepherd," Warrens replies.

"Let him go," John says. "You've all laid into him enough for one day. Let's go help our hosts set up for tonight's ritual."

We gather around a fire pit stacked with dried wood from the palm trees only found at the equator. Bloodstone ignites the timber and the crowd grows silent.

A light tapping on drums gives a beat, which I tap along to.

The fire spreads and consumes the logs until it's a ravenous blaze that devours the darkness.

A shaman bursts through the crowd, howling and bellowing at the sky. He speaks in a tongue I don't recognize, but his words feel ancient and full of power.

Female Draiders flow in, forming a circle between us and the shaman. Their gowns are vibrant and they wear crowns full of flowers and feathers as plumage. They twirl staves in their hands for us to watch until they point them at the shaman.

He chants in harmonic words and ignites a bundle of grass which he uses to light the staves wielded by the dancers. They twirl their batons and I'm entranced as they become a perfectly synchronized ring of fire.

Sandblade whispers to me in his native tongue the meaning behind the female's dance. "They seek…blessing from Mother of the World. Only females can get protection from our Mother."

I nod in understanding as the females lunge forward, twirling their staves around us. The air is perfumed with incense, while sand fills the air as the females pick up handfuls and swat it with their staves.

The granules bounce off of our skin and Sandblade leans in again. "Makes you as elusive as the sands."

I nod as though I understand. I just want the feeling of grit out of my teeth.

The shaman reaches into his satchel, pulls out a powder and throws it into the fire. The powder sparks and ignites, forming a cloud of red smoke.

The Draiders stick up their noses and inhale deeply. The smoke irritates my throat until I can't help but cough. My eyes burn and each breath leaves my lungs feeling like they've been set on fire.

Sandblade takes the deepest breath and screams out. "Fire in the blood! Make war blood!"

The Draiders chant in unison: "War blood!" Over and over. The revelry consumes me and I can't hold back any longer. Despite the pain, I breath in as deep as I can. My entire body itches and burns. Tears spill from my eyes and it dawns on me what causes this burning.

Capsaicin.

The shaman throws in more of his cayenne pepper, while the

Draiders whip themselves into a frenzy. They chant 'War Blood' with such fervor that it crawls through my body like an infection. The fire seeps into my veins and I feel it consume me. I jump in with the Draiders, screaming 'War Blood' alongside them. Our cries echo in the desert, while our shadows dance on the dunes.

Lee jumps in with me, screaming 'War Blood' at the top of his lungs. The two of us whip the Horsemen into a frenzy, screaming the vicious chant. We march and dance our war dances, while the shaman smears a white balm on our faces. The balm brings relief, but my eyes are full of tears. Between the cayenne pepper and the fury channeled around this fire, I'm overcome with emotion.

Time gets lost in the midst of our revelry. I immerse myself in the mysticism of these creatures and I envy them for it. All of their mysteries are explained by beings in the sky, while in our search for answers we only find more questions which inevitably consume us.

The shaman chants next to the fire, calling upon the protection of Father Sky and their War God. He calls for the death of the priests, that their magic be ended and the children of this world to rejoin Father Sky.

We chant and dance long into the night, until the shaman reaches into his satchel and pulls out another powder. He throws it high and it crashes down, smothering the flame like a blanket. The blue smoke sweeps across the camp, and we're overcome by the urge to lie down and fall asleep.

A figure stands over me. I rise from the ground and feel it give way as my fingers push through the granules. The figure is grainy, as if it were made of sand. I rise up and stand next to him.

He turns and points at a star in the distance, the last one burning amidst the rising dawn.

A gust of wind blows past us, making the figure shift and undulate.

"Silas," the wind whispers. I look around, until I gaze upon a faceless shade. The breeze picks up and whirls sand around us.

"Who are you?" I whisper.

"The one who has watched you since your dawn. Yet only now you've chosen to listen to me."

"What do you want?"

Another gust rushes past us.

"Test..." The sand warrior turns away.

He whips back, bringing his blade down on me. I draw my own to defend.

Our blades clash, and the two of us battle in the dunes. The ringing of steel echoes along the cold wind into the sky.

The sand warrior points at the star in the distance.

"What is it?!" I scream.

The warrior whirls around and bears his blade down on me. I block for dear life, tired while he has unlimited stamina. However, he gets too close. I catch him by the wrist and impale him.

His face shifts from a shade to a mirror of myself. He holds his arms up triumphantly as the wind dissolves his hands

"Don't fear what is to come," The wind whispers. "Have courage and you shall never die..." He fades as the breeze carries him away.

I breathe deep and turn to watch the rising sun, but I don't feel alone.

I look around and realize there's a gathering storm in the sky. Lightning leaps between the clouds and thunder roars overhead. I'm lost in a trance until one of the lightning bolts comes right for me.

I draw my knife as I snap awake, but a figure overhead catches my wrist and covers my mouth.

"Shh..." Sandblade says before he pulls me to my feet.

Everyone is gathering their weapons and breaking camp. Everyone...except for the female Draiders. I look at Sandblade in confusion.

"If we leave without disturbing the females...the Mother of the World has blessed us."

I nod and gather my weapons. I run to catch up with the others, noting how my joints still feel like they're on fire.

"I wonder what it's going to feel like when we pee," Forrest asks.

The Draider with him puts his hand over Forrest's mouth and pushes him into the desert.

Sandblade hops onto a nearby speeder bike and motions for me to take the bike next to him. The engine groans in pain before we speed off into the desert. The horizon opens before us as we race across the razing red earth. I latch my mask on tight as the sands whip around us. My cloak flutters in the wind as we close in 190 kilometres an hour. An entire army of speeders charge the landscape, each face solemn and ready for battle.

The Draiders around me shift their bikes into higher gear and lurch past me, while I notice a shadow creep up behind us. I turn back and see a wall of sand following us.

"Blessed by Father Sky indeed!" Fitch chuckles into the comm.

We push our speeders hard for hours, struggling to keep ahead of the sandstorm.

A temple made of stone rises above the horizon as we close in. A massive fortress built into the mountain and lords over the neighboring river. White figures stand guard over her walls. I zoom in with my visor and see confusion in the faces of our enemy. They're not sure if they should stand and fight, or take shelter from the impending sandstorm.

A glimmer catches my eye and I realize that the fortress is shielded. Any other General would've turn tail and ran.

Not Fitch though.

Our attack force splits in two. I follow Sandblade, who takes us to a bridge on the eastern edge of the complex. I hear the sandstorm roar behind us, a bellowing titan set on devouring all in its path. I steel my resolve, yearning for blood.

Sandblade reaches into his satchel, draws an ion cannon and opens fire. The shield cracks and fizzles, but it holds.

"Save your ammo fellas, my boys have got this," Fitch says over the comm. A beam of light from the sky slams into the shield, and sounds like the planet has been split wide open. The shield dissolves, and the guards retreat into the sanctum.

"Father Sky wills that victory be ours!" Sandblade shouts as the sandstorm sweeps over us.

We veer a hard right and crank the speeder into high gear, but it's too late. Mine has too much sand and has overheated. I abandon the vehicle and charge for the east bridge on foot.

Not to be outdone, the Draiders abandon their speeders and charge on foot beside me.

A glint of sapphire catches my eye. Acting on instinct, I pull the charging Draiders down while the blast flies overhead.

"Damn priests have Xeclian guns!" I growl.

"Does everyone have them but us?!" Forrest asks.

"They said priests wield lightning which strip flesh from bone!" Sandblade screams in his language. "To die in battle with such a foe would be an honor!"

We leap back to our feet, while another blast comes for us. I leap for the wall, but one of the Draiders alongside me is vaporized in an instant. The searing heat radiates in the air, but the Draiders keep charging, unfazed by the blast. I draw my pistols and load them full of shieldbreaker rounds. I fire on the priest, and his personal shield collapses. Sandblade rushes in and ends his life.

He picks up the disintegration rifle and fires upon the priests within the sanctum while the sandstorm rages around us.

"No place to go but to fight them head-on," I say.

"We call this 'Death Ground,' " Sandblade says. "No retreat. No surrender. The Gods bless us so that we can rejoin Father Sky!"

We fight hand to hand with the priests as we take the bridge. They're as fearless as our compatriots, but not as hardened.

Sand spills between the columns as the storm rages outside. Across the walkway, a priest comes flying up and lands on the floor. I hold my pistol close until I see Warrens walk up the stairway.

"Not bad buddy!" I shout. Another priest steps out, taking aim with a disintegration rifle. I leap out and knock Warrens out of the way, while Sandblade steps in and obliterates the priest.

A storm of blaster fire rains down on us just before the Draiders leave the sentry post. The priests are firing down from caves inside the mountain, despite the sandstorm.

"I got this," Warrens says as he swings his gatling gun out front.

"GO!" He shouts. His gun roars to life as a stream of blaster bolts pepper the mountain side, giving us the cover we need to storm the inner sanctum.

We're blocked off by a massive metal door. I notice a keypad to the side and ask which of the Draiders thinks they can get us in.

One volunteers and rips the panel off the keypad. With expert precision, he manipulates the components until the door opens up.

"You guys will do just fine in space," I say to my technical friend.

Beyond the door the walls are made of ceramic and are a beautiful navy blue, decorated to look like the night sky. Intricate figures are carved into the walls and stone columns. The domed ceiling has a carved Draider whose outstretched arms hold onto the sky itself.

The floor features a mosaic of a female Draider who holds her pregnant belly close. The Draiders tread carefully, treating this place as sacred ground.

"Beautiful isn't it?" Fitch asks. More Draiders swarm in, led by Starfall.

"Sure is," I reply.

"Smart propaganda," He says as he looks around the room and points to a figure. "They have the Sun God mocking and fighting off Father Sky, while his brother, the Sand God stands watch over their Mother."

John, Lee and Shepherd join us at the heart of the sanctum.

"We've got the High Priests surrounded General. There's no way out," John says.

"Perfect. Let Starfall take 'em."

"*Shuh muh*?" Lee asks.

"The Draiders need to follow Starfall, not us," Shepherd replies.

Fitch looks at John. "Kid's smart. We got a whole mountain to deal with, but I hope we attacked hard and fast enough so they'll come to their senses and surrender."

"Only one way to find out sir," John says as he cocks his rifle.

"You're right. Starfall! Lead the charge!" Fitch orders.

The Draiders take the lead while the rest of the Horsemen link up with us. We sweep through the mountain, one room at a time in brutal hand-to-hand combat which leaves us exhausted by the time we reach the High Priest's chambers.

Starfall opens the door to the temple. There is a ray of light shining upon an ornate throne, where an elderly Draider is seated.

Our breathing is labored, but the High Priest only has a few soldiers left. His warriors are calm and serene. They draw their blades, which glimmer in the sunlight.

The High Priest looks down upon us with contempt and screams in his native tongue. "[You have defiled this sacred temple! Now there is no one to protect the Mother of the World!]"

Starfall screams back. "[Our 'Mother' has kept us caged! There are worlds full of trees, water and grass, yet you sit here and lord over the fertile ring]!"

"[These foreign devils have filled your mind with lies!]" The Priest screams. "[Rejoining the Gods is to disgrace them!]" He strikes his metallic staff against the floor and a blue orb of energy ignites on top.

"A modified Xeclian rifle," Warrens whispers.

"[You're parasites!]" Starfall screams. "[Feeding off our Mother while you leave the rest of us to scrounge in the sands!]"

"[Enough of your blasphemies!]" The priest roars. "[There is no atonement for you, only to spill your tainted blood!]"

Two warriors charge for us, but they fall to the shieldbreaker rounds in my pistols. The third one is too quick and closes in. I can hear his blade whirl through the air as I weave and dodge, but he's too fast.

An electric charge crackles in the air, and the swordsman in front of me dissolves into a pile of ash. I look to Sandblade, who flashes a mischievous grin.

The Priest's face becomes a mixture of fury and scorn. He whips his staff and points the blue orb at us.

"[The infidels shall not inherit this world!]" He snarls and fires the blast right for Starfall.

Sandblade leaps into the orb's path and catches it against his chest.

"[Unite the tribes! Let us rejoin Father Sky!]" He says before he's consumed by fire.

Bloodstone charges for the throne and seizes the staff. He grabs the priest by the throat and tosses him to Starfall's feet.

"[It is by my hand whether you live or die. Not by the Gods,]" Starfall says to his fallen foe. "[We control our own destiny, and we're going back to the stars.]"

Bloodstone wields the staff and obliterate's the priest's throne. The priest shakes with rage, clawing at the floor as he watches his faith being tested.

"[How do I break the spell which holds us captive?]"

"[Go to Hell you godless savage!]"

Starfall looks to Bloodstone who tosses him the staff. He strikes it against the ground and holds the blue orb over the priest.

"[Does the lightning do it?]" Starfall asks. The priest trembles and tries to scurry away, but Starfall pins him down.

"[How do I break the spell?!]" He screams as he holds the crackling sphere against the priest's leg. The elder Draider screams in agony and claws at the floor like an animal. His flesh blisters under the scorching heat until he gives in.

"[There!]" He points to the throne. "[There's a door behind it - the door to our sacred purity chamber.]"

Bloodstone shoves the rubble aside and finds a stone door.

"[Only the faithful can cross,]" the Priest says.

"Or a guy with a pneumatic fist," Warrens growls. Bloodstone lets him by and the big guy turns the slab to pebbles in a few hits. The two of them stand at the entrance and look down on Starfall.

"After you," Warrens says.

Starfall climbs the stairs and enters through the doorway. One by one we file into a dimly lit, pale blue room.

The room has carvings of the Draider's pantheon of gods along the ceiling, locked in a tale which has been lost to time. At the center is the faint glow of the reactor which keeps us caged on this world.

"Destroy it Starfall," Fitch says. "Be the one who set your people free."

The blue orb crackles in the air, bathing Starfall's stoic features in the soft light.

"It time we rejoin Father Sky!" He shouts in English and fires the orb into the reactor.

The machine whines and groans until it comes to a stop and the room fades into darkness.

Starfall orders all of us to bury the honored dead, including the priests. He has the High Priest perform last rites for all of the fallen, returning them to the Mother of the World. He has the remaining priests swear an oath of loyalty to him, and proclaim him the first sovereign of their world.

We arrive back at the camp as conquering heroes, but there is still a weight on everyone's shoulders. It's as if we were forced to kill our own brother for treachery. It may be justified, but that doesn't make the pain any easier to bear.

The females scrounge together all they can for a bountiful feast. The camp comes alive with song and dance, but we humans gather together for another purpose.

"General, we've been here for over seven weeks, and I've gotta have a report to justify why we've been here so long. Do you want the Core to know about the Draiders?" John asks.

Fitch takes a deep breath and looks out over the camp. "If we tell the Core, they'll either want to annex them or exterminate them. My money is on extermination since this is a desert world with few resources and a population that isn't afraid to stand up for itself."

We stand in silence, unsure of what to say.

"That is why they need spaceflight," Fitch continues. "They need a chance to escape, to colonize, to have a fighting chance."

"The Core will see this as you're helping a hostile alien race escape," Sulture says.

"Wouldn't be the first time I broke the Core's military code," Fitch replies.

"So what happens when the Core inevitably encounters the Draiders?" John asks.

"I don't know," Fitch replies. "They're not afraid of humans. They're not afraid of war. Bad combination for political negotiations. That's why I'm staying, and will help navigate the waters when the time comes."

"I'm worried it's a losing battle," Sulture says. "We may trust them, but the Core likely never will."

"There is one outcome which can work," Fitch replies. "If the Core gets into a war, a devastating one which threatens their existence, then they may get desperate enough to turn to the Draiders for help. In the meantime, I'm here to help them build a fleet, navigate through space and get them conquering worlds. This will give them leverage, and make them a valuable ally."

"A skeptic would say you're placing the pieces for the next war," Shepherd says.

"That's what politics is son. No winning, no losing, only balancing the scales to suit our times."

"Still doesn't help with my report," John says.

Fitch chuckles. "Tell 'em you helped a small band of fighters chase off some raiders. You laid low and learned more about guerrilla warfare than you ever thought possible."

"Speaking of 'laid low,' I sure made-"

"Forrest we don't want to hear it!" John snaps.

"Aww c'mon! I barely said anything while on this planet!"

"Not true," Sujay says. "You just complained incessantly inside the tent about your sunburn."

"You do look like a baby lobster," I say.

"Oh screw you Godfrey! Can't wait to get outta here and back into the black! All this talk about 'rejoining Father Sky' makes me realize how much I miss flyin'."

Warrens and the Draiders get the *Enigma* running after cleaning out the sand sucked through the intake. We gather around the ruling council to say our goodbyes.

"General, it was great to see you again," John says to Fitch.

"John, always a pleasure," He replies. "Thank you Horsemen for joining us. We couldn't have been done it without your help."

"You sure about staying here?"

"I belong with them," Fitch nods to the Draiders. "Besides, you boys have your own war to fight, and I wouldn't be of much use to you. My time to serve again will come, I still got some fight left in me."

"Any words of advice on dealing with our enemy?"

"Gather intel. Learn everything about them - who's in charge and where the money's coming from. Then expose them. An enemy that attacks from the shadows needs the shadows in order to exist. You shine enough light on 'em, and there will be nowhere left to hide."

EVALUATION

Godfrey's Journal, Day 266

It's been an eternity since I've last written. Our time in the Unknown Regions was full of challenges, yet I feel restored somehow. I am replenished and feel whole for the first time in memory. However, our absence has been noted. Madame Chairman Harris has been searching for us, demanding that we show our faces. Her recordings are erratic and panic-stricken. We've made too big of a name for ourselves getting involved with Neuron, and the lawyers are struggling to keep it quiet. I know that an IPC has the power to crush any news they don't want to get out. Why they're not going to bat for us, but blindly funded Overwell's orphan mutation program is beyond me.

John calls for us and his face is grim. "We've been recalled to Earth. Harris is going to personally perform an evaluation of the Horsemen Initiative in order to determine whether it's worth continuing the expense. She's also furious about the contagion which got loose aboard the ship and is demanding to know why we're transporting radioactive cargo - the Hadrian gems."

"I told you those purple rocks were going to get us in trouble!" Forrest shouts.

"The contagion was a freak accident!" I shout. "The canister sprayed after being *bumped*."

"Yeah," Murph says. "Besides, we ejected the virus from the ship and cured Silas."

"I get that, but Harris wants to know *how* Godfrey was cured."

It dawns on me that I never asked about the procedure which saved my life. Murph and Sulture share a look, before fixing their gaze on me.

"What?" I ask.

"We…had to use heavy doses of radiation Godfrey," John explains. "It was all we had available, but if that information was to become public, we'd be shut down for sure. I'm sorry we didn't tell you sooner."

"Were there any…side effects?" I ask.

"So far, no," Sulture replies. "We haven't seen any ill effects, and your body has responded well." While his answer is clinical, Murph averts my gaze.

John interrupts my train of thought. "It wasn't the right call, but it was the only one. Your body wasn't responding to the antiviral, and we had to get rid of the virus."

"Don't worry, the video files and research notes are all under a rolling encryption aboard the *Enigma*," Hacker says.

John sighs. "It may not be enough. We'll have to unlock everything if Harris asks us to."

"What?!" Hacker screams. "And compromise our security?!"

"Doesn't matter, you do whatever the people holding the purse strings tell you to."

An idea snaps into my head. "Why don't we ask her why NuGeno was funding Overwell's experiments? We put Harris on the defensive."

"I don't know if it'll work."

"C'mon John, we're not going to take this lying down."

"I'm not asking you to! I said I don't know if it'll work!"

"Harris is motivated to keep the Centurion experiments buried, along with the idea of renegade scientists operating inside her organization. Can't we have that same level of discretion?"

"I'll try to sell it, but no promises. The best we may be able to get is we show her everything we have aboard the *Enigma.* No download, no recording, no taking any files out of the ship with her. Is that something we can all live with?"

We all nod in agreement, knowing this is the best deal we're going to get.

The ship hisses as it lands and the ramp lowers down. Two suits come walking out, wielding pistols so advanced that our guns look like muskets.

A tiny woman follows, clad in a pant suit and her hair wrapped up in a meticulous bun. Her face looks stretched and her eyes are tired. Her skin is pale, as if she never leaves her ship. Always flying from one meeting to the next.

"The woman we're supposed to be afraid of," I whisper to Hacker.

"Like it or not, she's who granted our freedom, and she can take it away."

John takes Harris on a tour of the *Enigma.* She inspects everything aboard the ship from the navigation computers to the propulsion engines while a team of dock workers come in to unload the bioweapons vault.

In the middle of John's tour Harris' eyes grow wide once inside the special projects area.

Half-buried behind a pile of scrap, a large, metallic humanoid hangs suspended by dietride cables.

"John are you and your men building…mechs?" Harris asks.

"We're currently working to secure the materials. We don't have immediate plans for deployment."

"Did anyone at Ionics authorize this?!"

"No ma'am."

"John, this is what we've been talking about! You and your men conduct these reckless experiments and spend our resources so you can have a human-shaped tank?! What reason could you possibly need them for?"

"Lynn, we've encountered Grigylls, a regenerating hulk, a schoolyard full of enhanced mutations and barely made it out alive from those encounters. I know there is much worse out there and I'm not willing to sacrifice my men when they're smart enough to build that human-shaped tank as you described it."

Harris swallows hard and adjusts her jacket. "I know we've asked a lot from you and your men, but I can't justify the expense of the Horsemen Initiative to the Board any longer. At least not while you're off God-knows-where and won't tell us!"

"I understand that Lynn, but we needed to lie low while the Neuron situation blew over."

Harris sighs. "Do you and the men have any designs or schematics for the mechs? Innovative manufacturing processes?"

"I'd have to ask Warrens, the engineer, but I believe he said he was using nanite assembly. Why?"

"Well, the military is looking into developing mechs and if your team is successful with deployment, Ionics would be...crucial in supplying the military with such machinery. We can also maximize return through any manufacturing processes that can be patented."

I can almost see the credit marks in Harris' eyes.

"I'll be sure to keep you up to date with this Lynn. Godfrey, could you show her the laboratory and what you've been working on?"

I swallow hard, but agree only for John's sake.

I give Harris a tour of the laboratory, but she proves less interested. My sodium hydroxide solution was nothing more than of 'potential interest' by the industrial solvents department. She scans the room, looking for something to exploit, but I can tell in her gaze that she believes the laboratory is a sunk cost. A play set designed to keep rebellious scientists occupied, while her ivory-clad employees will get the credit if our research ever sees the light of day.

I bring Harris back to the meeting area, where the others have gathered.

"Quite impressive isn't it Lynn?"

"Oh yes, it's quite something, lots of potential interest," She replies as she reviews her tablet. "John, there is still one thing that concerns me, There is no record as to how one of the canisters had been activated during transport. Or how Godfrey was cured of this ravenous disease."

"We created an antiviral to deal with the disease," Sulture says.

"Bullshit," Harris snaps. "I read all of the documents connected with the Neogan colonies, and I know how deadly the Crimson Plague is. How did you cure him?!"

John sighs. "Radiation. We managed to use a heavy dose and wipe out the virus."

Harris glares at John. "I don't believe you! Radiation would compromise the thyroid glands, only enhancing the infection. Plus, the amount of radiation needed would burn his cells away."

"Synthetic transfusion," Sulture says. All eyes dart to him, and he looks back at me. "I keep a few pints of blood for each of us available in case of emergencies. I was able to stop the spread of the virus by draining the infected blood and utilizing a synthetic substitute until I could grow enough of what I had in storage to replenish his body."

Harris stares at Sulture, looking like she wants to call him a liar, but has no basis to do so. "John, I'd like to conduct an evaluation of your men individually."

"Lynn, I can vouch for the character of everyone on board."

"Boo-yah! Told you the big guy would keep me!" Forrest shouts. "Suck it chumps!"

Harris rolls her eyes. "I'm afraid that won't be good enough John. I wish to speak with the men individually and want to see the recording from Mr. Godfrey's procedure."

"That's *Doctor* Godfrey," I reply.

"Ohh snap!" Forrest shouts.

Harris glares hard at me. "You don't even exist anymore, so I can call you whatever the hell I want. John, please provide a recording of Dr. Sulture's transfusion procedure."

John and Hacker share a look.

"We don't have it," Hacker replies.

"What do you mean you don't have it?!"

"I didn't record it," Hacker says. "I thought one of my closest friends, a man who saved my life, was going to die and I didn't want us to have to relive that terrible accident."

"Do you know-"

"I can describe how it's done in great detail," Sulture interrupts. "Hope you brought something to write with Madame Chairman."

John leads Harris and Sulture to his office, where she conducts our evaluations. One by one she calls the others in. When I ask them what happened, they avoid my gaze or give me simple answers that get me nowhere.

Finally, my time comes. Harris calls me in, and I sit down across from her at John's desk.

"Mr. Godfrey, I'm concerned about your condition, and I'm not sure if it's worth keeping you as part of the Horsemen Initiative."

"What do you mean my 'condition?' Are you still on the hunt for how I was cured?"

"I'd like to have my team run some tests on you."

"You want to lock me away like an animal."

"I want to ensure that the virus is actually *cured* Mr. Godfrey."

"That's *Doctor* Godfrey. Show a little respect."

Harris' lip tightens and she takes a deep breath. "John said you can be difficult. Look, *Doctor* Godfrey, I don't need the next Typhoid Mary carrying a deadly virus across the galaxy and killing billions of people. It's bad enough you exposed residents on Aurelius Prime!"

"Why don't you trust that Sulture and Murph cured me?"

"It's not a lack of trust Dr. Godfrey, it's a matter of certainty. You running around contaminating the galaxy-"

"It's bad PR is what it is," I interrupt. "Doctors Sulture and Murph are far more qualified to deal with an outbreak of the Crimson Plague than any of your doctors are. But because your team can't be credited with the cure, Ionics can't milk us."

Harris sighs. "What exactly is your problem with this company Dr. Godfrey?"

"My problem is that you allowed NuGeno to actively fund Anson Overwell, a man who experimented on children, while you scrutinize the fact that I had a bad case of the sniffles."

"Dr. Godfrey, Ionics wasn't aware of the fact that Overwell was performing experimentation. In fact, his departure from Ionics was not under good terms. How he managed such a connection is beyond me."

"Somebody believes in his work. Next time you may wanna perform an audit on your subsidiaries. I know Ionics uses them to hide funds on other worlds, but keep better track of general activities. Especially when orphan children are involved."

Harris sighs again. "Our auditors are too busy investigating the expenses the Horsemen have been wracking up. Your legal fees alone make you the most expensive department to maintain!"

"You wanted a team of scientists to go in and act as cannon fodder when your guys fucked up. You wanted us to clear the way for further scientific exploration of new worlds, well guess what: we get things done. It may not be in the cleanest manner, but we bring you results. The Aurelian sector has not only calmed down, your shipping rates have gone down thanks to Neuron's management of the starlane routes."

"I will acknowledge that the Horsemen have done some good for Ionics. However, I still need to keep the safety of our stakeholders as top priority so could you please allow us to run a test and ensure that the Pulmonary Hemorrhagic Virus has been removed from your system?"

"I will only consent to Murph drawing the blood sample." I hated to admit it, but I could see her point in being cautious.

"Very well," She replies. She proceeds to conduct the rest of the evaluation, asking me a series of questions about the Horsemen Initiative. I make sure to use as many scientific terms as I can to sound credible, but most of our time spent is her searching for answers to where we've been. Harris concludes the evaluation with extreme politeness and is quick to follow me as I rejoin the others.

"Your men hold a deep sense of loyalty towards you John. You've always been able to inspire that in others. I've concluded that I'll allow the Horsemen Initiative to continue, however there will be more scrutiny on your activities - this will go across all departments of course. The men have expressed concern over a group called "The Combine" and we will investigate this immediately. In the meantime, Dr. Godfrey has agreed to give us a blood sample to ensure he is not contaminated with the Pulmonary Hemorrhagic Virus."

"Only Murph is allowed to draw the sample," I reply.

Murph's eyes grow wide, but he clears his throat and comes over to me. "You're the only one I trust," I say to him.

"Thanks bud," He replies. "I'll take care of you."

In the medbay, Murph draws a sample of blood under John and Harris' watchful eyes. He runs my sample through the machine, which confirms there are no remnants of PHV in my bloodstream. Harris seems convinced, and prepares to leave the *Enigma.*

No sooner than Harris' ship leaves ours, we receive an incoming call. John patches them through and Neuron appears on the holodisplay.

"Thought the old crone would never leave," He says.

"What is it Neuron?" John asks.

"Got a situation with the Combine's network. After billions of tests, I've concluded that it's impossible to crack their servers. We can't gather any intelligence within their central mainframe."

Hacker cuts into the conversation. "No server is impossible to crack."

"This one is."

"I think your programs are outdated."

"Keep thinking that boy. I'll let you find out the hard way. Also John, I've managed to find where they're housing the program you call 'Slipstream,' and I will pay a generous sum to have it destroyed."

Hacker brings up a screen full of code. "What?!" He screams.

"Told you," Neuron replies.

"What is it?" John asks.

Hacker tries to explain. "As the information travels across their feed, strings of code suddenly become a completely different string. It's like the original command just…vanishes. This is literally impossible! No computer can suddenly change a line of script!"

"In plain English?" John asks.

Neuron interjects. "Imagine I put in a request for access, but then Rome got sacked and plunged Europe into the Dark Ages. That's what is happening here. We put in a command, and we get random garbage back. We start to gather information about their shipping manifests, suddenly I'm seeing mathematical problems. Collecting accurate intelligence through the Combine mainframe is damn near impossible."

"Couldn't you reconfigure the mainframe or deploy a sentinel or-"

"Hacker, listen to me: it didn't work," Neuron says. "I've thrown everything I have at this thing, and it still won't crack. Something tells me this is a 'boots-on-the-ground' endeavor."

"Can you give us a planet?" John asks.

"Sure can," Neuron replies. "But you're not going to like what we found."

"Why's that?"

Neuron sighs. "The facility is on Raml, and is owned by Ionics."

Harris walks across the dark ship to deliver her report. She crosses the kitchen, but doesn't pay attention to what lies in the shadows.

"Did you get it?" A man's raspy voice asks.

"Jesus!" Harris gasps. "I hate it when you do that!" The smell of ozone lingers in the air before settling to the floor.

"Answer the question Lynn."

"They lied to me. All of them, right to my face," She says before she pulls her phone out of her pocket. The crystal clear device lights up as she pulls up a video.

"I knew they would lie to me so I retrieved their video feed myself."

"You can't blame them Lynn. No other team has cured the weaponized PHV I had detonated aboard their ship. All I care about is *how*."

"Let's find out together."

"Unbelievable!" The man gasps. "They've done it! They've reached the God-State."

"Not exactly," Harris replies. "He reverts back in the end."

"It doesn't matter!" He smiles from ear to ear. "This team has proven the theory, and shown that it's obtainable! All we need to do next is replicate the experiment on one of our own."

"We don't have the genetic component either. Nobody can get close enough to retrieve a sample."

"We'll get it, one way or another. The Horsemen Initiative is a rousing success!"

"They're onto the Combine sir."

"A little competition won't hurt anyone."

Harris sighs, then eyes the man carefully. "I hope you're right Dominic."

IT'S ALL IN YOUR HEAD

Godfrey's Journal, Day 283

Neuron claims he's located the origin of the Slipstream file and has given us the Combine's primary server network which is based on Raml. It's owned by another subsidiary of Ionics, the Core Communication Cooperative, a company responsible for interplanetary communication between satellite networks. However, Raml is a desert world with constant sandstorms swirling across the surface. We've been scouting the place for three days, parked among a network of satellites which surround the planet. The numbers indicate that Raml can't sustain life, but somehow the CCC managed to carve out their own facility, down below.

"Why are we still here?!" Forrest shouts. "I thought you guys said this planet was abandoned!"

"No we said the planet *looks* abandoned you *yi dwei da buen chuo roh,*" Lee snaps. "Now quiet down!"

"And alert who?! The sand people? Oh wait, we already did that one!"

John stands up. "Forrest, I get you're antsy, but if this is what Neuron claims it is, the amount of intelligence we can gather on the Combine will allow us to shut 'em down for good."

"Isn't that why we brought the computer nerd? So he can crack into their servers and grab the goods so we can get outta here?"

Hacker pounds his fist on his desk. "I just don't get it!"

"I mean, it's pretty simple. Break in, get the information we need and-"

"No, their security mainframe!" Hacker shouts. "It can't possibly be like this! 98% of their information evaporates into thin air, and I've tried everything to grab onto it! Even my AIs are finding nothing but dead ends."

"Sounds like you're not very good at your job," Forrest replies.

Hacker gives him a death glare. "What we're seeing *doesn't* happen. It's impossible for information to evaporate! Code can't hide in any kind of mainframe like this!"

"Neuron did say 'boots on the ground' would be required," Shepherd says.

John nods. "I know, but with these constant sandstorms, I'd hate to have us fly down in these conditions. The storm isn't letting up."

"Sir," Sujay calls out. "Based on my environmental scans, these sandstorms are near constant. They won't be letting up for some time."

The ship grows silent as we think of a solution to this problem. We can't get in remotely or from the sky.

"Did you try taking over some of their stuff?" Forrest asks Hacker. "You usually do that when we're in a bind." Hacker gives another glare, not even bothering to answer the question.

After the tension builds through the silence, we receive a signal from the surface.

Sujay checks the transmission log. "It's an emergency beacon. They're calling for help. They're even providing landing instructions."

"Landing instructions from a Combine base? Hate to tell you but TRAP!" Forrest shouts.

"Even if it is, we need to risk it," John says. "The amount of intelligence we could get on our enemy is well worth it. Forrest, follow the signal and take us planetside."

Forrest mumbles to himself, but does as he's told.

Sujay leaps up from his seat. "Sir, there is a cyclone forming in the midst of the sandstorm, and it leads right for the surface."

"Incredible," Hacker replies. "They're using technology to control the weather here."

"Follow it down Forrest," John orders.

"Still think it's a trap," Forrest says.

The wind roars and howls outside of the cyclone, but the descent goes down without a hitch.

We land outside of an obsidian complex which is surrounded by an environmental shield to keep the sandstorm at bay. It's almost hypnotic watching the sandy waves crawl around the shield, even forming drifts along the bottom.

"Remember, the air here is damn near poisonous, so suit up accordingly," John says. Once we're suited up we march outside and search for an entrance into the complex. The first thing we notice are the worn carvings along the outer walls, which give the place an alien feel to it, as though we discovered an alien archeological site.

On the roof there is a lone door with a keypad. Hacker keys in a code which was sent up as part of the distress signal. Lee and Sulture stack the door and once it's unlocked, are the first two in.

We file in, keeping close to the walls full of alien carvings. They're all humanoids with a prehensile nose like a tapir and are locked in scenes ranging from ancient battles to being caged inside of pods. Every last one of them has glass eyes too.

"What the hell is this place?" Sulture asks.

"An alien complex?" Shepherd asks. "Did we get the wrong signal?"

Hacker scans the carvings. "No record of them in existence."

"Creepy," I say and take point. I approach a terminal next to a set of doors.

"Think you can get a map or something outta this?" I ask.

Hacker walks up to the terminal. "I'll try."

"Damn it!" Hacker snaps. "The same 'evaporation' occurs here! I don't know if I can unlock it!"

"Keep trying!" John barks. At the opposite end of the building a small patrol droid floats by, oblivious to our presence.

"This is not natural," Lee whispers. "Sentry droids shouldn't be like *dairuomu ji*. They notice everything! This place is too easy to penetrate, too easy to move…unhindered."

"Lee's right, something about this place is off," John says. "Impenetrable defenses which aren't defending the base."

A hiss behind us, and the door opens up. Our guns click as we draw at once, but it's only an elevator.

"You figure it out Hacker?"

"No, it opened on its own."

"Then someone's manning the controls and letting us in."

"I told you: TRAP!"

"Probably, but we're going to face 'em head on!" John says as he climbs inside. We pile in, but notice that even the buttons are written in an alien script.

"Are we sure that this base was built by humans?" Sulture asks.

"We'll find out real soon," John replies.

"My gut says what we're looking for is on the bottom level," John says.

"The worse the secret, the deeper we bury it," I reply.

The squad searches the cold steel hallways for something, anything. This place feels as though it's been stripped to the bare minimum, as though machines are all that's mobile around here.

We turn the corner and notice three laser turrets mounted on the walls at the end of the hall.

"Turrets, high precision caliber too," Warrens says. "But why aren't they firing at us?"

"Maybe this place is abandoned," Shepherd says.

"I doubt it," Murph replies. "Place reeks of antiseptic. This place has been sterilized. *Recently*."

Shepherd inspects the wall. The entire surface is a mural dedicated to the tapir people.

"Are their eyes…cameras?" He asks.

"Yes," Hacker replies. "Whoever is here has been tracking us since we entered."

Sulture gets into Hacker's face. "Why didn't you tell us?!"

"Seemed obvious. Who would put in the effort of glass eyes for decoration?"

Shepherd notices something else. "There's grooves in the walls.

Looks like some carbon scoring too."

"What? Let me see that!" Warrens replies. The two of them follow the lines until they see something in the wall. "This grid here was made by mining lasers. The snout people designed this place to carve up anyone who walked down this hallway, from every angle too!"

"Can we disable them?" John asks.

Hacker scans the welding machines. "Something has turned them off. We've triggered the defense mechanisms, but a command sequence is overriding the defenses."

"Finally, a stroke of good luck!" Forrest says. He walks up to the doors at the end of the hallway and presses a button. The doors slide open, while he turns back and waves at us.

Through the doorway is a dimly lit room. The main source of light comes from glowing servers, which blink and whine as they inhale the air they need to keep cool. Each server is housed in a column that has ornate copper-colored trim snake along the edges of the display glass. The room is air conditioned, but feels clammy. Strange to feel so much moisture in a room housing computer towers.

On the far wall is a lone man who looks to have been sealed into the wall. Hundreds, if not thousands of cables come out of the wall and burrow beneath his skin, leaving black imprints where his flesh has grown back. Past his elbows and knees, his limbs are inside the wall, while his bald head, full of black cables, dangles in place. His eyes are puffy and his red beard glistens from the unknown number of tears he's shed since he was sealed away like this.

I approach him alone, because I feel like I'm in a moment of deja vu.

The man looks up at me, surprised to see another human. When I see his face my breath catches in my throat and my heart seizes in my chest. I know this man. He was one of my best friends growing up. A man I trusted with my life.

James Atler.

I take off my helmet so he can see my face.

"Oh my God, it's you," He says as he gasps for breath. There's a desperate whimper in his voice, as if he's yearning for death. "I sent out the distress signal some time ago and when you landed I disabled all of the security devices so you'd have a clear path through."

"Yeah, thanks for that."

"You're one of the Horsemen now huh?"

"Yeah, I am. What happened to you?"

"Turns out my theories about cyberneural interconnectivity were true," he says as a tear falls down his cheek. "Y'know it's funny, I was a bit thrown off when I saw the Horsemen roster because I saw your face but your name was different. Once I saw where your identity was altered, it all made sense."

"Who did this to you Atler?"

"This was my own doing," He sobs. "I was so close to making a breakthrough in my research, but my son got really sick. I poured everything I had into finding a cure, but the disease was too aggressive. Someone from the Combine approached me and said they could help."

"At what price?"

"Once I realized what they were doing with my neurology research, I tried to get out, I swear it! They took my son captive and said if I didn't work, then he'd die. Because of me, the Combine learned how to rewrite neural pathways with *software*!"

"Slipstream," I whisper.

"Oh Silas, it's become far worse than that. Now they've altered the program to the point where if they sense disobedience, the software erases memories and implants new ones so you forget everything but the Combine."

"That cursed program!" Warrens growls. "I wish I'd never found that metal!"

"What's your part in all of this now?"

"He didn't want me wandering off, so he took my arms and legs and plugged me into the network which manages the entire Combine database."

The rage burns inside me. "Who?! Who did this to you?!"

Atler looks at me, frozen. "I…I can't say his name. Not out of loyalty, but he ensured that I can't physically say the names of the leaders within the Combine. Think of it as a password protection."

"I could get Hacker over here and he can find it."

"It's not that simple. The network here on Raml is powered by neural activity. The signals are transferred along the neural pathway and switch between electrical and chemical so a computer would be of no use."

"That's it!" Hacker screams. "That's why Neuron and I couldn't get in!"

"I'm afraid so," Atler replies. "I felt the two of you probing my defenses, and I couldn't have let you in even if I'd wanted to. Another technology I was forced to invent," He sobs.

My blood boils. I want answers. I want to know who did this.

"Wait, you store the Combine's entire digital mainframe inside of your brain?" Hacker asks.

Atler looks up. "No matter how advanced we get, we can't replicate the intellectual capacity of the human brain. Microchips stopped being practical, then they developed cloud technology. Then we hit a wall, but the Combine found the next step thanks to me," He sobs again.

The walls around us begin to shimmer. Where we once saw servers, we realize it's a hologram. From the walls human beings emerge, all of them unconscious with as many cables coming out of them as Atler has.

"*Wo Bu Shin Wo Dah Yan Jing,*" Lee hisses.

"We don't believe our eyes either," John replies.

My eyes grow fuzzy and I stumble backwards. I see something which I know I've seen before. An army with the same face flashes before my eyes.

"They're clones," I say.

"Monsters!" Shepherd shouts. "They're using human beings to serve as their mainframe!"

The clones slip beneath the surface of the hologram to rest once more. Atler raises his head to us. "My goal was enhanced memory, and apparently the Combine had access to a cloning facility. While clones are genetically unstable, their neural capacity is sufficient to serve as part of the mainframe here."

"How many clones are here?" Shepherd asks.

"Hundreds."

"Can you set them free?"

"It won't do them any good. They're functionally brain dead and wouldn't be able to survive outside of here."

Sulture draws his pistol and aims it at Atler."What *can* you do for us?"

"I can tell you *some* things," Atler replies. "I can tell you the new program they use to brainwash people is called 'Cerex.' In fact, I can give it to you."

Hacker looks to John who silently nods. He plugs in one of his computers and downloads the program.

"If you have a hologram, I can show you how it works," Atler says. Hacker projects a hologram of the human brain for all of us to see. A small silver object goes inside, and we follow in.

"We place the device into the cortex and the hippocampus. As I said, my intent was to enhance memory, but the Combine leadership changed the code using the program you refer to as 'Slipstream' and they use a combination of neurochemicals and electrical signals to alter brain chemistry. If anyone betrays Him, old memories are wiped out while new ones are implanted to make them devout to the Combine."

"Who's implanted with this chip?" John asks.

"Everyone within the Combine."

"*Everyone?!*" Shepherd asks.

Atler bursts into tears. "I'm afraid so. We've had defectors who've lost their minds, only to come back as devoted servants with access to all of their skills as scientists."

Murph cuts in. "Aren't there side effects? That's as dangerous as a lobotomy!"

"The dissonance between remnants of old memories and implanted ones has driven multiple subjects insane. They're unable to emotionally process the fragments which remain."

"Do people know they're being implanted with this chip?" Shepherd asks.

"Most don't even know they have been."

"Who is He?" I ask. "The leader of the Combine?"

Atler tries to speak, but he seizes against the wall and his eyelids flutter. "I can't physically say His name."

"Then we need a list of *every* member of the Combine you *can* give us."

"What good will that do?" Sulture asks.

"If the Combine is as vast as they claim, and their leader can turn them all into devoted automatons at a whim, then we need somewhere to start. If we can't find the Combine leadership, we should go after the rank and file."

Atler seizes against the wall.

"I'm sorry, he's trying to get in. You'll be exposed in minutes."

"Then upload the list," John replies. Atler nods, and compiles a list of names, titles and positions. He uploads a detailed database onto Hacker's computer. We scan where these people are, where they work. There are thousands in the military, the Core government, Samson Research & Development and…Ionics."

"How up to date is this file?" I ask.

"It's a live feed."

I feel a knot form within my stomach. With all of these people who have access to chemicals, pathogens and other technology carrying a chip that could wipe away their memories…there's no telling of the destruction that can be wrought.

None of us know what to do with this information. We look to each other for guidance, but there is none to be found.

"Atler, can you wipe us from the Combine's database?" John asks.

"It's purely theoretical. I can't wipe out *all* information but-"

"Atler, I'm asking you to make us invisible to the Combine."

He seizes against the wall, which is disturbing. I wish I could help, but there's little I can do.

Atler comes back to us. "I can't delete your information, it's on a security level that's beyond my clearance."

"You run the mainframe!" John snaps.

"I understand this, but keeping your information secure is a top priority to those I serve. I can lead your programmer there, but beyond that he'll need to delete the information on his own."

"Good enough," John replies. Hacker plugs in his computer while Atler goes back under. Hacker types frantically, sweat glistening on his bald head. He scours the database for any reference to us and deletes it, breaching security multiple times in the process. Atler keeps the defenses at bay, but he's getting worn out in the process.

Atler snaps out of it, which forces Hacker out.

"I'm sorry," He gasps.

"I got what I could. Nobody has defenses like that - the ability to make everything shut down in an instant."

"It's when the synapses convert the electrical signal into a chemical one. I pulled as much as I could have you access, but..."

"We get it," John replies softly. "There's only so much a man can do."

The pain in Atler's face makes me yearn for justice. I want to hunt down who did this to him. He looks at me with tear-filled eyes, and all I can see are the black cables protruding beneath his skin. He's been here so long his skin has grown over them. They've become a part of him.

I look down at my pistol, wondering if it holds the answer.

"Killing me won't help," Atler says. "The network is designed to replace my memories and regenerate my body. The rest of the clones... their information will be uploaded to a backup network until a new batch of clones arrive."

"Where do the clones come from?" Shepherd asks.

"Trinitian - 6. They have a breeding facility there."

"That's the place where the military was gonna send Golden Boy!" Warrens says.

"Sure is," John replies. "Looks like that's where we need to go next. But how do we shut this place down Atler?"

"You'll need a malware program which will devastate the Combine's network. If you upload it into me, I'll send it through the satellite network to all of the mainframes. Then we can contain what's left by shutting down the uplink and letting the program run loose here."

"Hacker?"

"On it," he replies. "Got an AI I've been working on for months which will corrupt everything linked to this network."

"There is a caveat. If you upload something and it attacks this mainframe, my neural processor will activate and turn me against you."

"Can't we surgically remove the processor?" I ask.

"No. Attempts at removal either activates the processor or sends an electrical pulse strong enough to kill the victim."

"Bastards made it so none of their boys will come outta this alive," Murph grumbles.

"Who is this madman?" I ask.

His eyes are shaky as he tries to find the words. "You will know his face. He will use that against you. He will try to convert you just like he did us."

"Who?! Who else is with him?!"

Atler seizes against the wall. "I…can't say…their names. People we knew. Fallen friends. This is all a game to him. He will use whatever he can against you. All of you."

"Isn't there *anything* we can use against him?!" I shout.

"I'm sorry, but I won't be of much help. Corrupting the Combine's network will be the best place to start."

John puts his hand on my shoulder. I look back at him, and he wears an expression of grief that I know all too well.

"Upload the AI into me," Atler orders. "I'll spread it across the entire Combine network. After that, follow the layout I've provided because you'll need to run like hell."

I have hundreds of questions for Atler. All of them flood my mind at once, freezing me in time as the rest of the team gears up for our escape. I can only make out fragments of what Atler is saying, something about ionic clones and mechanical limbs. I search deep into my memories of who our nemesis could be. Countless names and faces, but this one eludes me. I don't know who it could be.

"GODFREY!" John's shout snaps me out of my stupor. Everyone is looking at me, waiting for a response.

Atler breaks the silence. "It was good to see you one last time. I wish you the best, and that you find the peace which has eluded you for so long."

Finally, one question comes to the front of my mind. "Where is your son?"

"He took him away to a place where even I can't see him. Someplace called Centurion Academy."

The team flashes me a grim look. I walk up to Atler and put our foreheads together.

I lie to him. "We'll find him, I swear it!"

"I know you will and I will provide you with everything I can, but when I tell you to run, do it."

"Goodbye Jim."

"Goodbye Ri-, I mean Silas."

Hacker rushes in and plugs in his computer. He takes over the satellite network and downloads as many files to the *Enigma's* mainframe as he can. Atler seizes against the wall, pulling as much as he can out of the Combine's network.

Atler convulses and slams himself against the wall for what feels like an eternity. Hacker spins and wields his dataset with complete mastery. The two work in tandem until Atler's eyes open wide.

"RUN!"

Hacker rips his cord out and we retreat. The clones behind the holographic walls come to life and claw at us as we try to escape. Their eyes are as black as space. The team brawls with the clones, punching their way out. I look back at Atler who is beating himself against the wall, almost like he's trying to free himself. His eyes are the same empty black as the others.

He's a shadow of the man I knew.

"Intruder alert!" His shadow screams. On the edges of the room there's a faint hissing from tubes being disconnected. Doors to pods are thrown off, and I see what Atler meant by the Ion Clones. They're bald, translucent figures whose veins carry ionised plasma which give them a terrifying glow.

We cut the first two down, but that only drives the rest into a fervor.

We come back to the hallway with the grooves carved from mining lasers…except this time they're active. They weave and shift, daring someone to make the attempt.

"It can't ever be a simple 'We're outta here!' and we just walk onto the ship can it?!" Forrest screams.

Behind us the Ion Clones lay down wave after wave of blaster fire from devices embedded in their wrists.

Warrens activates his personnel shield. "I got an idea!" He charges at the clones, grabs one of them and drags it towards the hallway.

"GET DOWN!" We dive to the ground as Warrens lifts the clone above his head and throws it into the hallway. The explosion rumbles the installation, and Warrens nearly collapses after blocking the blast. John leaps up and hoists Warrens over his shoulder.

"Move out!" The rest of us leap from the ground, while I can hear Atler's shadow screaming in the next room. His convulsions echo like thunder and drive us forward.

Shepherd and I guard the rear from the oncoming clones. I hear a whir from the ceiling. It's the hanging turrets.

I activate my personnel shield and brace myself so I can give the others time to get out of there. They open fire and deplete the shields within seconds. I back away as fast as I can, but the shield breaks. I feel a searing pain through my gut and realize I've been hit.

Just before I make it around the next corner, I see Atler's shadow howl at me and break free of his confines.

"Intruder alert! Seal all the doors!"

Once I make it around the corner, Atler's shadow towers over me in a mech suit.

"None shall escape the Combine!" The shadow raises his fists and comes down over me. I roll out of the way, while he smashes the floor.

Murph and Shepherd lay down a wave of suppressive fire, but the shadow's shields are too strong. I see the black eyes, but I still believe there's a chance my friend Jim Atler is still in there.

"What is my name? Who am I?"

The shadow snarls at me. "Silas Godfrey, the man who tried to get me to betray the Combine!"

Atler's shadow slams his fists down and looks me in the eye. "Now you will join or die!"

In his eyes I see nothing but pure evil. His voice is hollow, reciting words but unable to put emotion behind them. His soul was stolen by the monsters who created him, and I have no choice but to put an end to this.

I reach down and cock both pistols.

Then I draw them.

But the shadow was faster than I was.

He slaps me like a rag doll into the wall. The others turn and open fire, but he blocks with his arm.

I'm seeing stars and my ribs burn, but deep down I find the resolve to press on. I dive between the shadow's feet and open fire, but I miss twice. The shadow puts his foot on me and presses down until my ribs crack.

Sulture unloads a clip, trying to drive the shadow back. He's fearful of getting hit, because he's always blocking his face. He finally backs off of me, while Shepherd dives in and pulls me out.

"I will kill the traitor!" The shadow howls. He bats Shepherd away and seizes me in his steel grip. He clamps down and I feel more ribs break.

"Silas, you've experienced traumatic damage to your torso. Another blow and you will suffer irreparable internal organ damage," Emie says.

I can feel that one of my arms is free. I cock my pistol and shoot the shadow, my blast tearing through his shoulder. He looks up at me and screams, as if he's trying to force emotion to come through.

Hacker activates his suit's computer systems and tries to take over the mech armor for himself. The others fire on the shadow, trying to draw his attention.

He throws me at the group, who manage to catch me. I look into the shadow's eyes and I know somewhere in there our enemy is watching us.

"Cover me!" I scream.

"Godfrey! No!" John roars.

Hacker breaks through and takes control of the armor, forcing the hands to rest against the floor. I pick up my pistol and close in. The shadow snarls at me again before he regains control.

But not before I'm standing over him on the mech's collar.

"I'M COMING FOR YOU!" I wheeze into the shadow's face. I realize what it will take to put an end to the Combine. Thousands of innocent men and women will need to die and there's no way we can save any of them.

And their deaths all begin with James Atler.

I gasp for air and fire twice through the shadow's head. The mech collapses and I tumble to the floor. I tear off my visor and throw up. Blood is speckled throughout. Murph rushes in and pats me on the shoulder.

"Don't worry bud, it's all over."

"No it's not," I wheeze. "The war has just begun."

SEEING DOUBLE

Godfrey's Journal, Day 285

We barely survived our escape from Raml. We killed the remaining clones - both the mainframe and the Ion breeds, but we suffered many injuries in the process. Despite the pain, we're racing for Trinitian - 6 to wipe out the clone facility. I'm haunted by the blackness of Atler's eyes. I'm unsettled by how evil our enemy is. The fact they implant every one of their members with a chip designed to brainwash or kill...such evil needs to be destroyed. Warrens is traumatized by the program he's unleashed, and spends his time tinkering in the lab. The extent of the damage from this program is taking its toll, and he sees it as his fault.

Murph comes in to check on me while I recover in the Medbay. My abdomen is black and blue and a respirator keeps me breathing.

"Man, you survived a lot," He says. "Eight fractured ribs, one of which pierced your lung and three fractured vertebrae. You're lucky to be alive - after that kind of assault, chance of survival was about 13.3%."

"Look at you doing math," I reply. I'm tired from the drugs, but we have a mission. I need to be prepared for it. I try to sit up, but Murph pushes me back down.

"Sorry bud, no can do. John wants to talk to you anyway." Murph steps aside to leave the room, while John sits down next to me.

"I'm sorry you had to put down Atler like that. Nobody should have to kill one of their closest friends."

"That *thing* wasn't my friend anymore."

"I get that, but he helped us a lot. His sacrifice wasn't in vain. Sulture's running tests on his brain tissue to see if there's any way we can deactivate those chips."

"Wait, where'd he get a brain tissue sample?"

John sighs. "From your clothes."

I feel my stomach bubble as John explains that Neuron's helping out since we sold him the satellite network over Raml.

"Whatever we're up against, they promised they'd cure Atler's son and then sent him to that shit hole Centurion Academy. John, what are we up against?"

He sighs. "Someone who doesn't want loose ends."

"What's worse is I'm supposed to know who this freak is!"

"Do you?"

"No," I sigh.

"Hacker was wondering if you may know who the overseer of Trinitian - 6 is. Here's a profile we recovered on Raml." John hands me a tablet, and I recognize the man immediately. Another old friend of Jim and mine from our past.

"Syd Smythe," I curse as I hand the tablet back to John. "It's as if this guy targeted all of my friends during recruitment."

"Not surprising. Groups like these thrive on the social networks of their members. Come on, you can help us gather intelligence."

I stumble into the main area where the group is performing reconnaissance over Trinitian - 6. It's a small sapphire gem peppered with archipelagos wrapped in sunlit white sand beaches. Looks like a paradise.

"So…I'm going to relax on the beach while you guys save the galaxy from the clones." Forrest says. The entire crew glares at him.

"Oh c'mon! I can't take them! There's gotta be *thousands* if not *millions* of them down there! How are we supposed to take on all of them?!"

"We don't," John replies. "At least not yet."

"We could if we had mechs," Warrens growls.

John sighs. "Seeing what we've been up against, we can push forward. In the meantime, let's come up with a plan."

Hacker starts us off. With a wave he shows us a hologram of the cloning facility. Only 10% is above ground, while the rest is buried beneath the ocean. He points out that the ground floor is where the clones are picked up and shipped off to God knows where. Below ground he outlines the base by floor. There's an armory, electrical and life support, training modules and a nursery. The bottom floor is a mystery since he was unable to get any useful information. He switches to a group of clones in formation.

"I recognize their faces," Shepherd says. "They were created from people I knew, people I served with."

"*Ta muh duh*," Lee says.

"You likely knew the origin patients," Murph interrupts.

"Origin patients?" Shepherd asks.

"Clones are inherently unstable genetically speaking. Their risk for infection is 53% higher than a natural born human, so they harvest healthy cultures from the origin donor in the event one of the clones has a kidney failure, for example. Good news is they'll do everything possible to keep the origin patients alive."

"We have to rescue them!" Shepherd says.

"We may not be able to," John replies. "Our top priority is intelligence. Our mission is to extract Syd Smythe and see what he knows."

"Sir, it is our duty to-"

"Son, do *not* tell *me* about duty!" John snaps.

"Ha! Doodie!" Forrest shouts.

John growls. "Now I know you value human life and that you seek justice. I know those boys were ones you served with, and if we had the resources, I'd liberate all of 'em. We have to use what we've got to outsmart the enemy. Finally, my money's on if we tamper with 'em, they'll be killed."

Shepherd swallows hard. Logically John's right, but the kid's staring him down.

"Stand down Shepherd. That's an order."

"Yes sir."

Godfrey's Journal Day 287

Reconnaissance is the most boring part of my job. We watch the guards to learn their mannerisms and habits. One thing's for sure: clones are unbelievably dull. They're creatures of habit and don't bullshit with one another. The bald nitwits don't laugh or joke around. They only speak with each other when there's a shift change. There's no sense of camaraderie. Maybe it's because they don't know what to say to the same person. I don't know, seems messed up psychologically.

Hacker calls us into the meeting room and displays a hologram of a brain in the center of the room.

"I've run multiple scans on the clones below because of a comment that Atler made," He says. "Here is a projection of a clone's typical brain activity." The hologram reveals where the neural activity is concentrated.

"Why so much activity in the right posterior cortical and the hippocampus?" Murph asks.

"Does that mean something?" John asks.

"Well activity in this region means the individual is more empathetic and emotional. It's very sensitive to the needs of others."

"It could also mean they're xenophobic and will kill outsiders without hesitation," Sulture replies.

"I'm glad you mentioned that Murph. Here's a scan of a normal human brain." Hacker projects a second brain next to the clone's. There's more neural activity from every region of the brain, whereas the clone's is more concentrated.

"Interesting," Murph says. "The normal brain is 23% larger."

"True, but that's not all." Hacker brings up three more brain scans and layers them all on top of the clone brain.

Their neural activity matches up perfectly.

"What?! Impossible!" Sulture screams.

"What does it mean?" John asks.

Murph cuts in. "Even clones have individual thought patterns. They may ask different questions or one can interpret a gesture slightly differently. The only way this scan could be possible was if all of the clones were the *exact* same person, which is theoretically impossible. Nobody's raised with the exact same circumstances."

"That's not all," Hacker says with a wave. Three different profile pictures are displayed. "These are all different specimens. Genetics should play *some* part in their mental configuration."

"Any theories?" John asks. The rest of us look to one another. We've got nothing.

"Mind control?" Forrest asks.

"Go on."

"Well, if Godfrey's buddy is right and they altered that learning program Slippery and if they're all implanted with chips, maybe they changed one enough so that one guy can control them all."

"That actually sounds plausible," Hacker replies. "Aside from how you butchered Slipstream."

Sujay rolls his eyes. "Oh sweet Vishnu, we're going along with one of *your* theories?!"

"It's about time!" Forrest cheers. "Does this mean I get a beach day?"

"No," John replies. "It means we need to prepare for extraction!"

At dusk John has the *Enigma* lie in wait for the next transport ship to take the clones off world. The minute one crosses our path, we fire off a round of electromagnetic inhibitors which stop the engines cold. From there we climb aboard and knock out the crew members. John pilots the ship, while he tells Forrest he'll give the all-clear for when they can land.

John navigates through the pristine airspace and searches for a dock with minimal supervision. Hacker works to cut the video feed, grateful that the systems on this planet aren't being controlled by clone brains.

John docks the ship at one of the receiving terminals. He whispers something to Warrens, while Lee slaps me in the shoulder.

"You ready *lao sheong?*"

"Sure," I reply. I breath hard through the pain. I won't allow myself to slow down when my friend's lives are on the line.

"Then let's go!" John roars from the back. The door slams open and we charge out. A handful of guards see us, but we cut them down. We find a stairway which will keep us away from prying eyes. We file down into the depths until we reach life support systems. We take out the handful of guards in the room. Within moments, we control the lives of a clone army.

On the screen are thousands of pods with clones inside them. Another screen shows them all dining together, a third shows them in combat training.

"Do it now," John says.

Sulture removes two vials from his belt and inserts them into the ventilation systems. Hacker turns off all filtration systems and lets the pathogens run rampant. Sulture calmly inserts two more vials into the vents. We watch the screens until one of the clones grabs at his throat and collapses. More cough and choke until they too collapse.

"What about the origin patients?" Shepherd asks.

"We couldn't differentiate between the clones and the boys," Murph replies. "Sorry David."

"We can't do this! Otherwise we're no better than they are!" He howls.

"We need to thin the herd and find the scientists responsible," Sulture says.

Hacker searches the camera feed, including recordings from the past twenty-four hours. "There's Smythe!" He shouts. We take down his position and move out.

The alarm triggers as we leave life support. The lights switch to red as the speakers call out 'Contamination Alert.' Hacker takes point and leads us through the complex to where Smythe should be.

A clone guard calls us out. We fire a few rounds, but he's still standing. It's only when he holds up his hand we realize why.

It's an Ion Clone.

He fires a blast, while Warrens steps in front to block with his shield. The bolt tears the shield apart. We return fire, dropping the plasma-blooded freak.

Murph retrieves a sample of the clone's blood while Sulture runs a scan on his fingertips.

"The plasma is burning off all the virons," Sulture says.

"Hopefully there aren't too many of them," John replies. "Let's keep moving."

Hacker guides us back through the stairway to the laboratory where Smythe was being recorded. We stack the door, throw it open and call for all of the scientists to get on the ground.

Except that nobody is standing.

We spread out and search the laboratory. Each body is still warm and their lab coats are splattered with blood.

"Here's Smythe," Hacker says. I go to the front, and laying in a pool of his own blood is my old friend with a bullet wound right through the head.

"Wonder why they were all executed."

Papers fly across the tables as though a wind blew through. Doors slam shut and the locks click in place.

"Because they didn't immunize the soldiers," a slithery voice hisses from the shadows. The figure steps into the light. It's a bald Asian man with pale blue eyes. Six ion clones swarm in, their energy blasters trained on us.

"*Wuo duh tian ah,*" Lee says. "General Quan Sito, you *lio coh jwei ji neong hur ho deh yung duh buhn jah j'wohn.*"

"How dare you refer to a Colonel of the Core as a son of a stupid drooling whore and monkey?

"*Fuhn pi.* You died at Zhao's hand. I suppose that's why you got demoted from General."

Quan chuckles. "You only thought he killed me."

"Even then, the Core would've arrested you along with the other tyrants on Ophridia."

"They did, but my benefactor saw…other plans for me. Like luring you and your friends into this trap. Once again Xing Ming Lee, you overreach."

"Why is your organization creating an army of clones?" John asks.

Quan shifts his gaze over to John. "A war is coming, and an army is needed to defend the Core."

"Who do these copies answer to?" Murph asks. "Someone must control them."

Quan looks over each of us, sizing us up. "I do."

The clones rush us. Their ion blasters whine as they power up. Lee disappears using his cloaking device while the rest of us dive into a brawl for survival. I draw my knife and swing at the one closest to me. They flinch whenever we hit them, but barely. It's as if they're suppressing their ability to feel pain.

I look at Quan, who is watching our every move in fascination. There's a maniacal look in his gaze and then I realize it.

"He's suppressing the pain of the clones!" I shout. "It's why they keep coming!"

The clones attacking Murph and Shepherd fall away and focus on me.

"Very observant Dr. Godfrey."

I notice a reflection of light flicker behind Quan. Just as Lee is about to land the killing blow, an ion clone shoots him in the back. The cloaking machine sparks and Lee materializes out of the air.

Quan turns around. "Such a habit Lee. You overreach. I have many eyes and many ears at my command." He reaches down and picks Lee up by the neck.

I attack the three in front of me, while Murph and Shepherd attack from the back. The ion clones aren't giving up.

The one in front powers up his palm blaster. I spin towards him, loop my arm around his and pull the arm until it's pointing at one of his buddies.

The other clone ducks out of the way and I curse under my breath. The bastard almost got hit, but I realize that Quan is looking at me as he chokes the life out of Lee.

He's *focusing* on *me*.

"John!" I scream. "Have Forrest and Sujay bomb the front door!"

"We can't yet! We need our getaway!"

"Trust me!"

"Henry to Eagle, Henry to Eagle! Knock on the front door! I repeat: knock on the front door!"

"Eagle is en route!" Forrest replies.

"Murph! Shepherd! Go after Quan! Don't worry about me."

The two let go of the clones and charge Quan. His other clones break off their attack and circle around him.

Warrens howls and shifts his armor plates into his fists. He attacks the ring of clones, sending two flying and breaking one's jaw.

A rumble echoes across the base and Quan looks into the distance. The clones near me get sloppy, making amateur mistakes. I pull on one's arm and stab him in the neck. The clone gurgles and for the first time in this battle, I see Quan straining to keep his attention on me.

Warrens swings wildly, breaking the ring of clones protecting Quan. He catches Quan's attention while Lee draws a knife and stabs it through the Colonel's arm.

Quan drops him and looks back at me.

The two clones fight with renewed ferocity, but Warrens breaks off his attack to help me. The two of us end the ion clones quickly, while Quan has nothing left.

"He said you Horsemen would've been a challenge to keep in my snare."

"Who?!" John asks. "Who said that?!"

Quan regains his composure as he backs towards the exit.

"On Ophridia, you may have been the 'Hunter,' but now we're hunting you," Lee says.

"Indeed you are," Quan replies. "But you will overreach. It's in your nature. And I will be ready for you."

Quan backs out through the doorway. Lee and I follow him, but there are dozens more ion clones lying in wait. They power their blasters up, but we slam the door shut before they fire on us.

"Trapped like rats!" Lee hisses.

"Hacker, seal the door!" John orders. The loud click feels like a nail has been driven into our coffin.

John paces the room. "We have dozens outside waiting for us. Only a matter of time before they breach the door."

"Is there a way to mess with their programming?" Shepherd asks.

"It's too late now," Hacker replies. "Once it's in their heads, it's beyond my reach."

"Shoulda finished the mechs," Warrens grumbles as he sits down. He looks around at the bodies on the floor.

"Hey Doc, could you do some field surgery?"

"Sure, what's wrong?" Murph replies.

"Oh it ain't for me," Warrens replies. He bends down to the floor, picks up one of the ion clones and slams it on the table.

"It's for my recently deceased friend."

Murph and Warrens dissect the ion clones, seeking to understand what makes them tick. We struggle to comprehend how the plasma state could be sustained without destroying the host. However, it's a miracle that the ion clones are still held together at all.

Sulture is looking through a microscope. "Their cells have nearly melted from being in such a constant high-energy state," He explains. "I would theorize that these clones are 'activated' and then sent into battle, unexpected to ever return."

"Is it possible to wait them out?" Shepherd asks.

Sulture shakes his head. "They'll melt the walls long before they fall apart."

"Great info Rooster, really appreciate the biology lesson," Warrens says as he reaches into the chest cavity.

"What did I tell you about calling me that?"

Warrens rips out a few devices embedded within the clone. "Help me get these faster and you can share your bio findings all you want."

Electromagnetic nanotubes carry the plasma through the body, while the reactor in the chest creates and stores the plasma. The other components are beyond my ability.

"What are you doing with those reactors?" Sulture asks.

Warrens puts his machine gun on the table. "Upgrading Rolanda. Giving her an unlimited power source."

The rest of us need to wait until Sulture and Murph dissect the remaining ion clones. Lee paces the room.

"I need to kill that *huen dahn*, he cannot run wild through the galaxy," He mumbles to himself.

The blasters echo outside and the walls are smoldering.

"You're running outta time Warrens," John says. The big guy gets less gracious about how he removes the reactors from the clones.

A piece of concrete tumbles down and splatters on the floor.

"They've breached the room!" Shepherd says.

"Just in time," Warrens replies. "Mind opening the door for me Circuit?"

Hacker swipes the holograms until we hear the lock click. More concrete splatters on the floor. Shepherd grabs the handle and rips the door open.

Warrens hoists his gatling gun onto his hip and opens fire. The reactors on his belt glow bright as they churn, sending plasma bots through his machine gun.

The ion clones are caught off guard, but they don't break rank. Warrens' gun fires at such a high frequency that the barrels glow red within minutes.

"Dammit!" Warrens screams. "Thought Rolanda could handle these plasma reactors, but I guess I was wrong!"

John and Shepherd open fire on the clones. Dozens of them have been killed, but many more keep coming.

"How many of these things are there?!" Shepherd screams.

"Enough that we need to find who's making these reactors!" John replies.

The wall protecting us has given out from the blaster fire, and the enemy is closing in on us. There's no way we can defeat an army boxed in like this. I think of a weakness. Any kind of weakness…

"Hacker!" I shout. "All of the clones have the exact same brain pattern right?"

"Yeah…"

"We know Quan controls them, so what happens if we take him out?"

Hacker projects a simulation and tests my theory. "If this is accurate, they should downgrade into a vegetative state."

"*Gao guhn*!" Lee shouts over my shoulder. "I'm going to hunt that *feh feh pi goh*."

"We all are!" John snaps. "We're not separating!"

"We need something to break the stalemate," I shout.

"This outta do it!" Warrens replies as he holds up five reactors strung together.

"Holy shit! Everyone take cover!" John shouts.

Warrens pulls the pin to a grenade and swings the string of reactors. He throws them into the crowd.

The pale blue explosion tears through the ranks and shakes the facility to its very foundation.

"Move out!" John roars. We charge through the fallen wall and search out the psychic commander.

We find him rubbing his temples in an open room. Lee knocks him to the floor and holds a knife against his throat.

Quan coughs and looks admiringly at Warrens. "Well done using the reactors. No wonder why you were able to conquer that savage land."

"*Bee-jway*!" Lee hisses. "No more words for you."

"You may want to hear my last ones."

"*Ta ma duh*, what is it?"

"One of you is missing, and I know where he is." We look among ourselves, taking a silent head count.

"Where's Shepherd?!" John howls.

"He went to save the origin patients, but he'll never make it past the others. I see him run through my halls. They will catch hi-" A sadistic grin spreads across Quan's lips.

"*Go hwong tong*!" Lee presses the knife against his throat.

"Lee don't!" John cries. We look up and see a pair of the ion clones dragging Shepherd back to us. Their palm blasters are charged, a high-pitch whine. And they're pointed at Shepherd's head. More of the ion clones follow and inevitably surround us.

"Call them off!" Lee hisses.

Quan chuckles. "Once again you've been caught in my snare. It seems you and your friends never learn. I outlasted Yiu Mei and I'll outlast the Horsemen."

Lee pulls the knife away from Quan's throat. Our hearts sink as he withdraws, but he keeps his hand on Quan's shoulder.

"Shields up," Lee says.

We look around in confusion, but the clones turn vigilant, drawing their blasters on us.

Quan's eyes grow wide. "You sneaky little-"

We draw our shields as the clones loose a volley on us. I watch Lee get hit twice as he pulls a bloody knife from the back of Quan's skull. He falls to the floor, while the room falls silent.

The clones are still standing, but their heads are sunken and their empty gaze is at the ground.

Murph leaps into action to help Lee, who's suffered two traumatic hits to the torso.

"Eagle, we're ready for pickup," John says into the comm.

"Eagle is on its way to save the day!"

John glares at Shepherd, who emerges from beneath the two clones unscathed. The kid must have quick reflexes.

"Murph, when Forrest and Sujay arrive, take Lee onto the ship and patch him up. The rest of you, come with me." John reaches down and grabs Shepherd by the collar.

We follow John through the maze of collapsed clones, either through disease or being braindead. We wave in front of their faces and shove them over to make sure this isn't another trap.

"John, what are you doing?!" Shepherd asks.

He walks silently through the facility until we reach the pods containing the origin patients. Their vital signs indicate they're still alive.

"They survived," Sulture gasps.

"They have their oxygen filtration system buried deep underground," John replies. It was as if he knew the whole time.

John throws Shepherd at the foot of one of the pods. "There they are. The people you put us at risk for."

"We have to do what is right!" Shepherd screams. "We can't leave them to suffer like this!"

John steps up to one of the pods. "During the war, the medics would keep the soldiers who wouldn't survive preserved in one of these so he could serve as a donor in case we suffered traumatic injuries. It was a way for a soldier to give up his life and protect his brothers. The catch was if you got in one of these pods, you would be put into a vegetative state and you wouldn't ever come out of it." He callously pulls the plug and we watch as the body inside the pod convulses before going limp.

Tears fall down Shepherd's face as he watches his friend die inside the pod.

"We are against an enemy that will stop at nothing to accomplish their objective," John growls as he pulls another plug. "They experiment on whoever they want whenever they want. They kill those who don't cooperate and force our brightest into working for them. If I hadn't gotten to you first, I'm certain they would've tried to recruit all of you too. So when I rescue one of you and you disobey my orders-"

John cuts himself off by unplugging another patient.

"And in doing so put my entire team at risk I take personal offense to that." He walks up to Shepherd. "Do I make myself clear soldier?!"

Shepherd whimpers like a beaten pup. "Yes sir. But why didn't you tell us?"

"Would you have believed me?"

The group falls silent because we know the answer. John turns away and walks towards the exit. "Warrens, Hacker. Get us some samples of the tech inside the ion clones. We're going to track down who manufactures them."

ION SCION

Godfrey's Journal, Day 288

Hacker and Emie took over the reactors embedded within the ion clones as we left Trinitian - 6. Hacker detonated them all at once as we approached atmo, and the entire cloning facility was vaporized in an instant. An ominous mushroom cloud lingered behind, while the sea rushed in to claim everything beneath her tranquil surface. Shepherd is shook up and Lee is still trying to recover. Forrest complained about how he didn't get a beach day. A new kind of resolve has taken hold of John, one that seeks to hunt down our enemy. The rest of us worry that we're gearing up for a fight we cannot win.

John holds up a broken plasma reactor. "Hacker, do you have a location of where these things are being made yet?!"

"Emie and I are cross-indexing all known locations to work on this type of reactor, or which emit the correct energy signature."

John and Warrens manipulate a hologram of the plasma reactor to break it apart into the individual components. The two men scour the device for any clues to its origin.

"These polymers are advanced," Warrens says. "Plasma isn't easily contained and these guys seem to have it figured out. There's gotta be some gene editing for their bodies to handle this. What do you think Rooster?"

Sulture glares at Warrens. "Yes, the clones had their genes edited in order to tolerate the exposure to plasma. However," He grabs one of the components in the hologram. "The electro-magnetism of the plasma wreaked havoc on the iron in their blood."

John was visibly losing patience, but he took several deep breaths to calm himself.

"Found it!" Hacker shouted. He pulled up a hologram of a planet with only a few lights on the surface. "Thanks to Atler's database and some intelligence collected by Neuron, we learned the foundry is located here on planet CMS-127."

"CMS?" I ask.

"Core Military Station," John replies.

"It appears to be a fully automated factory where they churn out these reactors non-stop," Hacker says.

"So bots are making these parts?" Warrens asks.

Hacker sighs. "Yeah, and it's under contract from the military."

"That outta make it easy to shut down," Warrens replies. "Just dump an EMP on 'em."

"If we do that, we can't hijack the foundry and get our mechs built," John says.

Warrens chuckles. "You're right, that's a much better option."

"We're building mechs?" Shepherd asks.

"To combat future threats, Warrens, Hacker, and I have created what we refer to as the 'Epoch Experiment.' Our goal was simple: to build four exoskeleton mech units which represented the four horsemen of the apocalypse and would wield immense firepower."

"Who's piloting them?" I ask.

"We've been careful with our decision, but we believe that Lee, Sulture, Godfrey and myself would be the best pilots for these devices."

I look over at Warrens. "You didn't want to pilot one of your own weapons big guy?"

"Nu-uh. That metal orb messed me up good, and gave me cluster phobia inside of machines."

"What about me?!" Forrest screams. "Why can't I pilot the robot suits?"

"Because we need you to pilot the ship," John replies.

"But that makes me the *most* qualified!" He screams.

"Doesn't matter Forrest, my mind's made up. I will be the mech of war, Sulture will be pestilence, Lee famine and Godfrey death."

John brings the three of us to talk with Warrens on how we want the mechs to be built. The moment I heard that I would be representing the mech of death, my mind thought of the Hadrian gem and wielding its terrible power as a weapon. I've learned through past experiments that we can wield its devastating energy to great effect. I argue with John and Warrens for hours, but they finally relent, believing that Warrens can build a chamber lined with lead which will protect me from the gem's radiation.

Sulture has a another question after our discussion. "How will these machines be operated?"

Hacker steps up. "I've built four unique personalities templated after Emie. However they'll need names."

"How about getting cute and using names with the first letter for the Horsemen?" I ask. "So I'll call mine 'Dorothy.' "

John chuckles. "I like that idea. I'll go with Wendy."

"Fenfang," Lee says.

Sulture clears his throat. "Phoebe."

"Excellent," Hacker replies. "The AIs can maintain a level of autonomy when there is no pilot. If she goes down, the suit goes prone, unless the pilot is inside. Each mech will be biometrically sealed so that only the wielder can access it. Not even I can break through those locks."

Warrens displays four concepts of the mechs via hologram. Lee's is a light and nimble four-legged humanoid shape with chemical canisters lining its arms and shoulders. The program shows the mech flying over a field of crops and the spray dissolves them in an instant. Sulture's mech is humanoid and equipped with heavy weaponry, but it's also equipped with large vents that can expel diseases across the battlefield. What really sets it apart is the mech's face is a plague mask, with beak and all. I get the creeps just looking at it.

John's mech has a head shaped like a battering ram and missile launchers on both shoulders. It also wields an impressive cannon for one arm and a gatling gun on the other. My mech has a dome-shaped head with a reactor in the chest that glows violet. The mech is able to unleash the energy churned in tandem with the Hadrian gem and create a 'death pulse.' The energy can also be focused into a canon on the left arm for a more concentrated blast.

"How long will it take to make them?" I ask.

"If I can get the foundry dialed in with Circuit's help, less than a day," Warrens replies.

We descend to the surface, landing at the loading dock of the foundry. Two drones which are nothing more than a hovering bar with dangling arms come out to greet us.

"Shipment ready to be received." It's Emie's voice coming from the drones.

"Load up the parts we have in the ship," Hacker says. "We have our own section of the foundry."

The factory is a quiet hum of activity. Robot arms swivel and turn, piecing together one component after another in an endless assembly line that creates a dizzying array of machines for the Core military. No wonder why they were able to beat the Coalition so easily.

Hacker uploads Emie into the mainframe, who doesn't waste any time taking over a section of the foundry where we can be left to our own devices.

"Why are there no guards?" Shepherd asks.

"There were a few antipersonnel defenses, but I managed to disable them," Hacker replies. "Very few people know about this planet, and it's inhospitable. Nobody but the brass with proper clearance will ever find this world."

The forges ignite and slabs of metal are carried over, then dropped in to be melted down. Warrens uploads the schematics into the mainframe, just in time for the nanite assemblers to kick in. The melted metal particles float through the air, being collected and shaped by invisible nanites. It looks as though our armor is being built out of thin air. Other robotic arms work in the background, repurposing their components for our own use.

Hours pass in boredom as we wait for the mech units to be built. The robotic arms move in a seamless system of piecing the mechs together, until a few of them come to a stop.

"Hacker…?" I ask.

Emie's voice cuts in. "I'm afraid that I'm being shut out. A hostile program is attempting to seal me away."

Hacker looks at his holographic dashboard. "Someone else is here!"

Emie cries out to us, but her voice crackles until she fades away. The factory comes to a halt, all of the conveyors and robotic units freeze in place.

A slithery voice cuts through the air. "Trespassing, repurposing, or rather, *stealing* government property and infiltration through means of an artificial intelligence. I wonder which of these I should choose to detain all of you." The man is decorated like a military general. He has sandy hair, but his face is scarred with burn marks. What is really terrifying are his eyes. They're pitch black ocular implants with a red iris.

"General Hawkes?!" John and Hacker shout in unison.

"Indeed, I am watching over this facility because I knew that you and your team of miscreants would come. I've seen the damage you've caused our organization and I won't watch from afar any longer. I had you in my grasp, but I was ordered to let you go. I won't make that same mistake again."

"You were *ordered* to let us go?"

"Indeed I was. Our leader was convinced the Horsemen would bring some much needed 'competition' to our ranks. However I believe the damage you've caused negates whatever supposed 'benefit' your team has brought."

"Sounds like we're doing a good job," I reply.

"Hmm. Typical arrogance, can't see the full picture. You think you're helping mankind, but all you're doing is prolonging their suffering by denying them their chance to evolve."

"What evolution?!" I scream. "Sticking a reactor in a clone's chest doesn't qualify as evolution."

"Our efforts involve multiple endeavors. We've set out to perfect mankind, and we'll experiment with every means at our disposal."

"Does your mission involve using innocent people in your

experiments?" Shepherd asks.

"Most of them are volunteers, but why waste the genetic material of miscreants? Especially when we can program the specimens born from them?"

"You're monsters!" Shepherd shouts.

"Sacrifice must always occur before real innovation can take place."

"You can't shake this man's belief Shepherd," Hacker says. "He's a zealot for the Combine's cause."

John steps forward. "Hacker's right. This man is one of the most demented in the Core military."

Hawkes flashes a sinister grin. "Jabal, I see that you've finally gotten the approval of a father figure you've sought for so long."

Hacker draws a pistol and fires. One of the robotic arms grabs a component, and tosses it to intercept the blast.

Hawkes grins again. "You may have great skills developing artificial intelligences Jabal, but I'm afraid this time my program is superior to yours."

"Great, let me guess your next move," Forrest says. "You're going to sic a bunch of your blue-glowing minions on us?"

Hawkes chuckles. "I do have some here, but rather than rely on unsuccessful ion clones, I'll utilize something I can trust. I believe the Horsemen have come across the STARs before, yes?" A platoon of black-clad soldiers swarm in. Their black masks hide their faces, but their insignias and fighting abilities paint an all too familiar picture.

"We knocked them out before and we'll do it again!" Warrens shouts.

"Oh, you hear that men? Sounds like they're itching for a fight. Go give them one." The soldiers charge in.

"Hacker, get those mechs built! I don't care what it takes!" John barks. "The rest of you, in with me!"

We crash into the mob of soldiers. They fight at an experience level we can't match, but we need to buy Hacker the time he needs to get the mechs online. My moves show some experience, but most are out of desperation, fighting dirty by breaking limbs and striking any vulnerable spot I can find. No one else is faring much better. I hear Warrens' grunts as he tries to take them down in one hit, but even he's getting tired.

A hard right knocks the wind out of my chest. I get up, but another strikes me on the left cheek. I try to break the cycle of blows, but there are too many of the STARs. I keep getting up, but they've taken to my dirty tactics, taking me out at the knees and hitting me more times than I can count.

I lunge at them, grabbing an arm and kicking another guy away. I snap the first one's arm, but another kicks me in the gut. I draw my pistol, but I'm disarmed and struck down by the butt of my own gun. I get up again, but I'm kicked into a wall. It seems that the program which creates these freaks has been perfected.

I'm cornered by three members of the STARs. I'm bruised, battered and feel blood filling my mouth from my busted lip. They close in, cracking their knuckles in anticipation of finishing me off.

A lumbering machine swoops in from the side and bats the three soldiers away. I gaze into the violet eye of the behemoth which kneels down before me.

"I thought I'd even the odds, Silas." It's a new female voice, and she opens the window to the cockpit. I get a second wind and charge amidst flying blaster bolts. I leap from the arm into the cockpit and the mech raises the arm to protect me.

"Hello Silas, I am Dorothy, your personal assistant for operating your mechanical device of death as part of the Epoch Experiment."

"Cool. Great to meet you. How do I operate this thing?"

"First we must engage in biometric synchronization," Dorothy says. "Subject: Silas Godfrey. Please remove your gloves sir."

"If I must," I groan as I rip the gloves off. I slide my arm up a shaft and grab a hold of the handles while the biometric scans take place.

"Now I'll show you how to operate the system, Silas."

The controls feel clunky at first, but within seconds my world is brought to life through an intricate interface unlike anything I've ever seen. I watch the other mechs come online, with one of the STARs attempting to hijack the machine. He's ripped out of the control center and thrown like a rag doll. John climbs in, laughing maniacally.

"That was perfect," He says. "Let's see what these things can do!" He unleashes his gatling gun on the STARs who break rank and scramble in retreat. I activate my weapons systems and open fire to get a feel for the machine. The controls are very similar to being inside a chamber device. I have two bracers, two plates on my shins and a thin wire crown which seems to read my every thought. I feel immersed in another world, as if I've become one with the machine.

"Biometric synchronization complete," Dorothy says. I pursue Hawkes and his team, laying waste in my wake. I smile with glee as I eliminate the STARs who had me pinned to the ground.

I hear Hawkes barking for reinforcements to defend the foundry. Ion clones pour in to defend, but this time I'm ready.

"Dorothy, activate the death cannon."

"I'm sorry Silas, but there are too many allied companions nearby. The minimum range we can wield any energy stemming from the Hadrian gem is 500 metres."

"Fine," I growl. "What other features do you have?"

"We could activate the program 'Harvest Mode.' "

"What's that?"

The metal on my right arm shifts until a massive scythe forms. I swing at the ion clones beneath me. I smile with grim satisfaction when the scythe switches sides so I can swing back and forth, carving up every clone in my way.

I look around the foundry, and all of the other mechs are tearing this place apart. Even with the automated defenses, this place wasn't built to handle four mechs raging inside.

As I pursue Hawkes and his men, the ion clones begin to take a different tact. One of them pounds on his chest and charges right for me as though he can take me down. His chest piece glows brighter the closer he gets. I follow my gut and put all power into my front shields.

The ensuing blast tears my shields apart, while the other clones catch on. They pound their chests and charge for me. I look behind me, and I'm still not far enough to activate my death pulse. However another hit from the kamikaze clones and my mech is done for.

I kick on my thrusters, which send me crashing through the ceiling, and then crashing back to the factory floor. The ion clones' skin is beginning to crack, and their bodies can't hold back the plasma reaction they've set off inside themselves. However, I'm far enough from the others to activate the death pulse.

I turn on the outside speakers. "Not bad boys, but let's see what a real explosion can do!"

A disc plate in my chest switches open, unleashing the atomic energy contained within. I activate the death pulse and watch a violet dome of electrical energy consume everything around me. I stumble back as I feel a wave of nausea, making a mental note to get some medicine in here.

The violet dome vaporizes the surrounding clones in an instant, devouring their flesh like a starving beast which licks their bones clean. The energy from their reactors can't be contained, which sets off a wave of explosions that shake the foundry to its foundation.

After the death pulse dissipates, I survey the damage around me. I'm surrounded by charred bone shards and warped reactors. It's a haunting scene of carnage where our revelry in destruction gives me a glimpse to our doom.

Several of Hawkes' men got caught in the blasts but he and the rest are on the verge of escape. I rush after them, trying to cut off their ability to leave the foundry.

I activate the canon on my left arm and fire at them, but they make it inside the starship. The blast wipes their shields out, and I signal the controls to fire again.

"I'm afraid I can't fire again Silas," Dorothy says. "I need to recharge the reactor, and this takes time."

"Damn it," I reply. I get an idea. "Get me as close to them as you can. And what's it called when you operate on your own?"

"Sentinel mode."

"Perfect, prepare to go into sentinel mode."

When Dorothy gets close enough, I activate sentinel mode, leap out of the cockpit and pursue Hawkes.

He stands over the cockpit to his starship while the STARs look back at me.

"Go on, finish him!" Hawkes shouts. "He's vulnerable now that he's out of the suit."

The STARs look at Hawkes as though they wish to defy him, but can't find the words. They look from him to me, and come at me in a half-hearted charge.

I draw my pistol and make quick work of the soldiers. I cock the gun and fire at Hawkes, but it only grazes his shoulder. He looks at me with contempt and climbs into the starship. Dorothy is distracted by the remaining soldiers, and Hawkes is able to escape.

The others fall in right as Dorothy finishes off the final soldier. The entire foundry is in ruins, with robotic arms twisted and half melted. The cost to replace the factory will be atrocious, and I can only hope that we dealt a serious blow to the Combine's wallet.

Hacker is the first one on the scene. "Hawkes get away?"

"Yeah," I reply. "But not like we didn't try."

"He's a slippery one. How'd you like operating the mech?"

"It felt like I had a second body, like I was the brain for the machine."

"Good," Warrens says as he walks in. "About time that four-dee program did some good."

John leaps down to the ground. "Whoo! That was great! Cannot wait to do that again!" He shouts.

"Life forms detected, and they are in danger of overheating," Emie says.

"Show us Emie," Hacker replies. His gauntlet glows, providing an arrow for us to follow. We search the factory until we come to a trap door in the floor.

We pull the door open and it's a dozen men and women who've been locked up.

"What're you guys doin' down there?" John asks.

"They're the engineers and computer technicians who run this place," Hacker replies.

"We were locked up when the General came in," one of them says. "He came in and told us to clear out."

"Any idea how long you've been down there?" John asks.

"Weeks," Another one replies.

"Damn, Hawkes is an asshole to everyone," John says.

"He's still out there too," I reply.

"We'll find him," Hacker says. "Now that we know he's out there, we'll find him."

"What do we do with these guys?" Warrens asks.

John takes a long look at the foundry. The lights flicker, there are random fires where the hydraulic fluid ignited, there's smoke everywhere and most of the robotic arms are too far gone to be fixed.

"Looks like you're hitchin' a ride with us," John says.

STOWAWAYS

Godfrey's Journal Day 290

We bring the engineers and computer techies aboard the ship for transport. It may strain our resources while we're aboard the ship, but deep down we know it's the right thing to do. John orders Hacker to run a background check on everyone we found to keep them honest. Turns out, they're all employees across different divisions of Ionics. The good news is, they weren't lying to us. It's nice to have an honest bunch for once.

It's my turn to take the guys their rations of food and water. They're a reasonable, understanding bunch and it's a shame we had to lock them up. However, given our fears of any possible connection to the Combine we have no choice.

I sit down to join the others for dinner, but the lights flash red overhead.

All eyes move to me

"It can't be," I reply. "I just saw them locked up."

"Yi dwei da buen chuo roh!" Lee shouts.

"They were locked up asshole!"

I bite back another curse. Why couldn't I be right about this? Why couldn't the stowaways have been docile and harmless for once?

I leap up from the table and make for the holding cell. The lights blink as I make my way through the ship, and every object casts a shadow, which makes my heart leap.

When I reach the holding cell, there's nobody inside. The door lingers open, no sign of forced exit.

The bastards simply walked out.

I click on my comm. "Horsemen, the stowaways are loose. This is not a drill. I repeat, this is not a drill."

John replies. "Godfrey, you're the closest to life support. Secure it."

"Will do. Godfrey over and out."

The lights flicker above my head as I walk through the ship. Try as they might, they buzz out, and the faint emergency lights flicker on. What I can't figure out is why the alarm hasn't been triggered.

I hear the door to life support open. A shadow darts inside and the door slides shut. I pound my fist in frustration. I peel off my glove and wave my hand over the lock.

It beeps at me in denial.

I wave my hand over again. Same result.

I click on my comm. "Emie, why am I locked out of life support?!"

Silence rings on the other end.

"EMIE!" I scream.

A scrambled signal fills my ears, but Emie finally cuts through.

"Sorry Silas, I don't know why the lock wasn't working. Please try it again."

I wave my hand over the lock. It clicks and the door slides open.

I pause before going in, my body on full alert. This will be the last time I fully disarm before dinner.

None of the systems have been altered. No sign of intrusion. There isn't even any noise.

Until I hear an exhale behind me.

A figure leaps out and swings a wrench. I hear the metal slice through the air, but I duck out of the way and sparks fly as metal scrapes on metal. The guy swings again, but I catch the tool. The two of us wrestle for control, battling until I push him into the light. His eyes are pitch black, a haunting reminder of the effects from the Combine. The man has become a Shadow, forcefully converted.

I click on the comm. "Contact made with a Shadow! I repeat: contact made with a Shadow!" I activate the alarm, but the Shadow didn't like that. His face contorts in pure rage and he roars a hollow scream before attacking me again.

He seizes my throat and I strike him as hard as I can. The red light makes him look demonic, complete with gnashing teeth. I keep hitting him, but he ignores my strikes. I take a deep breath, focus for a moment and strike him in the temple. He goes down, knocked out cold.

"Contact!" Warrens screams through the ship's comm. "One of those boys has gone bug-eyed on me."

"Where are you?" I scream back.

"He and I are throwin' down near the barracks - I caught him snoopin' around our weapons and when I turned him around he swung at me then tried to grab a pistol."

"Shit," John hisses. "That means we got six more of 'em rifling through the ship. Emie, put the ship on lockdown. Nobody walks through the door unless you know their face!"

"Right away John," Emie replies.

John dispenses with the orders to the entire team."Forrest and Sujay, get to the bridge. Sulture, relieve Warrens so he can check on engines. Shepherd and Lee, provide support to Godfrey, then you three hunt them down. Don't kill 'em, let's try to save these guys. And Hacker: *find* them through the video feed!"

"Bring them to the infirmary!" Murph says.

I lift the guy over my shoulder and carry him to the medbay. Murph is waiting with his surgical table prepped and holograms on display. He helps me rest the Shadow on the table and straps him in. He connects the life support pads and goes through the motions of brain surgery to reach the embedded chip. Emie calmly guides him where to go, while Murph slowly moves the controls.

I point to a hologram of a brain with a yellow blotch embedded in the center. "Is this where the chip is?"

"Yeah," Murph says. "It'd be a challenge even for the best brain surgeons in the galaxy. I'm just an unlicensed medical doctor with a knack for knowing the odds."

"How do your odds look?"

Murph looks up at me with grim eyes. "Not good."

Emie projects a hologram of Murph's operation. He closes in on the embedded chip, but the moment his instruments touch the device, an electrical signal disrupts the hologram. The body jerks and the heart rate flatlines.

"Damn it," Murph growls. He pulls up one of the holograms and reviews it to ensure he didn't make a mistake.

Warrens comes in through the door, carrying another Shadow with him.

"Got room for this runt?"

"Yeah, let's try removing his chip."

"Is that what happened to the last guy you tried it on?" Warrens gestures towards the table.

Emie interjects. "Patient died from traumatic electrical surge inside the hippocampus which resulted in termination. It is not due to Dr. McGinnis' handling of the equipment."

"Oh," Warrens replies. "Good to know I can count on you if I ever get bugged."

"Yeah yeah, right after I give you fifty see-sees of Vitamin STFU."

Just before Murph begins the procedure the ship rumbles, as though we're experiencing turbulence. The three of us look at each other in confusion.

"Warning!" Emie screams. "*Enigma* is on course for a collision with a dwarf star!"

"Forrest!" John screams over the comm. "What have you done with my ship?!"

There's no answer on the other end. The three of us share a look of panic.

"Shit," I mutter. We bolt out of the medbay.

"Warrens, please tell me you brought some guns."

"I got one for me."

"Oh, you suck."

"You think I didn't prepare for this?" Warrens asks. He waves his hand over a panel on the wall which flips around to reveal a pair of pistols and knives. I grab one of each and Murph does the same.

By the time we make it to the bridge, the rest of the team is already there. John is tending to Forrest and Sujay who are on the ground, out cold and bleeding from the scalp.

"Jesus Christ," Murph curses as he starts patching the two up.

Emie warns us again that we're heading straight for a dwarf star, along with a projected map and a time until impact.

"Can't you change course?" Sulture asks.

"I'm afraid the issue is a hardware situation Dr. Sulture, not a software one," Emie replies. "It also seems that whoever changed the hardware has installed a program which makes it look as though it's correctly installed to me. I'm trying to find the right configuration, but that takes time."

"That's fine Emie," John grunts. "Just find the stowaways."

"I'm afraid I don't have a record of any stowaways John."

"What the hell do you mean you don't have a record?!"

"All I have is our crew roster of eighteen. One of which is deceased in the infirmary."

"Son of a bitch," I growl.

Warrens tears open the motherboard to the ship. "Get in here Circuit! We gotta figure this out pronto!"

"I'm sorry," Emie says. "Is my information incorrect?" Her voice becomes distant and frail.

"We're losing her," Hacker says.

"Shut her down," John orders. "She's no use to us now. Get that malware outta her too! Murph, tend to the pilots - the rest of you, let's hunt down these freaks."

John leads us down the main corridor, wondering out loud where they would've gone to.

"Two are accounted for," I say. "One's dead and the other is sedated in the medbay."

"We'll have to split up," John says. "Just because we missed them on the first patrol doesn't mean they won't attack the engines or life support systems again. These bastards don't expect to come out of this alive. You don't go to such lengths to make our escape impossible and then hightail it outta here. Plus these 'Shadows' seem to be the focused type. Divvy up the ship and find them."

We list off where we're going, and I take life support again. Hacker turns off the alarm, but the red emergency light dominates the ship. Time is short, and we split off to hunt the Shadows.

My flashlight captures every shadow, the edges of my vision faltering on me. It's isolating, lonely. The walls feel as though they're about to close in.

In the distance, I hear the cock of a gun. The metal components click as well, the sound of someone who is passing the gun between their hands. Trying to get a feel for it. They're not used to it. I have the advantage of experience, but I'm not sure how far that will get me.

I take a gamble by turning off my flashlight. I slip out of my boots to silence my footsteps, and make for the clicking sounds.

I pull my gun on the Shadow hiding behind the carbon dioxide filtration system, but he bats it away as I shoot. He strikes at me hard and fast, far better at martial arts than I am.

"Did they upload Slipstream into your head too?"

The Shadow growls at me. He claws the air, showing me his martial prowess.

I roll my eyes. "Screw this." I shoot him in the kneecap, and he falls down while howling in pain.

"Who sent you here?" I ask as I stand over him.

"I'm here to kill the traitors!" He screams in a hollow voice.

I step on his knee. He groans in pain, but is trying to suppress it. I shine my flashlight into his eyes. "Didn't ask why, I asked *who* sent you."

He gives me a blank stare, like he doesn't know. "Infiltrate. Reprogram. That is all we were sent for."

I step on his knee again. "WHO?!"

He continues to stare, but a memory from his past life comes through. "The General spoke of plague outbreak. Vaccinated." He shakes his head. "Mission is to kill the Horsemen!" He grabs ahold of my leg, but I shoot him in the shoulder. He groans and still tries to reach me, despite his wound.

"Gotta hand it to your resilience." I strike him in the head with the butt of my gun and knock him out.

I click on the comm. "Murph, got another one for you."

I haul the guy back to the infirmary, where Murph is tending to Forrest and Sujay. Once inside, I toss the guy onto another metal slab.

"Any luck with Forrest and Sujay?"

"They've both got serious concussions. Even if I can get 'em awake, they're in no condition to be flyin'."

Hacker comes in through the comm. "I'm struggling to unlock the access to the operating system for the ship."

"Then we'll have to switch everything over to manual." John says. "But the real problem is I need a pilot!"

Warrens steps up. "I can do it sir."

"No," John replies. "I need you near the engine in case we need to stall the bastard out."

I step forward. "What if I do it sir?"

"Godfrey, you don't know a damn thing about flying."

"True, but given our situation sir, I'm afraid you don't have much choice. Tell me which knobs and levers to pull, and I can give you some muscle. Don't need to know what does what."

"Alright, get up here."

John and I take over the bridge. I wave my hand over the console which shows our collision with the dwarf star as imminent.

John clicks on the comm. "Hacker, can you shut down the hyperdrive?"

"No luck reaching it sir."

"Then Warrens, I need you to manually disable it. The rest of you, strap in because it's going to be a rough stop."

A violent grinding noise consumes the ship and within seconds we're all being thrown forward. John and I white knuckle the controls as we see the dwarf star fill up the windshield. If we'd waited any longer, we would've collided with the star.

John points at a lever and barks for me to grab it. He attempts multiple manual overrides of the controls, but every effort fails.

"Y'know, there was a time when we had to learn how to fly these things without software!" John shouts.

Hacker clicks through. "I'm unplugging the OS from everything. We're going to be on full manual in the ship."

"Perfect," John growls.

A steering column rises out of the console for me and I grab on, waiting for John's orders.

"Okay, we got the hyperdrive cut, now we gotta fight the star's gravitational pull. Fortunately, all we need to do is turn a few degrees, push the engines as hard as we can and we'll be free and clear."

"Can we push the engines that hard without the hyperdrive?"

"One problem at a time Godfrey."

He and I grab hold of the steering column and twist as hard as we can. The orange glow of the dwarf star fills the entire cabin and the two of us grit our teeth as we fight her pull.

"When will we know we've hit those few degrees John?"

"You'll just have to trust me on that."

Every muscle in my arm strains as we fight against the star's gravity. John tells me which levers and knobs to manipulate, but most of the effort goes into twisting the column. I can't tell of our progress, as the star dominates our entire view. However I notice a line of black space on the edge, which is slowly growing.

"Warrens! Is there any way you can give us a boost strong enough to rip away from the star's gravity without killing the engine?"

"I know of a trick," He replies.

The sliver of black grows, and we begin to edge away from the sun, but my arms are shaking too much.

"John, my arms are about to give in!"

"Just hold on!" He barks.

I throw all of my weight into it, pulling as hard as I can muster.

Warrens clicks in. "Punch it now!"

"Let go Godfrey!"

I release the column right as John activates the hyperdrive. The boost jolts us back into our seats, and the star fades away.

After a few seconds, John cuts the hyperdrive and we're thrown forward again. All of the cajoling leaves me feeling nauseous, while John crawls out of his chair and pukes into a trash bin.

"Warrens, cut the engines, we're floating here for a while." John orders. He stands up and looks down at me.

"You okay sir?"

"I don't have the stomach for flyin' like Forrest does. Punk makes it look too easy. C'mon, let's go check on how Murph's doing."

We walk into the medbay where Murph and Sulture are preparing for surgery. All of the Shadows have been captured and sedated.

"Status?" John asks.

"We're going to do what we can for these guys and see if we can reverse some of the damage," Murph replies. The two hold the patient down and drill into the back of her head. Murph keeps the display up, showing his progress for the surgery.

John points to a cavity within the brain. "Murph, are these scans up to date?"

He pauses. "Yeah. The chemicals eat away the parts of the brain the Combine doesn't want people to have access to. It's only going to get worse."

Murph carefully navigates through the brain tissue, seeking out the chip that caused all of this havoc. The scan reveals the chip, which is reduced in size by half.

"Why is the chip so much smaller?" John asks.

Sulture answers for Murph. "Because part of it dissolved, releasing the hormones and chemicals which altered the subject's brain chemistry. We're attempting to learn what we can from the remains."

We watch the scan as Murph reaches the chip. Just as he grabs the chip, and electrical surge flares out. The patient jumps, and the heart monitor flatlines.

"GOD FUCKING DAMN IT!" Murph howls.

"Grab the chip Murph!" Sulture shouts. "Just grab the chip!"

Murph rips the chip out, and throws it onto the neighboring table. Sulture moves to inspect it, while Murph kicks the tables around the room.

Sulture readies a schematic to be sent out. "Hacker, Warrens, I'm sending this to both of you. See what you can make of it."

"It'll take me days to break down the programs," Hacker replies.

John cuts in through the comm. "Is there a signal we can use to shut these down? Something is causing these chips to detonate."

"The electrical surge is detonated by proximity," Hacker replies. "If we mess with the signal, the chips have a tamper-proof protocol and they'll electrocute the subject."

"What about finding the control center and turning it off?" John asks.

"Sir, there is no control center," Hacker sighs. "Think of each chip as a server, and they're all hosting the network. Even if we take out one of them, the network still operates unhindered. The only way to bring down this network is to eliminate every single server at once! Plus the signal they use can only be accessed via the brain chip, so unless someone wants to implant one to listen in, it won't do us much good."

"Why only 'listen in?'" John asks.

"Because the only chips we've seen are receivers, not transmitters, we can't see what they're doing, let alone take control of it."

Shepherd walks in visibly shaking in anger.

"We have to save them," He says. "John we have to save them! What good are we if we don't?!"

Sulture rises up. "They signed up with the Combine, this is what they get."

"To execute them isn't our choice to make!" Shepherd snaps. "You think those guys wanted to be brainwashed and to send our ship crashing into a star?! They were men and women with families! People like us!"

John approaches him. "Shepherd I get that, but we can't put millions of people at risk by leaving them exposed to rogue agents of the Combine."

"There has to be a way we can fix this!" Shepherd howls.

"And what if there isn't?!" Sulture snaps. "Are you willing to let these people walk?! Are you willing to risk the lives of the innocent by letting these *cultists* run free?"

"Easy Sulture," John says as he gets between the two. "We need to be patient now boys. If we put all of our brains to the task, an answer will come. There are a lot of names on that list, and we must consider the ramifications *if* we even pull that trigger. We could wipe out the greatest minds of a generation."

The lights flash back on and the engines fire up. Emie comes online, greeting all of us and able to tell us apart from the stowaways lying unconscious next to us. Hacker comes in, and we all cheer for him restoring the ship.

He waves us down, and his face looks grim. "Now is not the time to cheer. I managed to overcome the program that took over our ship and what I learned is worse than I feared." He looks directly at John. "I learned that the chip, the neurochemicals, Cerex, all of them were developed in secret by Ionics."

All of us look at John, stunned. His face is calm and solemn.

"Then let's pay a visit to the Madam Chairman herself."

THE PURGE

Godfrey's Journal Day 311

We determine to take our ship heist directly to Harris. Ionics has been behind every encounter with the Combine and we need answers. The only way we're going to get honest ones is through Harris. John knew there was nothing more we could do for the Shadows aboard the ship, so he ordered Murph to put them down via lethal injection. It was hard for him to do, but Sulture explained that while the neural degeneration would inevitably kill them, it would take too long. John figured that none of the men deserved to be turned into Shadows, so the least we could do was put them to rest with their dignity and without struggle. We're closing in on Earth's orbit and are preparing for the worst.

John's pacing the ship again. We arrive over the glimmering city of New York, yet I've never seen him so anxious about a mission. He sees me approach and looks like he yearns to talk.

"I never thought it'd come to us confronting Ionics," He says.

"None of us did John. But we need answers and honesty from

people who've been short with both."

"Still doesn't make it easier."

"How do you think we should approach Harris with all of this?"

"We'll have to catch her off guard. We can't just march into her office demanding an explanation. I'm sure she has something canned. Plus if we're going to interrogate her-"

John cuts himself off as he hears the words leave his mouth.

"If we're going to interrogate Harris, we need to do so under cover of darkness. We can't let the cameras see us doing it," He says.

"What if only a handful of us go? We can minimize our exposure and if the mission goes to shit, you can claim we went rogue."

"Who here would put themselves at risk like that?"

"Well, I would for one. Answers mean more to me than the threat of jail or death. And I'm sure you can find others just as willing."

John calls in the rest and explains the idea of interrogating Madame Chairman Harris. He emphasizes that it's volunteer only and that if the operation goes south, we're on our own. Despite all of this, Lee and Shepherd volunteer.

The three of us gear up for a night operation, dialing in our equipment and preparing to parachute down through the city.

"Just remember: If anything goes wrong, you're on your own."

"We know John," I reply. "That's the third time you've said that."

"She'll be protected, either by ion clones or Core authorities."

"We'll have to act fast."

"Please don't dismiss her Godfrey. This woman can and will destroy us if she needs to."

"I have no doubt, John."

"There won't be any coming back from this," John says. "We'll lose all of our funding, and we'll be hunted by the Core authorities. Or the Combine. They'll all come after us."

"Who're you trying to convince John, you or us?" I ask.

He looks down because he already knows the answer.

"You're right. I always knew it would come down to something like this, but I never would've imagined Lynn would turn on us the way she did."

"That's the thing about betrayal, you never see it coming."

Hacker walks us through the drop and explains in grisly detail the hazards of jumping out of a ship at night. He syncs Emie up with us, who will act as our personal guide to the surface. Warrens tells us how to use our suits, and when we should deploy them. It doesn't look like much more than a few flaps between our limbs.

"Don't forget this," Murph says as he hands a syringe to Lee.

"What is it?" I ask.

"A little dose of truth serum. Seems like we can't take her at her word."

John walks us to the dock doors. He can barely hold his head up. We all feel used, betrayed and angry for how Ionics has turned on us. When we look up, everyone is in the loading dock with us. We know deep down there's no turning back from here. Once we do this, we go all in.

The door opens wide, and all I see is the dark of night. We take one last breath before the plunge.

Lee charges for the exit and leaps out. Shepherd follows close behind. I step to the ledge and look back on the crew.

"Horsemen until the end!" I scream at them. They howl in agreement, and I leap out of the ship.

Beneath is the sprawling cityscape ignited by billions of lights. The concept of night barely exists within the city anymore, and I laugh as I realize night vision wasn't needed.

My visor comes online and tracks Lee and Shepherd. I pull my arms in and lean in to catch up to them.

The wind howls against my ear and my armor drags against the air.

Hacker clicks in through the comm. "Comm systems check, can everyone hear me?"

We all confirm, one right after another.

"Okay, your rate of descent is good. Your trajectory shows you should deploy in about 30 seconds."

When falling from the sky, each second feels like a lifetime. To top it off, there's speeder lanes to avoid. Hacker counts down, which doesn't help the situation. I feel a knot form in my stomach, but I force myself to think about striking back at the Combine. Harris is one of their leaders, I know it.

"Three…two…one! Deploy now!" Hacker screams.

We force our arms and legs open and the flaps catch. Our descent slows and Lee guides us towards Harris' condominium. It's a rare event when she actually uses this place, but we were ready for when she did.

We weave through the local traffic and activate our magnetic grips within our hands and feet. I reach out to the building, and my hand catches before the rest of me does, threatening to tear my arm from its socket.

I slam into the building, while the others cling on with ease. Lee scrambles up to the window and deploys a small device which looks like a four-legged spider. The machine suctions itself to the window, while the legs extend and cut out a rectangle of glass big enough for one of us to slide through.

The glass pane starts to fall, but Lee reaches out and grabs the spider. My heart leaps into my chest as he swings back, but his other boot secures him as the wind howls around us.

Shepherd scrambles up and crawls through the window. He draws his pistol, checks the room and waves us in. I climb through and hold my hand out to Lee for the window. He struggles to hand it to me, and the gale-force winds don't make it any easier. As I grab hold, the wind catches the sheet of glass and almost rips me out of the building. I pull as hard as I can muster, while Lee leaps inside.

I slide the glass pane into place while Lee throws on some kind of adhesive. The two of us draw our weapons and search the condo, and Emie informs us she's suppressed the intruder alarm.

From outside the front door, two shadows step up against the threshold and open it. It's two men clad in black suits and wearing dark sunglasses. They draw their pistols and tiptoe in, closing the door behind them.

Emie's scans reveal that the pistols they're wielding are a variation of the Xeclian disintegration rifle and their glasses also have night vision capability.

They turn on their night vision just as Shepherd activates a flash grenade. By the time they realize what he's done, it's too late.

The grenade goes off, but one of the goons fires off a blast.

Which hits me square in the chest.

I gasp for air, but the place reeks of ozone and death. Shepherd is kneeling over me, checking my vitals. My chest is also throbbing.

"What happened?" I ask. I see a few pieces of dust floating in the apartment.

Shepherd looks up at the dust. "You got hit in the chest and then there was-"

"Then the *tian di wu yohn* lights went out," Lee says. "Probably a side effect of the blaster."

Shepherd pulls me to my feet. "I feel like I just took a battering ram to the chest."

Lee waves at the shoes by the door. "Don't worry, we took care of the *luh suh*."

I struggle to catch my breath. "C'mon, it won't take long for people to see the power's out here. Let's get this done and over with." I open the door to Harris' bedroom, who's retrieving a pistol from her safe.

Once she realizes there are three of us in her apartment, she points her pistol at us. "What is the meaning of th-" Lee leaps over the bed, disarms her and drags her across the room. Her squeals are muffled by his gloves, but he ties her up into a chair.

"What do you criminals want?! Money?! Jewelry?!" She shouts.

"Answers," I reply. Lee ties off Harris' arm until her vein is exposed and injects the truth serum into her. She looks around her apartment, curiosity gnawing at her as to who we really are. She's as determined at being silent as we are while the serum courses through her body.

"The police will be here any minute you know," She says. Droplets of sweat are forming on her brow. Lee comes up and tells me she's ready for questioning.

"What is the objective of the Combine?"

Harris sighs as she tries to find a different answer. "To achieve the God-State."

"What is the God-State?"

"Where an individual becomes pure energy but has enough will to retake physical form. Complete mastery over matter." Harris focuses on the carbon scoring on my chest.

"How did you survive that blast? Those guns were custom-built by the Xeclians." I could tell that Harris wished she hadn't said that last part.

I ignore her question because we can't get distracted. "How much has Ionics funded the Combine?"

Harris chuckles. "John's boys huh? I figured most of you would stoop to this level, but I never thought he would. Still on your crusade against the Combine."

Shepherd leaps in front of me. "They experiment on innocent people! And you implanted chips inside them which either brainwash or kill them!"

A devilish smile forms on Harris' lips. I pull Shepherd back.

"Let me handle this," I say to him. "She doesn't believe she's wrong so your cries of injustice are falling on deaf ears. You're showing you're angry and that your head's clouded. Stay focused."

I return to Harris who can't stop smiling. "How much has Ionics funded the Combine?"

"You're naive to think at this point Ionics is the only one behind the Combine. It belongs to Samson, most of the Financial IPCs, the military, hell most of the Core Senate has bought in!" She shouts. "We're *everywhere*, even the Horsemen Initiative is an extension of the Combine."

Shepherd leaps forward again. "That's imp-" I hold up my hand to cut him off.

"Why even create the Horsemen?" I ask.

"We needed competition within the ranks. Innovation would only succeed if we pitted you against each other. We knew it was a risk, but when we saw how much progress was made on both sides, we knew it was the right decision."

"You manufactured a war between us?" Shepherd asks in disgust.

"We engineered competition, *boy*," Harris snaps. "You're the ones who turned it into a war! Once you attacked our servers and cloning facilities, most of us in the council voted to terminate your operation. However it wasn't unanimous, but General Hawkes couldn't stand to allow your group to continue operations so he went rogue."

"What does everyone get out of this? The God-State?" I ask.

"Immortality you moron!" She snaps. "Extending our lives through clone bodies or uploading our minds to chips and continuing on as AI- that's not living! Those are copies which inevitably degrade over time. The God-State is where we transcend the flesh and become beings of pure energy!"

"How do you intend to accomplish this?"

"Your team already has."

"What? That's im-"

Hacker interrupts through the comm. "You guys have police on the ground coming in. They're investigating the power outage at the building."

"Shit," I hiss. I'll have to decipher what Harris means later. Right now, I have to get to the point of our mission.

"Do you have a system that controls the chips embedded in your scientists?"

Harris glares at me, trying to resist giving an answer.

I cock my pistol and hold it up to her head. "I won't ask again."

"Is this really worth it? Disavowing the company that spared you and-" I strike Harris with the butt of my gun.

"Answer my goddamn question."

She spits blood at me. "The only way you can access those chips is if you were given one by the council. And even then, he can kill you on a whim-"

Harris' eyes roll back into her head and she convulses before going limp in her chair.

"SON OF A BITCH!" I click in through the comm. "Murph! Is there anything I can do?!"

He sighs. "I'm afraid not bud. It takes them out at the base of the skull, frying them in an instant. No comin' back from that."

"Warrens! What about the chip itself? Can we still use it?"

"It's as fried as her brain is."

"Can we fix it?!"

"It's over Casanova, they've won this round."

I look out across the city and see the Ionics building glimmering in the distance. "Maybe not." I turn around and force open Harris' eyelid.

"Emie, record biometric signature." She scans the eye and beeps when she's done. I do the same thing with her fingerprints. "Emie, also prepare a voice emulator to match my voice to Harris."

"Right away Silas."

"You've become a *guay toh guay nown* Godfrey," Lee says.

"Damn right I've become a schemer. Let's go to Ionics!"

We glide to the street level and hijack a speeder. I drive like a man possessed, hellbent on my enemy's destruction. I ask Emie to find me a route to Ionics' R&D building.

"What is your plan Godfrey?" John asks.

"Sir you wouldn't approve anyway. We need to move on the fly for this one!"

"Godfrey, I will not allow you to put this team in jeopardy! We will figure out another way!"

"No! We keep falling into their master plan. Not this time. It's time we do something they don't expect!"

I pull up in front of a dimly lit cube of a building and draw my pistol. I smash the front door and scream for the security guards to get on the floor. I tell them that if any of them call the cops or lock the building down, I'd hunt them and their families down. Lee follows and ties them up.

I download the building's layout and march for their secret tech division.

An AI cuts in through the building's comm once I reach the door. "I'm afraid I can't allow strangers to enter this division."

I whisper to Emie: "Activate the voice emulator."

"I'm not a stranger you moron! I am Madame Chairman Harris, and I demand access!"

"I'm afraid I require a biometric scan Ms. Harris, as your stature doesn't match our records."

I scan my visor, but the machine protests, claiming the need to see my actual eye. My mind races, trying to come up with something, but the machine pauses, then accepts my credentials and opens the doors.

"What was that about?" Shepherd asks.

Hacker replies through the comm. "I tricked the machine. I don't know what Godfrey's up to, but he's not giving in."

The room is dim and empty. A few crates are scattered around, but there's nothing on the surface to notice down here.

"Silas, what are we doing down here?" Shepherd whispers.

"Quiet! The AI is listening. We're searching for the vault."

"What vault?"

"Every corporation has a vault they keep their most closely held trade secrets in. Ionics is no different, and my gut tells me there's something in there we can use."

Sulture clicks in through the comm. "You're a fucking idiot Godfrey! You're basing the stake of this mission on your *gut*?!"

"In a past life, I was one of the division heads in Research and Development. I know how Corporations like these work." I pass a terminal computer, turn it on and seek out the vault.

I find a safe embedded within the wall, and press my thumb against the lock. The dial spins until the door clicks open to reveal a handful of small devices contained inside. One of them is kept inside a slim plastic tube. I hold it up to the light and see the silver cylinder I was hoping to find.

I open the tube, take the capsule and plug it into the computer terminal.

"What is this?" Hacker asks.

"It's one of those chips with a transmitter inside. We now have a working unit and can get inside the Combine's network."

"Only one problem: whoever uses it will either be converted or killed."

"Then patch me through to Warrens. We can take out the part that delivers pheromones."

Sulture cuts in. "You weren't listening were you? These things contain stem cells which connect the user with the Combine's neural network. They force the brain into creating the neurochemicals, they're not dispersed. And before you ask, if we take out the stem cells the chip is useless. There's no other way to connect to their network.

"So right now we're programming stem cells?" I ask.

"It seems that's what the terminal wants to do, so yes," Hacker replies.

"You're telling me you can't put *something* into that script?"

Hacker sighs. "I'll try something, but I can't guarantee anything. Until I met these people, I thought conversion from software to biology was impossible to gap, but these guys found a way."

The script runs for a few more minutes and the capsule is ejected from the terminal. Back inside the safe is a gun which is designed to implant the chip. I take the gun and load the chip.

"What are you doing?!" John asks.

"Sir, we need to do something."

"I will not have you putting yourself at risk Godfrey. Not until we have more time to learn the programming."

"There's nothing to learn!" I scream. "They know who we are and will stop at nothing to kill us! We either destroy them or they'll destroy us!"

"Godfrey, I get you're upset, but we need to look at the grand strategy-"

I cut John off. "I'm beyond upset! I signed up to help you clean shit up and perform science experiments, not watch clones self-destruct or learn that a secret organization implants their members with a chip that brain washes or electrocutes them! They took our team and bastardized our mission! It was all one big experiment to them and we were the fucking lab rats! So you're right John, I'm pissed and I want to tear this organization apart!"

Sulture cuts in again. "Godfrey you will be putting yourself and the team at grave risk. Not only that, you're putting the best minds of our generation at risk for your little vendetta."

"Said the xenocidalist."

A pause lingers over the line. "My point is, think this through. If you turn on us we will have no choice but to kill you."

"Then draw your fucking blasters."

"Godfrey! I order you to put that gun down! Don't do it!" John shouts. His orders are desperate, but I know that we have no other choice. In order to destroy the Combine, we have to become the worst monsters imaginable. There are hundreds of good reasons why we should let them live. Thousands of reasons to leave them alone, but only one to kill them all, and unfortunately that's the reason that matters the most. In an instant, every single person within the Combine can be converted or eliminated with a thought. And when converted, they won't hesitate to unleash the greatest horrors upon mankind for the sake of 'Evolution.'

I put the injection gun against the back of my skull and pull the trigger.

I feel the chip burrow deep into my brain, and I almost pass out from pain.

However, I realize that my perception of reality has changed. I can sense the others in the Combine. I can feel their presence.

A mad chuckle echoes from behind.

"I've finally got you," He says. I hear his voice, but I can't see him.

"You're him, aren't you?" I ask.

"After all the defiance you've shown, you were the last one I suspected to join us."

A sharp pain tears through my head, threatening to split it open.

"The migraines will pass shortly. You're processing all who's here. The enhancements take a bit of getting used to."

"Do you always host orientation like this?"

"Not for most of them, but I made an exception for you. Still a smartass as always I see."

"Who the hell are you?!"

"In time you'll know. But, you have something I want."

I concentrate on finding the others. I reach out and pull them in.

I can feel him wriggling in my head like a worm. I try to focus. Try to drown him out so I can concentrate on the mission.

My mind stretches as far as it can go. I feel all of them, like we're in an overcrowded room. I gather them together. All of them. They have no idea we're all here like this, there's endless chatter. The headache is getting worse.

The comm line cuts through. "Maybe if we electrocute him-"

It was Hacker, but he sounded so far away.

"Won't work," the man's voice says. "When those stem cells are in, they're a part of you."

I have almost all of them, but it's crowded. Too crowded here. I keep trying to find the rest, but my head hurts. I'm getting dizzy.

"Shouldn't strain yourself when you're so new. It'll make you tired before I take over."

I keep focusing until I have all of them together. I can't believe it. It worked.

"Well, that was a good effort. Congratulations, but now you fall to me."

There's a lingering silence. I don't feel any different.

"What? Impossible! Why isn't the program taking over?"

A woman's voice comes through. "We thought it was prudent to remove that sequence and replace it with something more friendly. Your move Silas."

It's Emie. Hacker did it. I focus on the minds I've gathered, feeling their presence for one last time. No one should've had to do this.

"There are still ways I can deal with you. You take my army and I'll find another."

I activate the kill sequence against everyone in the Combine.

A crack of thunder slams into me, and in an instant I feel completely alone.

FALLOUT

I hear a rhythmic beep which matches the pattern of my heartbeat. A shallow breath forces a deeper one, and the stale air catches in my throat. I look around and I'm confined to a bed with atrocious wood paneling.

John is sitting on a chair next to a window sipping on some coffee. The smell is delightful and makes the morning feel more welcome.

I shift in bed, and John notices. He calls the team, and Shepherd, Murph and Forrest rush in to see me, while the rest trickle in.

"What the hell's goin' on?" I ask.

John swallows hard. "Godfrey, you've been in a coma for the past three weeks."

A wave of heat rushes over my face and I feel my stomach churn from the revelation.

"It's a miracle you're alive bud," Murph says. "Nearest we can tell, that chip detonated inside your head. Your chances of survival were 0.003%."

"Woo-hoo to horrible odds," I reply.

Murph continues. "After it had detonated, we were able to remove the remains, along with the stem cells. I think you implanting it yourself is the only reason you're alive."

I look around the room, studying the wood paneling. "Why does it look like we're in someone's cheap cottage?"

Sulture glares down at me. "Well since you had the brilliant idea of renouncing Ionics and placing yourself at death's door-"

"Sulture!" John snaps. "What he's trying to say Godfrey is that due to your condition we had limited options since we were in a race to keep you alive. Fortunately, thanks to Hacker, he was able to arrange for this safe house through The Grid. The police are after us because of Lynn's death, along with the break-in at Ionics R&D."

"It's worse than that," Hacker says. "They're getting the galactic bureaus involved because of all the people who suddenly dropped dead. They're keeping it quiet, but they've launched an investigation into Ionics, with General Hawkes leading the charge."

"And the *Enigma* has been placed on the no-fly list," John says.

I push myself up. Everyone is looking at me, waiting for me to say something.

"You guys get that there was no good option here right?"

"We could've found a way," Sulture hisses.

"Yeah but how long would it have taken you?!" I snap. "The Combine was hunting us and they've almost eliminated us six times! They were winning up until I used one of the transmitter chips and eliminated 99% of their rank and file in an instant!"

"Casanova's right," Warrens says. "The pressure's off of us, for now."

"No, it's probably going to get worse than ever!" John interrupts. "Without protection from Ionics, Hawkes will be able to hunt us unhindered. Thousands of scientists, soldiers, military officers, and even politicians all fell over dead in an instant. The people in power are out for blood, and they won't rest until they find their scapegoat."

Sulture speaks up. "It'll also be impossible to calculate how many years we've been set back on scientific progress-"

"For fuck's sake shut the hell up Sulture!" I scream. "The mission of the Combine wasn't for the betterment of mankind, they were seeking immortality. You heard it from Harris' own mouth. And seeing how quickly their leader dispatched Harris, someone within his inner circle, my guess is he isn't about to share his gift with humanity."

"How can we be certain?" Sulture asks.

"Because I heard him when I went under!" I snap.

The room falls silent.

Forrest shrugs. "Well if nobody else is gonna ask…what did he want?!"

"He said that I have something he needs. He tried to take over, but Emie managed to stop him."

"That was pure dumb luck," Hacker says. "Our tech is far too young to actually manage any sort of bio-encryption. Programming stem cells…only Xeclians go that far."

"Regardless, what would I have that the leader of the Combine would want?"

"Access," Hacker replies in condescension. "Your credentials will get you anywhere in the ship and he obviously wants access to our research."

"But we're not researching immortality," I reply.

"Doesn't matter," Sulture replies. "Our notes, our files, everything we have on board can be interpreted and used for different purposes. A cure can be the inspiration they need to achieve immortality."

"We need to focus on the new battlefield," John says. "We don't have many allies and any protection we did have is gone. Even our funding has dried up. Ionics and the Core government are on the war path, and I fear that they're closing in on our position."

A well of guilt swirls inside of me. "Then let's hunt down the last of the Combine. They're weak, and we're on an even playing field."

"They still have the advantage of anonymity," John says.

"Yeah, they get the advantage of being able to hide in plain sight," Sulture replies.

"Y'know, I'm a little surprised that when I turned on the kill switch, your brain didn't get fried too."

Sulture's face burns red hot. "You son of a bitch!" He lunges and grabs me by the neck. I slam my arms down, breaking his hold.

"What would you have done Sulture?!" I howl. "You seem more disappointed the Combine is dead than alive!" I leap for him, but Warrens catches me.

Shepherd and Murph restrain Sulture and John gets in between us. "Now is not the time for this bullshit!" He roars.

"Yes it is John!" I roar back. "I did the unspeakable. I killed thousands of our enemy with a single thought, but everyone here acts like I butchered their families!"

"That's not what we think Godfrey," John replies. "Our concern lies in not knowing the long-term ramifications of your actions."

"Well no one here tried very hard to stop me! Ionics, the Combine - they used us! They played us and I did something about it. I'm not proud of what I did - I will burn for all the lives I took, but you either accept what I did or turn me over to the fucking cops because I know at the end of the day they wouldn't have hesitated if those chips were in our heads!"

"You're right Godfrey," John says. He motions for Warrens to let me go. "I hoped it didn't have to go this far, but it did and we'll deal with the fallout. We'll become what we set out to be: the men who protect humanity from the monsters."

Hacker pushes his way through. "Looks like you'll have your chance sooner than you thought." He pulls up a hologram which shows thousands of naval warships heading for Earth.

"Earth space is being invaded."

"By what?" John asks.

"Grigylls," Hacker replies.

"One army for another…" I gasp.

INVASION

Godfrey's Journal, Day 334

Panic has seized the heart of every citizen on Earth. An armada looms overhead, swallowing the sky like an engorged leviathan. It threatens to strike like a hammer to an anvil, and untold devastation will be wrought on the Core's homeworld. Earth's most hated enemy is about to unleash everything they've got in an effort to crush us in one blow. There's never been a force like this over Earth's sky. It's quiet in the streets now. People have taken to hiding, waiting for the end to come. Just as I see the last person scamper indoors, the carrier ships open, and thousands of fighter jets spill out.

"Hacker!" John shouts. "Have you gotten through to the Defense Minister yet?"

"No sir, the Grigylls have jammed our communications, but I'll keep trying."

The rest of us grab everything we can, packing our bags and prepare to leave the safe house. Buildings are a bad idea when bombers are about to fly overhead.

"I've reached Defense Minister Reynolds!" Hacker shouts.

"Excellent, patch him through," John orders.

The holo shifts into a display of a man who looks about as happy as a Defense Minister could be with his planet under siege.

"Maximillian, my name is Colonel John C. Henry, Commander of the Horsemen Corps. We would like to volunteer in the effort to defend Earth, but we're marked men by the authorities and the military."

An explosion rattles the city outside. Reynolds holds a firm gaze, the two men staring each other down.

"My Generals tell me you and your men are dangerous, Henry. That you can't be trusted. That you're terrorists marauding as folk heroes."

"What do you think sir?"

Reynolds sighs. "The only reason I took this call is because you also served under General Fitch. I don't know who to believe, but I've got one hell of a situation outside." He groans in frustration. "I'll issue an order that you and your boys are to be left alone for the duration of the battle. The enemy of my enemy is my friend. After that, we'll have to reassess. How does that sound?"

"Like the best deal I'm going to get," John replies. "We'll take it sir. Thank you, we look forward for the chance to prove ourselves."

"And Henry," Reynolds says.

"Yes sir?"

"The Core military is a big place. I can order a ceasefire on you and your boys, but a lot of mine lost their lives which are being blamed on you. I'll do what I can, but in reality I won't be able to protect you out there."

"We understand, thank you sir." John shuts off the feed and turns to us. "We have to do what's right, even when it ain't easy."

"We get that," Forrest says. "But do you expect me to fight bajillions of Grigylls in that thing?!" He points to the *Enigma.* "You couldn't at least have haggled for a fighter ship?! Sujay could have!"

"It's true, I could have. Just remind Reynolds that we could be killed by his own men and-"

"I think it's time we hit the skies boys."

We scramble aboard the *Enigma* and blast off into the sky. Orbs of light fall from the sky, incinerating skyscrapers, while thousands of fighter ships swarm above them.

"Hacker, can you get us an uplink into Central Command?"

"I can try, but they're still jamming all signals. It'll be spotty at best."

"Sir, do you mind telling me your plan? Y'know, the pilot who's flying a ship with no guns?!"

"The ships the Grigylls have sent down are only a fraction of their entire fleet, and I suspect the Apollo Guard is launching an assault against the armada's main force as we speak. Our job is to isolate and cut off the fleet down here so that Central Command can focus on the main force outside of atmo."

"Oh! I got it!" Forrest shouts. He grabs tight onto the steering column and veers toward a small ship lying outside of the fleet.

"All you bozos with big metal bots - get inside them because they're the only thing around here with offensive firepower. Well except for my pe-"

"Oh sweet Vishnu, so not the time."

"Where are we going?" I ask.

"See that little guy hiding on the outskirts? That's your jammer. We get him, boom! Everyone can talk to each other again! Now suit up boys!"

We look over at John, who flashes a grin. "Suit up."

We charge into the loading bay and climb inside our mech suits. Forrest flies as close as he can to the carriers, I activate Dorothy and prepare her for delivery. I can hear the reactor churn to life right as we're about to pass the first carrier, and I hear the latches click open, releasing me. I hold on tight through the free-fall, bracing myself for a new battle.

The mech unfurls and the thrusters activate just before I make impact. Ships buzz all around, firing at me, but my shields are unfazed.

"Dorothy, let's test the cannon out against them."

"Right away Silas."

The reactor whines as power is fueled into my left arm. The Grigylls on board are scrambling to mount a defense, but I hope these machines are as powerful as we've been led to believe.

I want to *see* these monsters die.

I unleash the cannon, which tears right through the bridge. I push down and the blast cuts the carrier in half. I hit their reactor which triggers a chain reaction and causes the ship to explode. I ignite my thrusters and jet out of there, while the remaining fighters get caught in the blast.

Through the distance I see John decimate the communications scrambler ship. The mech comes alive with chatter with everyone able to talk now.

Sulture cuts in through the comm. "How am I supposed to eliminate a ship with this thing? My weapons are designed for organic beings."

"Already thought of that Rooster," Warrens replies. "Tell Phobe to switch to inorganic warfare."

He follows the instructions, but is still confused.

Hacker cuts through. "Now instead of a normal pathogen, you're equipped with a terminal computer malware which I guarantee none of the ships around you will be able to stop. Lee, you'll have the same setting, but your mech will carry the ability to fire a concentrated EMP at the target."

"*How shi sung chung*!"

"Glad you like it."

"*Da kai sa jeh*!"

"Yeah! Let's go get em'!" I howl.

Another voice cuts in through the comm. "Colonel Henry, this is General Marshall of the Apollo Guard. We see how you and your boys are handling those troop carriers down below and would be honored in bringing some of those skills up here to assist us."

Forrest squeals. "The Silver Bow Boys?! Those are the best of the best! Most people don't know it because we rarely call on them, but they're Earth's very best aerial guard!"

John chuckles. "Forrest, why don't you fly the rest of the crew up there and see what you can do to help them? We'll meet up when we're done here."

Forrest gasps. "You mean it?! Oh boy oh boy!" The *Enigma* disappears beyond the clouds while the four mechanized Horsemen are left with the remains of the fleet spearheading the invasion.

John clicks through. "Okay boys, most of these ships are destroyers and battleships. Full of firepower and covered by fighters. Fight smart."

Each of us takes on a different ship, wielding our mech suits to annihilate the Grigyll warships. We're small enough to evade their guns, yet able to deal catastrophic damage. The forces on the ground are mounting a defense, which is leaving us stuck in the crossfire. Their cannons pound the Grigyll warships even as we fight them. We focus on attacking the ship's engines, where we can't be targeted by the enemy's guns.

The Grigylls catch on to our strategy and the fighters turn their attention to us. The reactor churns in my chest, and just as a squadron gets too close, I activate the death pulse. The pulse serves a secondary purpose as an EMP, and I find grim satisfaction watching the fighters fall to their doom.

I fly to the next ship, while the destroyer behind me slowly floats toward the cityscape below. The fighters are still in pursuit. Three swoop down and fire in front of me. I draw my shields, but I'm surrounded. I try to ignite the pulse.

"I'm sorry Silas, but the reactor needs more time to recharge," Dorothy says. "I'll try rerouting power to the shields, but they're depleting fast."

I notice that Lee is also on the ship with a squadron of fighters closing in on him. We regroup and get back to back, but the fighters have us surrounded.

"*Ai yah tien ah*," Lee says.

"Same here, and I gotta wait for my reactor to recharge."

Just as we're about to be overwhelmed by a wave of fighters, blaster bolts rain down from above. I look up and see a squadron of silver ships using the sun as cover. One of them flies right past us.

"WOO!" Forrest shouts through the comm. "Gimmie one of these bad boys with Emily's help and I'll be the best fighter pilot in the galaxy!"

Hacker sighs. "I don't even know if it's worth correcting him anymore. If he doesn't get it now, he never will."

A fighter comes in, guns blazing and I leap in front of Forrest to protect him with my shield. He flies over me and dives for the other fighter.

"Yeah teamwork! Oh, I can't get over how great it is to be in one of these again!"

Forrest flies off and leads a squadron of fighters to take on the bombers. More from the Apollo guard break through Earth's skies, and it becomes apparent quickly that the battle is going to be a rout. Earth's advanced technology is simply too much for the antiquated ships the Grigylls pilot. The bombers begin to retreat back outside of atmo.

"The bomber squadrons are on the verge of collapse," Forrest says.

Sujay clicks through. "I wouldn't be so sure. It looks like they're rallying and regrouping for another run."

"No way! They're clearly breaking, otherwise their flanks would risk the dive since they possess the altitude!"

"Nu-uh! They've figured out that they don't have a speed advantage so they're rallying to gain the altitude and have the backing of their frigates! They'll send the cannons streaming down on us if we follow them!"

"You should've seen how my cannon streamed all over your mom-"

"You leave my mother out of this! We're in the middle of battling an invading fleet and all you can think about is another stupid 'your mom' joke?!"

And so began the seven minute diatribe between Forrest and Sujay about what Forrest did to Sujay's mom. They never thought to shut anyone out of the conversation through the comm network, no they just kept bickering like they always do. I'm half convinced that the reason why those two fight so well together is because the constant arguing distracts them from the deadly realities of aerial combat.

John clicks through. "They're regrouping outside the reach of Earth's cannons. General Marshall has a chance to hammer those reptiles with his artillery."

Marshall cuts in. "We're hittin' them as hard as we can Colonel. I'd appreciate it if you and your boys rallied up here to help us out. I just got word that Earth can handle herself."

"You heard him Epoch squad, let's move out!"

The four of us ignite our thrusters and prepare for space combat.

As we breach atmo, we were never prepared for the full size and scope of the Grigyll fleet. Thousands more warships slowly fall in, and what we saw down below was only the tip of the spear.

"This is where heroes become legends gentlemen," John says.

"You can say that again!" Forrest replies. "WOO!" He leads a squadron right into the fray, taking the invasion fleet head on.

John signals General Marshall. "Sir, how did this fleet get past the Ares Defense?"

"That's a question *I* still don't have an answer to Henry. In my opinion I think someone on Mars let 'em through. Those martians are some tough sons-o-bitches, and I'd be hard pressed to believe they'd give anything up without being told to."

John turns to us. "Looks like we still have allies around here. Now, let's descend into Hell."

"We're right with you sir," I reply.

The four of us split up and charge for the leading warships. Small flares from the ensuing battle rage overhead, and the Apollo Guard is losing ground. Guns are firing on all sides and despite being unable to hear the battle rage, my blood boils at the sight of these disheveled ships.

I activate my cannon and carve a line down the back of the ship. The exhaust mufflers fade into darkness and the ship comes to a halt. I climb atop, waiting for the reactor to recharge and go after the next ship. The Grigylls inside fight a losing battle of their own as they attempt to seal the ship up, but the hole I carved is torn open by the vacuum of space. Dozens of Grigylls are ripped out and float by, dying in seconds. It's the first time I see our enemy during this battle. The first time I see their beady eyes and don't feel fear, I feel a deep primal hatred as if it were coded within my DNA. I want the others to see their comrades floating in space, and to feel helpless as they watch them die.

But that comes to naught as their cannons fire at me, the blasts driving right through the carcasses. They don't care. They only yearn to see me die, even if they must destroy the bodies of their allies to do so. A new Grigyll war has been unleashed, and this time I don't think the Core will give them the chance to live.

An oncoming frigate veers to avoid the dying ship I stand over. I kick on my thrusters and charge, trying to evade the small guns which line the ship. Two ships from the Apollo guard fall in to cover my flanks and destroy the enemy guns. I have Dorothy reach out and connect with their commlinks.

"Thanks for your help boys."

"It's the least we could do sir. Your mechs are taking each of these ships one at a time. Anything we can do to protect you, we'll do it."

"Glad to hear, but don't wait for me when I get to the engines. Take cover, and tell the others we'd really appreciate you escorting us."

"Sure thing Commander Godfrey."

I fly behind the frigate and carve out the top two propulsion engines and let space do the rest of the work. It's like cracking a shell and watching everything spill out. If there's one thing we're going to make the Grigylls feel, it's terror at the sight of the Horsemen.

The other ships catch on and their fighters start battling to the last to defend their engines. My shields take a lot of hits, but I either hit them with my death pulse or a squadron from the Apollo Guard saves my ass.

I switch tactics and search out an air carrier. I want these monsters to *see* what we can do to them. I veer off and fly inside the carrier. I have Dorothy record video of me breaching their shields and slaughter the marines who try to stop my advance. I carve them up with my scythe, but there are too many. I unleash a death pulse, which vaporizes them into charred skeletons. More of them swarm in, shooting me with their blasters. I adjust the controls to create a larger blast and fire another pulse.

Except nothing happens.

"I'm sorry Silas," Dorothy says. "I can't allow you to fire the pulse in quick succession, the internal shields must recharge in order to prevent you from exposure to radiation."

"Damn it, override the settings!"

"Silas I can't-"

"I *order* you to!"

The control panel changes status and I unleash another death pulse which consumes half of the ship. I feel a wave of nausea overtake me, but Dorothy injects me with some anti-radiation medicine I created.

The lights overhead go dark. I consider that good enough. I send Hacker the video feed and tell him to have it set to repeat and shown on every Grigyll screen across the fleet.

The battle rages for hours as we slowly turn the tide. I wield my death pulse to devastating effect, but it takes a heavy toll on my body. I'm overloaded with anti-radiation medicine and I've pushed the mech far beyond recommended limits. The Grigylls press hard, even firing in the midst of their own in an effort to get a shot at us. Warships from Earth join the battle, driving the Grigylls back even further.

Hacker clicks in through the comm. "There's something off about the Grigyll ships."

"What is it?" John asks.

"I can't tell from their scripts, but it looks as though they're powering up their warp drives and-"

One of the Grigyll ships overhead launches directly into a Core battleship at warp speed, splitting the ship in half.

Another Grigyll frigate does it to a Core carrier. The bastards are launching themselves at the Earth fleet so they can get away. I ignite my thrusters to go after the first warship, but something holds me back.

It's John.

"If you try to go after them and they launch into the Core fleet, it'll be a suicide mission."

"We have to do something!" I scream. I notice out of the corner of my eye three fighters close in on us. They dive down and fire on John's six.

"John, your six!" I howl.

He turns and fires with his gatling gun, but they don't stop. My sensors indicate that John's shields are on the verge of collapse. I try to fire with my canon, but the reactor is still charging.

A frigate next to us opens fire. I try to intercept the blast, but I don't reach John in time. He's knocked to his knees, and his shields are depleted. The fighters launch their bolts.

My heart freezes when I see three of them pierce John's chest.

"NO!" I howl in agony. I set my canon to overdrive and shoot the fighters, carving them in half. The frigate fires on us again, but I grab ahold of John and pull him back to the bridge for cover.

"John are you alright?! I'll get you back to the *Enigma* where Murph can patch you up."

John coughs up blood. "No Godfrey. They got me in the heart and the liver, I'm a goner."

"No!" I scream. "You can't leave us John! I won't let you!" The ship beneath our feet rumbles as the frigate's cannons hammer the other side.

More fighters sweep in to finish us off, but I launch right at them.

"Dorothy, a death pulse!"

"Silas, I must warn you-"

"Just shut up and do it!"

The reactor churns and rumbles angrily against my heart, and the violet bubble sweeps through the ships, sending the fighters tumbling into the abyss. My stomach feels as though a vise has clamped down and refuses to let up, but I turn around and fly back to John.

"C'mon! Let's get out of here John!"

"No, their fleet is getting away," He growls.

"Shut up and let me fly you out of here!"

"Silas, my suit has a built-in inversion matrix and I'm going to use it to eliminate what's left of the Grigyll fleet."

I feel my insides shatter like glass. "You can't do this to us! We need you to lead us John! *I* need you!" Hot tears rage down my face as I watch my mentor, my friend, prepare for his demise.

John signals General Marshall. "Marshall, pull your men back. I'm ready to activate an inversion matrix that will take care of the Grigyll fleet, but your boys need to get out of there."

"No John! Keep fighting! Now is not the time to surrender!" I scream.

"Silas, I've taken the Horsemen as far as they can go. As my last act as commanding officer, I, John C. Henry name Silas Godfrey, Commander of the Horsemen Corps."

I should be honored, but all I feel is a hallow emptiness.

"I won't know how to lead them!"

"You know everything you need to Silas. Dorothy, get him outta here."

"NO! You won't do this to me!" I scream. I try to move my controls, but they've locked up on me.

"I'm sorry Silas, but John has an override protocol I must follow."

"STOP THIS! SOMEBODY STOP THIS!" I scream.

John floats above the ship right as the frigate rips through her remnants. He blasts off into the distance, ahead of the fleeing Grigyll warships. A gray light flashes in his place, and the ships at the front are pulled into a black abyss.

The synthetic black hole drags the entire invading fleet into a maelstrom of crushed metal. The ships launching at warp speed are ripped in half, while the remaining ones are turned into a metal heap. Fighters even come back in an attempt to escape, but their engines stall as the gravitational pull becomes too much. They too are dragged in. I stand far beyond its reach, yet I still feel the pull, as if a dark lord is trying to bring me into his domain.

When all is said and done the fleet is gone. Vanished into the unknown, and so is my leader. My teacher, my friend. John is gone, having sacrificed himself so that our enemy couldn't get away.

When the gravity well subsides, my stomach churns from the sight of John dying and the effects of the Hadrian gem. I open the waste hatch and vomit in my suit. I notice tiny flecks of blood, but I flush it out.

Our commlink fills with cheers of victory from the Apollo Guard and Earth warships. There are no cheers from the Horsemen. My throat is raw and it feels like nails are being driven through my stomach. We regroup at the airbase where the *Enigma* is stationed. I lock in and power down Dorothy. My eyelids are so heavy. The door opens up and I catch my reflection in a mirror. I look ghastly, as if all color had been drained from my face.

I see the others, who all look at me. I try to wave at them, but I trip over my own feet and stumble into darkness.

SOLACE

I'm standing in front of a house in the middle of a suburb. The rain is pouring, and his name is on the list. I sigh deeply, resigned to the task ahead. I grab a hold of the handle and press down slowly, until the latch releases and lets me inside. My cloak hangs heavily on my neck and clings to my armor, while my visors are covered in beads of water. The door is unlocked and I slip in as quiet as a ghost.

The family is sitting down to dinner. I've felt his presence before, but I've only seen him now for the first time. They don't know I'm here. I walk around the table, looking at their trinkets and photos of locked memories from happier times.

"Please don't hurt my daddy!" It's his little girl. She's looking right at me. I feel exposed, unable to hide from her big, gray eyes. She looks so hurt, and reminds me of how I'd always wished for a daughter.

He sits there, eating one scoop of food after another. I don't know who he is.

"They experimented on children!" A voice screams. It's mine. "He's on the list. He needs to die!"

My mind swirls in conversation with itself.

"Please don't hurt my daddy!" The girl is more determined this time.

"I have no intention to-" Before I can finish, he sees me. His eyes burn with pain and in an instant, he falls over, dead. A droplet of blood trickles from his ear, but aside from this, you'd have no idea of the cause.

"Daddy!" Her shriek pierces my ears. She looks up at me with red, puffy eyes and screams at me. More screams follow and before I realize it, I'm drowning in the howls of every family member who found their loved ones snatched away in an instant.

"Their names were on the list," I reason. They all had to die.

I gasp and almost fall out of bed.

The overhead lights are oppressive and the room smells sterilized. Tubes are coming out of me everywhere. I run to a nearby sink and splash some cold water on my face. When I look up into the mirror, I see the little girl.

I take the mirror, rip it off the wall and slam it against the railing of my bed. The Combine took everything from us, including John.

Jesus Christ. John's gone.

I rail the mirror against the bed, shards of silver fly everywhere. I hear the wood splinter, but I keep slamming the frame down in a desperate effort to make something feel more pain than I do.

"SILAS!"

The scream jolts me out of my stupor. It's Murph and he's in his white coat with an MD badge.

"Where are we?!" I growl.

"We're with the Apollo Guard, inside their medical facility."

I want to scream. I want to rage. At the same time I want to dig my own grave and hide until the end comes.

All this time I thought I was strong enough to hold it together. I thought I could handle adversity, but my soul withers and my thoughts are turning corrosive. It's tainting my blood, turning everything to hatred. Hatred of the Combine, the Grigylls, hell even hatred of John for recruiting me in the first place. I should've stayed on Titan and accepted my sentence. I shouldn't have joined the Horsemen.

"Hey bud, how about we clean up the bed and you try lying down?" Murph asks.

I catch my reflection in one of the mirror shards. I look like a ghastly wretch with sunken eyes that are barely held together. The Hadrian gem has taken it's toll, and I find myself wondering how am I supposed to lead the Horsemen?

Murph waves in a few nurses who clean up the bed and pick up the pieces of mirror. I approach the bed, slip beneath the new sheet and yearn for death to take me.

"How about I get a cute nurse to look after you huh?"

"Sure Murph, sounds great," I reply. The truth is, I want him to go away. I want to wallow in my pity. So much death. I close my eyes and see the faces behind the Combine. I see the scorched bones of the Grigylls. Yet I'm still here.

"Is it safe to come in?" A nurse asks with a sly grin. She's a blue-eyed brunette with her hair held in a simple ponytail. Her eyes are calming, while there's a strength in her voice.

"Sure, just watch your step."

She sucks in a breath through her teeth when she sees the mirror. "Nobody liked that thing anyway. It was big, bulky and made us all look ten pounds heavier."

I can't help but chuckle. "I had some pent-up frustration."

"Well, Dr. McGinnis says you've been through a lot the last few weeks. If I were you, I'd be asking for something stronger than these painkillers. Like whiskey."

I chuckle again. "What's your name?"

"Angela, but you can call me 'Angie.' "

She takes my arm and gently reinserts the IV port. I catch the faint smell of her perfume, a comforting warm vanilla.

"I'd tell you my name, but you probably already know it."

"Oh yeah. The higher-ups rushed you in to treat for a new kind of radiation poisoning. None of the doctors knew what to do, so Dr. McGinnis stepped in. They ordered us to give you heroes whatever you needed."

"Hero," I scoff. "I don't deserve the title. All I did was kill a bunch of lizards."

"That's not how we see it. You helped rebuff an invasion force that threatened Earth itself. If the Horsemen hadn't intervened, the Core government would be in shambles. Now they're launching every ship we have to go to war."

"We're at war?"

"Yeah, the Core declared it the day after the invasion."

"How long have I been out?"

"It's been five days since the attack."

I sit and let the thought sink in. Another coma that I barely survive. I don't know if something out there is watching over me or refusing to let me die.

"I'm surprised at you," Angie says.

"Why's that?"

"Dr. McGinnis warned that you'd try to be flirtatious."

"You sound disappointed." I flash her a grin.

She smiles and tries to hide a blush. "Just sayin' it might make my day."

"Maybe when I'm a bit less ghoulish."

"Deal," She says with a gentle smile. It gives me comfort, but my eyelids grow heavy. I can feel sleep pulling me under.

An invasion fleet is over Earth. An armada of Grigylls seeks to conquer the human race, but I won't let them. I fly out and attack them on their ships. I charge against an army, but I'm routed in an instant. One of them leaps over the others and his claw slashes my throat.

The scene resets. John is next to me. The two of us open fire on the Grigylls, but we're overrun. I watch helplessly as they dog pile him and tear him to pieces.

A thousand scenes unravel in my head, each one with the same ending: John dies. Each time is different, but the end result is always the same. I feel trapped within a realm I can only describe as a black hole. I claw for a way out, but there is no escape. I slide further into the abyss, but I feel a spark of anger ignite within my chest. I feel the anger grow, becoming an inferno that is consuming me from the inside. My skin flakes away, revealing a raw, pulsing energy like what the ion clones possess. I feel all the energy being pent up, and my anger only makes it grow. I want to unleash it all and burn the Grigylls for what they've done. I feel the gate open in my chest, releasing my own death pulse.

I'm shaken awake. The air smells of ozone and sparks of electricity flare in the air. The lights flicker, while my hands feel ashen. I claw at the bed, trying to escape, but I've been strapped down. My anger rises and a small lightning bolt leaps from my fingertip.

I look to the window and nurses are staring at me in shock. The alarm is blaring overhead and Murph charges into the room.

"Murph, what is happening to me?!"

"Side effect from the radiation bud." He draws a syringe and plunges it into my neck. My anger rises again, but my limbs and joints become too heavy for me to lift. I feel darkness pull me back into the lull of a forced sleep.

"Good morning!" Angie chirps. I shake off a groggy stupor, wondering where the straps are.

"Wasn't I strapped to the bed?"

"What?! No! You must have some weird dreams."

"Huh. Could've sworn it was real."

"Last I heard from the doc was you got some desperately needed rest. You're lookin' a lot better too!" She hands me a mirror, and I look to have rejoined the land of the living.

"Dr. McGinnis said you boys lost someone close to you. Mind telling me who he was?"

"He was our commanding officer, a Colonel who believed in all of us. He molded and shaped us into a band of warriors when the rest of the galaxy had abandoned us. He sacrificed himself to take out what was left of the Grigyll fleet. His last order was to name me as commander of the Horsemen Corps."

"Sounds like quite an honor."

"It is, but I don't know if I can lead them. I don't think I'm ready."

"Few who're given the mantle of leadership are. I think the others care for you more than you know. They've been waiting on your recovery for six days."

I watch Angie in fascination as she moves around the room. Her smile is lighter than a feather, and her eyes feel like she can see and accept me for who I am. She's the type of woman I've longed for my entire life, and perhaps in another time our paths could've crossed sooner. My mind plays with the idea of giving up the Horsemen, naming another successor and staying here with Angie. I could disappear again and form a new life. I've done it before, I can do it again.

"Angie, will you have dinner with me?"

She turns and looks at me in surprise. A smile spreads across her face. "I'm afraid the hospital has a strict policy against us dating patients."

"Then be a bad girl and break the rules. I'm way more interesting than any schmuck you'll find out on the street."

"Hmm, good point. Okay, I'll sneak a second helping up here and we'll have dinner together."

True to her word, Angie brings an extra large tray of bread and soup. While it wasn't special, it still beat the slop we ate aboard the *Enigma.* Would I still serve the same food aboard the ship? Many other such questions linger in the back of my mind, but I force them out as I enjoy this meal with a beautiful woman.

"So what made you become a nurse?"

"It's funny, growing up I couldn't stand the sight of blood. But…an accident with my sister forced me to get past it."

"What happened?"

"A speeder accident. She was impaled and her leg got cut off. The medics found me trying to put her back together." A tear glides down her cheek and I brush it away with my thumb.

"What made you join the Horsemen? I'm curious as to what could convince any of you to join."

"We all have our stories. I was a chemistry professor who was bitter and resentful for a life lost. I sabotaged student's work to see if they'd stand up for themselves. I convinced myself I was there to protect all of the nuclear, chemical and bio weapons locked in Titan's vaults, but I was too afraid to leave. My exploits against students went too far, and I faced life in prison. Thanks to helping cure a stranger from being poisoned, John was able to find and grant me my freedom in exchange for my service to the Horsemen."

"Wait, who was the stranger?"

"My teammate, Hacker."

"Wow, incredible how we end up in some places isn't it?"

"It is."

"What'd you do before you were a professor?"

"I worked at Chemron, one of the largest manufacturers of industrial solvents in the galaxy."

"Did you like it there?"

"Not a bit. They did a lot of shady stuff and manufactured most of the chemical weapons used during the Unification Wars. Leaves a sour taste in your mouth."

"I imagine. Why become a professor?"

"Chemistry was all I'd known. I was driven into the field by my father, who saw Chemron as the be-all end-all gateway to the scientific community since every laboratory needed our cleaning solutions."

"I take it by your tone that you and he didn't get along?"

"That's an understatement. He was a greedy, selfish prick obsessed with what went into his pockets. I got rid of him from my life and that was it."

"Is he still alive?"

"No, he died in an accident." I chuckle. "I don't really know why I'm telling you all of this, it's not like you need to know my life story."

Angie smiles at me. "Maybe not, but isn't this what life is about? Getting to know each other and connecting?" I look down at her lips and I notice she looks down at mine. I lean in and kiss her, tenderly.

When I pull away, she smiles and kisses me back.

The two of us switch between sharing stories and kisses for hours, never stopping to look at the time. We bare our souls to one another and I become connected with Angie on a level I've never known.

Our kissing leads to the two of us making passionate love. Never in my life had I felt such desire for a woman or the feeling of acceptance than with her. I became obsessed with her body, kissing her everywhere I could. We fall asleep wrapped in each other's arms and I make my decision just before I fade to sleep.

The next morning, Angie slips out of bed, but not without me noticing.

"You probably need to go." I can hear her force the strength in her voice. I take her hands and kiss her fingers before looking deep into her eyes.

"I'm going to stay here with you Angie."

Her eyes shake as I look into them. I can hear the thoughts

debating in her mind. "Are you sure?" She asks.

"More sure of this than anything." I kiss her sweet lips. "I'll go out, tell the others and name a successor."

"Okay." She smiles. "I'll go get Dr. McGinnis."

Murph comes in with a fresh set of clothes. "How you doin' bud?"

"I feel much better. How's everyone else?"

"Not good. There's a lot of tension with the team."

"About…?"

"You being in charge."

"And what do you think?"

"I think you'll be fine. Isn't me you have to worry about."

"Let me take a wild guess who."

"Yeah," Murph sighs.

The two of us walk back to the *Enigma.* As the others fall in line, I feel the butterflies and yearn to run away.

Not this time. This time I face the Horsemen and tell them I plan on staying with Angie.

Sulture walks up to the two of us, a fury in his eyes. He strikes me down without saying a word.

"More interested in getting yourself off than leading us?!"

Shepherd and Warrens leap onto him, while Sulture thrashes like an animal.

"You have no right to lead us Godfrey!" He screams. "If you'd protected John we wouldn't be in this mess! Everything around you dies!"

I feel a trickle of blood from my lip. I rise from the ground and look down at Sulture, pure contempt pouring out of his eyes. As I look down on him, I realize why John chose me to lead. Sulture gives in to anger and will tread over anyone who gets in his way. The others look to me, seeking my response.

I realize I can't leave these men. We've sworn an oath of brotherhood, and now that our leader is gone, that oath is more important than ever. I can't turn my back on them. I can't turn my back on John's final order. And while it pains me, I must break this to Angie.

"Lock him up, I'll deal with him shortly," I order. Warrens and

Shepherd drag him away, while Lee and Hacker look down at me with the same eyes of contempt.

I turn to Murph. "I need to say goodbye to Angie. I'll be right back."

"Sure thing, Sir," Murph replies. "You heard him boys! Let's get ready to roll out!"

I search the hospital and find Angie. She notices my eye.

"And they didn't take it well."

"No," I chuckle. "This was from me being named commander. Angie I-"

She puts her finger over my lips. "I understand. I don't like it, but I understand."

"How'd you know?"

"Because it's a promise to keep," She says. "The Horsemen are in danger Silas. Protect them."

"I will," I reply. "And when this is all over, I'll come back for you Angie. I want to be a part of you forever."

"You will always be a part of me Silas."

I climb aboard the *Enigma* and go to John's…I mean, my office. I pull out my old journal showing its wear from our travels.

Godfrey's Journal, Day 342

One night as passionate lovers will serve as a better memory than the death of a flame which slowly burns out through the night. That's what Angie and I will become: a memory that cannot be contaminated or corrupted. One that will only become more perfect as time passes on...

SCHISM

Godfrey's Journal Day 343

I face my greatest challenge yet. It is up to me to lead the Horsemen into the unknown. Our team has divided into two camps. Hacker, Lee and Sujay are all ready to follow Sulture. Murph, Shepherd and Forrest are with me. Warrens will remain neutral and follow whoever is in charge. Sulture has been locked up for the day, but I need to decide what to do with him. Such insubordination must be punished, but I also need to heal this team. It is my mission to unite them under one banner and accomplish what we set out to do. It's now or never.

"Emie, turn on the computer," I order.

"Sorry Silas, it's locked via bio-encryption. Place your finger on the keypad."

I do as Emie says, and the computer goes through a long reset process since a new user has been detected.

"Voice input."

"Commander Silas Godfrey." Even hearing it out loud I still can't believe it.

The screen lights up, and brings in every application I'll need. There's also a notification that I have a message. I try to click elsewhere, but Emie says I can't do anything without listening to the message first.

I click the link, and the screen fades to black. A recording of John takes its place and automatically begins to play.

"Godfrey, I'm sure you've been left wondering why I put you in charge, and that others are questioning this decision."

"Tell me about it," I reply as I rub my chin.

"The truth is Godfrey that your ability to lead the Horsemen was apparent to me. You have good rapport with the others, even if that's not obvious now. You must show them why you're to be respected, but don't abuse your power. You will want to maintain your friendship with the men. Don't. You must keep a healthy distance because they can't see you as anything less than their leader.

Your first mission is to unify the Horsemen. I believe that you're the only one who can do this without destroying them. Treat all of them with honor, justice and respect. In time, they will fall in line as long as you show leadership. Prove you're the bigger man, even when you don't want to be.

Next is the far more difficult mission. You once said that our purpose has been bastardized, that the Combine has ruined everything the Horsemen stood for. You're right, and now you must be prepared for what comes next. Your new mission is to destroy the Combine at all costs. They are the greatest threat to our galaxy, and the Grigyll invasion is a part of their master plan, don't be fooled. I have in here everything I've collected on the Combine at your disposal. Our enemy is wounded, but far from destroyed. Unfortunately, all they've done is replaced their army of scientists with an army of Grigylls to protect their leadership.

I wish you the very best of luck, Commander Godfrey. I may not be here anymore, but adversity forces us to grow in ways we never thought possible. I know you'll make an excellent leader and in time your leadership will surpass my own. But know this: there will be times when it feels like the entire galaxy will conspire against you. I chose you Godfrey because I know that deep down you want to fight until the bitter end. That no matter what comes against you and the Horsemen you won't surrender. There's probably a part of you that still believes you're that professor on Titan, always running away. Now's your chance to become the man you were meant to be. Goodbye and good luck Commander."

John salutes me in his video and I do the same. A tear glides down my cheek, a mixture of pride and shame swirling in my blood. I look out into the dark skies and feel strength flow back into me. My heart aches from John's passing, but I'm forever grateful to not only have known such a great man, but to have called him a mentor and a friend.

I realize among the stars are billions of people counting on us. Counting on me. I have eight of the most brilliant men in the galaxy aboard my ship. I can't wallow in pity or run away any more. It's time to face this mission head on, and not flinch in the face of fear, just like John would've done.

I head into the meeting room where everyone is waiting. All eyes fall on me, wondering what I'll do next.

"Shepherd, Warrens. Go get Sulture."

"Yes sir," the two reply.

"The rest of you, fall in for a meeting."

Everyone but Hacker does so. He keeps working at his station.

"Hacker, fall in now!"

"Just a minute," He scoffs. It's clear he's taking his time and has decided to go at his own pace. I storm up to Hacker, grab him by the shoulders, throw him against the wall and seize him by the throat.

"Defiance to me is defiance to John!" I roar. "He named me as his successor and you will honor that!" I shove him in line, while a look of shock lines everyone's faces. Shepherd and Warrens wait at the doorway with Sulture who still has a look of defiance.

"Bring him to the center." They do as instructed, and leave him bound in the middle.

"On your knees," I order.

Sulture stares into the distance and doesn't move a muscle.

"I wasn't asking!" I growl as I kick out the back of his leg.

"His pistol," I order while holding out my hand.

Shepherd pulls the gun from behind his back and hands it to me.

"Silas," Murph says.

"It's Commander now!" I snap. I turn and face the men. "We've been through a lot together. We've been to hell and back. We've survived much worse, and we'll survive this. In the military, striking an officer is punishable by death." I cock the gun, and the men gasp. Sulture closes his eyes and his breathing has gone shallow.

"Is this what you sacrificed everything for Sulture? To die on your knees for something as trivial as striking your CO? Would your son look up to you for this?"

Sulture's lip quivers and tears flow between his closed eyelids. His face glows a fiery red, but I can feel him breaking inside.

"Will my death honor your family's memory?" I ask. I unlock his binders and hold the pistol up to him.

His red eyes look at me, a mixture of confusion and anger.

"Go on, take it. If this is what will make their deaths mean something, then kill me."

Sulture takes the pistol and inspects it to see if it's real. He looks at me, then at the pistol. His eyes shift to the floor and he holds the pistol back up to me.

I take the gun and hand it off to Shepherd. "Execution won't help us. It won't unify us at a time when we need unity more than ever. John is gone and he isn't coming back. We must rise up to take on the Combine and destroy them once and for all!"

Sulture rises and takes his place in line. There is a resentment in him, but I don't think he'll try anything stupid.

"Now, let's go run some drills. You've all gotten pudgy on civilian food while I was out." The others groan out loud.

I'm the first one back in the gym and I dive in to our drills with renewed enthusiasm.

After a long workout session, I go into my office and raid John's liquor stash. I carry the box out and toss a bottle to most of the guys, and I hand one to Sulture.

"Let's reminisce and tell our favorite John stories," I say. We tell about how he found us, all his quirks and what made him a great CO. Sulture drinks silently in the background, watching me as I joke with the others. I hold up a toast to him, but he gives the same stone-faced look I know all too well. I grab my bottle and walk up to him. I need to know the source of this resentment.

"Let's talk."

"Fuck off Godfrey."

"That was an order, not a request."

"Pulling rank now huh?" His words have a slur, and he stumbles as he stands up. We head into a side room.

"Would you rather I shot you through the head?"

"Sometimes, yes."

"Why?!"

"You're reckless. You let John get killed and you killed all those scientists with your goddamn brain!"

"What would you have had me do Sulture? Take John's place?"

"You'll never be the Commander he was." Sulture's glassy eyes show no restraint in their hatred of me.

"Thanks for the feedback, but it was your temper that made me accept the position."

"What?"

"I was prepared to walk away. I was ready to start over and live a new life, but when you walked up and struck me. I realized that I couldn't allow myself to defy John's last wish."

"You son of a-" Sulture takes as swing at me, but I catch his fist and seize his throat.

"I let you live once today. Was that a mistake?"

"You're a fucking abomination," Sulture hisses. "You should've died on that table."

"Sorry to disappoint," I reply. I release him and he gasps for air. "Think of your family and why you joined the Horsemen. The reason why you're here hasn't changed, only management. And rest assured Sulture, I'll consult with you and the others just like John did. I've held your life in my hand twice, and twice I've given it back."

"You just keep me around because you need something from me."

"Maybe," I reply. "Or, maybe I respect and admire your intelligence and *need* you to be a part of the team."

Sulture glares as though he doesn't believe me. I grab him by the throat again. "Or maybe you're right. Maybe you'll push me too far, break my sense of mercy and I'll kill you outright." He chokes and gags, trying to break my grip. His eyes turn red and his gaze turns desperate.

"But you're right. As of right now, I still need you," I release him again. He falls to the floor, sucking in air. "Now, go sleep off the alcohol."

I don't know if I reached Sulture or not, only time will tell. I hope he learned that I'll do whatever is necessary to get him to learn his lesson. However, there's still someone else on the team whose allegiance I need if I'm ever to succeed. I find him also drinking alone, but he's tinkering with his software.

"Hacker, let's talk."

"What is there to talk about?"

I get in his face. "Your fucking attitude!" His hands curl into fists, but he takes deep breaths to control himself.

"John's dead. We need to move past it."

"You don't understand," Hacker replies. Tears glide down his face as he struggles to hold himself together.

"He was like a father to all of us."

"It's not just that!" Hacker snaps. "You're reckless! You react based on your gut, not on facts! If we keep operating that way, we'll die for sure!"

I swallow hard, suppressing my urge to fire back. "What's done is done, we must accept it and live with the consequences. Having said that, I will take into consideration all evidence when making a future decision. But when I make a decision, I expect you to accept it."

"You're talking too good for a drunk man," Hacker says.

I grab the bottle and take a long swig. He chuckles and takes another drink.

"I know it was you who recommended me to John."

He takes another drink. "Yeah, well you saved my life. Couldn't let you rot in prison on Titan."

"I almost left, y'know."

"Yeah, I do." He sighs. "It wouldn't have worked."

"Why not?"

"Because the Grid is compromised. Ionics owns them. Part of the deal to get General Hawkes off our backs when John and I were cornered. If you were to have approached the Grid again for an identity wipe, they would pass that information to the Combine leaders and they'd track your every move."

"And since we cut ties with Ionics, we won't have access to their information anymore either."

"We might get some tips from old friends, but yeah, we're functionally cut off. We're also broke too."

I look at Hacker with confusion.

"Ionics was the lifeblood of this operation. They funded everything we did. Right or wrong, our ability to operate hinged on them. We don't have any resources, so why John favored splitting apart didn't make any sense to me."

"Because he knew we'd figure it out."

"There's not much to figure out. Ionics cut all of our funding after hundreds of employees dropped dead and they pinned it on us. There's nothing left."

A thought dwells on me. A secret buried within my past that I would've preferred taking to my grave, but now it's clear we need it.

"Does anyone else know about this?"

Hacker takes another drink. "No."

"I have an idea. We'll convene tomorrow and discuss it with the rest. In the meantime, get some sleep."

I leave the room, not knowing if I really solved anything or not. My eyelids grow heavy and the alcohol is starting to hit. I need to get some sleep as well.

I come across Shepherd, who is drinking and staring out the window. He's oblivious to my presence until I sit down next to him.

"How're you taking it?" I ask.

"It's been hard," He says as he watches the sky. Outside are beautiful plumes of nebula clouds dancing along, intertwining with one another. It's a myriad of colors - violet, green, goldenrod, blue and red all mixing together in a twirling display.

"Beautiful isn't it?"

"It's breathtaking," I reply.

"It's easy to miss something like this until it's gone. I like to think that John brought it to us."

I grunt and nod. The two of us sit in silence and watch the nebula pass us by.

"You have to lead the Horsemen," Shepherd says in a shaking voice.

"The team will fall apart if you don't."

"How do you know?"

"Because you're the only one who keeps us in balance. The others are extremists, and none of them will listen to me. You know how to keep them in line. I mean, I almost shit myself when you gave the pistol to Sulture, how'd you know he wouldn't shoot?"

"I didn't. But I figured that if he shot me everyone else would beat his ass."

"You can't do that shit Silas!" Shepherd snaps. "You can't be that reckless!"

I chuckle. "You're the third guy today to tell me that. Maybe there's something to it."

"You're damn right there is! But you saved us! You saved us from the Combine's army."

"I replaced one army with another. Unfortunately the Grigylls are much worse than the Combine."

"You made a decision and you stuck to it. That's the leadership we'll need going forward. John was great at getting us to see something from all sides, but now we need someone who will act and galvanize us into action. We all like and respect you, even if I'm the only one who'll say it."

Maybe I should've given John more credit. He brought me in without allies or friends and I was able to connect with all of the men here. They became my brothers, but now they're forced to accept that I'm in charge. I can either hide or rise to the challenge and accept the mantle of leadership. Decisions need to be made, and not every decision John made was popular either. We must be able to live with the consequences of our actions. I smile as I realize John's plan, and I finally feel the honor that I've been bestowed with.

"Thank you Shepherd. We need to get some sleep, so don't stay up much longer."

"Yes sir," He replies. "And Silas?"

"Yeah?"

"You'll be a great commander. The rest will come around. We all believe in you, even if I'm the only one willing to say it."

"Thank you David." I turn and head into my office, finally having heard the words I'd desperately needed to hear.

LEARNING HOW TO INVEST

Godfrey's Journal Day 344

Hacker made the facts crystal clear by showing me our bank account. Zero. Zilch. Nothing. If we were to continue as a team, we'd need financing, and as it stood, nobody needed a band of mercenaries at the moment. We were too hot for the military, and still aren't on the best of terms with them. Hacker figures we have enough to last a week before we restock on food, water and oxygen for the ship. After that, we'll have nothing left.

I ask Hacker to gather the rest of the men, while I perform a search on one of the tablets. After almost ten years, the vault is still there. Unaccessed, untouched. Opening it will make my worst fears come true, but the circumstances have changed.

I shut the tablet off and join the others in the common area. Their eyes all fall on me, wondering what this is about. I bring up the tablet and show a star map of us traveling towards the Arkellian sector.

"Hacker has brought it to my attention that we're broke. Severing ties with Ionics meant cutting ourselves off from corporate funding. We still have too many enemies in the military for me to believe that we can sustain ourselves on merc contracts."

"I know some people," Warrens says. "I'll reach out to 'em."

"I appreciate the offer, but I have a plan which will set us free financially for good."

"Wh-wh-why are we heading to the Arkellian sector?" Forrest asks.

"What's out there?" Shepherd asks.

Sujay shivers out loud. "Arkellia houses the most closely guarded vaults in the galaxy. It's where the rich and powerful store their money - including the Core government!"

"I got it!" Forrest shouts. "How about I just take one for the team and marry a really rich old woman? I'm okay with her being my sugar momma!"

"Forrest, that won't be necessary," I reply.

"Aww c'mon! What woman wouldn't want this?"

"Any woman," Sujay replies.

"Well that's funny, because your mom refers to me as white chocolate delight and-"

"Forrest, stop there," I order. He fluffs his collar and sits back down.

I scroll across the screen until a schematic of a vault comes into view. It has a number and some statistics connected to a live feed from the Galactic Arkellian Reserve, the bank where it's housed.

"What is it?" Warrens asks.

"The way Arkellian banks work is they store all information and personal possessions inside these vaults."

Sujay interrupts. "Yeah, and they guard them with men who are more heavily armed than soldiers!"

"It's true we'll have to knock a few guards out," I reply. "However, we can cut the door open and crack their central computer, which will allow us to download billions of credits. Worst case, we screw up and download a sum in the millions."

"I doubt an Arkellian internal computer will be that easy to crack," Hacker says. "I also don't believe we'll be able to get away with that much before the authorities show up."

"No, Godfrey's right," Forrest replies. "The banks are so heavily armed that they don't feel a need to have any military stationed nearby. The banks *are* the law on Arkellia and if your competitor was getting robbed…"

He pauses, but nobody responds. "Well, there's no reason to help the other guy keep *his* dough."

"Why this vault?" Sulture asks from the back. He wanders into the circle as though he's intrigued.

"The vault belonged to one of the founders of Chemron," I reply. "Decades' worth of income, stock share dividend payments and other bonds purchased all amount to billions in untold wealth."

Hacker gasps. He ignites his gauntlet and brings up old video footage of a skyscraper on fire. "It would've been one of those who died in that mysterious explosion fifteen years ago."

"The very same," I reply. "And he died without an heir. The timer above the vault counts down to the twenty-year anniversary when there has been no account activity. When that ticker hits zero, the bank keeps everything inside for itself. Clean, quiet and unreported income."

"How do you know so much about this Silas?" Shepherd asks.

"I worked at Chemron, remember?"

"You knew an awful lot about the bank accounts of the executives," Hacker says.

"It was required for my position. Hacker, collect the schematics of this bank. Their floor plans, security details, I want to know the guard's names! Warrens, I want you gearing up to cut off the vault door."

"Yes sir!" He shouts.

I turn and almost run into Shepherd who's standing with his arms across his chest.

"This isn't right Silas and you know it. We shouldn't have to steal like common pirates."

"We're not exactly friends with the military right now so getting contracts is damn near impossible."

"We relied on a corporation for our existence before. I don't want us to rely on the Core either. This heist will make us self-sufficient permanently."

"You seem so sure that it'll work. How do you know?"

"Because after busting our asses against monsters and mad scientists, robbing a high security bank seems...easy." I leave the conversation, walk to my office and grab one of my notebooks. I thumb through the yellow pages until I find the half-sheet full of numbers that I hoped I would never have to use. I look over the crumbling piece of paper. The numbers have faded, but can still be seen. I fold the paper, put it into my pocket and toss the notebook back into the box.

I go to Hacker's chamber, where he's searching out information on the bank.

"What do you know about money laundering?" I ask.

"I know how to follow the trail."

"Perfect. I need you to open 30 bank accounts, probably more. Scatter them. Put AIs in charge of managing the money, I don't care. If we have to perform billions of micro transactions, that's fine, just make it all disappear."

Hacker waves the simulation off. "There's so much you're not telling us about this mission sir, that I find the risks overwhelming. For example, setting up these fake accounts. In order to not arouse suspicion we need weeks, not days. And that's all assuming this will work! What if it doesn't?"

"All I need is to get in front of that keypad, and I can take care of the rest."

I turn to leave, but Hacker jumps down from his platform. "What is it you're not telling us?!"

I look back to him. "Just get it done. Once I'm in front of the keypad, I can take care of the rest."

We get clearance to land on a docking station above the bank. Ships are not allowed below the platform and neither are weapons. Three heavily armed guards come out to serve as our escorts for the elevator.

"We need to confiscate all weapons and will need to check your account certificates."

"Now!" I order. Hacker activates his armor and works to take over the elevator controls. Lee comes up behind one of the guards and takes him hostage, while Warrens leaps on the second one. I draw my pistol and hold it to the last one's forehead while he raises his hands in surrender.

I have Murph, Sulture and Warrens swap armor with the guards and then tie them up on the platform. Hacker takes over the controls before the soldier in the sentry post can call for reinforcements.

With the security platform under our control, the bank is ours. We ride down the platform into the bank. There's gold everywhere. On the door handles, on the walls, on every railing, even the pens are a gold color.

We open the door and the manager greets us with the warmest smile. I draw my pistol and fire into the air, daring the inner guards to challenge us. The Horsemen spread out and with our weapons trained on the guards, they don't put up a fight. We gather everyone against the wall, giving the usual speech that if they don't do anything stupid, nobody will get hurt.

I grab the manager by the collar and tell him the vault number I'm looking for. His eyes grow large, but he doesn't dare defy me.

The massive robotic arms descend into the depths below the bank until they rise up with the vault in hand. It's a massive black box with no discernible input system of any kind. I don't take my eyes off the manager since I can't risk him pressing an alarm button.

Once the vault is revealed I grab him by the collar and take him to the rest. I tap on Warrens' shoulder.

"You're up."

I take his place while he carries a bag of tools he'll use to get that door open.

"You'll never get it open," the manager says. I point my pistol up and shoot.

"That's your first warning! I won't give another to the group!"

The minutes tick away and feel like hours, but Warrens finally gets the door open with a deadened thud. The vault's hinges are glowing orange, and the acrid smell of molten slag dominates the air.

I turn to Hacker. "Do you have your equipment ready?"

"Yeah," He replies. "Are you sure about this?"

I wish he hadn't said that. Now they'll try to use it against us. Warrens comes up and swaps places with me and Hacker. The two of us go to the vault, where a server terminal blinks in silent watch. Above it is a small keypad meant to direct the contents.

"Silas!" Hacker whispers harshly. "You didn't tell me this was biometrically sealed!"

"Relax, just connect the external port and tell me when it's activated."

He scoffs, but does as he's ordered. Within minutes we have a small satellite dish pointing towards the *Enigma* which will route the signal off-world.

"It's ready."

"Good." I take off my glove and go to the keypad. I signal the comm to reach everyone. "Up until this point we've had all the time in the world. Now things are going to get heated. Get ready." I press my thumb to the scanner, and within seconds, I have full access of the contents inside of the server. I pull out the folded piece of paper and hand it to Hacker.

"Here is a list of the accounts contained inside the vault. Empty all of them and spread them between the accounts created off-world."

Hacker stares at me, dumbfounded.

"We don't have much time," I remind him.

He snatches the paper away and begins typing on the keypad, unlocking the vault's secrets. The money is transferred through the uplink, dispersed between our accounts.

I check my watch, waiting on the time.

Forrest clicks in through the comm. "Godfrey…I mean sir, we're seeing multiple ships inbound for the - oh jeez! They're firing at us!"

I hear Forrest and Sujay yell at each other to get the shields up.

"Get outta there," I order. "You may have to meet us at the front door."

"No! Don't let them move!" Hacker screams.

"I don't think we're gonna be able to do that either sir," Forrest replies.

I look through the front windows and multiple ships land in the street, oblivious to the traffic behind them. Ion clones crawl out and are heading towards the building.

"Looks like we got a platoon of blue-bloods comin' for us!" Warrens growls.

"I figured this would happen," I reply. "The GAR is a front controlled by the Combine. However to keep up with security laws, even they cannot break the contract of an account. It's easier to murder and wait it out rather than risk having your license revoked by the Core authorities."

"Doesn't look like they're being subtle with your murder," Sulture says.

"No," I sigh. "They're not. Positions!"

Warrens swings his gatling gun out and fires on the incoming clones, making the glass rain down in small shards. Most of them coming through the front are annihilated before they make it to the door, but the ones on top of us aren't as subtle. Emie has denied them access to the elevator, but they shoot out the terminal with ease.

I turn to the manager and put a pistol to his head. "There must be a manual override to the elevator down here. Where is it?"

"I'm not telling you-" I shoot a woman teller next to him in the arm, who screams out in pain.

"Try again," I growl. "Next shot kills someone and I don't think your employees are as dedicated as you are."

"It's behind the manager's desk!" One of the tellers shouts.

"See?" I turn, leap over the desk and lock the elevator controls. The platform stops, but the clones fire on the glass containment unit.

Sujay clicks through on the comm. "Sir, we are taking a lot of fire from their ridiculous palm blasters and they're getting that look in their eyes where they want to blow themselves up with us!"

"Then get Shepherd and have him kill some of the bastards!"

"Sir, we may have to flee."

"Do *not* let them flee!" Hacker snaps. "We need the ship to route these transactions."

"Emie, wake Dorothy, Wendy and Fenfang up."

Three avatars appear on my screen and three female voices fill my ears, asking for my orders.

"Ladies, target anyone with an ion clone energy signature. Terminate with extreme prejudice."

"Right away Commander," all three reply. The three mechs come to life and unfold at the top of the platform. They slaughter the clones without mercy, but more ships are inbound. The skies overhead become a battlefield, with our automated mechs leading the charge.

I go to Hacker. "Where are we at?"

"It's a lot of friggin' money," He replies. "But we're about halfway."

One of the clone ships out front explodes and the clones have their hands full dealing with the mechs.

Forrest clicks through. "Sir, things are getting really heated up here. There's over two dozen ships inbound! I don't know who you insulted, but even I've never had this many ships come after me! I think we need to get out of here!"

"Do not move!" Hacker hisses.

"Well if you want your butt to get roasted then you can stay here, but I think we need to high-tail it outta here!"

"Forrest, what is the longest you can hold out?" I ask.

He whines on the other end. "Maybe five minutes…? But you're putting the ship at risk!"

I look over at Hacker.

"I'll do what I can," He replies.

"We'll try to be ready by then."

"Hallelujah!" Forrest screams.

"Why can't this shit ever go according to plan?" Hacker asks.

"Actually, it's going exactly according to plan," I reply. An ion bolt singes the floor near us, and I see a handful of clones have shot through the elevator tunnel. I return fire, but they duck behind the glass. I shield Hacker, but the clones are hammering at us from above and to the North wall. The bank is in shambles, but there's a tinge of satisfaction on the manager's face. He loves seeing us struggle and the volume of support he got from his benefactors.

Explosions rock the elevator platform overhead and the *Enigma* takes heavy fire.

Forrest clicks through. "Sir, if you really want to keep this ship," he swallows hard. "And us, we need to abandon the platform."

"Don't move!' Hacker snaps again.

"Why is it taking so long for you to *download* something?!" Forrest asks. "Isn't that something we mastered centuries ago?!"

Hacker growls under his mask.

"Where are we at?" I ask him.

"90%."

"Route or store the rest through your suit. We can use some cash on hand." I click the comm to Forrest. "You two can evacuate."

"Woohoo! Sweet freedom!" Forrest screams. The engines kick on and the *Enigma* flies off, leaving the clones in the dust.

"Dorothy, Phoebe, guard the *Enigma* and help her get to the front door." I use a laser to signal our position, using one of the vehicles out front.

"Right away Silas," the two reply.

"Fenfang, blast the assholes up top with an EMP."

"Wait! Don't!" Hacker shouts.

The mech lands on the elevator pad overhead and releases an orb of energy that fries the clone's glorified pacemakers, killing them in an instant. The lights flicker for a moment, and then the bank goes dark.

In spite of the darkness the vault is still lit up.

"Military grade storage, and backed up with a top of the line battery," I explain. "I told you these things were indestructible."

Hacker sighs in relief and performs the final transactions. "Done."

"So are we. Forrest pick us up out front. The rest of you, let's move out!"

The three mechs shove the ships blocking the entrance, while Forrest lands the *Enigma* in the middle of the street. More clones come out from the crowd, but we manage to beat them onto the ship.

I click on the comm. "Ladies, let's get outta here."

"Right away Silas," they all reply. The mechs curl into a ball and roll back into their docking stations.

"Good afternoon gentlemen, this is your pilot speaking. Please fasten all seatbelts and secure all valuables, pilot is not responsible for lost or stolen articles during takeoff. Where to boss?"

"I don't care where we have to go or what you have to do, just lose them!"

"You shouldn't have given him permission to do that," Sujay says.

Forrest blows a raspberry. "We'll be fine! Off we go!" He shifts the ship into high gear and sends us roaring into the sky. A handful of ships pursue us, but after some wild maneuvers from Forrest, we shoot off into warp space.

Cheers howl from the hold over our major heist, while Hacker comes to me with a stone cold gaze.

"What the hell was that?!"

"Now what?" I ask. The hold grows quiet, everyone wondering why

Hacker seems so bitter.

"That keypad in the vault was biometrically sealed! How in the hell did *you* have access? And don't tell me it was skin cultures or duplicated thumb print - you knew every last account number in the vault. This whole mission there's been something you're not telling us and we need to know what it is!"

Fine way to learn that Hacker can't handle secrets being kept from him.

"You're right. You all deserve to know. My father was Hugo Daniels, the founder of Chemron. It was his vault that we breached today, however before he died I'd had my genetic signature added to the vault's records so that I could access the funds anytime I needed to. However, a security consultant warned me that if I did so, it would rouse suspicion, even an investigation, so he advised I should only access the vault when I absolutely needed to."

"That can't be," Sulture says. "Hugo Daniels didn't have an heir. His son died in the Chemron explosion."

"That's the official story the media put out, which is the truth, but not all of it. I didn't know it at the time, but Chemron was organizing the foundation of the Combine, with my father as one of the founding members. The more we see of the Combine, the more I realize how much of a hand my father played in creating our enemy. Raiding the vault today only confirmed my suspicions - that the bank was acquired after his death in the hopes of securing his wealth."

"That still doesn't explain how you were his son," Sulture says.

"Chemron did many shady business deals. During the Unification Wars, they sold chemical weapons to both sides, and happily sold to despots like Yiu Mei. I was an up and coming Vice President at the time, and I confronted my father about it. He made multiple threats against me, from disowning me, to threatening my life."

"Jesus," Shepherd replies.

"Yeah," I sigh. "My father more than once referred to me as an 'inferior specimen.' He believed that biology still created too many defects and would've much rather preferred a clone of himself to hold conversation with, except cloning was still an unstable science. Anyway, I needed proof of what was going on, so I collected evidence of the weapon sales, even captured video of our scientists performing experiments on human test subjects."

The team gasps and becomes eerily quiet.

"Nothing stuck. This was before the Grid, and the board had enough contacts within the Core government to bury everything. During the day the board would smile and welcome me with open arms, but beneath their veneer was the desire for my death. I learned that I was being followed by hitmen. I hired a security consultant, a man named Rick who served as Hacker's number two at the Grid.

"I wondered how you knew him," Hacker replies.

"Against his advice I took matters into my own hands. We set up an alternative identity named Silas Godfrey, while I created a bomb which I planted inside Chemron's board room. During the meeting, I detonated the bomb, with the blast centered on my chair to eliminate any suspicion from myself and convince the authorities there were no remains to be found. The entire board was eliminated and after an extensive investigation by Core authorities, the culprit was never found. Rick finished the job by switching out my identity, transferred all of my father's assets into the vault and assisted with my escape. I went on the run for a few years until the investigation died down, but I reappeared as Silas Godfrey at Titan University, a chemist ready to pass on his knowledge to the next generation."

The team stares at me, in shock over the revelation.

"I struggled to connect with my father too," Hacker says.

"It wasn't a struggle to connect. He resented my existence. My mother was his secretary and he…" I pause and swallow hard. "I was a bastard son that shouldn't have been born. I was a cover-up, something Hugo hid from his wife because *their* son died. What I'd discovered later was that Hugo's son was a clone of himself, and the procedure wreaked havoc on his body. He'd paid for extensive medical procedures on me when I was a toddler to harvest genetic material which was used in an attempt to repair the damage, but it wasn't a permanent solution."

"Why'd your mother allow this?" Shepherd asked.

"She didn't know. Hugo and his doctors convinced her I was gravely ill and the procedures were my only chance for survival. He manipulated her constantly and when she'd had enough of him, she died in a speeder accident. I believe that he had her killed, but I've never been able to prove it. Shortly after, I was offered a position at Chemron and worked my way up, hoping to collect enough evidence to bring him down. I think the position was to keep an eye on me so that I couldn't tell anybody."

"So how does all of that lead to you collecting billions in a vault?" Forrest asks.

"Pretty simple really. Hugo didn't have an heir, and when a genetic match is submitted, they're added to the will. My name was added to the vault, but Hugo was notified. He was going to have me killed, but I acted first."

"So much family drama!" Forrest exclaims. He rubs a locket hidden behind his shirt, while the rest of the men seek to understand all that I've told them.

"I don't expect anything by telling you guys this. I figure it's best for you to know for context, but also to risk everything for the sake of this team. I want us to be independent and free from the influence of others. We control our destinies now."

Warrens speaks up. "Well, I only got one thing to say now."

"What's that?"

"Looks like the first round's on you, Commander."

DOMINIC SALVATORI

Godfrey's Journal, Day 353

It's almost been a year since I joined the Horsemen. We've had celebrations for everyone else on the team and have picked up a new military contract from the Core. Our celebrations are cut short when Hacker brings me a message from someone even he can't trace.

"Obviously, they want to remain hidden," Hacker says.
I read the message and then upload it to the central display.

Dr. Silas Godfrey,

I am impressed with your efforts against the Combine. I believe it's time that we finally meet and discuss the future of science. Our fates are intertwined and I need to know exactly who it is I face. Meet me at your favored meeting spot, Nero's Cove on Aurelius Prime. And come alone.

-Dominic Salvatori

"Who is he?" Shepherd asks.

"He's a recluse," Hacker replies. "One of the galaxy's wealthiest men yet doesn't grant interviews, talk to the press, there isn't even a picture of him on any network."

"Used all his money to buy privacy," Murph says.

"How does he know about the Combine?" Shepherd asks.

"Well," Hacker replies. "He owns a large stake in Ionics, Samson and has hundreds of fronts, all somehow connected to the Combine. Either he's their leader or a pissed off investor."

"My bet's he's their leader," I reply. "But we won't know until I talk to him."

"I think that's a *really* bad idea," Forrest says. "This dude is the king of the glow clones and you're okay eating with him alone?!"

"I don't want to go alone, but he'll know if I bring backup. I'm sure he's expecting it."

"Golden boy's a hell of a sniper, and Kung Pow can go invisible. Why not take them?" Warrens asks.

I look over and the two men nod, accepting their stations.

"Alright, it's settled. Forrest and Sujay, set a course for Aurelius Prime. The rest of you, let's plan an ambush for our fabled King of Clones."

It's a quick three days before we arrive on Aurelius Prime. As I pack up to leave, I notice that Forrest is standing outside my office.

"What is it Forrest?"

"Well, since you insist on going on this suicide mission without backup and all that -"

"Get to the point."

"If you survive, will you bring me a plate of fries?"

"Fine."

"Milkshake too?"

"You're pushing it."

"Aww c'mon! Do you have any idea how long it's been since I've put horrendously greasy food that will fill my arteries with buttery-clogging goodness?! Look at me! I'm wasting away!"

I roll my eyes. "Forrest, put your shirt down. We both know you're not starving to death."

"I will if I go on a hunger strike!"

"You'd go on a hunger strike for fries?"

"I will now! And the milkshake! Thanks for the idea boss!"

Nero's Cove. Still got the same smell mixture of body odor, grease, and tobacco smoke. I find an empty booth and try to keep a low profile, but Brocker howls for joy when he sees me. I swear he's wearing the same shirt he was the last time we were here.

"A massive plate of your famous fries Brocker." He scribbles down my order and howls into the kitchen.

Forrest clicks in through the comm. "What about my milkshake?"

I click the comm off. I watch the rooftop of the building across the road as Shepherd gets into position. His armor gleams in the setting sun, but I turn my attention back to the restaurant.

A waitress brings me my plate of fries, which clatter on the table. I realize I don't even know who I'm looking for, so I grab some and start munching.

A figure slides into the booth across from me. A tall, lanky man with wild hair and frantic blue eyes. His icy eyes pierce right through me, and I realize I've seen those eyes before. In fact, I know them all too well.

"It can't be," I growl.

"Hello son," He replies.

I feel my stomach churn and my face flush in anger. I feel weightless for an instant and force myself back into reality.

"I killed you."

"That you certainly did." He reaches over and grabs a few fries.

"You don't look anything like you used to."

"Well reconstruction on a shattered corpse is bound to change a few features. Fortunately I had the means. My partners believed I was too valuable to let die. Congratulations on your newfound fortune. I was quite perturbed to discover that my new genetic identity couldn't unlock the vault. Imagine my surprise to learn that you were able to."

"Why change your name?" I sneer.

"I didn't know who was with me and who was against me so I changed how I handled my affairs. My identity was part of that. I wasn't going to partake in the public eye, and orders were given through my inner circle."

"Just like the old days."

Salvatori scoffs. "You've always sought to destroy everything I've built."

"Maybe if you stopped experimenting on people. What are you even after anyway?"

He grabs a few more fries and watches me as he eats. "Immortality. I suppose I should be thanking you Richard-"

"It's Silas."

"Not to me," He snaps with a chilling gaze. "As I was saying, I should be thanking you. Had it not been for you, I wouldn't have experienced death. I saw what it was like to stand on the edge of the abyss. The edge of nothingness. I'd never felt more alone or empty than in that moment. Eternal numbness. A void."

"That's called hell, which is where you belong."

Salvatori curls his hand into a fist until his knuckles turn white. "My efforts at immortality were concentrated before, but when I experienced death first hand, I poured every bit of energy I had into it. Investing in laboratories, funding research, even giving a black budget to miscreants like you. I made all of you compete by giving you banners to champion all while you ran experiments to find the answers I sought."

"Sorry that your grand experiment failed."

"It didn't, I just changed the inputs."

"Yeah, swapping an army of zealous scientists for Grigylls."

"Monumental scientific progress has only been achieved during wartime. The Manhattan Project, The Warp Drive Reactors, Neutron Star Material Forging. All of these discovered during wartime. I will find immortality in this one."

"You sound awfully certain."

"One of my teams discovered the God-State. It was accidental, but they found it. All I need to do is replicate the conditions. Now I have the renewed resources to do so. Once again, I should be thanking you."

"You're a madman."

"And you lack vision. Take this restaurant as an example and look around you. Mouth breathers. They may as well be primordial bile I'd find in a swamp. They'd tear each other apart if given the chance. I'm seeking to rise above the pettiness. Seeking to become a being fit to rule and provide guidance to these lost souls."

"Like the guidance you gave me?"

"You were unfit."

"Because I wasn't a duplicate of you. Did you even tell your wife that your baby was your clone?"

He stares at me with hard eyes, telling me everything I need to know.

"There will come a point when mankind must learn we can't defy nature," I say. "You especially. Last time you did, it almost killed you."

"Yet I'm still here, proof of science overcoming nature."

"I suppose knowing that nature will overcome is what makes me unfit."

Salvatori rolls back his sleeve and taps on his wristcomm. "If you believe in nature so much, let's see how you overcome this challenge."

"What did you just do?!"

"Latest development in man-made evolution." A gray hulking beast breaks out of a building and charges into the streets.

Salvatori grins. "Our process isn't perfect, but it has yielded successes in areas we didn't expect. Now when it comes to facing this foe, you wouldn't dare fight it personally. You'd wield that monstrous mech powered by a substance that is far from natural. My teams on Hadrian have attempted to harvest the material, but they can't get anywhere near it. Tell me where you would draw the line between natural and unnatural in all of this?"

I notice the raging hulk below has an ion reactor glowing in the center of its chest.

"We couldn't have developed the endoplasmic solution which serves as their bloodstream without your research decades ago. More *unnatural* science I suppose." His condescending tone is getting on my nerves.

Salvatori takes a few more fries and looks out the window while I slide my hand overtop a steak knife.

"Maybe I should breed a line of clones with *your* material. Then I'll have an army which can handle that rock."

I feel a fury rise that I can't stop. I grip the knife and slash at Salvatori's throat. Just before the blade makes contact, he flashes out of existence. I look around the restaurant, wondering where he went. He reappears next to the booth, grabs hold of my wrist, knocks the knife loose, takes it and stabs it through my hand, pinning me to the table. I force myself not to scream and tear my hand further.

"Don't interrupt," He hisses as he sits back down across from me. "I know the Hadrian rock was the key to your cure after the *Acer* incident. What I can't grasp is how you survived."

"Just lucky. Let's talk about how you phased out of existence a moment ago."

Salvatori scoffs, then points to the back of his head. "My implant grants significantly more abilities than the rest do, transdimensional teleportation being one of them. Now focus on the topic at hand. I don't believe for a second your survival was a 'miracle.' Your team accomplished the impossible."

"How do you know about the *Acer* incident?" I pull the knife out of the table and toss it aside.

"I give all of my teams impossible challenges at one point or another. Amazing what can be accomplished when a comrade's life is at stake."

I think back to the *Acer* vault and remember when the canister lifted its lid up and sprayed me in the face. A pang of insight rings in the back of my mind and I look up across the table.

"You rigged it to detonate."

"Of course I did," He scoffs. I hold my injured hand and flick on the comm through my wrist controls. "Sometimes you need to push scientists in order for them to make noteworthy discoveries."

"And I was acceptable as a casualty?"

"Pure coincidence. The breakthrough achieved was groundbreaking. They didn't just cure you they-" Salvatori cuts himself off as he notices Shepherd's laser searching for its mark.

"Fools!" He growls. The laser dot disappears and I turn to look out at Shepherd. One of the ion clones has him in a chokehold with a knife to his neck. I look out at Lee, and an ion clone has a hold of his invisible form.

"You really are an inferior specimen if you think that would've worked on me!" Salvatori barks. "All that will happen now is your anarchist and golden boy will die with their throats slit!" Everyone looks over at us. Some of their comm units jingle and they check them amidst our family drama.

"No! Wait!" I plead. "Let them live."

"Why?!"

"You want to know how they cured me right? I won't cooperate if you kill my men."

He glares down at me. "No. You didn't follow the rules."

Blaster bolts fire all around us, one of them hitting him in the shoulder. The two clones fall over, with bullet holes in their foreheads.

Salvatori growls. "If you want to save these mouth breathers, then play heroics on the surface." He nods to the beast and then teleports away.

I click on the comm. "Hacker what happened?"

"I issued a fifty thousand credit bounty on each of the clones and Salvatori. That's what happens in a restaurant full of mercenaries."

"Good work. Lee, Shepherd are you alright?"

"Good here," Shepherd replies.

"*Wuo duh tian ah* that was a close one," Lee says.

"Excellent, get back to the ship." I leap out of the booth and run for the exit. "Get me eyes on that creature!"

I put on my visor and see a massive ion clone wreaking havoc in the streets. The beast is bigger than anything we've ever encountered before, and blaster bolts aren't penetrating his skin.

"Deploy Dorothy!" I order.

"Wait a minute! What about my fries?!" Forrest screams.

"Salvatori ate 'em."

"You let him?!"

"Well I had a knife stuck in my hand so I couldn't very well stop him."

"What about my milkshake?!"

"Again, had to worry about two of my men having their throats slit."

"That's no excuse!"

"*Chur ni-duh!*" Lee hisses.

A handful of soldiers fight back against the beast, but it swats them away like ants, barely even noticing they're there.

"What is that brute?" Sujay asks.

"Its like Goliath," Shepherd replies.

"Let's see what it can take," I growl to myself. Dorothy unfolds right as I close in.

The beast slams into the ground in front of me. It's as tall as the mech unit. It gnashes its teeth and swings its gorilla-like arms. The veins pulse with the plasmic blood. The scythe blade looms overhead and strikes the goliath in the shoulder. The blade pierces his skin, and it bellows out in pain. It turns and fires a palm blast at the scythe, but it does nothing to the metal. Dorothy pulls it aside, giving me a clear path. It charges its palm blaster and fires at me, but its blasts only hit dirt.

I make it inside Dorothy and take the controls. I pull the scythe out and watch as the wound heals over in seconds.

I click on the comm. "Subject name: Goliath. Has the ability to regenerate in seconds. Impervious to normal blaster bolts." I notice out of the corner of my eye several mercenaries with Xeclian disintegration rifles open fire on the beast, but they ripple against its skin like water droplets. It chases after the mercs.

"Subject is impervious to Xeclian rifles, I repeat: subject impervious to Xeclian rifles. How is this possible?"

Sulture clicks through. "Subject's epidermis appears to be as structurally solid as a diamond. No light can get through. Given its rate of regeneration, contagions won't be of much help."

I look at the scythe and chase after the goliath.

There's a wave of static over my comm and a voice forces itself through. "Enjoying one of our more perfected specimens?"

"Is this what you hope to turn yourself into Salvatori?"

"Joke all you want, this creature will lay waste before you can even puncture its flesh. There is a secondary benefit…"

Just as I close in on the goliath, it turns around and unleashes both palm blasts at me. I don't raise the shields up in time, and the suit takes heavy damage.

"Why not use your miracle blast?" Salvatori asks.

"Dorothy, shut him out."

"I'm afraid it won't be that simple son."

"Hacker…?"

"Even he can't keep me out. I operate far beyond your elementary methods of scientific study." The goliath closes in on me. I make a wild swing with my scythe and knock the beast into a building, but it doesn't seem fazed.

"How about a trade? You give me Sulture and I'll kill the specimen."

"Why Sulture?"

"He cured you. I'm sure he regrets that now, since you lord your authority over him."

"Shut up!" I scream.

"My associates thought you invulnerable, but you're nothing without my protection!" The beast looks at me with yellow eyes and charges, but I fire at it with my defense blasters. None of them even slow it down and I'm struggling to gain my balance. It leaps and tackles me, tearing pieces off my suit.

The beast looks at me through the glass, but holds back.

"Last chance," Salvatori says.

"For what?"

"You or Sulture. One of you comes with me willingly or I kill until one of you is left."

An explosion rocks over me and the goliath goes flying back. I look over to see Warrens standing with the door to the *Enigma* wide open and holding a rocket launcher.

I leap to my feet and swing the scythe down on the goliath. It catches my blade and holds it, centimetres above its chest piece.

"Dorothy, charge the cannon."

The goliath shoves the scythe away and leaps to its feet.

"It won't work," Salvatori says.

"Hacker, cut his feed."

"You never listen. I-" His voice disappears.

The goliath roars at me and charges.

"Dorothy, spear!"

The scythe adjusts and becomes a spear and I jam it right into the goliath's gut. The beast screams in pain, pushing forward and trying to tear my suit apart.

"Full shields up Dorothy." I point the cannon at its wound and fire.

A violet blast brighter than the sun fills my windshield. I hear the goliath roaring outside, but I watch as piece by piece the ferocious monster is consumed by violet light. A force hungrier than the goliath consumes its muscles, evaporates its blood and withers skin from bone. I watch those yellow eyes vaporize in front of me, the rage-fueled spirit driven back to whatever hell created it.

Dust lingers in the air, a fine chalk which covers everything. I survey the damage, but deep down I know there's little I can do to help. We caused all of this carnage, but can't stay to clean it up. Salvatori and the Combine know about the Hadrian gem, and we must destroy it.

I activate my thrusters and rejoin the *Enigma* in the sky.

Everyone is looking at me, their faces silently demanding answers.

I take a deep breath. "Dominic Salvatori is my father. Well, his alter-ego after I killed him years ago. His goal is immortality and he believes that the Hadrian gem is connected to achieving it." I look over at Sulture and Murph.

"What did you two do to me?"

Sulture swallows hard. "I did what I explained to Harris. I used synthetic blood until I-"

"NO!" I snap. "What did you *really* do? Why is Salvatori convinced the gem cured me?"

"Because it did Silas," Murph replies. "We found that the gem was made up of crystallized astatine which when diluted enough killed the virus attacking your lungs without vaporizing you. It still wreaked havoc on your organs, and we had to work nonstop to replace what was lost with hastily grown tissues."

A part of me still doesn't believe him, but at the same time I don't believe Murph would lie. "Is there any other potential use?"

Murph and Sulture look at each other. Murph is the first to answer. "It's possible that with the Combine's resources, they could turn it into a plasmic power source as a replacement to the current material."

"Jeepers!" Forrest shouts. "And we thought the original buzzy clones weren't bad enough! If they can turn someone into a skeleton with their blasts…"

"There's no telling what kind of havoc they'll cause," Shepherd finishes.

"Yeah! Wait, Godfrey did you say that Salvatori was your *father*?!" Forrest asks.

"As he explained it he somehow lived through the explosion which I thought killed him. He's the mastermind behind everything and he's on the hunt for immortality. He's a man possessed and won't stop this time."

"But...how did you not notice him?" Forrest asks.

"At first, I didn't. He's been reconstructed. His stature is similar, but he looks like a completely different person. Except for his eyes, which still resent me."

"What do we do now?" Shepherd asks.

"Who knows physics?" I ask.

"I do," Warrens replies.

"Good. We're going to figure out how to destroy a planet."

THE DESTRUCTION OF HADRIAN

Godfrey's Journal, Day 375

Dominic Salvatori has left us with no choice. We must seek out and destroy the planet known as 'Hadrian,' the place where we found the gem, a substance which destroys everything it touches. Yet in this capacity for destruction is the very substance which cured humanity's deadliest disease. Murph even explained to me the possibility of my body being immunized *by the astatine, that it has cured me of all disease…permanently. It's only a theory with little science behind it, but I doubt Salvatori is going on pure science any longer. We've scoured the junkyards for parts, and even found a forger who could rebuild my suit as well as Wendy, the mech of war. We're also in the midst of deliberating on a doomsday device which we know will cost a small fortune. Turns out, having billions lying around is quite nice.*

"Oh, you can't be serious…" Sulture hisses. His glare dares us to challenge him "If such a thing were even possible-"

"We know the physics is possible Sulture!" I growl. "We ran all the numbers."

"It's true," Murph says. "Their math is spot-on."

"Do you know what the fallout would be from destroying a planet?!" Sulture screams. "How ecosystems on other worlds could be affected?"

"If it stops the Combine from acquiring the Hadrian Gem, I don't care what the consequences are!"

"And you really think you'll be able to build a machine of such magnitude out of scraps?!"

"Don't tell me what I can and can't build Rooster!" Warrens snaps. He brings up the projection. A pair of claw-like devices fly into place over the poles on Hadrian.

"Gravity wells. You're playin' a dangerous game Casanova."

"Play out the simulation Warrens," I order.

One of the machines is activated, and accumulates an amount of force beyond what I can fathom. The wells are switched on and off in an alternating pattern so the force drills through the planet until the surface cracks.

"Sulture, if the crust cracks, will that be enough?" I ask.

"No. To achieve the devastation you're seeking, you must keep going until the crust has been eradicated."

Warrens nudges my shoulder. "Sir, I don't know if the gravity wells will survive once the crust cracks. All of the spraying lava could wash them out or the chunks could take them out."

"May not matter," Murph says. He takes the keyboard and types something in. "Look what happens when you account for the altered gravity state of the planet."

The simulated planet collapses on itself, with the mantle spilling out into space. Whole sections of the world catch within the gravity well and it becomes a churning mess of lava and rock.

"What about the damage to neighboring planets?" Sulture asks.

"No hospitable ones," Sujay replies.

Sulture stares at the simulation, still uncertain.

"Think about all we know about the Hadrian gem. Can we risk more people being exposed to it like I was?"

Without missing a breath Sulture responds. "No, we can't."

It takes a long three weeks of scouring junkyards to build the gravity wells, but we get a set of working prototypes which, according to Murph and Warrens' calculations, will do the job.

It's another two weeks before we make it to the Hadrian system, a frontier world that's still under firm control of the military.

"Scans of the planet?" I ask.

"Three confirmed military bases sir," Sujay replies. "All belong to the STARs."

"ATTENTION!" A voice blares over the comm. "This is a restricted area. Leave now or we will be forced to investigate your ship."

Forrest and Sujay both turn toward me. "Hold in place. Hacker, activate the cloaking devices and deploy the gravity wells. Sujay, give Emie the coordinates of the poles."

"Wait, we're going through with the mission?" Shepherd asks.

"Are you questioning my orders?"

Shepherd stirs in his seat. "I'm asking about the lives we'll be taking. Shouldn't we at least alert them?"

"*Buhn dahn,*" Lee hisses. "You think they alerted us when they nearly sent me into a coma?!"

"Golden boy may be onto something," Warrens says. "If we kill a bunch of the STARs, we won't be able to help out the war effort against the Grigylls. The military will hang us."

I seethe below the surface, but I don't dare show it. Of course the men are right, but I can't allow Salvatori and his puppets to get away with mining the astatine compound unhindered.

"Forrest and Sujay, pull as far back as we can so that we can still communicate with those gravity wells."

"Too late, we've been spotted," Sujay says.

"Do they know it's us?"

"We haven't told them anything," He says.

Hacker explains further. "Electronically, we're invisible, but the military won't like it if we don't tell them who we are."

"And I suspect it won't take much to identify the *Enigma*?"

"No sir," Forrest replies. "We're practically sitting ducks against the military right now. Probably running our schematics against their database of criminals and before you know it there we are!"

"Can we jam their systems?"

"Oh man you'll get in trouble for that one!" Forrest replies.

"That's a yes. Hacker! Jam their signals!"

"Already on it. Infecting their satellite network now."

"Oh sweet Vishnu, if the STARs catch us…"

"Quiet Sujay, you're not helping," I growl.

"This is Core Military airspace and you are trespassing!" The voice rings through the comms.

"Their signals outside of us are jammed sir."

"Thank you Hacker." I feel a migraine pressing against the back of my eyes. I have no idea how we'll get out of this. I don't know what to do. John would've known what to do in this situation. I watch the gravity wells flying towards Hadrian, wishing that the planet could shake itself to bits.

An idea sparks.

"Hacker can you forge reports of irregular seismic activity? Tie the tremors back to deep mining and blatant disregard for safety procedures."

"This is your last chance!" The military voice howls. My breath catches in my throat and I need to make a decision.

I configure our communications to upload a virus to the ship's mainframe the moment I start talking.

"This is Commander Godfrey of the Horsemen Corps. We're under directive by Defense Minister Reynolds to investigate this research facility."

The officer scoffs. "We don't have to share anything with you. You're lucky we haven't opened fire yet."

"They're unlocking their missiles now sir," Hacker informs.

The officer continues. "I spoke with Reynolds recently and he had nothing to say about any investigation. We know who you are Horsemen, and we know you're lying."

I type on my keypad an order for Hacker.

"Fine. We came here to tell you that you'll be tempted to experiment with the astatine. You may even be ordered to do so. We're here to tell you that only death follows that rock. No good comes from experimenting with it."

"You're all still standing."

"I can give you all of our research on the subject. Save you and your men the trouble. Word from Salvatori is none of your men can get near it."

Rage flows through the officer's eyes. "Alright, I've had enough of this. First lieutenant, fire when ready."

"I wouldn't do that," I reply.

"Watch me!"

"Forrest, Sujay! Shields up!"

The ship lingers for a moment, with a confused look from the officers on the other side, but then a blinding light consumes the ship. The force hits the shields and we're all knocked off balance from the ensuing blast.

"What the hell happened?!" Warrens shouts. "No way we got through their shields!"

Hacker climbs back into his chair. "We took over a part of their ship and locked their missile clamps. When they fired, they detonated inside."

"Hacker were you able to pass that virus through their communications network out here?"

"All local communication stations are being shut down as we speak."

"And the documents?"

"Emie's filling them out right now."

"Perfect. Everyone, to your stations!" I order.

"Sir, we've just been pinged by another ship," Sujay says. "Make that three more. Apparently they know about the explosion."

I curse under my breath. "Time until the gravity wells are in position?"

"At least ten minutes," Hacker replies.

"We don't have that kind of time."

"You're telling us!" Forrest says. "We don't have the shields either, one smack from them and we'll be smushed like a pancake!"

I roll my eyes. "Are their communications jammed?"

"Yes sir," Hacker replies.

"We have no choice. I need to mobilize the mechs. Lee, Sulture, let's move! Shepherd, you'll pilot Wendy. Congrats, you're the new Horseman of War."

The three men wordlessly run for the mechs and fly out to meet the Core ships.

"The Core is charging their weapon systems," Sujay says.

"They're not even going to negotiate," I growl.

The ten minutes crawl by. My stomach is in knots as I watch the mechs buzz around the STAR ships, dismantling them piece by piece. By the end all three ships float along, dead in space thanks to the precision the mechs grant us.

"Gravity wells in position," Hacker says. They've followed Sujay's coordinates exactly. Warrens keys in the final commands. I recall the mechs and wait until they've docked.

"Gravity wells 80% powered up sir," Warrens says.

All eyes turn to me. I feel the weight on my shoulders, just like last time. My head aches when I remember how it felt to gather all the members of the Combine for my culling. How in an instant I felt thousands all around me and then completely alone.

Here I am, killing thousands all over again.

"Begin," I order. I notice the small pieces of debris floating past the *Enigma*.

Warrens powers up the gravity well located above the northern pole. An orb of force churns above the planet, below a device we can't even see. It looks like a cyclone, the gravity well turning the planet's magnetic field against itself.

"Anyone ever wonder what the ethics are of destroying a planet?" Shepherd asks. I shoot him a glare.

"Not now."

Warrens releases the cyclone of force and activates the southern gravity well. The swirling becomes a maelstrom, pulling more of the magnetic field into its grip. Warrens switches the wells, the orb shooting back to the north. It moves through the planet like a shadow with no effect on it at all.

The debris floating outside of the ship starts to float back toward the planet. Warrens switches the wells and the cyclone flies through the planet. We get lost in the spectacle, mesmerized by the transformation taking place. Bits of rock and dirt are knocked away, then waves strong enough to bump the ship occur. Everything starts flying toward the gravity wells. Even our ship is starting to feel the pull.

A dark cloud churns across the surface, and Emie warns us of the lack of oxygen in the atmosphere.

Sujay turns to me. "Do you want death tolls sir?"

"I'm certain I'll know soon enough," I reply. My hand is shaking, and I'm visibly trembling from condemning this world to be destroyed.

The orb of force slams into the planet, cracking the crust. Magma flies through the atmosphere and off into space, while the rest is pulled southward. The ships in front of us float back toward the planet.

"Forrest, pull back."

Warrens interjects. "Sir we can't go any further or we'll be out of range."

I swallow hard and keep watching. "Keep the reverse thrusters on then."

"Yes sir," Forrest squeaks.

The planet is struck again, visible cracks forming across her surface. I turn to Warrens.

"Make sure those gravity wells don't make it out of this, understood?"

"Yes sir," He replies.

The glowing veins pulse and throb, the planet barely able to hold itself together. It takes a few more rounds, but now the tectonic plates crumble beneath the strain. Each piece is swallowed into the vortex and ground to dust. Every wave takes more with it until the planet splits apart.

"Turn on both wells. Tear the planet to pieces so they can't mine the asteroids."

"Yes sir," Warrens replies.

The wells drift away from each other, pulling the pieces of Hadrian apart in a devastating tug of war. The magma melts most of the crust before hardening in the vacuum of space. The wells pull against each other, straining the planet in their relentless grip.

"Sir, we need to release the well or we'll risk an inversion matrix!"

I feel my blood run cold. "The point of quantum singularity." I look out at the gravity wells where it appears the fabric of space is warping.

"Forrest! Get us out of here!"

"Music to my ears!"

I go up next to Warrens. "Set the southern gravity well one notch below the northern. That way they'll collide and release the stored energy."

"Yes sir."

"Everyone strap in!" I howl. We buckle in as Forrest turns the ship around and prepares to make the jump to warp speed. Warrens adjusts the dial for the gravity wells and we all watch. Even at this moment of untold destruction, we can't look away. The gravity wells fly toward each other compressing their energy into a smaller and smaller point, until we have a supernova.

A bright light shines behind us, but we fly off into warp space before we can see what comes next.

I take my first deep breath since this started and I feel a hot tear glide down my cheek. As the ship stabilizes, I realize that I have a death grip on the arms of the chair.

"I sent the report to the Ministry of the Environment moments before the planet fell apart," Hacker says.

A voice cuts through the comm. "Now you've done it you ingrates."

I rub my eyes. "Problem Salvatori?"

"Since you destroyed one of my most substantial investments, I'll be in need of replenishing my funds."

"How?'

"Well, before they were locked in the vault. However since *you* had access…"

"Good luck finding the money."

"I already have. Good luck financing your rogue operation." His comm clicks off.

I look around the cabin in a panic. "Hacker?!"

He's in the chamber checking our accounts, having heard everything. "It's gone. He took all of it. Every account, empty."

I pound my fists against a table and scream in frustration.

The ship is silent, nobody knows what to say.

"Sir, we have an incoming transmission," Hacker says.

I feel like I've been punched in the gut. I don't want to talk to Salvatori. "Decline the transmission."

"I don't think that's a good idea. It's Senator Meredith Lindstrom from Avestan and she's requesting aid."

"I'll take the call in my office." I close the door and flick on the screen. There is a woman whose hair is too tall and she's wearing armor overtop of robes, as though she were acting in a Roman play. Her auburn hair is decorated high, and her emerald eyes are vibrant.

My mind is in a fury, but I try to remain calm. "You must be Senator Lindstrom."

"Thank you for taking my call Commander Godfrey. I'm reaching out to the Horsemen on behalf of the people of Avestan. It seems that the Grigylls have made us their next target to pillage in an effort to finance their war effort. As you know we're a peaceful planet full of artists and musicians, not warriors. We're in need of experts to help us organize a defense force."

"Isn't that something you should ask from your government Senator?"

"I've petitioned the military multiple times, and I'm afraid they're waiting until the Grigylls invade and tear my planet apart before they make their move. You see Dr. Godfrey, if the authorities wait until my people have evacuated their homes-"

"Then the Core troops can loot and pillage and blame it on the Grigylls."

"Your words, not mine."

"We will pay you handsomely as consultants, but I don't have many allies in the military at the moment."

"How far out are the Grigylls?"

"My astronomers tell me they're three weeks out."

"You know we can't train a militia in that timeframe."

"I don't expect you to. However, we're prepared to give you a generous advance to ensure that our militia receives some of the best arms and ammunition you can in that timeframe." Senator Lindstrom keys in something on her computer and I receive a number with a lot of zeroes.

"Please help us Dr. Godfrey. The Horsemen may be the only ones who can."

SOULLESS MERCENARIES

Godfrey's Journal, Day 384

I asked Hacker how we could secure a planet's worth of armaments. He informed me that the only individual who could fulfill such an order was Neuron. We approached the droid pirate, and a tense negotiation ensued. Neuron believed that purchasing such an arsenal was impossible, especially with our timeframe and the war raging. Hacker pointed out that we were close to the planet Xeclia, home of the galaxy's most powerful weaponry. It took everything in us to convince Neuron that this deal was worth his time. Fortunately, his greed won out.

We met at an outpost known for dealing in black market Xeclian weapons. Our encounter with the dwarf-sized aliens was brief, but etched in memory. Their language is rapid and too foreign for me to understand. Their skin was pale gray and their eyes looked ready to pop out of their heads. What got me the most was how cold and clammy their skin was.

As difficult as it was to negotiate with Neuron, the Xeclians proved twice as stubborn. There may have been an embargo on their weapons before, but due to the war effort, restrictions were lessened. It didn't matter to them that we were buying these for a Core Senator, they were holding out for the highest price. Neuron took matters into his own hands and made the Xeclians buckle through intimidation of his droids.

On the way to Avestan, we came across a fleet of Grigylls, who still manned ships from decade's past. I urged Forrest to get there faster and to buy us as much time as he could. We'll be lucky if we get a week before this fleet shows up.

Descending to the surface, our fleet looks ragtag compared to the polished and pristine metal that gleams from the capital, Melusine. The cities are also protected by latticed shields which look damn near impenetrable.

"That is an Aegis class shield!" Warrens says. "I'd love to get the parts and integrate them into our armor. Not even ion blasts can break those."

The Melusines hesitate to open for us, requiring the intervention of the Senator herself to let us through the shield dome.

A crowd gathers around the ships. All of the people wear immaculate robes bright with color, their eyes curious to see what we've brought their world.

Upon seeing us, some of them gaze at us with disgust. Our faces look more weathered and aged than they do.

"Just what we need, more soulless mercenaries," One of the men growls. More of the men grumble at our presence, cursing their need for us. They storm off into the more eager ranks still surrounding us.

Neuron's droids walk out of the carrier ships and unlock the vaults for the eager crowd. A handful of officers try to control the chaos, but the need for these men to prove themselves is too strong.

The militia unpacks the carriers full of weapons, and right away I notice a problem. Their bellies swell at the waistline and they're reluctant to handle anything with grease on it. Their faces are young and full while ours are stretched and worn. Our hair is dulled and threaded with silver while theirs shines in the sun. I motion for the Senator to join me in her office.

"Your men suck."

Her face conveys hurt, but understanding. "The Core gave us a year to get everyone ready for combat, but the invasion came much sooner. Is there anything…?"

"Not in the timeframe we have. They need to understand what we're up against, what's at stake."

"They *know* what is at stake Commander Godfrey."

"I don't think they do Senator, otherwise you'd have drill instructors training them non-stop! Your…conscripts will fall against this tidal wave of slaughter!"

"I will not apologize for how our people live Commander! We were established as a haven for the nonviolent. We never imagined an invasion of this magnitude. To raise a fighting force we had to-"

"Turn to mercenaries, yes your people made that very clear."

"I'm sorry for that. They don't know what you're capable of. I do."

"I get that Senator, but nine men can't hold off a planetary invasion."

"Do what you can in the meantime."

I return to our quarters with the rest of the men while Neuron's ships depart. Sulture is watching the men outside, his eyes heavy with skepticism.

"They have as much a chance as Forrest becoming Einstein in the next thirty seconds," He growls.

"Hey!" Forrest shouts.

"I agree with Rooster," Warrens says. "Boys are too pudgy. They're gonna break."

I sigh, because I know he's right. "How do we even the odds?"

"Against a planetary force?" Sulture asks. "Disease."

Murph comes in. "It worked once, we can do it again."

"If I had their genome, I could wipe them all out," Sulture replies. "Right now it's trial and error."

"How would we get it?" I ask.

"Get me a dead Grigyll, the right AI to sequence its genes and time."

"How much time?"

He looks at me as if I should know the answer. "Two years, maybe three."

"Why so long?"

He looks at me again in disgust. "The Grigylls were born from an alien recombinator. No telling how much it eviscerated the human genome."

I look up at the sky, knowing that thousands of enemy ships are en route to us. "Do you have any pathogens that would work against them?"

"None for certain. Their biology is too different to tell."

"Let's focus on respiratory then. You still have some genetic material from our previous encounter correct?"

"We have enough to test some pathogens against it."

"Good. We need to use every advantage we can get. Hacker, find the layout of the ships the Core used during the last Grigyll wars."

Four days pass and the Grigyll ships arrive. They come in slowly, covering the sky with their dominating presence. Despite the age of the ships, they will still hold up against anything the Core uses today.

The people around us look and point into the sky, amazed at the sight. They chatter amongst themselves, murmurs of Grigyll brutality they heard during childhood.

Sulture looks around "These men reek of fear."

"I'd figure that you of all people would empathize."

Sulture glares at me, then turns to the men. "That was our problem. Everyone on Angkor was covered in the stench. The military, the men. It was only when we rose up against them that the planet became tolerable. These inbred blue-bloods need to face these beasts in combat. Maybe the Grigylls will cull the weak and-"

"Enough! We're here to help these people, not watch them get slaughtered."

"Sometimes tragedy gives rise to our best."

"Or our worst. You're telling me you wouldn't trade all you've learned to get your wife and son back?"

Sulture glares at me in contempt. He doesn't answer, he just walks away.

Three more days pass and the Grigylls haven't made their move. They linger above us, waiting for something.

"Come on already! Let's get it over with so we can spend that moolah!" Forrest says.

"What are they waiting for? They should know by now they'll probably win!" Sujay says.

"Enough!" I growl. "I won't tolerate us voicing defeat! We must prove we can do the impossible!"

"How are we gonna do that?" Forrest asks.

"Sulture, do you have the modified Crimson Plague virus ready?"

"Ready as it will ever be. There's still the ship's on-board biohazard security measures."

"Don't worry about them." Lee says. "Fenfang and I will take care of that."

"Warrens, you get the Aegis shield tech integrated with all of our toys?"

"I upgraded the ship, the mechs and then some. These gauntlets are the strongest personnel shields I've ever tested. Stop blaster bolts, bullets, even EMP-proof. Put 'em on!"

I slide on the leathery glove and activate the device. A half-metre long beam projects out and forms a shield that towers over me.

"Looks good. Hopefully these will hold up against their fleet. Forrest, Sujay, ready the *Enigma.* We're going to infiltrate and infect their troop carriers."

Forrest and Sujay soar the ship into the sky, taking us directly into the Grigyll fleet. Their ships linger, omnipresent and menacing. The two pilots keep our cloaking device active as we navigate through the maze of ships. We find a troop carrier to test Sulture's batch of pathogens on.

Lee and Sulture climb into their mech suits and deploy in the midst of the fleet. I admire their courage as they fly between frigates which make no attempt to knock us out of the sky. Just like in the battle over Earth, they tag team the carrier ships, Lee knocks out the electrical defenses, while Sulture injects the Crimson Plague into the ventilation systems. The weaponized virus will decimate the antiquated defense sealants. The troops inside don't have a chance.

Out of the corner of my eye, the fleet adjusts their guns and point them in our direction. Fighter ships spill out of the carriers by the thousands.

"Have we been spotted?" I ask.

Sujay turns to me. "They know something's wrong, but they haven't spotted us!"

"It's because of that right there!" Forrest shouts, pointing at the troop carrier Lee and Sulture had attacked. The lights inside the ship flicker off, and it veers into a neighboring frigate. The silent destruction causes the fleet to go into high alert. Our comm network fills with growls and grunts.

"Lee! Sulture! Back to the ship!" I order.

"We can infect more of them!" Sulture replies.

"The *Enigma* can fly much faster than you. Now move!"

The two mechs return, but thousands of ships are coming right for us.

"To the next carrier!" I order.

"Sweet Vishnu, you can't be-"

"You heard the man Sujay! Let 'er rip!" Forrest jams the throttle down and the ship launches directly into the oncoming fleet.

Everyone else takes a seat and straps in, while I hold on for dear life. The pilots weave and dodge the other fighters, but one of them strikes our shields, which don't even flicker.

"Nice work with the shields Warrens!"

"Thank you sir!"

Forrest and Sujay find the next carrier, but some of the fighters catch on to us.

"Time to carrier?"

"Sixty seconds," Sujay replies. I turn to Lee and Sulture.

"You're up!"

The two unbuckle and run for the mechs. A hand grabs my shoulder. I turn around and it's Shepherd.

"We've gotta protect them!" He shouts.

I nod in agreement and turn to the pilots. "Give us five minutes out there. Try to lose the fighters, then come back and pick us up!"

"Aye aye sir!" Forrest says.

Shepherd and I suit up and deploy right after Lee and Sulture. The two of them go for the troop carrier while Shepherd fires off his gatling gun at the oncoming ships. I charge my reactor and take aim for the fighters still chasing the *Enigma.*

"Dorothy, I need you to time the blast just right so when those fighters pass over us, we can shoot them down."

"Yes Silas. Calculating now."

Shepherd covers me until the reactor is fully charged. The *Enigma* is racing away and two fighters are in pursuit. I activate the cannon and fire on them, slicing through the hull. We pursue Lee and Sulture to give them cover, but they seem to have everything well under control.

We attack over a dozen carriers, and have hopefully eliminated thousands of troops. There are still thousands of ships lingering over Avestan, but now they've begun the invasion of the planet.

The frigates and destroyers fly into position and unleash one barrage after another against the cities below.

Amidst the invading fleet, we take the long way back to the surface, crossing the dark side of the planet. Even on this side of the sparsely populated world, the cities are still covered in the same violet domes. Now the Grigyll strategy becomes apparent. They were hoping to outlast the Avestanian people in a siege.

The nav board blinks out at us and Sujay swipes in on the reading.

"Sir, a second fleet is coming."

"*Da shiong la se la ch'wohn tian*!" Lee screams. "It twice as big as the first one!"

There cannot be enough riches on Avestan to sustain a Grigyll invasion force of this magnitude. "Sujay, zoom out on the star map!"

He swipes his hand until I have a better view of the surrounding systems. Avestan is on top of one of the key star lanes which leads directly into the Core. If the Grigylls conquer Avestan, they'll have a staging point to launch more invasions into Core space. Judging by the size of the invading fleets, they'll stop at nothing to conquer this world.

"We have to get back to the surface! Now!" I order.

Forrest works the controls and sends us into a dive just ahead of the invading fleet. I struggle to hold on for dear life for over an hour. It's grueling, but we make it back to the surface ahead of the invaders. I storm past the defenders and the half-hearted militia Avestan has assembled. I search most of the capital, but I finally find Senator

Lindstrom.

"Commander Godfrey."

"You need to contact Defense Minister Reynolds and demand that he send a fleet *now*."

She looks at me with wide eyes. "The military has refused-"

"There is a *second* invasion fleet coming that's twice the size of the one looming overhead! If Avestan doesn't receive reinforcements, the planet will be a wasteland within a week! Call Defense Minister Reynolds and don't stop until he sends a fleet."

A crack that echoes like thunder rumbles overhead. I run outside to see a barrage of ion blasts coming right for the city. They explode against the shield and fizzle out, making a spiderweb of lightning. The sky ignites from other ships firing down upon us. Each time the shield is hit it edges closer to collapse. Their blasts strike the outlying fields, turning rolling hills into cratered scars on the planet's face. For the first time in a long time, I pray. I pray that the shields hold, I pray the Core sends reinforcements and I pray that the people of Avestan live out this siege.

Godfrey's Journal, Day 392

It's been seven days since the Grigylls have laid siege on the planet. The once green meadows have become mounds of charred dirt. Nobody here has gotten a full night's rest - the bombardment has made sleep an elusive concept. Still, the Avestan shields hold, unbreached, although I suspect the technicians are overwhelmed and overworked. The Grigylls have switched tactics now. They're bombarding only the shields and have sent massive carriers to the surface. It's only a matter of time before the ravenous beasts spill out, a tide that few can stop. Senator Lindstrom reached Minister Reynolds and he said that he'd send aid, but no one has come. We're all alone here, forced to face the beasts on our own.

Three carrier ships land outside of the city. The militia rallies together, forming a defensive phalanx encircling the city. The doors to the ships open up and thousands of Grigylls charge out. Some open fire on the barrier. Others activate an energized claw weapon which rakes at the shield.

Hacker has Emie tap into the city shield schematics. "The barrier… it's wearing down. How can this be after surviving a week-long siege?"

Warrens has the answer. "The barrier is designed to disperse energy across its surface and into the ground. With the constant barrage from these lizard-boys, it can't distribute the energy properly. It's better at impacts than a constant assault."

"What if we open it a crack?" I ask. "Funnel them in and make their numbers count for nothing."

"Then we better buffer those doughboys, otherwise the line will break," Warrens replies.

"Hacker, you convince the technicians to open the barrier on our twelve. Let them in and the Grigylls will do the rest."

"Yes sir."

"Emie, take control of the militia's comm networks."

"Right away Silas." Within seconds I'm connected to every soldier in Avestan's militia.

"If you want your families to live, all of you gather to me." I send out my location and in minutes the militia falls in around me. Men are walking across the city, but we don't have time for them.

"We're going to open the barrier. On the other side lies a creature we only knew in our nightmares. They will slaughter you, they will tear you apart with their bare hands and they will not stop until all of you are dead. Yet remember that you men are the ones who will protect your families. The Core isn't coming to save us. We are all that stands against annihilation! Who will fight with me?!"

The men howl a deep, primal roar that echoes across the city. More of the militia file in to form the ranks. They set up their barriers, readying themselves for when the city shield is opened.

"Coming down now," Hacker says.

"Let them come!" I growl as I cock my rifle.

The barrier opens and the Grigyll standing behind it gathers a sadistic glee. The beast charges in, but I fire with my Xeclian rifle. The bolt vaporizes the creature, turning it into a skeleton. More of them pour in, funneling through the barrier exactly as we'd hoped.

Warrens charges up his gatling gun and unleashes a torrent of blaster bolts at the oncoming enemy. A 'V' shape formation emerges, the men cutting down the Grigylls with ruthless efficiency. Their bodies pile up, but there's a new level of fanaticism inherent in the Grigylls, something we've never seen before.

One of the men in front is bitten by the beast and it rips a hunk of flesh off his neck. The realization hits me like a hammer.

"The Grigylls have been starving their soldiers for this battle."

"Despicable savages," Sulture growls.

They attack the front of our flanks, and have learned to deflect the xeclian blasts with their energized claws. However there are still thousands of Grigylls outside of the barrier, attacking it.

"The barrier is at 23% and dropping!" Hacker says. "The funnel isn't working!"

Just below the clouds I notice a frigate ship taking aim with its gatling gun.

"Hacker, deploy the mech units we bought to the West side of the city. Deploy the epoch mechs too!"

The gatling gun opens fire and within seconds, the barrier shatters in a deafening echo. There's a moment of silence as both sides realize what had just happened.

"Back to back! Everyone back to back!" I scream through the comm. The men at the end of our 'V' are taken first, overrun by the hungry Grigylls who smell fresh meat. Their hunger gives us a chance to kill some of them as they feast, but dozens more fill in the gaps.

Sulture is backing away to get in formation, but one of the Grigylls comes after him with a machete. The beast swings wildly and Sulture dodges, but he trips and falls to the ground. I sprint over to help him.

The savage draws the blade back with Sulture lying on the ground. I leap in and block the blade, but it carves my rifle in two. The Grigyll comes after me but I strike it in the eye, stunning the creature. It bites onto my arm, while I draw my pistol and blow its brains out.

The beast falls back, and I take his machete as my own. I hold out my hand to Sulture. He can't seem to find the words, but in his eyes I find acceptance.

During our clash the Grigylls have assembled an artillery cannon and are preparing to fire upon the troops fighting for their lives.

I charge into the line of fire and ignite my personal shield. The cannon unleashes a torrent of glowing orange bolts and I intercept them. The shield is strong, but it's being depleted at a rapid rate and each bolt feels like a rock pelting my arm.

I lose track of time, but each second feels like a lifetime as I try to hold up against the onslaught. My shield is on the verge of collapse when I notice the weight get lighter. I look up next to me and Sulture has interlocked his shield with mine, spreading the energy blasts.

"We face them together, sir."

A figure moves in behind me and interlocks with my shield on the other side. I look back and its Warrens.

"Couldn't let you have all the fun!"

One by one the rest of the Horsemen file in and interlock shields until we form a phalanx that stands against the entire Grigyll army. A united Horsemen defending a people from annihilation, the very unit John had hoped to create.

I howl into the winds. "For John!"

The rest howl with me, and the militia concentrates on the artillery battery. Within seconds the unit is scattered, which gives us the opening we desperately need.

A bomber soars down overhead, laying waste upon the charging Grigylls. More come, with fighters soaring in to defend them. A battle erupts in the skies and we realize that we're no longer fighting alone.

"Reinforcements!" A soldier shouts. "Reinforcements from the Core!"

We counterattack against the scaly bastards, and show no mercy. The bombing forces them to scatter, leaving them to retreat across the meadows and into the forests. They're rooted in this planet now, and it's going to take a lot of effort to dig them out.

An officer's ship descends upon the Senator's headquarters. Other ships land around us and platoons of infantry are dispatched to the front. They charge after the Grigylls, but are also focused on getting them out of the city first.

Inside HQ the place has been overrun by soldiers and officers commandeering the place for their own ends. At the end of the hallway are Lindstrom's chambers, where I see her speaking to someone sitting down. Her mood lightens when she sees me.

"Here is our hero now. If we hadn't deployed the mechs he purchased, the entire city would've been overrun on the western flank."

The figure spins around in the chair and I reflexively grab the handle of my pistol.

"Commander Godfrey, this is General Hawkes," Lindstrom says.

"We've had the pleasure of meeting," Hawkes replies. "I'm…quite aware of Mr. Godfrey's…bravery."

Between his demonic eyes and sadistic grin, I half expect a snake to slither out of his mouth.

"So you're the General Minister Reynolds sent?" I ask.

He chuckles. "No, once I knew how dire the situation on Avestan was, I insisted in coming here. Glad to see how you held the line. Gave us the time we needed to deploy and destroy." He smirks at his little rhyme.

"Excuse me, but I must oversee our next assault. Commander, Senator." He nods to us and takes his leave.

"Reynolds sent *him*?" I ask.

Lindstrom gives me a strained look. "I know. The worst part is he was the General pushing hardest *against* sending troops to Avestan. I don't understand why he's here."

"I have a theory," I reply. "The Horsemen and General Hawkes don't have a friendly history. I suspect that he may be after us."

Lindstrom swallows hard. "He was always one to manipulate a situation. The militia will watch over you as well. They know who stood out there to defend them. And General Hawkes isn't the only one with allies."

I smile at Lindstrom, trying to find comfort in her assurance, but she only has a militia, while Hawkes controls the deadliest branch of the military. The skies of Avestan turn dark and I watch the neighboring cities smolder in the distance.

ENEMIES ON ALL SIDES

Godfrey's Journal, Day 418

It's been over three weeks since Hawkes and his infantry have landed on Avestan. We may have succeeded in keeping the Grigylls out of the capital, but they obliterated the neighboring city, Erato. The cityscape smolders and the Grigylls have held it with an iron fist. No matter what we try, we can't root them out. They've secured a stronghold and fly soldiers in daily. They've dragged us into a guerrilla fight, forcing us to retake the city block by block. All of the human forces are worn out - the militia, the infantry, even us. Every time we gain a foothold within Erato, more Grigylls are transported in to fight and retake our gains. Hawkes has been pleading with the Core to send reinforcements, but they're tied up elsewhere. Today we've made it to Erato's city center and our goal is to ambush the transport ships when they bring down reinforcements.

We hole up inside City Hall with a platoon of militiamen. I order them to take a break and as soon as they do, my men start grumbling.

"I don't understand why Hawkes hasn't ended the stalemate here,"

Hacker says.

"Incompetence?" Sulture asks.

"Hardly. Blackhat Hawkes always sent overwhelming forces against the rebel fleets. He sent one-third of Earth's fleet to break the Coalition's siege of Khonsu during the Core Invasion."

"I remember that battle," Warrens says. "It was a slaughter."

My comm device rings. It's a call from Senator Lindstrom, and I answer.

"Yes Senator?"

"Commander Godfrey, I have information that I can only trust with you."

"What is it?"

"I don't believe Hawkes has been requesting reinforcements from the Core."

"What makes you think this?"

Lindstrom sighs. "Politicians spend their entire lives collecting and leveraging secrets. If I reveal this one, I forfeit my life. The Horsemen is the only group to cross his path and survive."

I want to tell the Senator to get to the point, but I let her continue.

"I have allies within the Martian forces who've informed me that Hawkes ordered *every* defense outpost to stand down right before Earth was invaded by the Grigyll fleet. I didn't know if I could believe this, so I had the matter investigated quietly. My findings were even worse than I anticipated. Hawkes has allowed dozens of systems to be ravaged to further the war effort. I've pulled all communications Avestan has made with the Core over the past two months and Hawkes hasn't made a call once. I'm sending you and your team everything I've collected. I believe Hawkes and his men are on to me, and I can't risk taking this secret to my grave."

I check my comm. I've received the files Lindstrom sent me.

"Senator, have you ever heard of the Combine?"

She pauses. "I've been approached by their agents, but I have no interest in some disjointed cabal."

"What part does Hawkes play in all of this?"

She looks at me as though the answer is obvious. "By allowing a war to start, all of the entities get their wartime contracts, funding their scientific research. In exchange, the Combine gives the best enhancements to the STARs, Hawkes' personal army."

Behind Lindstrom, there's a banging on the door. It's an officer calling for the Senator to surrender and that she is under arrest for treason.

"Watch yourself Commander Godfrey. They're going to come for you next." The door explodes open and the transmission ends. I growl and punch a nearby door. The other Horsemen rush over to me.

"We must kill that traitor Hawkes," I growl.

"Eliminating one of the Core's most prominent Generals won't go unnoticed," Hacker replies. "The Core will hunt us."

I turn to Hacker. "What did you call Hawkes earlier?"

"Blackhat Hawkes?"

"What does it mean?"

"He makes people disappear, never to be seen again."

I look out at the sky above us. Dark clouds loom overhead, the Grigyll ships blocking out the sun. I call out to the men that we're going to march back to Melusine.

Hacker tugs on my shoulder. "Sir, we've just intercepted a transmission issued by Hawkes to the six-oh-eight. Emie, play it back."

"I'm afraid General Hawkes has issued charges of treason and conspiracy in collaboration with the traitor Senator Lindstrom."

"That's it!" I growl. "Emie, launch the mechs. We're taking this war to him!"

"I'm afraid General Hawkes has issued a lockdown on them and the *Enigma*. A hostile artificial intelligence is preventing me from accessing the ship's operating system."

"That's a shame," Shepherd replies, looking away from his sniper scope. "Because we could use reinforcements. The Core Infantry is on the move and they're heading right this way."

I access my comm unit. "Squadron forty-three, all of you return to my position!"

The squadron assembles within minutes.

"What is it Commander?" One of them asks.

"We have a common enemy now. General Hawkes has arrested-"

Blaster bolts pound the concrete pillars. One of the infantry raises his rifle and shoots the unsuspecting militiaman.

"Everyone inside!" I order. The militia runs in and I turn to the

Horsemen. “Hand to hand combat only. The Core won't get any video of us shooting at her soldiers.” I draw my knife and wave the men in.

One of the infantrymen gets the draw on me and orders me to turn around.

“Such a shame the infamous Horsemen had to murder these innocent militiamen.”

I activate my shield right as he takes the shot. I knock his rifle away, grab the kid and slit his throat.

“Such a shame you grunts didn't pay closer attention to martial combat,” I reply. The kid gurgles his last and reaches for me as I kick his rifle away. I turn and walk inside the crumbling city hall building.

“Find me an exit! Won't be long before the grunts have us surrounded!”

“We've got one sir!” A militia soldier cries out. He's cut down by gunfire through the window. The assailant reaches in and shoots at us, but Lee pulls him in and stabs him in the chest. The kid has a pained look on his face.

“We got a way out sir!” Warrens howls. We make it to the south exit while Shepherd surveys the area with his scope.

“Not quite. Grigylls are on the move now.”

Hacker releases an orb-shaped droid into the air and displays a hologram onto the ground. To the North are hundreds of Core soldiers coming this way. To the South, dozens of Grigylls are preparing for an assault.

And we're caught smack in the middle.

“Warrens, ready your gatling,” I order. “We head South.”

“Sir?!” Sujay asks.

“At least we *know* who our enemies are to the South.”

“You heard him,” Sulture growls. “Let's hunt some Grigylls.”

Warrens takes point and readies his gatling. We form a tight-knit unit while Murph and Sujay watch the rear. The city looks like a broken husk with shattered buildings and lifeless streets. Bodies are everywhere - the people who refused to leave are now a ward for all to see what it means to defy the Grigylls.

They crawl out from the buildings, gleeful that we'd wandered into their midst. We take cover while the Core infantry tracks us. Some of the Grigylls go after them, but we hold their immediate attention.

"Light 'em up!" I order.

The city descends into chaos as three factions fight in a ferocious bid to stay alive. I look to the South and I see a hill that towers over the town. My gut tells me that's where we need to go. I can't explain it, so I put all my focus on driving South.

The Grigylls keep the Core infantry at bay, but they're still gaining on us. The lizards seem to come from out of nowhere, but that doesn't stop us from cutting them down. The sky is a dim yellow, with blackened clouds swirling overhead. A warship breaks through the clouds and heads for Erato.

"There's the troop carrier!" Warrens cries out. He pulls a bundle of rods which become a tripod that drive into the ground. He pulls components out of his armor, fiddling with his gun until he's transformed it from a gatling to a missile launcher.

"Cover him!" I order. We drive back Grigylls who look half-starved and are more ferocious than anything we've seen so far. Warrens mounts the missile launcher to the tripod and activates the cannon. It screams in anticipation, sucking the oxygen out of the air until the reactor glows white hot.

"Firing!" Warrens cries out. The cannon erupts like thunder and the static ion blast soars directly into the troop carrier. All of the lights flicker until the ship goes black. The behemoth howls and the clouds grasp at the ship, each airy finger unable to keep the machine in the sky.

"It's plummeting!" I roar. "Head South!"

We charge for the hill to the South, watching the ship above us slowly falling. Blaster bolts fly all around us. The ship crashes into a building, but the infantry isn't slowing down.

We break through the borders of the city, running through the green grass. The city lies in ruins as the ship crashes, twisting and melting steel all into one. We see the hill. We see the place we can run to.

Except another aged Core warship flies over our heads and hovers above the hill.

My heart sinks as this ship slowly spins and the troop carrier door opens.

Bolts torch the grass around us. Hundreds of Grigylls that either survived or ejected from the falling ship are now coming for us. We're surrounded by enemies, Grigylls on one side, Core soldiers hunting us on the other.

I look at the Horsemen and a quiet nod is all we have for our final goodbye. We get back to back and brace for the next onslaught.

At the top of the hill, the carrier has opened up and a few soldiers come spilling out. They're reptilian, but not Grigylls.

Draiders.

Alongside them are brown-clad soldiers, all of them charging right at the Grigylls.

The Draiders keep low, wielding double-bladed swords and run right around us, crashing into the horde of Grigylls at the base of the hill. The Grigyll ferocity is no match for the Draider discipline as the two battle and stain the planet with their blood.

More troop carriers land along the edge of the hill. Each of them spills out hundreds more Draiders, every one of them yearning to prove themselves against the larger Grigylls.

One of the browncoat soldiers stops by us, noting my confused, yet relieved gaze.

"General Fitch has received Avestan's call for aid. We came as soon as we could and he told me to tell you that we're eliminating the Grigyll infestation on this world once and for all."

The sky overhead erupts into a firestorm, with hundreds more ships landing, creating a rising tide of reinforcements. Fitch's fleet attacks the Grigylls with merciless precision, annihilating the enemy forces.

One way or another, Avestan is being retaken today.

"Horsemen! Charge!" I order. We turn and run back into Erato, rejoining the Draiders and eliminating every Grigyll in sight. The Grigylls are merciless in their savagery, but the whirling blades of the Draiders give them a deadly reach their enemies can't match.

The city is a smoldering ruin, but in the following hours we retake Erato. Fitch's fleet drives the Grigylls out of the skies, while the Core soldiers meet the Draiders for the first time.

"What are these things?" A Core soldier asks.

His CO cuts him off. "Doesn't matter, Horsemen, you're under arrest-"

Everyone's comm unit goes off at the same time. It's a message from Defense Minister Reynolds. The curious soldiers play the message.

"The Chancellor and I have issued a proclamation. None of these new alien species, the so-called 'Draiders' are to be harmed. They fall under the dominion of the Sentience Protection and Yield Act and will be granted protection status until formal review by the Ministry of the Interior."

The CO glares at me. "The Horsemen are still under arrest-"

A Draider holds a blade up to his throat. The soldiers all look to the CO, wondering what to do.

"We escort them to Fitch," the Draider says. His English is rough, but unmistakable. The Draiders and browncoats surround us, and we march back to Melusine. The Draiders tell us their tales of rejoining Father Sky, and how they've fought against 'the fallen.' They see the Grigylls as a race that were abandoned by the pantheon and have become demons who feast on flesh. Not too far off the mark.

Once inside Melusine, the city swarms with browncoats, Core infantry and the Avestan militia all commingle together. The browncoats have started organizing the militia, giving them the discipline they desperately need.

Inside the palace, Core officers are being arrested, while staffers are being released. At Central Command, Fitch stands tall, issuing orders in the midst of the chaos.

The Draiders and browncoats separate and stand at attention for Fitch, before switching into a gauntlet for us to walk through. I take the lead and approach the General. His face is solemn and full of sorrow.

"Welcome back Horsemen."

"General," I reply with a nod. "What brings you here?"

"We received your calls for help. When it became clear the current residing officer wasn't going to allow for aid to come, we took matters into our own hands. As you can tell, I've brought friends with me."

Out of the corner of my eye, I notice a Draider approach us.

Starfall.

"Once word got out that Starfall had defeated the priests and was able to rejoin Father Sky, the planet's tribes fell in line," Fitch explains. "Now we have an ally who hates the Grigylls as much as we do and I intend to explain that to all the talking heads back on Earth."

Starfall looks to us. "So many humans among the stars."

"We've been flying a bit longer," I reply and then turn back to Fitch. "Did you know we were here?"

"I did. We received some chatter of the Horsemen mounting a defense on Avestan followed by a lengthy report on General Hawkes instigating this new war."

Senator Lindstrom walks into the room. "Oh General Fitch, this is Silas Godfrey, Commander of-"

"Senator, the Horsemen and I have a history, no introductions are needed here."

Lindstrom looks at me. "Well, it seems you know everyone. I'll go check on my staff."

"How do you-"

Fitch grins. "Her father served under me. Great man who would do anything for his homeworld. I see his daughter took after him. There's a lot of cleaning up needed within the Core and I believe I've stayed away long enough. Avestan is where I start."

One of the browncoats tosses a cuffed General Hawkes to our feet. Fitch notices our confused gaze.

"I'm afraid General Hawkes was missing upon my arrival," He says. "I have no record of him being here so we can only label him as MIA, presumed dead."

"You sniveling traitor!" He hisses.

"I fight for Earth, not the factions that have corrupted her. I've stood by long enough, now it's time to do what your generation couldn't: save the Core. Horsemen, I believe you're the ones who found him correct?"

I draw my pistol and cock it. "Yes we did sir. And General?"

"Yes?"

"It's great to have you back."

FITCH JOINS THE WAR

Godfrey's Journal, Day 451

Fitch has taken us aboard the Monolith, *granting us amnesty against the other Core Generals. We've been en route to Earth for weeks now, so that Fitch can speak with the Minister of Defense and his staff personally in regards to the Draider situation, with Starfall acting as their representative. His soldiers are hardened boys, some of them too young to have finished school. I asked Fitch about this and he explained that people on the outer edges contribute what they can, whether that be food, fuel or volunteers. He then went on to say that the Horsemen weren't the only ones to fight monsters, but left it at that. He said that his army would be a great bargaining chip and a useful ally in this new war. He has us tell him everything we know about Hawkes in preparation of arguing a case with the Ministry. Fitch dismisses the rest of the Horsemen and has kept me in his quarters.*

"I take it you've discovered who the puppet master is?"
I swallow hard. "Yes sir."

"You know 'im?"

"All too well. He's my father."

Fitch lets out a sharp whistle. "That must sting. But at least now you have an advantage against him."

"Excuse me sir?"

"He underestimates you. Anyone who builds an organization this large and secretive has control issues and the moment he realizes he can't control you, you've won."

"He's still got a legion of followers that have infiltrated every layer of the scientific community *and* the military."

"Well now we'll have allies deep in the Core as well." Fitch rises and watches out the window.

It's another few hours after we land before we make it to Central Command. Behind the closed wooden doors the most powerful minds in the military are discussing strategy and plotting their next move. However, four aides halt our progress and are focused more on a technicality than on the war.

"I'm sorry sir, but your name isn't listed," One of the staffers says to Fitch. "It's not even in our system. The meeting in progress is heavily classified and you can't enter."

"Like hell I can't! Are you more concerned with the guest list than the fate of the Core son?"

"I'm sorry General…" The aide looks down at his tablet.

"Fitch! It's Fitch boy! I was serving this government when you were in diapers sucking on your Momma! Tell me again that I can't enter."

The aides try to stiffen themselves. "We're under strict orders to not disrupt this meeting."

"Don't worry son, you won't be the one disrupting them." Fitch shoves the aids aside and throws the doors open. Starfall and the rest of us follow in close behind.

The members of Central Command rise up and two guards pull their pistols on us. Fitch snatches the pistol and disarms the guard with a left hook. Two more charge out, ordering him to drop the pistol.

"That's enough," Defense Minister Reynolds says. "Stand down gentlemen." He approaches Fitch and extends his hand. The two share an unwavering handshake. Reynolds is shorter than I expected, with big brown eyes and his matching hair swept back. There's a touch of gray, which makes him look like a kid compared to the elderly generals surrounding him.

"What brings you to Central Command?" Reynolds asks.

Fitch holds his hand out behind him, signaling Starfall. His cloak is white with a crimson trim, and he looks at Reynolds without any fear in his eyes.

"I have discovered a race of humanoids deep within the Unknown Regions. I come here to present them as allies to our cause. I also come to offer my expertise in fighting the Grigylls, for I've been battling them for the past twenty years."

A balding general with a white mustache struggles to look at Fitch over his shoulder. "You don't deserve to be here Romulus. You're a deserter."

"Said by a ring of men who ruled the military when *I* enlisted. You fought a war that didn't need to be fought because you couldn't face criticism! And what's worse is you didn't fix anything! You kicked the can down the road by supporting oppression and now you're a decrypt government scrambling for soldiers. I offer you legions of reinforcements and you dare call me a deserter?!"

"I'm afraid Fitch is right," Reynolds says. "We are in dire straits with recruitment."

Another one of the generals speaks up. "Of course you side with him since you served under him."

Reynold's eyes burn, but he holds back. It's obvious why a younger man was appointed to the Ministry, the Generals needed someone they believed they could bully.

"General Roth were you not the one who supported all of General Hawkes' maneuvers even though he was secretly betraying the State?"

Roth's jaw drops so far even his bushy mustache can't cover it up. "We were all betrayed by him…"

"Well now I'm here to replace him," Fitch says.

General Nimitz stands up in outrage. "And are we to forget your act of treason in killing a fellow officer of the Core? An Admiral no less?"

Reynolds holds up his hand. "This is about the fate of the Core General Nimitz, not your son. I will convince the Chancellor that a pardon is in order. General Fitch, will you join us in Central

Command?"

"On one condition. The Draiders are acknowledged with a full treaty as allies of the Core, with the same rights as humans."

"How do we know they're benign?" Roth asks.

"They just liberated Avestan, a planet the rest of *you* refused to go to! I won't live to see them exploited like what you did to the Xeclians!"

"Not like it did much good," Nimitz says with a sip of brandy. "I'm half-convinced they'll side with the beasts soon enough."

"Consider it done," Reynolds replies. "We'll have a treaty drafted now."

The Generals spend hours arguing with each other, locked in a power struggle. Fitch argues on behalf of the Draiders, and finally gets the others to break. They agree to his terms, recognizing the 'Draidarian Empire' as an equal to the Core and pledging to a mutual protection pact. The other Generals glare at Fitch in resentment. There's mumblings of how and where to proceed in the war against the Grigylls.

"Perhaps Fitch can investigate the matter," Nimitz says.

"Investigate what?!"

Nimitz swipes at the holo display. "Intelligence shows what we believe are cloning vats deep within Grigyll space on a planet codenamed 'Aeris.' Do you believe you can break this stronghold Romulus?"

Fitch swallows hard as he surveys the map. "That's a bold push into Grigyll territory."

"You said yourself that we must drive in deep and then cut off the surrounding worlds. Hop from planet to planet. Or are you scared of the execution?"

Fitch takes a deep breath. "Give me my armada. Those boys will drive the Grigylls back so hard they'll be seeing stars. I'm also bringing you General Nimitz."

His eyes look as though they're trying to pierce through Fitch.

"Once this planet is conquered, your army can hold it. You're quite good at holding the position. Does that sound like a plan to you

Minister Reynolds?"

"An excellent balance General. Godspeed to both of you."

We board the *Monolith* which lifts off and reconnects with the rest of Fitch's fleet. Nimitz's 306th Army mobilizes and follows as we brace for the long voyage into Grigyll space. Fitch's men escort Nimitz to his quarters.

"I was worried you'd been outmaneuvered sir," I say.

"I merely tied Nimitz's fate to ours."

"Perfect. Now if you can show me how to tie Salvatori's fate to mine."

"It already is. Which reminds me, I have some information for you on where he is. Help me with this mission and I'll show you what my intelligence analysts found."

I try to hold back, but a grin slips through. "Sounds like a deal."

"It's funny. I once told John when things were falling apart that the only way to get our unity back as humans was to keep spreading and exploring. I joked about a crew who could make the next push. Smart fellas who could actually figure shit out."

I feel myself grin. "Like scientists?"

Fitch looks over and shares a grin. "Never would've guessed he'd take it to heart. But now I see why John formed your team. It wasn't about exploring the galaxy, we don't need any help with that. It's about making things right. John knew what the Unification wars were about: bureaucrats seizing power away from the people. On top of it, he made one of the biggest offenders, Ionics pay the costs. Brilliant man."

"So the Horsemen Initiative was John's master plan? To what end?"

"To bring down the shadow government that has infiltrated and ruled the Core for the past thirty years."

Godfrey's Journal, Day 471

We finally reach the planet codenamed Aeris. It was a long six week journey, and I fear that Salvatori is getting stronger every day. Every day we're not hunting him gives him the chance to regroup, to convert others to his cause, or to experiment and accomplish the God-State. I fear we're running out of time.

Aeris looks like a young world, one that Earth was in the process of terramorphing before the Grigylls took over. The *Monolith* scans the surface, searching for the alluded cloning facilities. We come across a laboratory with a nuclear power plant built in. Along the ground are thousands of glass-like coffins.

"Horsemen! What is this structure?" Fitch asks, pointing to the glass boxes.

"Those are clone vats sir," I reply.

For the first time, even Fitch is unsettled. "Clones. Last thing those beasts need is to figure out how to copy themselves."

Sulture grunts. "Clones are easy. They're all subject to the same immune deficiencies as the host. One viral strain will wipe out a legion of them. That and we can secure the Grigyll genome. Wipe them all out."

"You make a good point Dr. Sulture. Let's explore the surface and secure that genome for the Horsemen!"

Man and Draider alike howl, ready for battle.

We descend to the surface which is far quieter than expected. The two armies march out and hundreds of vehicles pour out of the ships. We drive across kilometres of dead city streets with war-torn buildings and rubbled roads. After an hour of driving, we reach the facility. The laboratory bears Samson Research and Development's logo, but the place is covered in dust and grime. Nobody's maintained the place for years.

"This is it," Fitch says. "Pull over."

Our convoy pulls into the abandoned-looking laboratory and surveys the outside. The cloning pods are huge, connected in stacks three stories high and covered in grime.

Hacker releases two drones to assist in scouting the area. The place is overrun with core infantry.

"What happened here?" I ask.

"It's a setup," Fitch replies.

"How do you know?"

"Haven't seen one Grigyll track since we got here."

"Who would do this?"

"I got an inkling," Fitch growls. "But I need proof."

One of the boys calls out. "General Fitch! You've gotta come see this!"

We rush deep into the laboratory. The building has been hollowed out, a victim of multiple bombing runs seeking their target.

In the center of the laboratory is a crater, where tracks from machines had recently tread. The equipment looks as though it'd been abandoned in a hurry. It's scattered and parked in random places. The dirt is piled high around the crater and smells fresh.

Despite all of my instincts, I approach the pit.

A projection of Salvatori rises up. "You destroyed my army, now I destroy yours." I smash the device displaying him before he can taunt us any further.

I look down into the silo buried deep within the earth. It's a dark void, but there's a strange hum that echos from below. There are dozens of tunnels that snake outward from the pit. The hum gets louder, and a glow ignites. I feel a strange pull on my shoulders. The air around me has changed. It's being drawn *into* the silo.

The pull grows stronger. Flecks of dirt fly in, and the other men are struggling to resist. Hacker looks at his wrist comm and his eyes snap to me.

"It's an inversion matrix! Run!"

"A *what*?" Fitch asks.

My mind scrambles to find the right answer. "It's basically a controlled black hole!"

"Aw hell, and we're kilometres from the ship!" Fitch's men hop into their trucks and take off while Forrest skids in.

"Looks like it's up to the pilot to save the day again!"

Fitch and I look at each other, but we know we don't have a choice.

We hop into Forrest's truck with Sulture and Shepherd.

"Where are the rest?!" I scream.

"Our good pal Sujay has 'em! But we've got a planet to flee from so strap in!" Forrest jams his foot down on the gas and the truck roars forward. Soldiers behind us fly backwards, unable to escape. The hum becomes a deafening roar as the portal of destruction threatens to swallow the world.

Pebbles on the road start floating before they're pulled back towards the void. Sand becomes rocks and then boulders are torn from the earth, all launched behind us. Forrest dodges an incoming boulder, desperately trying to outrun the black hole.

Another deafening crack echoes across the plane. We look around and see a skyscraper shift and collapse in the distance. The street a block over cracks and crumbles into dust, before being sucked down the tunnels.

"What is happening?" Fitch roars.

I remember the tunnels surrounding the pit. "They tunneled beneath the roads. All of the air is being sucked out, creating negative pressure that the hollowed-out earth can't hold!"

"In English?!"

"This entire city will crumble to bits in about five minutes!"

"You heard him Forrest! Give it all you got!" He turns on his comm. "All units aboard the *Monolith* get that ship ready for immediate takeoff. We're coming in hot and I want whoever is in charge to ensure we can take off the moment I arrive.

Forrest looks back and flashes a thin smile, then turns back to the road. He swings a hard left, barely avoiding the foundation of a skyscraper and our road collapsing into ruin.

"All units aboard the *Monolith* converge and arrest General Nimitz! I don't care what he says, I'll deal with the Core!"

Forrest weaves from one street to another. Now the skyscrapers are crumbling, with pieces of steel falling and then flying off to be sucked up. Each one of them is like a flying hammer, which we barely avoid.

It feels like an eternity, but we arrive at the *Monolith.* Visions of John's death flash in my mind as we make our escape run. There are still more trucks behind us and I fear that Fitch will need to make the call to let them go.

"C'mon boys! C'mon!" Fitch whispers to himself. We drive into the loading dock, but the ship powers up in preparation for takeoff.

Fitch gets on his comm. "Hold on, we've got a few more!"

One of the soldiers clicks through. "Sir, we can't wait any longer or we'll get sucked in."

"Stay here or I'll personally escort you back to that black hole."

Forrest looks at me. "I don't think he's bluffing." I roll my eyes and turn my attention to the other soldiers. We wave them all in, pleading for them to drive faster. Two more trucks containing the Horsemen drive through, so we're all accounted for.

Three more trucks of soldiers drive in, but the remaining ones are lifted off the ground and pulled back. Fitch reaches out to help, but I pull him back into the ship.

I click on his comm unit. "Time to go!"

The *Monolith* roars to life and lifts off. The thrusters whine and growl as we struggle to break orbit. The ship works three times as hard to pull away. We consider ourselves lucky as the 306th is swallowed into the abyss.

Fitch pulls himself to his feet. "Where is he?!"

We follow the angry General into his ship where his soldiers are struggling to cope with what they'd just witnessed.

"At your stations! All of you!" He howls. The men scamper like mice, pretending that it's just another day. Two soldiers wave him down, and bring him into the interrogation chamber.

"What the hell was that?!" Fitch roars.

Nimitz is devastated. "You…you…"

"Were supposed to go alone?! Yeah I know. Figured if I took enough of *your* boys along, your master would hold back. Who else is under his control?!"

Nimitz looks up at Fitch and a lone tear glides down his cheek. He looks at me and his body convulses. Fitch grabs him by the shoulders and tries to slap him out of it, but Murph steps in.

"He's gone sir. It's something we're all too familiar with."

"What was Nimitz promised?!" Fitch's eyes look frantic.

"Immortality," I reply. "Salvatori promised him immortality in exchange for his service." We look at the monitors around the room, which show Aeris crumbling in on itself. Within minutes, the planet is no more.

Fitch storms off, but I follow him into his quarters. He doesn't try to keep me out. He throws two of his glasses at the wall, then pours himself a drink three fingers tall and swallows it whole.

"We lost a lot of good men out there. This? I've never seen anything like this."

"Unfortunately sir, that's our enemy."

"There are no limits to his destruction."

I never thought I'd see it, but Fitch is visibly shaken.

"I can't protect you from that. I can't even help you," He growls. "This is not a war I know how to fight. However, you and your boys can. You can fight him on his level. You need to hunt down every last trace of this group and wipe them out.

"How? He's always one step ahead of us! He anticipates everything!"

Fitch pulls a tablet from his desk. He looks at it and hands it to me. "General Hawkes kept meticulous records. Go dark. Disappear without a trace. Keep yourself so hidden that even I can't find you."

"How?!"

"You boys are skilled enough to do this. All you need is a map of the Combine's inner network, and now you have it." Fitch hands me the tablet.

"This was to be used by the Core for Hawkes' investigation."

"Screw the damn Core boy! They won't go after your father - you have to! I'll help however I can, but your war belongs in the shadows, a place I don't know how to fight."

I analyze the contents of the tablet. Every organization the Combine owns is in here, along with financials, rosters, experiment notes and progress reports. All of it updated in real time.

I look up at Fitch.

"As I said, meticulous. Now, go end this war."

ROIL

Godfrey's Journal, Day 1,806

It has been almost five years to the day since I'd joined the Horsemen Corps. For years we've been tracking the final remnants of the Combine. We've hunted and eliminated the council, however Salvatori still eludes us. He's all that's left. We've destroyed his factories, bombed his laboratories, robbed his finances and burned his research. We've caused the financial collapse of Ionics and have exposed the puppet master for all to see. He's vulnerable and has been driven deep into Grigyll space, no doubt performing experiments on the rampaging lizards. That's fine by us, because Defense Minster Reynolds has paid a tidy sum for us to retrieve the Grigyll genome on a planet codenamed 'Roil' and create a disease that will exterminate the Grigyll race.

Sulture has been struggling for years to find a disease which will wipe out the Grigylls, but slowly enough that it can spread between planets. He believes the key is extending the dormancy, but another challenge lies in the genetic structure of the Grigyll itself. Since the species was created by a microscopic recombinator, their genes are in a near-state of constant evolution, making a disease that will destroy the species that much more challenging.

It's quiet aboard the Enigma *now. We've shared all of our stories, jokes and memories. There's not much for us to talk about except the next mission. In truth, we don't need to say much. Brotherhood entails a certain comfort in each other's presence, even if no words are exchanged.*

The star map shows our path to Roil, a ravaged wasteland that's been a battlefield for the entire war.

"You actually believe the reports?" Sulture asks. "After all the false leads?"

"I have to believe at some point we'll find what we're looking for. Besides, these ships that just landed are equipped with biohazard vaults."

Sulture snickers. "I'll believe it when I see it."

"*Ping ming,*" Lee says.

"He's right," I reply. "Getting this genome will be the fight of our life." The cameras show dozens of Grigylls patrolling the area.

"Do we have to fight for it? Can't we just download the program remotely?" Shepherd asks.

Hacker answers. "A valid question. There is a surprising amount of encryption within this facility. I wonder if they're using Xeclian tech for their research. The only way we're getting that genome off world is to manually download it from their terminal. And that means we need to get inside." All eyes fall on me.

"Standard drop through atmo. Warrens get the coffins ready. Once we're through the stratosphere, we can eject. From there we'll rendezvous at the coordinates on the map." The numbers are sent to their comm devices. "Forrest and Sujay, keep the boat afloat."

"Finally! An order I agree with!" Forrest shouts.

"Warrens, Shepherd, you'll be heavy infantry support. The rest are with me. Lee and Murph, I'm having you two take point, while Sulture and I will guard Hacker."

"And lastly, pray to whatever god you worship that we find the Grigyll genome here. This is the key to ending this infernal war. Now, let's go kill some lizards!" Sulture screams. Warrens seals us in the pressure chambers affectionately called coffins. We're launched from the ship and plummet about five kilometres. The howl from the wind is awful and I'm completely reliant on sensors telling me where I am. When the coffin splits, it's ripped apart and I'm bathed in the icy air.

The flaps on my armor connect and I join the others as we soar to the surface. Our sensors map the terrain and give us a path we can use to hit the laboratory. There are some trenches they've dug in, but it's nothing we can't handle.

We extend our flaps and slow down, landing on the outer edges of no man's land. The two sides have staked their positions and now fight for this pockmarked piece of dirt. Lee takes point, eliminates the sentries and leaps into the trench maze.

We file in, tracking everything through the sights on our guns. It's quiet in here. Too quiet.

A Grigyll leaps out and grabs Murph by the throat. Without even batting an eyelash he draws a knife from his side and plunges it into the forearm. The beast cries out, but doesn't let go. Murph twists the blade holding eye contact the entire time. He finds the right tendon and cuts, which releases him. He pulls his rifle back up and fires two shots, killing the beast.

"You alright?" I ask.

Murph shakes it off. "Never better." The gunshots cause the Grigylls to pour out from caverns dug behind our position. They charge in with a bloodthirsty ferocity. We move as fast as we can to our target, but we're surrounded in no time. Lee and Murph dive into a path to the left, while Sulture and I face Grigylls shooting from both sides.

I turn on my infrared and give the order. "Lima Alpha Foxtrot!"

Sulture spins around to protect my six while I do the same for him. We stand shoulder to shoulder, shooting until we're clear on both sides. I look over to him and he gives me a small nod.

"Let's move!" I take point while Lee and Murph bring up the rear.

We utilize our GPS coordinates and navigate through the maze within the trenches. We take out only the Grigylls in our way, sparing those hidden elsewhere.

We make it to the laboratory, taking positions behind overturned tables and furniture. The place is grimy, but fortified. Our enemies growl to one another, alerting our presence. We eliminate all of them on the first floor and then perform a sweep. I'm about to give the all clear when one of them leaps out and tackles Lee.

He gets an arm free, elbows it in the ribs and snaps its neck in one fluid motion. The Grigyll falls over and Shepherd rushes in to secure the area. Hacker walks up to the central computer while the rest of us circle around to protect him.

The laboratory is quiet, except for explosions outside. A series of bombing runs from the Core threaten to shake this place to pieces, but the Grigylls fire back with antiaircraft weaponry.

"Does the Core know we're here?" Shepherd asks.

"Nope," I reply.

"Should we alert them?"

"Nope."

"Sulture, I need you to review this sequence," Hacker says. The two stare at a display of a DNA sequence until Sulture finally answers.

"This is it."

"Great," I reply. "Pack it up and let's get out of here! Calling an extraction."

I click on my comm and signal the *Enigma.* "Alpha One to Eagle. We are ready for extraction."

"What's the magic word?"

"I swear to God Forrest…"

"Always remember that I'm the one who flies this-" His voice is cut off by the sound of him choking.

"Forrest?!" I scream.

"Don't worry boss," Warrens replies. "Someone's gotta put Curly in his place."

"Rude!" Forrest gasps. "We're en route."

The gunfire intensifies outside. Black-clad figures charge towards our position. We raise our guns, ready to fire at whatever comes our way.

"Forrest where are you?!" I growl.

"We're almost there! These AA guns *are* high caliber y'know!"

"That's what your mom said about me," Sujay replies.

"What do y'know? Sujay finally got one! I'm so proud of you-"

"Forrest, we have soldiers charging at us, and we can't tell if they're friendly!"

"Right, right. Give us three minutes."

The soldiers breach the doors and we're both staring at each other with guns raised. They recognize that we're humans and the CO lowers his gun and raises his hands in surrender. I can tell right away from their uniforms they're STARs.

"Glad to see some humans here instead of the defective 'guanas."

"Yeah, real glad," I reply.

"Which unit are you with?" He asks.

"We report directly to Minister Reynolds," I reply.

"Yeah, he's ordering us all to make an aggressive push."

One of the soldiers points at our shoulder. "Sir, their armor."

The CO looks and a flash of disgust seizes his face. "Horses' Asses!"

The *Enigma* stops overhead and drops the extraction cables. They draw their guns and we draw ours.

"It doesn't have to end like this," I say. "Let us go and we won't be any trouble. None of us need to get hurt."

I hear a slight beep from all of the soldiers. "You should've thought of that before you killed all those soldiers four years ago."

I draw my guns and open fire "GO!" I order. Murph, Hacker and Lee all click onto the cables and are pulled up while Sulture and I lay down a wave of cover fire.

"Sulture, get out of here!" I order. I get a clear shot at the CO. I shoot him through his chest, but the wound heals within seconds.

"GET OUT OF HERE!" I scream to Sulture. His eyes grow large and he pushes me out of the way.

Right in line with the CO's shotgun.

I watch in horror as Sulture is knocked back, blood splattering on the floor.

I leap to my feet and charge the officer.

His shotgun erupts a second time.

It feels like a ball of molten lead is swimming in my stomach, but I look down. My armor is in tatters, but there's no damage. Instead, there's a violet glow. The heat I feel swirls for a moment, but then it begins to spread, fueling my rage.

"Doc give you something or is it homemade?" The CO asks.

My gloves itch, too much for me to ignore. I tear them off and my fingertips are glowing purple. A spark leaps between my fingertips. I look up, the soldiers are scared.

My hands shake in rage, my blood feels like it's boiling. I concentrate, trying to temper this, but I feel like I can't any longer.

I howl in anger and streaks of lightning leap from my fingertips. I target the CO, who disintegrates into a pile of ash before me.

The other soldiers try to run away, but I bring my wrath upon them, unleashing wave after wave of torment. One after another they collapse into a pile of ashes, leaving behind only cindered bones until there are none left. I look at my reflection, and my eyes have a bright violet glow to them, like I'm possessed.

As quickly as it came, the wave ceases and I return to normal. I turn around and to my horror, Sulture is lying on the ground. I run to him and check his wound.

"Through the liver, no coming back from that," He says. He coughs up blood and looks at me.

"I'm sorry…for everything Godfrey. I'm sorry for having been an ass. I'm sorry about the experiment."

"What experiment?" I ask.

"Murph will explain. The Combine targeted us because of what we did to you."

"Stop talking like that Sulture. We'll get you out of this. We need you to help wipe out the Grigylls."

"My lab notes detail the virus I intended to create. Murph will know how to do it. You can do it too."

"Shut up!" I scream. "You're doing this with us. We need you!"

"I'm sorry again Godfrey. On Avestan when you saved me, I understood why John chose you to lead. I thought it was to tie our fate to yours, but on that battlefield, I understood why."

I grab the rope and tie Sulture to it. "Murph will patch you up and you'll help us-"

"Godfrey," He interrupts. "I want to see Katrina and Joey again. I've caused enough damage in my life."

I put my forehead against his. "It was an honor to have served with you Dr. Adam Sulture."

"It was a privilege to have been led by you Dr. Silas Godfrey." His gaze turns to the sky and I watch the light fade from his eyes. I click on to the extraction cable and signal to pull us up.

The others haul me up with faces of relief which quickly turn to anguish as I pull Sulture's body onto the ship. I rip my mask off and the tears in my eyes tell the story for me. Murph's face turns to horror. He cries out in agony and leaps for the body. Warrens catches him and pulls him into a hug, holding him tight. He gives me a light nod as tears glide down his cheeks.

Forrest and Sujay come rushing in, but they're stunned by what they see. Forrest tries to say something, but he can't find the words.

"Get us out of here," I order. The two rush back to the cockpit to get us out of the no-fly zone.

I carry Sulture's body into the medbay and place it onto the table. Shepherd comes in behind and helps me strip Sulture's armor. The two of us clean the wound and put the body of our friend to rest. We treat him with the care and respect of a lost brother. After we've finished, Shepherd sees the pain in my eyes and hugs me, all of us struggling to cope with our loss.

It's hours before Murph comes to terms and finally joins me in the medbay. His face is stained with tears and he looks upon the body as though he can't believe his own eyes. I rise up and stand next to Murph.

"His last words were that he was ready to see Katrina and Joey again."

Murph's cries turn into a sob and I hold him for comfort.

Hours pass and we join the rest of the men in mourning. There aren't many of us, and every one lost is a friend. We approach the circle. Warrens and Shepherd slide apart, offering us a seat.

"Golden Boy is leading us in some final prayers for Rooster," Warrens explains. Shepherd's service is simple, but harmonious. We go around and share our memories of Sulture. In this time we come to remember him as a loving husband and father. He was meticulous, with such an eye for detail that he missed nothing. A zealot unhindered by what others believed could be done. Inventive with an unquenchable thirst for knowledge.

In the end, all of our tales stood as a testament to a man who would stop at nothing for the people he cared for.

We place him into a homemade coffin, lock him onto the track and Sujay flips the switch. The coffin is launched into the black, a fitting end to a man who stood taller than all of us. One of the greatest minds in a generation is finally at rest, even though we wished he could've helped with one more mission.

The next day, I pull Murph aside as there was something that was still bothering me.

"Sulture spoke of an experiment performed on me and that you would explain."

Murph sighs. "When you contracted the Crimson Plague, We'd mentioned before that we had to blast you with radiation in order to keep you alive."

"Yeah."

"Using radiation to kill a virus is like using a nuke on a house to kill mice. It's beyond overkill."

"What about the 'Synthetic Transfusion' Sulture described?"

"He made it up. The truth Silas is in order for you to survive the radiation we had to bond your DNA to the microbes found inside of the Hadrian gem. That was the transfusion process Adam described."

I'm stunned into silence.

"We were desperate bud. Nothing was working. Your odds of dying increased 1.4% a *minute*. When the bonding was complete, John ordered us to hit you with a concentrated radioactive blast. When we did..."

"What?"

"It'd be better if you saw it. Emie, show the Hadrian Transfusion test."

"Dr. McGinnis, I am not authorized to show this video in the presence of Dr. Godfrey and I-"

Murph interrupts. "Override authorized. Show him the clip Emie."

"Right away Dr. McGinnis." A screen lights up and video footage of me lying in the medbay fills the screen. The team is surrounding me and they're covered in hazmat suits.

"This is just after we'd finished the cellular bonding."

On screen I notice the monitors measuring my vitals are erratic. My breathing is labored. The team brings in a slapped-together x-ray cannon with a piece of the Hadrian gem serving as the power source. They wheel it next to me and get into position.

Murph hits the switch and the lights flicker. The team looks to each other, amazed that I survived. However, the same violet glow I saw on my stomach appears. The team asks themselves what is happening. The health monitors go erratic, and the camera flickers. John orders everyone out of the room. I start convulsing and Murph tries to help, but he's dragged out. The convulsing turns into a seizure and my eyes open. They're glowing and my iris has turned violet just like before. Electrical charges glide across my skin until I unleash a wave of energy, destroying everything in the room, including the camera.

Murph turns to me. "It took us weeks to understand, but nearest we can tell is when your body is hit by a large amount of energy, you create an electrical discharge with the same energy signature as the Hadrian gem."

My thoughts begin to race. "So when I was shot at Harris' apartment-"

"The energy blast was absorbed into your body, but you redirected it back at the assailants. It's a miracle Lee and Shepherd survived being in the same room. It's also how you survived the electrical discharge from Salvatori's chip you implanted in yourself. Your body discharged the energy and caused half a block to black out. It took three weeks for your system to recover, but you survived a traumatic electrical pulse."

"The God-State," I whisper. "Is this what the Combine was after? This experiment?"

Murph nods his head.

"So…what? Am I immortal? Can I be killed?"

"Silas, Adam and I have been running tests on your blood for years. Based on our calculations, while you're 94% less likely to die through normal means, your cells were exposed to ten times the amount of radioactive energy as a normal human. The strain is causing your body to degrade on a molecular level, just like the ion clones. It's as if your body is a battery, you've been plugged in for too long and you have no means of releasing the excess energy so you're being worn down trying to contain it."

"Can we build something where I discharge the excess?"

"We've run those tests. While I haven't found the limit, if too much energy passes through your system, your physical state will disintegrate and you'll become a being of pure energy."

"But with no ability to put myself back together, I'll cease to exist."

"Yeah." Murph holds his head down in defeat.

"Does everyone know this?"

"They know about the ability to discharge energy, but not your degradation."

I can feel anger swirl within. Murph's face shows the first sign of relief, no longer tasked to shoulder this lie any longer. "Why did you guys keep this from me?!"

"John asked us to. He believed that if you knew you'd run away or sacrifice yourself for the good of the team, which would make you vulnerable against the Combine. As long as you were here with us, we'd be able to help and protect you."

My mind is buzzing with questions, however one echoes louder than all the others. "The degradation. How long do I have?"

"A year. Two tops. The symptoms will appear as organ failure. Your ability to contain the energy will diminish and anything organic you touch will turn to ash. You'll eventually just…fade away."

My thoughts race, struggling to cope with the diagnosis. I've been handed a death sentence, and my insides become a bubbling caldron of angst and fear.

"No, this can't be," I reply to Murph. "I can't possibly be some 'conduit.' I was cured using Sulture's synthetic transfusion."

"Silas, we didn't know what we'd done until it was too late!"

"You cured me using the synthetic transfusion. That's it!"

"Silas, no we didn't! We performed an experiment in desperation and traded one death sentence for another!"

I feel my inner walls crumble. I turn around and throw all of the glass equipment off the bench. "You made me a freak! The result of an experiment which showed we were no better than the Combine!"

Murph backs away from me. "I'm sorry Silas."

"Sorry?! You bonded my DNA to an alien microbe, then blast me with deadly radiation and you're sorry?! What did you think would happen?!"

Tears flow from Murph's face. I can't find his reason. I can't understand his logic.

"The worst part is the entire team knew. Get out."

"Silas I-"

"GET OUT!" Murph backs away and leaves the medbay. I stare at the shattered glass and look at Sulture's silent body and weep. The others are traitors to me, I don't want them around. John manipulated everything to keep me alive longer, in the dark about my condition and have the rest of the team 'follow' my lead. They didn't respect my leadership, they followed out of a sense of pity for the sick man who could fall apart at any moment. Then there's Salvatori who unleashed the plague in the first place…

Salvatori. My father, the man obsessed with conquering death. He once told me we'd achieved the God-State, but I didn't believe him. We clearly aren't able to harness what this is. Perhaps my father can.

"Emie, I need you to compile and send a message for me. This must remain top secret, you will only disclose to me."

"Of course Silas. What is your message?"

"Find Dr. Dominic Salvatori and tell him I want to make a deal."

The medbay doors open and the rest of the crew is silent to me. They hold their heads in shame, Murph clearly having warned them of what he told me. I walk into my quarters and lock the door. I unleash hell within the room, breaking glasses, throwing books and kicking over tables. How could they do this to me? How could men I considered *family* do this?!

I realize that I'm holding a picture of John in my hand. A voice nags at me, wondering what he would do. I can only aspire to be like him, a man who couldn't be rattled. It all feels so pointless. The war against the Grigylls, the Combine, it's only brought about untold destruction. I think back to when I'd corralled all those people under the Combine's control. I remember how it felt to have everyone there one moment and gone the next. There's no telling how much I've set the human race back on scientific progress. Maybe it'd be better for me to simply fade away and leave my ashes to the wind.

Hours pass in isolation and my stomach rumbles so loud I can't ignore it. I've received a transmission from Salvatori on Centaura, but I haven't responded.

I grab a tray of food and call the men together.

"I found Salvatori," I say. "He's on Centaura using lithographic machines, which is firmly controlled by the Grigylls. Centaura is so heavily fortified, even the Core is afraid of invading."

"We're coming with you Casanova, like it or not," Warrens says.

"Why? Because John told you to?"

Murph grabs me by the shoulder. "Silas, we've been following *you* for *years* now."

"Yeah," Forrest says. "Besides, we're...we're brothers. All of us."

Hacker comes in. "We started this together, we'll finish it together."

"Till the end sir," Shepherd salutes.

"You all my *se duhng*," Lee says.

All eyes fall on Sujay. "Oh, I don't really like the idea of dying, but I figure after five years with you jokesters, I'm bound for enlightenment. Let's do this!"

OPERATION ARTEMIS

Godfrey's Journal, Day 1,841

Murph and I spend the next five weeks experimenting with genetic combinations for a virus which will eliminate the Grigylls. It's a slow, meticulous process which tests my patience. We read through every page of Sulture's notes half a dozen times, but even then we have hundreds of failures. Murph explains that using enzymes to break hydrogen bonds apart, combine them with other genes and sealing the bonds back up is tedious work. In the end, we manage to create a strain which will spread far and kill the host. Every test we've run against this strain has succeeded. However, there is still one challenge ahead of us.

"How do we get it into the population?" Murph asks.

All we needed was the right strain. We can take this genetic code, plug it into Salvatori's lithographic machines and we have a plague engine.

"Does that really work?"

"Emie, show the projections." Murph's eyes light up in fear as Emie crunches the numbers. Assembling a virus is simple and doesn't require a lot of material. The lithographs will be able to create virions by the billions in minutes.

"Sir, we're being approached by another ship and they sound grumpy!" Forrest says.

Sujay cuts in. "That's just because you can't understand their language you insensitive clot! They were actually really polite. It's Bloodstone and he's bringing a strike team of Draiders aboard sir."

"Excellent! Let them board!" I rush out of the medbay and into the central room.

The Draiders march on board the ship, carrying Xeclian rifles and advanced armor beneath their colorful cloaks. The garment looks to be from a different tribe, and I mention this to Bloodstone as we greet each other.

His hoarse croaks make me realize how much I'd forgotten. Fortunately, Emie was able to translate. "[Yes, these brethren here are of the river tribe, guardians of our people's water. After we rejoined Father Sky, they pledged their allegiance.]"

"We're honored to have you on board, but why are you here?"

"[General Fitch received your intelligence report about Centaura. He sent us to scout this land and prepare for invasion.]"

"Very well. You're more than welcome to join us."

Our initial scans of Centaura show a planet that's been wracked by war. The terrain is scarred, yet fortified. The land can't sustain crops, but at one time it flourished. It's the planet that fought until the bitter end against the Core, with the resistance finally dying down just in time for the Grigylls to invade and take over.

Bloodstone's hand is on my shoulder. "[With your permission commander, we would like to lead the warriors into an oath to cleanse fear. The demons feed on it.]"

I look to the other Horsemen who try to hide squeamish gazes and turn back to Bloodstone.

"Go ahead."

We take a fixed position, aligned with Centaura's sun. Bloodstone pulls a crystal mace from beneath his cloak, a glittering artifact which has seen thousands of rituals.

He orders us to kneel, while the others bring us a cup half full of a black liquid that's thick as tar. The Horsemen look at each other in curiosity while I sniff it.

It's molasses and something else I can't identify.

One of the Draiders croaks at me."[Don't drink it yet! Only when the high priest calls for it!]"

Bloodstone requests that the lights be turned off, which we oblige him. We bathe in the warm glow of the incoming sunlight and our friend pulls a prayer book from beneath his cloak.

He recites a medley of incantations, chants and prayers in a dialect that I don't recognize. The words he utters feel ancient, as though lost to time but have been reclaimed. There are multiple pleas to Father Sky and others in the pantheon I can't discern.

Bloodstone holds his mace out, filtering the rays of light flowing into the ship. The room explodes in a shimmering bath of tones and colors. He recites his chants until the sun goes behind Centaura, creating an eclipse.

He puts down the mace and raises the cup into the air.

"[Father Sky, purge all fear from us as we travel through your dominion. Make us worthy of defending the Mother of the World from demons. Cleanse and purge all fear so we shall not pollute your dominion.]" Bloodstone finishes by drinking deeply from his cup until it is empty.

The other Draiders howl with pride and follow his lead. The rest of us toast to a successful mission and pour it down the hatch.

Thick molasses coats my tongue, but after I've finished my drink I realize what the chemical I couldn't discern was.

Sujay holds his stomach. "Oh these blithering mystics poisoned us!"

Forrest laughs. "You're such a weak-" And vomits all over the ship.

It's Ipecac.

Everyone aboard the ship vomits for the next ten minutes in a cruelly literal desire to purge all fear from the body. Our cleaning bots are overwhelmed and the smell is horrendous.

"Man these croakers have a penchant for abusing themselves," Warrens says. "First the red pepper, now this. No wonder why they don't lose."

"I dunno, I think it worked!" Forrest says.

"You were just griping about how you were going to die," Sujay replies.

"Yeah, but since we're about to charge a heavily fortified planet full of aliens that want to eat us for breakfast to defeat a mortal enemy we hate beyond all reason, I feel pretty good!"

"Perfect," I reply. "Let's prepare to breach atmo."

The skies are cluttered with debris from tattered satellites that had been used during the Unification Wars. A blast hits blind on the starboard side.

"Great," Hacker hisses. "They repurposed some of the satellites and sent them back into orbit."

"Another death-defying challenge for us to evade!" Forrest cheers. "Here we go!" He pushes on the throttle before anyone is ready and dives for the planet.

We surge past Centaura's outer defenses, but every stage has another set of armed satellites. It'll be a miracle if we make it through in one piece. The *Enigma* may be fast, but she doesn't have much in firepower and if we're going to make it through, we need all the guns we can muster.

"Launch the mechs in sentinel mode," I order. "Tell the girls to give 'em hell!"

"Releasing the mechs," Sujay replies. All four are deployed around us and unfold as we fly through the atmosphere. Immediately they open fire on the base, which is equipped with heavy anti-aircraft guns.

The mechs weave and dodge the incoming missiles which become a wave of light assaulting us. Forrest and Sujay are trying everything to avoid taking fire, but the shields are almost depleted within seconds.

Sujay turns back to me. "Sir, we can't take much more! We either break away or we'll be destroyed!"

I look around us and know that I don't have any choice left. I have to do everything I can to protect this team. They're the only family I've ever known.

"Dorothy, fly in front of the ship."

The mech of death kicks up the thrusters and flies in front of us. The mech's shields buy us some time, but we're not close enough.

"Wendy, lay waste to that turret on the ground! Give us some cover!"

The mech stops and floats in the air before launching six missiles which rain down on the turrets. After the smoke clears, they resume firing back at us.

"Damn it!"

Hacker looks over at me. "There was a saying during the war that no Core fleet could've breached Centaura's fortresses."

"Not much help!" I snap. I watch Dorothy's shields collapse and her arm get torn away. Within seconds the mech is peppered with holes and falls away, no longer able to protect us. I call for another mech to protect us, but the ship suffers a direct hit, and we go into a freefall.

"Hold on guys! Let's hope Momma Forrest can protect us!" Forrest rips off his gold chain and ties it to the throttle.

"Sweet Vishnu or Mrs. Forrest protect us! I don't care who!" Sujay screams.

The alarms blare, the lights switch to red and everyone straps in for a rough landing. We struggle to hold on and the ship crashes into a field of jagged rocks. My head is launched back, and I feel the blow right before I sink into black.

I come to, and there are a band of Grigylls searching the ship. Some of them are equipped with blue chest pieces that match what the ion clones wore. I move as slowly as I can and unfasten my seat belt.

One of them catches me and fires with a blaster. I feel the searing heat in my gut, which I channel into my hand. If this is what's going to kill me, then I'm taking as many with me as I can.

My glove turns to ash and a violet lightning bolt leaps from my hand. The Grigyll that shot me is vaporized and the others are scrambling to react. I leap from my seat onto one that has a chest piece and punch it as hard as I can. My hand ignites with pain, but I feel what it's like to become a conduit to unlimited power. My other glove's ashes fall away as I obliterate every Grigyll inside the ship, along with the small platoon keeping watch outside.

I gasp for air after it's over. My flesh is paler and my arms look like the skin has been stretched against the bone. Everything hurts, but I ignore the pain and get the squads mobile. I go into the cockpit and see that Forrest and Sujay are both bloodied. I nudge Forrest and his head tips away, where I see blood trickling from his ear.

I turn to Sujay and he's been impaled by shrapnel from the ship, his lips covered in blood. I turn back and see the others. I nod my head and the crew struggles to hold it together. I feel a hot tear glide down my cheek in a struggle to hold it all together.

"We're doing all of this for them," I growl. I stoke the fires of rage and force myself to focus on the mission. I only hope that the souls of these two brave pilots can forgive us for not giving them a proper memorial.

Night has fallen upon the planet and we charge under cover of darkness. Emie guides us to the fortress where we believe Salvatori is hiding.

"Emie, I have a final journal entry I need you to record."

"Right away Silas. Whenever you're ready."

We breach the hill to Salvatori's foundry. The air surrounding the place is ionized and it's a hive of activity. The inside looks like an electrical storm and I fear that Salvatori's grand experiment is almost complete.

Bloodstone taps me on the shoulder. "[We will eliminate the sentries. Make them blind to us.]"

Before I can give a response the Draiders slip away, hunkering down and using the hills to disappear. We take the other side, eliminating sentries and guards. Turrets fire upon us and we're forced to take cover. Warrens pulls out and puts together a missile launcher. He fires at the nests, which still stand despite his firepower.

"Let's knock on the front door while we're at it!" He growls. The launcher belches a stream of fire, knocking out the entrance. Hundreds of Grigylls pour out, firing at us. We're trapped like rats, unable to escape unless we can break their line.

Warrens switches his missile launcher to a gatling gun. "I guess this is where we charge 'em right boys?"

A handful of Grigylls slide down the hill and surround us. They have us in their sights, but after they communicate with each other, I realize that none of them are aiming at me.

I draw a grenade, pull the pin, but hold the lever in place.

"Take us to him or I wipe all of you out!"

The Grigylls look at each other, uncertain of what to do next.

"You know what I can do, I won't ask again."

One of the beasts growls to the others and waves us in. I motion to them that I'm keeping my hand on the grenade's lever to keep them honest.

Salvatori's laboratory is impeccably clean, which comes as no surprise to me. The lithographic engines are unimpressive, they're massive overhead silos with a small terminal at the base. He's at a computer chamber, tracking the war effort on both sides, with one screen focused on whatever he's crafting within the engine.

"Give up on the intelligent races Frazzle?" Warrens asks.

"Hardly," Salvatori quips. His hair is wild and erratic with eyes to match. He looks half-starved, his quest consuming him. "The rebels built this state-of-the-art lithographic engine just before the Core invaded Centaura. They placed all of their dwindling resources into this one chance to assemble matter into weaponry and droid soldiers. All of my resources went into this machine and I knew that if I came with the same technology as what I presented the Core, I'd be accepted in a heartbeat."

"Loyalty doesn't mean much then," Hacker says.

"Sovereigns need not be loyal to those they rule."

"*Rung tse song di ching dai wuo tzo*," Lee says.

"Soon enough I'll be the only God you know and rest assured you'll be taken away."

"How does it all work?" Shepherd asks. "Your grand plan?"

Salvatori glares at him. "Meager minds may not appreciate, but I'll enlighten. First is quantum transition through space." He disappears, but then reappears behind Shepherd.

"The second is lithographic regeneration, or giving form through perfect replication of genetic material. The third is assimilation of energy through biological tissues." Salvatori holds his hand out to me.

"Exactly what my son has promised to me if I let all of you go."

The others look at me in shock.

"I know the pain you feel Richard. I know what it's like to stare into the black abyss. Eternal nothingness. I can heal you."

Murph leaps forward but a Grigyll seizes him. "Silas! He won't do it! Remember everyone else he used!"

The Grigylls seize everyone.

"You said they'd go free," I growl.

"This is only a precaution. They'll interfere out of their primal regard for you."

"I guess that was the main difference between us Dad. You saw caring for someone else as weakness!" I throw the grenade at him.

Salvatori teleports away just in time, while Lee and Murph are able to turn enough so the Grigylls holding them are smoldered in the blast. The two men are wounded, but they can still fight.

"Murph! The Chimera!" I point to the lithographic engine and he nods to me.

The Grigylls on the upper levels fire down at us, while we break free and take out the Grigylls holding us hostage. Murph taps on the controls and is about to switch the canisters out, but Salvatori reappears right next to him.

"MURPH!" I scream. Salvatori pulls a knife and slices his throat. His face is frozen in horror as he collapses and drops the chimera strain.

"You monster!" I howl.

"And you're a fool!" He snaps. "A boy who had potential turned into a brute incapable of appreciating what you've discovered. Together we could have achieved the God-State. Now I'll just take it for myself!"

"Not if I can help it Frazzle!" Warrens fires at Salvatori with a rifle, but he disappears right before the bolts can hit him.

Lee charges for Warrens, plunging his knife right where Salvatori emerges.

Salvatori cries out in pain, but he disappears again. Warrens and Lee try to fight him off, but between the Grigylls firing down and Salvatori flickering between the two, they're cut down in less than a minute.

Hacker tries to provide support with his rifle, but Salvatori flickers in front of him, knocks the rifle out of his hands and shoots it right into his chest. He looks to me before he falls backwards and I feel utterly helpless.

Shepherd holds his rifle close and questions whether to shoot Salvatori. He looks at Shepherd, daring him to do it. An idea goes off in his head and Shepherd turns his gaze to me.

"Do it," I reply.

Shepherd takes his rifle and shoots at me. The energy bolt catches in my chest and I feel the searing heat crawl through me. I concentrate and fire at Salvatori, lighting bolts leaping from my fingertips.

He screams in pain while his arm burns away, but he teleports before I can finish him off.

I look over at Shepherd. "The Chimera!" He charges for the machine, but I lose sight of him when I see Salvatori rematerialize only a few metres away. He's breathing hard, but particles around us float towards his arm. Within seconds he has a fully formed arm that is burning red hot. He cries out in pain, but that turns into a cackle of triumph.

"Forgot to tell you, I was able to create my own lithographic engine and enhance my implant."

I feel a wave of fear take hold. My skin is cracked and flaking away. This can't be how it ends. I can't allow Salvatori to win. My hands fall to my sides, but then I see my answer on the floor. It's an industrial electrical cord powering the engines. Salvatori may be able to re-form himself, but if I can burn him faster than he can regenerate…

I leap at the madman and grab him by the neck.

"Look at you! You're showing your true form…a diseased mongrel. Unworthy. Unfit."

I pick up the cord. "No, just low on energy." I bite into the protective case and expose the underlying wire.

"What are you doing?! I can make us immortal! I can heal you!"

"I don't need to be healed. I think it's time to take you back to the world you cannot rule."

I sink my teeth into the current and feel a surge of power. A wave of energy erupts, passing through me into Salvatori. His implant shorts out and try as he might, he can't teleport away. I tighten my grip even when my feet turn to ash. Salvatori thrashes against me, trying to break my hold, but when he hits me his hands become dust. He searches for an answer, but I have him trapped. The mind that always had an answer now has none. His gaze becomes fixed on me and I see a look I've come to know very well, but never thought I'd see in my father's eyes.

Fear.

I take one last look. Every Grigyll around us dissolves into ash, same with the fallen bodies of my brethren. I wish I could've saved them, but at least now we'll all be able to rest together.

I feel the energy welling in my chest. My father is gone, scattered to the elements. He always spoke of death as a black abyss, but as I fade away, all I see is a shining light.

EPILOGUE

The squad floods into the wreckage. General Fitch stands tall and looks up at the destruction which leads into the sky. Overhead, large plumes of smoke rise from the silos and thousands of Grigylls lie dead among the surrounding hillsides. Inside the wreckage they had been turned to skeletons without even a fleck of flesh on their bones. Intermingled with the dead are a handful of human skeletons.

A private calls out. "General! You'll want to see this!" He points to a canister, locked into the foreign machine. He recognizes that the display is showing him a genetic sequence, but can't understand much else.

"What is it?"

"Basically sir, they turned this place into one massive plague engine. Only seems to affect the Grigylls because it's been running for days."

"Let it keep running then."

Bloodstone croaks in the distance, pulling on sheets of metal that make up the silo.

"Excuse me son," Fitch runs to the Draider.

"What'd you find?!" He asks. Bloodstone points inside of the silo, a cavern carved out from a welding rod.

He gasps. “Shit, c'mon, pull him out!”

Bloodstone replies in hushed tones, but drags out a man with blonde hair. The medic sweeps in and checks his vitals.

“He's alive sir.”

“Son of a bitch,” Fitch grins.

The man coughs, his lungs searching for air. His eyes open, full of confusion. He searches for a friend, but only recognizes the General towering over him.

“The last one,” Fitch says. “Help him up!”

The soldiers pull the blonde man to his feet. His armor is scarred and covered in ash, but he holds his head high with pride.

Fitch pats him on the shoulder. “Climb aboard the *Monolith* Commander Shepherd. For your heroism, we'll take you wherever you wanna go.”

Thank You for Finishing the Book!

Reviews Are the Lifeblood of Authors and I'm No Different…

Please Submit Your Honest Review On Amazon.

Finally, Subscribe to the Odyssey Journal For Short Stories, Events, and Upcoming Book Updates! Only at www.benjaminshartman.com

www.ingramcontent.com/pod-product-compliance
Lightning Source LLC
Chambersburg PA
CBHW022242020726
47496CB00004B/1028
* 9 7 8 0 9 8 6 0 5 8 4 5 5 *